"MacKenna: Confrontation"

Part Five Of The

Ic'nichi - Human Chronicles

Continuing The

Second History Of The Interstellar Concord

By,

Robert A. Boyd

For

"Kelly"

"Prologue"

p'ved'm'trnna Circle
near the main spaceport, d'enchia
323 Common, 20th B'matapur:

His knock on the door was answered by an elderly fem who greeted him with an uneasy look. "Yes?" she asked. "What do you want, First Degree?"

He gave her a courteous formal ear twitch as he mentally compared her to the intelligence file he reviewed that morning. She was still attractive in a stately way, despite the years. It was hard to credit all the adventures they'd been through: their record read like an action thriller, which might explain her pensive expression. This wasn't going to be easy, so he tried to be as polite as possible. "I need to speak with him, *nn'etd*, if I may. It's an important matter."

"Very well," she said after a moment, and held the door open for him reluctantly.

Their grotto was comfortable, if basic: the sort of place a senior 'Dark Grays' Elder and his bondmate would live in after a distinguished career. It was in a comfortable nest close enough to d'enchia's spaceport that they could hear the shuttles take off. Unlike most such grottos, theirs was crowded with human artifacts brought back from earth over the years. His *t'plk'asira,* embossed with enough honors to raise an eye ridge, was hung opposite the door between a large map of earth and another of the Ic'nichi and human spheres of space. Below that was a bookshelf filled with human volumes. They gave the place a wild, exotic air strangely out of synch with such a mundane setting.

"He is in his study," she said. "Would you care for some refreshment?"

"You are kind, *nn'etd*, but I am on duty."

"C'traBenla?" a voice came from behind one of the doors around the the room. "Who is it?"

She gave him a glum look, then turned. "It's for you, love." She obviously wasn't pleased, not that he could blame her.

4

One of the doors opened, and he was confronted by a bulky, elderly mal who considered him with some surprise and no enthusiasm.

"Ki-Eldest I'eiBida?" He gave the elder a crisp formal tail wave. "First Degree B'monTrea, sir, Fleet Intelligence. I have been instructed to ask you to come to the 'Dark Grays' circle."

He was positively dismayed. "Is it that bad?"

"Yes, sir."

"I'eiBida? Do you have to?" she asked, plaintively. He gave her a guilty look. "Nothing good has ever come of fooling with those humans."

He offered her a humorless smile. "I can think of one good thing, at least." They met at the Ic'nichi embassy on earth, fifty-three years ago.

"If you please, sir, will you come to the circle? I have a car waiting."

He shook his head sadly, although he had probably been expecting this visit. "I'm retired. I've been out of the herd for five years now. What good can I do at this late date?"

B'monTrea hesitated; he knew how the Ki-Eldest felt about this. Best get it over with. "Something's come up, sir," he said, simply. "We're reactivating him."

She reacted with a gasp of dismay, and retreated into the kitchen. I'eiBida studied him glumly for a long moment, then replied with a pungent human expletive.

*****

5

"Chapter One"

"Hey, peewee, wake up."

His head jerked up. The first thing he focussed on was a Master Chief Petty Officer standing over him. His first reaction was anger. He'd always been sensitive about his height—he was a half-head shorter than the next larger recruit, who was no giant himself—and after being harassed and shoved around like cattle since six AM, his temper finally snapped.

"Hey, yourself. Don't call me that!"

The Chief's frown was like an approaching thunderstorm. "What'd you say, *boy?*"

Shit, his temper did it again. It's never easy being the runt, and like a lot of little men, he had developed a hard edge in his seventeen years. He'd already backed down one big lug in this herd of recruits by his sheer uncomplicated willingness to take on all comers. Yeah, but a Master Chief Petty Officer was something else entirely, and this one was a hulking brute with hard eyes. He'd probably spend his tour in the brig after he got out of the hospital, but he couldn't back down now; not and hold on to the self-respect he'd earned in a hundred schoolyard scrapes. Too late to do anything but follow through.

"I said don't call me that, Chief." He clambered to his feet, back against the cement block wall as the boots on either side scuttled away from ground zero. "That's impolite. And the name isn't 'boy'. It's MacKenna, Brian A."

§

"Interesting." The lizard-like Ic'nichi Learnéd *pondered the two, who were paused momentarily in a tense tableau-a-deus so he could study the scene in more detail. "Most interesting. Not only the difference in authority levels, but in physical size as well." He glanced curiously at the elderly man standing next to him. "He must weigh twice what your earlier self did."*

"I was a rash young punk back then," the old man muttered.

§

"Your name is 'Shitbird', mister!" the Chief snarled. "I'll wipe you off my ass and flush you down, you give me any back-talk!"

The kid matched him eye to cold unblinking eye. "The name is MacKenna. Brian A. Sir."

It had been a long time since this Chief took sass from anyone under the rank of Captain. He glowered at the kid standing before him who...rank or no, size or no, this kid was calmly prepared to whip his ass or die trying. He could see it in his eyes. It was a look he hadn't seen much of in recent years, and he'd been in long enough to know true gilt when he saw it. He sure as *hell* hadn't seen much of it around here lately. The war was not going well, and even the Navy was drafting now. The recruiting staff at the Cleveland Naval Reserve district headquarters were entirely 'administrative duty': hollow-eyed men with shaking hands, missing limbs, and other less obvious problems. The look in this kid's eyes was like a chill wind which took the breath away and warned of storms on the horizon.

The ice broke after a long, tense moment. "Yeah, well, maybe so." The Chief pondered the youngster, and in spite of himself he was impressed. "I'll give you a word of advice, kid," he said confidentially. "You got a set of stones on you. You learn to keep it tight, and you'll go far in this-here Navy."

§

"This directed dreaming is something," the old man said, bitterly. "I'm not enjoying this, you know."

"This is the last of your memories, Brian, so this will all be over soon."

"As if that's a comfort."

§

They watched in silence as the young Brian MacKenna endured an endless day of Navy hurry-up-and-wait while he was examined and inoculated, formed and filed, indexed and cross referenced, subjected to a perfunctory security screen, and finally loaded on a bus with fifty-four fellow sufferers bound for Boot at Great Lakes. As they left, late that evening, he faded into an exhausted sleep.

§

"Is that it?" the old man asked after the scene around them froze.

Learnéd P'demDren turned and considered him for a moment before answering. "Yes, that was the last. Unfortunately, the technology wasn't all that good back then. The original recording left a lot to be desired, and we have no way to fill in the gaps. Everything prior to this is nothing more than vague impressions and isolated bits."

"I needed to go through all this again?" They had politely argued this matter back and forth for months.

"I'm sorry Brian, but we had to rebuild your psyche as near to the original as possible in order to gain the same results. Regretfully, that meant reliving your long and unpleasant life, but the process should be done now."

It was all old news, not that it made this any easier. Mac was still bemused and slightly horrified to learn that he died forty earth years ago, and existed now only as a recording of his memories. At times, he felt like a ghost in a haunted castle, doomed never to rest for his sins.

"Seventy-five years of bloodshed," he muttered. "God." He pondered the scene: the Cleveland Naval Reserve Center in the mid-21st century, now somewhere under Lake Erie after the city was nuked during the Collapse. "Why did I have to come here again?" He gave P'demDren a bleak, hostile look. "This ain't natural. Nothing good can come of it."

"You might feel more confident if you cast off this virtual image, and adopt that of your new body."

Mac turned on him bitterly. "Hey, this is me. This is how I looked when I died, and it's all I have left to cling to. Allow me that much."

P'demDren watched him silently for a long moment. Mac knew he regretted all this, what they had to do, why he had to suffer; the Ic'nichi were that human at least—or perhaps 'nonhuman' was the better word. "All I can say, Brian, is we had to do this," he said at last. "I wish it wasn't so painful for you."

Mac brooded silently for a bit, withdrawing into himself to tune it all out, if possible. In a way it was his own damned fault. A man's actions—a man's karma—bear on his soul unto the Hour of his Judgement. Sometimes, if a man is truly, horrifically unlucky, the weight of his sins will follow him beyond the grave. Seventy-five years of bloodshed: seventy-five years of combat experience all through the Collapse, and beyond. Humanity's greatest soldier. A Goddamned statistical fluke who threw dice with Death and beat the odds so many times that the dice kept rolling Snake Eyes even after he died of old age. The weight of his sins.

"Yeah. Life's a bitch, ain't it?"

"Brian..."

"T'hell with it. Shut this damned thing off."

§

As usual, he felt a brief disorientation when they switched off the virtual reality system. He pulled off the eye piece, and lay on the hard doctor's table for some time staring listlessly at the cloudscape ceiling tiles. As usual, his eyes ached, and he had a sinus headache. As usual, he was so depleted and emotionally drained that he just didn't care any more. The Ic'nichi technicians removed the bulky helmet, and he eventually got up the gumption to rub his eyes and run his fingers through his close-cropped hair to scratch his scalp.

"So how was it, Brian?" I'eiBida asked.

Mac sat up with an effort and stared vacantly at him for a moment. His return from the dead landed him in some sort of top secret Ic'nichi lab; typical of any hospital, really, with pale green walls and hospital furniture and medical instruments with glowing lights and squiggly lines marching across their screens. I'eiBida stood out among all the Ic'nichi Learnéds and military types attending him: clearly in command, expecting and getting the deference of military and civilians alike. Mac shook his head, bemused: I'eiBida was a junior staff officer last he remembered; now he wore enough hash that the other 'Dark Grays' kept a wary distance from him. The uniform was a bit tight in spots.

"I'll manage. I always do." He clambered to his feet and stretched to get the stiffness out of his back. Part of that was laying on that damned table all day; part of it was the constant low-level tension he endured from being caught up in this preposterous fix. He relaxed with a sigh, and looked down at I'eiBida. He still wasn't used to standing 195 centimeters tall, or with how *small* the Ic'nichi seemed. "So now what?"

"I understand this completes your formal restoration." I'eiBida examined him closely. "How do you feel? Any mental confusion? Disorientation?"

Mac pondered that. "No. I feel fine."

"No memory gaps?"

"No." More's the pity. "But I itch like hell."

That was another thing he had become used to over the last three months. From what I'eiBida told him of their plans, he was to infiltrate earth after apparently being a fugitive for some time. They limited him right from the start to one shower a week, and he wore the same clothes day and night since he awoke. He could smell himself, he was greasy, and his skin was raw with jock itch.

He rubbed his chin absently; his beard was almost long enough to groom. "So where do we go from here?"

"Assuming the Learnéds will sign off on your treatment, we can proceed with your briefings." I'eiBida turned expectantly to the three Ic'nichi physichs who oversaw his rebirth, and to Doctor Eddington, who advised them on human biochemistry.

"We'll want to run another standard series, but based on results thus far, I expect he should be finished shortly." Eddington was an elderly black human with thinning snowy hair and an odd accent: East African, Mac had learned. He heard Eddington worked with him before, not that he, Mac, remembered. He might have had something to do with recording his memories before he...died. For some reason, he shied away from knowing; some things are better left buried, even if the ghost isn't allowed to.

§

Several grueling hours of psychological screening later, and Eddington pronounced the verdict. "He appears to have absorbed the last input, and is reintegrated in all respects."

10

"As near as you can figure, anyway," Mac grumbled. This mind recording gimmick was a wild-ass blue sky project if ever there was one. He had little confidence in their *understanding* what they wrought.

"As near as we can figure," Eddington allowed. "The recent advances in stabilization are working better than we hoped."

Mac answered with a resigned sigh. "Wonderful. So can I take a shower now?"

"I'm afraid not, Brian," I'eiBida said. "If things go according to plan, you will be committed within the next two days. You need to maintain appearances, so to speak."

"Yeah." Appearances: like someone on the run, sleeping under bridges and cadging food wherever he could for months. "That's another thing. It's about time you filled me in on this plan of yours."

I'eiBida studied him for a long moment. "Yes, Brian, it is. Please forgive me for not briefing you sooner, but we were worried about how the details would affect your reintegration."

That had the insane logic of most secret rationalizations. "Well now they're done with their voodoo, and I need to know, so you need to 'fess up, pronto."

I'eiBida hesitated and looked around cautiously. "Walk with me, Brian."

§

They left the others in the lab, and headed down the corridor leading to his quarters. It had the same antiseptic hospital feeling as the lab, with polished tile floor and drop ceiling and landscape art on the walls, except being designed for the horizontal Ic'nichi. He long since got in the habit of walking slightly bent over. The mix of the familiar and the alien was hallucinatory at times, and added a creepy feeling to his constant angst.

"You people seem a lot more paranoid than what I remember," Mac complained after bumping his head on a light fixture for the third time. "Why can't you just tell me back there?"

"We have a security breach. The 6th Office planted a mouse somewhere on the Staff, so we have to be ultra-cautious."

"Hence that bullshit about interfering with my rebirth?"

11

"Partly, although it was a genuine concern." I'eiBida paused and looked at him. "Tomorrow we'll have the first of your briefings. The situation is deteriorating, so now that you have completed the reintegration, we need to start you galloping on the problem. You'll know all the ugly details then."

Mac considered that with no enthusiasm. "Its been forty years now. Haven't you learned how to get along without me yet?"

I'eiBida seemed to feel guilty at that. Mac knew he was pained by all this too. "We have a unique problem this time, Brian. This is one only you can deal with."

Mac's angst finally overflowed. "Why should I care?"

"Because of who you are, Brian," I'eiBida said, softly. "Lives are at stake, and you can't refuse to help and live with yourself afterward."

He was right, damn him. "Why me? Why did you have to bring me back? Haven't I paid my dues in full?"

"I'm sorry, Brian. I would have opposed that recording at the time, but I was still nobody back then. The Staff felt your skills were an asset which should be preserved for future need, and there was this new technology for them to play with." He hesitated, seeing the anger and bitterness in the large human's snout. "If it means anything, we wouldn't have brought you back except we face a crisis. And you can rest assured I have the grunt to see you get a fair shake this time."

Mac gave him a sharp look. "This time?"

I'eiBida hesitated, caught by his momentary slip. "We...brought you back once before, twenty years ago," he admitted at last. "A human colony was under attack. You were able to contact the aliens, and talked them out of destroying earth and d'enchia both."

Mac's eyebrow crept up. "That bad, huh?"

"It's fair to say you prevented the extermination of both races. You felt at the time that it made up for the horrors of your former life."

Mac shuddered. "I'eiBida, *nothing* can make up for that." There was a painful silence, then he asked, "What happened last time, afterward?"

I'eiBida hesitated for a moment, then turned away. "The...transfer technique wasn't perfected at the time. The transplant eventually failed."

Mac understood the implications, all too well. "So what about this time?"

"We believe we have the method perfected."

"Believe?"

I'eiBida turned to him again. "All we can do is hope. For what it's worth, once this is over, you will be well provided for. I made sure your future will be secure."

"I don't give a flying purple *damn* about the future! It's my past I'm worried about. Do you think I want to live with that lifetime again?"

"I don't pretend I understand what you went through, Brian. We simply aren't as violent as you humans, nor have we gone through anything like your Collapse. All I can do is whatever I can to help you cope with those memories. You have my promise."

Mac looked at him silently. "Well, thank you for that, anyway," he said at last.

§

His quarters was a single room with a restroom annex. The furnishings and fixtures were human, except there was no sink, and the shower stall was locked. The door was not locked, but two 'Dark Grays' stood watch outside around the clock, and escorted him wherever he went. Once they were safely in his room, I'eiBida laid it down: short, sweet, and to the point.

"Another me?"

"I think you can see why we are so obsessed with security now," I'eiBida said. "Someone at Fleet Staff has been turned, and leaked the recording to the 6th Office."

"God, what a bunch of screw-ups," Mac grumbled.

"We are still trying to figure out how they managed that. There has just been the one copy all this time, and it was among our most closely guarded secrets. But the big concern is what this will do to the balance of power between the two races."

"Uh huh. And you figure this is bad enough to bring me back from the dead, not to mention you out of retirement?"

"You know better than anyone how much your skill and experience can affect the balance of power. Intelligence figured if the humans have a copy of you, we will need one as well to restore the balance."

"But you don't agree?"

"Having two of you will only ramp up the intensity of any conflict. Our overriding goal is to prevent a war between d'enchia and earth. Neutralizing their recording is the key to reducing the possibility of a conflict, and the intensity of one if it does come. That should be our strategy."

'Neutralizing'. Mac sighed inwardly; his old counterpart picked up a lot from the humans over the years. Still, he was right. Points to I'eiBida. "You must need a wheel barrow to carry your balls in." His plan was brilliant; insanely brilliant; the sort of finesse move which would cripple the opposition if it worked, or get them all killed if it didn't. Which it would be was a toss-up.

"It's the only chance I can see to short-circuit the Alliance's war plans." I'eiBida paused and studied Mac's features. "What do you think?"

Mac settled on the bed and eyed him skeptically. "You really think this will solve all our problems?"

"I don't know, Brian," I'eiBida said, honestly. "But we have to do something, and the 6th Office is the source of the contagion, so to speak. You'll understand Fleet Intel's paranoia after your first briefing tomorrow."

Mac gave him a hard look. "Damned spooks and their cloak-and-dagger games." The itch in his scalp got the better of him, and he scratched vigorously. There were traces of dandruff and blood under his fingernails. "Why the hell did you get mixed up with those clowns, anyway? You were a good soldier once."

I'eiBida sighed. "It was inevitable I guess, with my experience at the embassy. I was Herd First Fleet Ops, in line to become Eldest 'Dark Grays', but they transferred me to the 'spooks' eighteen years ago because I was needed there."

Knowing as he did how the military mind worked, Mac saw the untold story behind that: I'eiBida screwed up somewhere, but he was too useful to dump, so they shuffled him off to a position out of the chain of command. Perhaps it had to do with the last time they 'reactivated' him; he felt a twinge of guilt over that.

"I don't know if your plan would keep earth from starting a war," he said at last, gently. "But it could make it a lot less painful."

I'eiBida shook off his funk. "They will certainly be disconcerted by losing their copy of the recording, and intimidated by our ability to make more copies of you."

His unique one-and-only life was being turned into a production commodity, which wasn't comforting. "Perhaps. It could help, anyway."

There was another uncomfortable silence, then I'eiBida changed the subject. "Have you reviewed your persona today, Brian?"

"Fer cryin' out loud, I know it all, already."

"Colonel Alvarez, the head of 6th Office special operations, has been diagnosed as clinically paranoid. If you make any slip which arouses his suspicion, it could go badly for you."

Mac studied the history, speech patterns, and mannerisms of his body's former occupant for over a month now. They must have watched his alter-ego for some time; video-taping him, monitoring his phone calls to record his voice, taking careful note of every habit and every little gesture, and drilling them into him relentlessly. Methodical, Ic'nichi Intelligence. Mac sometimes felt like his reborn persona was a blend of the two.

"Reinhart Krauss, born in Dresden, age forty-seven..."

"Accent."

That damned German accent; I'eiBida hounded him about it right from the beginning. It seemed preposterous for them to school him in human dialect, but Ic'nichi speech ran six times faster than human; their linguists had the ear for the most subtle detail, and drilled him day and night.

"Reinhart Krauss, born in Dresden, age *sieben-und-vierzig*," he said in resignation. "Former citizen of zee Kingdom of Altmark, now forcibly 'rationalized' into zee Bavarian Confederacy." He gave I'eiBida a disgruntled look. "I haff a price on my head from zee old homevolk. You could haff picked a better lab rat."

"How much? The reward."

"Fifty thousand Kroner, for treason against Bavaria."

"Go on."

"Anyway, I'm a field op for the 6th Office..."

"Accent."

Mac sighed. "I am *der feld operatif* working under zee cover of a trade representative."

"Hearing rumors is..."

"Stepping in it."

"And solid news is..."

"Zee ugly."

"Mixed race humans are..."

"Sausages." Mac held up his hands. "Enough, I'eiBida. Give it a rest, huh?"

§

By rights, after what he'd been through lately, Mac should have crawled into bed, pulled the covers over his head, and slept like a baby. But he was too wired and distraught to sleep, so he wandered out into the central courtyard of the top security research center where he was 'reborn' a scant three months ago. It was late: they put in long days. Two of the moons were visible through scattered clouds, and as he watched, he could see the faint lights of orbiting starships passing overhead. There was a moist feel to the air, like it might rain later, blending with the aroma of flowering plants: tart for native species, sweet for earthly transplants. The place was decorated with flagstone walks, trees, and colorful bushes around an ornate fountain. There was a small gazebo with a wrought iron table and some human and Ic'nichi chairs in a plaza next to the fountain: a pleasant place all round, especially now in the cool of the evening.

He stood staring at the fountain without really seeing it as he brooded over the bizarre twist of fate which put him in this fix. He'd paid his dues back when he was alive—*God*, did he pay his dues!—but that wasn't good enough, it seemed. It didn't take a military genius to see he was their quick-fix, their easy out to cope with problems which would otherwise require thought and sweat and bloodshed. What was worse, there was no way out, not even dying, again. They brought him back before, and for all he could see they'd bring him back over and over whenever they needed a Superhero to hold their friggin' hands. There are some things worse than dying: living with the past was one of them.

Eventually his nicotine craving got to him. He absent-mindedly dug a half empty pack of cigs out of his pocket, scraped the self-lighting end of one on the side of the pack, and stood staring at nothing while the smoke wreathed around him. As comforting as it was, it was disturbingly *alien* as well. He never smoked a day in his life; was a holy terror about it back when he captained the SSN Seattle, and later when he was in charge of Space Fleet. And here he was, a weed junkie, complete with the chronic cough and the raspy voice and the cravings which got to be overwhelming at times. And it all seemed so natural; a jarring reminder that he was a ghost haunting the living corpse of a human spy.

"Well, Admiral, I see you are up late." It was Eddington, who had shed his white lab coat for a colorful East African native garb which disguised his stoop-shouldered posture and made him seem more like a native elder than a fugitive endocrinologist.

Mac gave him a hostile look. "Checking up on me, doc?"

"No." Eddington settled against one of the gazebo posts, and considered him. "Actually, I thought you could use a sympathetic ear about now."

"God, you have no idea..."

"If it helps, your reawakening was a lot easier this time. The first time was rough."

Mac drew on his cig, and stared at him. "No, doc, the memories are rough. Being alive is rough."

"I read a lot about your career. I don't suppose you are thrilled to be alive again."

"You think?" Mac took another hit, tossed his cig in the fountain, and slumped on one of the wrought iron chairs.

"Things on earth are not good these days. The Alliance has mutated into a nightmare. War is brewing." Eddington gestured vaguely to the heavens. "You must have noticed all the ships in orbit. Both sides are arming feverishly."

Mac watched absently as a glittering array of lights—one of the orbital shipyards—passed majestically overhead. There were other lights moving silently against the background of stars. Ships and orbital weapons platforms: d'enchia was being turned into an armed camp.

"It'll be bad."

"Yes, Admiral, it will. I'm no military man, but from what I'eiBida told me, a war between our two races will leave both in ruins."

Mac watched the silent show with deep misgivings. "Yeah, it will, if we're lucky."

Another cluster of lights was passing overhead. As they watched, one of those lights blossomed and began drifting away from the rest: a starship leaving orbit.

Mac turned to him. "What good can I do? I'm just one man, and my skills must be out of date by now."

Eddington sighed. "I don't pretend to know these things, but Fleet Intelligence thinks you can help, and I'eiBida agrees. I trust his instincts in this."

"For that matter, aren't we in the wrong place? As much as I like the Ic'nichi, we belong to the human race. That's where our loyalty should lie. We should be on earth trying to deal with this from inside, not helping them with their war plans."

"I'm afraid that is not a realistic option for either of us, so we have to improvise as best we can." Eddington pondered him somberly for a long moment. "Sometimes loyalty means charting your own course, even if it seems like the wrong course to many. I did that long ago, when we reactivated you the first time."

"And you wound up in exile for it."

"I did. I don't regret it, since it gave you the chance to save both species."

Mac pondered that. "And now I get the chance to do it again? What are we facing that the 'Dark Grays' can't handle?"

"It's...complicated." Eddington shifted uncomfortably. "I'm not being mysterious on you, Admiral. They'll fill you in tomorrow, and it will be easier to accept that way."

"That's no comfort."

It wasn't. His rebirth in the body of a top human agent was ominous. This mission would be deep penetration; a dangerous, desperation play. He was used to being expendable for the greater good; had been since Boot Camp over a century—*Jeez*, it *was* over a century—ago. But not knowing *why* always rankled him. He understood the need for compartmentation, but he never did like it. What did they expect from him?

And who was this Colonel Alvarez, diagnosed as clinically paranoid, and what was the 6th Office? According to memory, there *was* a 5th Office, but it was disbanded years ago when he commanded Space Fleet. Were they reconstituted as an interstellar covert action arm of the Alliance Protective Agency? He was no spook, had always despised the cloak-and-dagger commandoes for their idiotic games and their obsession with secrecy. Somehow he got the feeling he was ill-equipped for what they had in mind. Somehow, the gut feeling said he wouldn't live through it.

"At least you can take comfort knowing we wouldn't have done this lightly. We need you, Admiral."

He looked askance at Eddington. "Yeah, that's the hell of it. Nothing succeeds like success."

"Brian..."

"Screw it. I'm for bed."

§

"...Con, sonar, still nothing, sir."

The dream came again, like it did so many nights: his darkest nightmare rising from the past to haunt his sleep. He clung convulsively to the periscope handles, watching in horror as the enormity of his failure swept through him like a chill wind. The glow was well beyond the horizon, but the dim red lights in the con were overwhelmed by the blinding glare which came down through the periscope from above. He managed to click a filter in place, but the glow was still painfully bright. The light faded as he watched; faded and rose into the air; a vast white pall over the city they were guarding. As he watched, another white light burst beyond the horizon, growing and rising like an obscene parody of dawn.

19

"Singapore, sir?" their Kiwi Number One asked.

'What a waste,' was his first rational thought. 'What a miserable, senseless waste.' A third burst of light joined the prior two. His hands trembled.

"Con, sonar. We're getting something now, sir."

"Oh, dear God..." Greg Baker, the Third Lieutenant— one of his—muttered. They could hear the rumble through the hull from eighty klicks away.

'Thirty million defenseless refugees, for no good reason.' And it was his fault. He was tired, his crew was tired, the boat was tired. All he did was succumb to a moment of weakness, sent them off to the northeast into deep water where they could go deep and get some rest. All he did was let down their guard for a moment, leaving the threat axis to the north open. A fourth burst of light appeared. It was sickening. Whoever did this intended to destroy all life on the island. Thirty million people...

"Con, sonar, I'm getting something off to the west. It's a long way off, but it sounds like a small warship."

That hit him hard. His decision to move into deeper water left them out of position. If he'd stayed on the ball, patrolling the threat axis down from China, they would have been waiting right there for the intruder. Those thirty million refugees would have lived. He failed them. He failed in his duty.

"Con, sonar. The computer says that warship is a Taiwanese frigate."

A guided missile frigate: one of the few serviceable warships in the Asian Theater, in the hands of one of the factions slaughtering each other on the Chinese mainland...or fleeing to some imagined safe haven...like Singapore... Their deaths were his fault. Thirty million of them. He slacked off, took a course out into deep water so they could have a quiet watch for once...

"...Lives are at stake. You can't refuse to help and live with yourself afterward..."

"Sir?" The scope had been up a long time now. Number One was getting anxious...

§

...he awoke, and lay staring at the bedside clock. His bedding was soaked with sweat, his heart pounded, and he was crying. The horror came back as waking reality, and he wept bitterly as the magnitude of his failure overwhelmed him. In some quiet corner of his mind, he knew he should have gotten over it after all this time. He lived with his shame for years while he commanded Space Fleet there in Singapore during the Contact Crisis. He should have gotten past it. But he hadn't. He hadn't.

Eventually he was cried out, again, and lay in a fetal curl staring at the wall. It wasn't over. It would never be over. He would go on paying his dues time after time, living with the memories and the nightmares down through the centuries.

"...Lives are at stake. You can't refuse to help and live with yourself afterward..."

The weight of his sins. He bitterly cursed his fate; the Ic'nichi; his own uncompromising sense of duty; that tough seventeen year old kid. Couldn't they have left well enough alone?

"...Lives are at stake. You can't refuse to help and live with yourself afterward..."

"Shit," he muttered.

He finally drifted off to sleep again. Mercifully, the dream didn't return.

*****

21

"Chapter Two"

"Good morning, Brian," I'eiBida greeted him when he came to escort Mac to the briefing. "Are you feeling well today?"

Mac sat up in bed with a weary grunt. "I'll manage."

I'eiBida considered him for a moment, but didn't make anything of it. "Well, the waiting is over. Today you will receive all the answers."

Mac was in no mood for idle chit-chat. "Freakin' Christmas in July," he muttered as he reached for his shirt laying on the floor at his bed side. That worried him vaguely once he thought of it, since he used to be meticulously neat, a habit learned in his years in the subs. When a crewman starts getting sloppy, it usually means his morale is slipping. But there was nothing he could do about it, so he finished buttoning his shirt, pulled on his shoes, grabbed a quick snack from a supply of human zero-G rations they kept on hand, and followed I'eiBida down the hall.

§

It seemed Payday came in spades around here: his first formal briefing was attended by the Eldest of the 'Dark Grays' in person, along with a retinue of Staff and Fleet heavyweights including no less than Elders Home Defense, Second, and Fifth Squadrons. There was another herd from Fleet Intelligence who packed every bit as much horsepower. They filled the center's cafeteria, which was hastily rearranged around an open area with a display monitor and an easel; the two factions separate with a noticeable gap between them. The installation was cordoned off by 'Dark Grays' ground forces, and the cafeteria itself sealed by security types on every entrance. Everyone's ID was scrutinized carefully, and even he had to be vouched for.

"God, what a circus," Mac grumbled as he surveyed the crowd.

I'eiBida gave him a sardonic ear twitch. "I believe you humans call it a 'rogue's gallery'."

"You got that right." He looked around the room again. "There's some heavy hitters in this bunch."

"The heaviest. You can see how seriously we take this."

"Hmph."

Things finally settled down, and I'eiBida started the ball rolling with a quick review of the current state of Ic'nichi and human diplomacy. It wasn't comforting.

"To summarize briefly, the problem we face is caused by a political faction on earth known as the Purity Movement. The Purity Movement emerged from the old Anti-tech environmental terrorist movement, which was finally suppressed some twenty earth years ago. They gained effective control of the Alliance Parliament eight years ago by a mix of voter fraud, scandal-mongering, and outright violence, and they maintain control through their core of party loyalists, known as the 'Tan Shirts'."

"The security core of the Purity Movement is the 6th Office, which evolved from a party apparatus into a government agency at the time. They established a world-wide network of informants and secret police, and have been instrumental in suppressing the political opposition. They also control the 'Tan Shirts', who have evolved into a paramilitary organization known for violence and intimidation. The core of their ideology is that mixing of human ethnic groups is to be avoided. Each ethnic group has their appropriate place in the 'racial sphere'—with the European caucasian ethnic group as the supervising and governing class."

Mac nodded morosely. It was hardly anything new.

"The current trouble began when the 6th Office used its influence to extend their racial policies off earth to include us. Tensions have risen steadily for several years, and the prospect for war is growing acute. The present crisis emerged when the Fleet Staff lost control of the recording of Admiral MacKenna's memories, which we believe the humans used to create a MacKenna of their own."

"You Intelligence types are all too eager to wag ears at Staff," Eldest W'neMven grumbled.

I'eiBida confronted him. "It happened. The recording was in your keeping all this time, so it has to be one of your people who was compromised and leaked it to the humans."

"A matter which we will correct, in both particulars," Eldest T'verTra, the leader of Intel said. W'neMven glowered at him, but didn't reply.

"What we need to do now is find a way to neutralize their copy of the recording," I'eiBida went on to the room at large. "The best chance for that is the covert mission we are discussing."

"Keep in mind your role in this is as his handler," W'neMven said, sharply. "Defense strategy will be made by the Fleet, *not* by Intel."

I'eiBida confronted him again. "And please keep in mind, W'neMven, that I have worked with the humans since you were a hatchling. We must finesse this if we are to avoid mutual slaughter, and we have the practical experience of working with the Admiral, which means fleet Intel should be chanting the pace."

Mac was impressed, since anyone who could dress down the head of the 'Dark Grays' publicly—on a first name basis at that— must pack some serious weight. As he watched the tense confrontation between the Fleet on the one hand, and Intel on the other, he began to get a feel for how much weight I'eiBida carried.

"We?" W'neMven snapped. "You, you mean!"

"Very well, me," I'eiBida said, evenly. "I have more practical experience with the humans, and with the Admiral, than everyone else in this room combined. So who is best qualified to address human strategy issues?"

"Agreed we should apply the Admiral where his knowledge can do the best good," Eldest T'verTra said. "But if the humans apply theirs for fleet operations, we pretty much have to as well. This scheme of yours was not what we originally intended, and I for one doubt if it will work."

"As do I," W'neMven added.

"Putting the Admiral in Plans will be playing their game," I'eiBida told them. "Having two of them will only heighten the destructiveness of a war, and may well goad the humans into starting one."

"But..." T'verTra started, but I'eiBida rode him down.

"The one thing you *never* do is let the enemy set the rules. The Admiral's greatest asset is his ability to come up with unorthodox answers. Right now we need an unorthodox solution if we are to avoid a general conflict which may see d'enchia attacked with stellar bombs."

Most of them flinched at the thought. "Our planetary defenses are the strongest ever, and we are improving them by the day," Home Defense protested. "Plus we can reinforce with fleet elements if we suspect a move by the humans."

"Fixed defenses can always be broken. All they do is buy us time, and probably not enough time to rally the fleet if they are dispersed to cover the colonies." I'eiBida addressed the room at large again. "In any event, no defense is air tight. A saturation attack on d'enchia will be a disaster. Even if we stop ninety percent of their missiles, the few which get through will wreck havoc."

"That's assuming they *do* launch a saturation attack," W'neMven retorted. "Why would they commit their entire strategy to one strike?"

Mac spoke up. "Because neutralizing d'enchia will end the war. That's what I would do."

They all looked at him in surprise. "We are not such monsters, *human,*" Home Defense said, scornfully.

"No, but they are."

I'eiBida picked up the theme. "We cannot risk an attack on the home world, no matter how solid our defenses. Our best bet is a preemptive move against the 6th Office, and the best way to make such a move is for the Admiral to infiltrate and sabotage the recording project as the opportunity presents itself."

"Granted a preemptive move is best," Eldest T'verTra said after a bit. "But this plan of yours is *er'trxxda*. He could never accomplish it, and if they don't kill him, then they will have two MacKenna's."

"If we launch a preemptive attack against earth, it should be a fast raid to knock out their defenses," W'neMven said.

"Earth's defenses are tough enough to require a general fleet action," I'eiBida said. "That will trigger the war we hope to avoid. A precise covert action is our best bet."

"This is getting us nowhere," Second Squadron complained. "*'The more leaders, the less decision'*: the Sixty-Second Maxim of the Defenders, you will recall." W'neMven bridled at that, as did several of both staffs.

"Well then, may I suggest, since we all hold the Admiral in such *high* esteem," I'eiBida threw a pointed glance at W'neMven. "Let's put the matter to him."

"Good point," Fifth Squadron said, with a speculative look at Mac. "I would like to hear his opinion in any case."

I'eiBida turned to him. "Admiral?"

"I'eiBida is right," Mac said, reluctantly. "A general conflict is not what you want. If I can avoid that somehow, then that's where I should be."

"This is *cc'v'renk,*" W'neMven complained. "We are strong enough to fight the humans. If we are to take the Admiral's advice, let us launch a preemptive strike against earth's defenses. We can knock out their shipbuilding capacity, and likely get several of their ships as well. Then we can dictate terms to this *Purity Movement.*"

"We aren't *that* strong," I'eiBida said. "And while you might eliminate their long term war-making ability, they will still be capable of a short term revenge campaign."

"And it will surely provoke them into whatever counter measures they would still possess, sir," Home Defense added.

W'neMven waved angrily at a large chart set on an easel in front of them. "Well if we're going to do anything, we need to do it now while we still have the advantage. See for yourself, human!"

Mac gave him a jaundiced look, then considered the chart:

	Ic'nichi		human	
	active	under construction	active	under construction
Cruisers	6	2	6	4
Old Cruisers	4		3	
Long Range Patrol Ships	8	4	10	4
Patrol Ships	15		7	
Old Patrol Ships	12		5	
Fleet Logistics	10		6	4
Fleet Scouts	2	1	4	2
	=57	=7	=43	=14

(Human Language Translation)

The numbers were impressive. Earth's shipbuilding capacity had advanced by leaps and bounds in the forty years since he died. The Ic'nichi had advanced as well, but the numbers plainly showed they were playing belated catch-up.

"Well, *Admiral*," W'neMven said, pointedly. "You have seen the fleet numbers, would you care to give us your interpretation of them?"

Mac turned and gave him a jaundiced look. "It's not good. You're badly outdated, your fleet balance is way off, and you don't have nearly the fleet train you need."

"We have a solid advantage of numbers..."

"No, you don't; nor firepower, either. You are falling behind in heavy fleet units, for starters. Both sides older ships will pretty much be limited to local defense, which knocks out a disproportionate number of yours. That leaves you a slim majority in patrol ships at best. You're ahead on logistics tonnage, but not that much ahead; not enough for the size of your operational force; and you are way behind on scouting elements."

W'neMven's ears were half wilted in anger. "We plan to use our long range patrol ships for scouting."

"Which disperses your fleet all to hell and gone. You need to maintain concentration. Recalling the fleet will take too long if earth makes a sudden move."

Mac noted as Second and Fifth Squadrons both nodded silently. "What's more, they're outbuilding you two to one, with a major emphasis on logistics and scouting. That suggests they're planning a long range raiding strategy with several self-contained squadrons. Once they get into your space, they'll be free to terrorize your colonies, and you'll play hell tracking them down. It'll drag on forever, and that's a sure recipe for disaster."

§

The briefing dragged on forever as the argument raged. Finally, when tempers were played out, they paused for lunch, and Mac and I'eiBida slipped out into the corridor to find a bit of peace and quiet.

"Well that went nowhere," Mac grumbled as he sagged against the wall.

"You forget our cultural predilection for quibbling," I'eiBida told him with a humorless smile. "They are all seasoned professionals who have studied the human problem for years; they simply need a little time to sort it out in their minds and they'll come around."

"Human problem, eh?" Mac gave him a sour glare. "You got that right. So how does it look?"

I'eiBida brooded. "Not good. It took all my influence to get this conference convened to begin with, and we're making precious little headway with W'neMven."

"So what's his story?"

"Territory. W'neMven worked hard throughout his career to get where he is, and he resents anyone trying to tell him his job; Intelligence in particular."

"The guy's a battleship admiral if there ever was one. Your fleet needs a complete revamping."

I'eiBida gave him a stern look. "Please keep in mind that our usual need is for light forces to do routine patrol and rescue work."

"This situation isn't 'usual'."

"I'll...grant you that. Actually, he's an excellent leader. He's done a lot to shape the fleet up as this crisis unfolded." I'eiBida paused for a discreet glance at the Fleet Eldest. "He was one of my candidates back when I taught Human Studies at the Academy: good academic record, and a fast riser with extensive service in both Fleet and Staff."

"But?"

I'eiBida offered a resigned ear twitch. "But, like a lot of us, he just doesn't grasp how dangerous you humans can be. He sees this in terms of ships and logistics; he doesn't really understand how much your skills and killer instinct can shift the balance of power. If the Alliance deploys a copy of you, we'll be seriously outclassed."

"Hence my untimely return from the dead?"

"Yes. Actually, the idea came from Intel. T'verTra reactivated you out of sheer desperation to serve as a consultant, and he isn't thrilled at my idea for a covert earth mission."

"Can we count on him?"

I'eiBida sighed. "Probably not. He doesn't like this enough to stand up to W'neMven. He's a stubborn *un'tdar.*"

"And you don't agree with your intel people either?"

"Like I said, too much conventional thinking. We need to break herd and run wild with this, or you'll just make things worse. Fortunately, you're good at coming up with unorthodox answers. It's the one redeeming quality I see in all this."

"They're going to attack you," Mac said, firmly. "It's only a matter of time. Can't they see that?"

"By all common sense the Alliance wouldn't, so goes the thinking. We still outnumber your fleet, and our stellar sphere is far larger than yours, so it will be harder for them to hunt our forces down. To Staff's point of view, they won't start a war because it makes no sense."

"They don't know us very well, do they?" Mac brooded for a bit. "Looks like I better give them 'the talk'."

§

The meeting reconvened a short while later, and I'eiBida took center stage again. "Now that we have gone over the basics, I think it wise to get a human perspective on this mess." He gestured to MacKenna. "Whatever merits you may credit the Admiral with, no one can deny he knows the darkness in humanity's soul far better than any of us. So I would like him to address you on the threat."

"I hardly think we need to be instructed on the threat posed by *humans,*" W'neMven complained.

T'verTra eyed Mac skeptically. "Nonetheless, he must have a perspective far clearer than anything we have, and it never hurts to hear all points of view."

"I agree, sir," Fifth Squadron said. "We should hear him out." Home Defense nodded in agreement.

W'neMven gave them an icy glare. "Very well then." He turned to Mac and folded his arms in a hostile gesture. "What can you tell us that isn't already painfully obvious, *Admiral?*"

"A lot. I'm a human, remember." Mac clambered to his feet with a sigh, stepped into the center of the room, and confronted them all. "These are the fanatic dregs of a maniacal cult, and

29

they've tasted political power," told them bluntly. "They seized power in what amounts to a political coup, and there's no limit to what they'll do to hold onto it. We fought the Anti-techs for decades, but it really turned ugly when they got into Parliament: they ceased to be an ideological force, and became a political force. Politics does something dark and ugly to the human soul. It's no surprise they went bad."

"So how do their racial policies fit into their politics?" Eldest T'verTra asked.

"The first thing any dictator does is pick one faction of his society and give them all the privileges; they'll fight to protect their own advantage, and thus prop up the dictatorship. It's the oldest trick in the book."

"That doesn't make sense," W'neMven complained. "Why fractionalize their society? It undermines their authority, and weakens them for any potential conflict."

"They maintain their authority by sheer intimidation. And as for fighting a war, the actual fighting will be done by a relatively small force of true believers. The rest will support the war effort out of fear."

"We don't have anything like the racism the humans do," I'eiBida added. "They are so easy to polarize and divide that it's a wonder they haven't slaughtered themselves long since."

"They did so before, more than once," someone commented. "Perhaps they will do so again with a little encouragement. We could tailor our strategy to promoting another Collapse, since things on earth are already so tense."

"They might at that," Mac said. "But later. Right now they can rely on a war scare to keep the masses in line."

T'verTra considered. "Granted they would use these methods for domestic control, but why pick a fight with us?"

"Because the one thing any dictator needs is enemies," Mac told him. "That's how they justify their crimes: they're trying to suppress the foreign devils and those traitors who support them. To a racist régime, you're the perfect BoogyMan."

W'neMven sighed. "What you say is obvious, but I'm afraid I don't understand it."

"They're making you Ic'nichi out as monsters, aren't they? An *unspeakable* alien menace capable of who knows what. And I'll bet there have been all kinds of sensational 'officially denied' rumors going around about the horrible things you do to hapless humans. Right?"

"Um...yes. How did you know?"

"I've seen this a hundred times before. Trust me: it works." That produced an ugly murmur in the crowd.

"Wouldn't your people speak up against it?" T'verTra asked. "Perhaps not at first, but surely your intellectuals would complain eventually."

"And be branded as 'soft' on some creeping alien horror? The best way to neutralize a political enemy is to make him out as weak on the threat, or even in league with them. It gives the Purity Movement the perfect excuse to round up 'traitors' who are aiding the enemy with defeatist talk."

"But why would they start a war over their own propaganda?" W'neMven asked. "From what you say, we're better for them as an ongoing menace."

"That only goes so far. And, yes, they will come to believe their propaganda after a while. Maybe the top dogs will know better, but the rank and file are the sort of losers who will buy it whole hog, and the leaders will have to cater to their paranoia to keep them in line."

"There are many in the Chamber Of Ancients who still believe a negotiated peace can be maintained," W'neMven said, doubtfully.

"I'll bet they've been pressing your government for concessions, on fleet strength, for one. Haven't they?"

W'neMven looked uneasy. "They have, for some time now."

"And the Chamber has been making concessions to buy them off, haven't they?"

"They were, until recently."

"Bad move. Making concessions only goads that sort on; look up Neville Chamberlin in earth's history, and you'll see what I mean. They'll keep pushing until you're too weak and demoralized to resist. Take my word for it: war is coming, and it won't be long before it gets here." There was a further stir among the ranks as

31

they tried to digest the uncomfortable truth. "They won't attack right at first, but they are clearly making preparations for war." Mac returned to his seat. "The growth of their fleet shows that."

"I have some news coverage from earth which will support the Admiral's argument," I'eiBida said once Mac was finished. He slipped a video cartridge into the player. "I personally culled these scenes from our recent diplomatic intelligence."

"I was wondering what you were looking for," T'verTra grumbled. "That's all useless low level material; we have days worth of it."

I'eiBida gave him a wry ear twitch. "The humans have an old saying about not seeing a forest for all the trees. You just have to know what to look for."

The video opened with a demonstration in progress. Thousands of people crowded along a major boulevard, with the road to their front and all the side streets blocked by lines of riot police. Despite their numbers and their obvious anger, the demonstrators seemed peaceful and orderly.

I'eiBida supplied narration, raising his voice over the muted roar of the crowd. "They can't hide the extent of the demonstrations, so they have agitators turn them into riots which they then suppress."

A fight broke out along the forward edge of the mob. The camera focussed in as a group of demonstrators rushed the police line, forcing them back with clubs and fists.

"You'll notice how the civil authorities generally try to contain the demonstration." The scene shifted, and I'eiBida used a wooden pointer to highlight another group joining the assault on the police line. "But once the rioting starts, the 'Tan Shirts' take over, and their methods are very different."

The scene deteriorated as the mob surged out of control. The riot police fell back, and several columns of 'Tan Shirts' in riot gear emerged from the nearby buildings. It was a perfect ambush. For all Mac's war experience, the violence was sickening to watch. A rumble of dismay came from the Ic'nichi around them. Another scene showed 'Tan Shirts' brutally beating and shooting helpless demonstrators. One was actually run over by an armored car.

"Those are the 'Tan Shirts', huh?" Mac muttered. "Shit, they're a fine collection of Neanderthal thugs." He turned to the others, who watched the video in horrid fascination. "That looks like old Nazi propaganda footage. They slaughtered millions to support their racial theories."

"...I...don't think we realized the significance of those videos," T'verTra said in a hollow whisper.

"There aren't as many demonstrations these days as in the past, since the population is becoming increasingly cowed," I'eiBida said. "The news reports always portray the demonstrators as extremist elements trying to disrupt earthly civilization."

"Demonize the opposition," Mac grunted.

"Lately the emphasis has been more on treating them as revolutionaries. The level of violence has been increasing." They watched in grim silence as a young Hindu, his face soaked in blood, was dragged away by the 'Tan Shirts'. "And while it is never mentioned on the news programs, they have been detaining thousands of people without charges."

When the video was finished, I'eiBida brought out several large photos which he propped up on the easel. "This is a shot taken from our courier in orbit. There are detention camps like this springing up all around earth."

Mac studied the photo of a huge fenced compound with thousands of people sitting or laying in an open enclosure surrounded by a deep ditch flanked by guard towers.

"God, they've got things messed up." Mac gave I'eiBida a bleak look. "Those are like the Nazi camps built for Russian prisoners of war: no shelter, no food, no services; just dump them there to starve to death."

Another photo showed bulldozers burying hundreds in mass graves. "How do they get away with that?" W'neMven murmured. He was clearly appalled, as were all of them.

"They control the media, the telecommunications, and the internet," I'eiBida said. "Their propaganda is relentless, and their informants are everywhere. The 6th Office is all too ready to scoop up anyone who asks questions, so those humans who are willing to resist are being systematically weeded out."

Mac nodded grimly. "Someone's been studying history," he said out loud. "They're using the most ruthless techniques of the Third Reich and the Soviet Union. They're damned effective, I can tell you. I haven't seen the like since the Collapse."

"You can see why we're so worried," T'verTra said.

Mac turned to him. "You should be. People who do stuff like that are capable of anything, and that racist mindset is always trouble. There's no doubt about it: war is brewing."

"And do you think you can stop them?"

Mac sighed. "I don't know. I'eiBida's plan is likely your best bet to reduce the level of violence, but I'm not sure what can short-circuit their ambitions. You better take a worst case outlook and keep building ships as fast as you can."

§

I'eiBida came to see him in his quarters later in the evening. "Well, Brian," he said. "They agreed. The mission is a 'go'."

Mac thought about it for a bit, and felt surprisingly calm about it. "All right. How soon do I leave?"

"As soon as possible. The situation is deteriorating fast."

"At least I'll be able to take a freakin' *shower* once I'm on the ship."

"I feel your pain." I'eiBida wrinkled his snout and gave him a wry grin.

Mac slumped and shook his head in despair. "God, this is one ugly sumbitch. We have a real gift for self-destruction, don't we?"

"Sadly, you do."

"I...can't fault your people for being afraid, I'eiBida, or for bringing me back to help. I just don't know what good I can do."

"Which does bring up a personal matter, Brian," I'eiBida said, softly. "Something I should have asked you earlier. As much as the humans are in the wrong, and your efforts will hopefully prevent a disastrous war, you'll be fighting against your own people. Can you do it?"

That was the big one: Mac fought with it for some time, trying to decide where his loyalties lay in light of what was happening on earth, and what he might be called upon to do. As wrong as the Purity Movement was, as twisted as the Alliance had become, it wasn't easy to turn his back on a lifetime of duty. "To such an extent as is necessary to prevent or limit a conflict," he said at last, carefully. "Beyond that, I'll have to reconsider."

I'eiBida nodded thoughtfully. "I wouldn't ask any more from you, Brian. Or any less."

§

Main spaceport, d'enchia:

Ensign KilPatrick was tired and sore after a long day of hauling supplies down for the human diplomatic enclave. He had a sinus headache, his flight suit itched and chaffed, and he could smell himself. His legs and back were stiff from sitting in one spot all day, but the shuttle was refueled and reloaded so fast that they hardly had a chance to take a head call, and there wasn't enough room to do the porkin' *Hula* in this crowded cockpit. This was their seventh shuttle run of the day, and he figured they faced at least two more. He longed for the meager zero-G shower and a few hours' sleep on the transport. Word was the movement of supplies would soon be back up to speed, which meant they would likely go back to six runs a day starting tomorrow.

"Fuel pumps?" His copilot, Ensign Perez, was checking off the flight list.

"Um, turbos at full, ramjets on standby, main engine on standby."

"Navigation radar?"

"Active. Track shows clear."

They were standing at the end of the taxiway ready to turn onto the runway, their turbines whining, running lights blinking.

"Capacitor?"

KilPatrick fought off his lethargy and checked his gauges. "Eighty-two percent." Enough to get them into orbit since their earth-bound cargo was lightweight foodstuffs for the Lizard embassy in Geneva.

"That will do, I guess. Checklist complete." Perez slid the clipboard under his seat and touched his throat mic. "Human shuttle flight two-zero-seven to d'enchia control, requesting clearance for take off."

The reply, in excellent Swiss, came back almost at once. "D'enchia control to *human* shuttle two-zero-seven, you are cleared for take off." It might have been their imagination, but that word 'human' seemed almost derogatory.

"Copy, d'enchia control. *Human* shuttle two-zero-seven departing."

"Damned Lizards," KilPatrick griped as he tweaked the turbine throttles and steered the ponderous shuttle around until it faced down the runway. "Lets go get some fresh air..."

"*Madre Dios!* What is that?" Perez pointed to their left.

A faint figure—a human—staggered out of the gloom onto the runway, and stood waving frantically to them in the glare of their landing lights.

"What the hell is he doing out there?" Perez asked.

"Idiot," KilPatrick muttered. "Get off the road."

They watched the agitated figure for a few seconds before they began to wonder what was happening. "Where did he come from?" Perez asked. "Something must be wrong."

"I don't like it." KilPatrick said at last. "Chief, come up here!" he called down the narrow gangway leading to the cargo bay.

Their cargo master took a look at the intruder, uttered a choice obscenity, and went back to open the starboard hatch. No sooner did he, then the stranger forced his way on board.

"I am Krauss, 6th Office," he snapped. "Take off at once!"

"What are you..."

"Zee Lizards are after me." The stranger waved at the open hatch. "You need to get me off planet. Take off now! Zat iss an order!"

The Chief threw a distracted glance into the gloom outside. There were lights moving across the field in a broad sweeping pattern. The intruder was shaggy, hadn't bathed for some time, and had a wild look in his eyes. This looked like major paperwork, and the Chief didn't want to get caught in the middle it; not when the 6th Office was involved. He hauled the hatch shut and yelled to KilPatrick to take off.

*****

"Chapter Three"

November 9, 2148 AD:

The transport arrived in earth orbit eighteen days later. Mac hovered at one of the viewports, watching the planet below and remembering. Things had changed in the last forty years, and it showed even in orbit. There were more city lights down there, and through a borrowed pair of binoculars he could just make out ocean-going ships as they plodded along the ancient trade routes like ships have done for the last five thousand years. There were more of them, and they were larger.

Things in space changed, too. Orbit Dock had grown from what he remembered, and when he studied it, he could see bits of the original structure which were rearranged and added to over the years. The space yards nearby held the partly completed hulls of six ships, and two more which seemed to be in for overhaul. Two more seemingly operational ships—a destroyer and a cruiser—drifted off the other side from the space yard, the cruiser taking fuel from a tankage lighter. Both were larger and more formidable-looking than the ships of his time, bristling with missiles and fire control antennas. Earth's shipbuilding capacity grew by leaps and bounds since he died. There were more work craft skittering around larger clusters of building materials, and the orbital tank farm was more than doubled in size. He was impressed.

The Ic'nichi courier ship floated near Orbit Dock, while their supply ship orbited some five degrees ahead, with one of its shuttles just docking. That reminded him that I'eiBida would be waiting for him at Singapore...

§

...*"The Alliance has made substantial gains in consolidating earth in the last forty years,"* I'eiBida told *him during one of their briefings. "Most of their expansion has been in the Middle East, Southern Africa, and South America, with limited gains on the Chinese mainland. They now control a bit more than half the earth's land mass, and about two-thirds of its population."*

"How tight is their control?"

"It varies. The Alliance was generally accepted in the areas they annexed, although there were some politically unstable regions."

"Was? How about 'is'?"

I'eiBida's ears twitched uneasily. "Since the Purity Movement gained power, the unrest is growing in many areas, notably those with large non-caucasian populations. Some regions have been severely repressed, and Peacekeeper units are widely deployed to maintain order."

"Can we use that?"

"We thought about it carefully, but we don't see how we can harness that anger and fear. There is a lot of rage building up, but the Purity Movement has been most effective in stamping out isolated outbreaks. That anger may grow to pose a threat in the future, but we have no way of tapping into it..."

§

..."Excuse me, Mister Krauss?" It was a crewman, who spoke with all deference. The 6th Office field operatives didn't display any rank, but there was no mistaking the subservience in that 'Mister'. "The Captain said to tell you your shuttle is ready, sir."

True to form, Mac didn't bother to thank him.

It turned out his shuttle was crewed by the same team which brought him up from d'enchia; one Ensign KilPatrick and company, who waited anxiously as he took a seat and strapped himself in. The shuttle was empty: no doubt Colonel Alvarez arranged a special trip for his benefit. No doubt these three would be interrogated at length to get their take on his miraculous appearance once he left them. It might explain their nervousness.

The trip down was routine. The shuttle was larger than the ones he remembered, and cut into the thin upper atmosphere a lot more smoothly. He sat alone in one of the crash couches on the upper deck, and the enforced isolation gave him time to think about his mission, and about earth. The briefings he received from Ic'nichi Intelligence weren't comforting...

§

..."The Peacekeepers are being shunted aside by the growing 'Tan Shirt' forces, and we believe the Purity Movement intends to supplant them completely in the long run. Their capabilities and morale are severely impaired by calculated neglect while the 'Tan Shirts' have received the bulk of the military resources."

"Political troops, like the SS during the Second World War," Mac said in disgust. "It will go a long way to assure the Purity Movement's permanent control."

I'eiBida nodded. "As far as we can tell, Space Fleet has not been politically compromised to a great degree as yet, although that process is under way. It seems your presence is still felt in Singapore; they have resisted politicization thus far, although it can't last."

It was some small comfort. "Good for them."

"Indeed. But don't count on them for help; few people on earth dare oppose the 6th Office these days..."

§

...They came out of the overcast, and flew over the water along the shore on final approach to the spaceport. Out the left window, Mac could see the Alliance Navy base—what was left of the old harbor district—filled with service ships, patrol craft, and three frigates. In his day one frigate and four gunboats were stationed there, and they were constantly hurting for logistics...

§

..."Southeast Asia is still a lawless region despite the Alliance's efforts over the years," I'eiBida told him in another briefing. "Malaysia in particular is gripped by quasi-religious fanaticism, and is in a state of near anarchy. It's a very dangerous place, and you should keep a wary eye open for random incursions."

"Which means security will be tight."

"Yes. There are checkpoints and patrols everywhere, and the spaceport and Navy base proper are well protected. Singapore has a large garrison, as much as the Alliance can spare, and sea-mobile operations go on all the time..."

§

...The spaceport runway had been lengthened and repaved, and there were more hangers, workshops, and office blocks then he remembered. The whole was surrounded by chain link, barbed wire, and more guard towers. Just beyond the spaceport fence was a sprawl of residential blocks for the spaceport and Navy personnel, surrounded in turn by its own guarded perimeter.

The shuttle touched down, bringing him back to the present.

The weather was cool and humid when he left the shuttle, and there was a chill breeze. The hardstand they parked on was wet with recent rain; the monsoon season had come once again, and the sky was ugly. Mac tucked his hands in his pockets and hunched against the chill as he surveyed the surroundings. The place looked much the same as always: weathered slab-fab office blocks, rows of cinder block warehouses, and steel frame hangers much like any military base anywhere in the world. There were more and larger buildings, and more truck traffic, but the sense of *deja vu* was overwhelming. It reminded him sharply that he was a ghost from an innocent past come to haunt the present.

A limo with two apes in three piece suits and sun glasses—on an overcast day—were waiting for him. Mac knew intimidation when he saw it, and dismissed them with the thought that they'd have to do better to impress a real military man...

§

...*"Colonel Alvarez commands the Special Operations wing of the 'Tan Shirts', their elite security apparatus. From what we have learned, he is feared even among the Purity Movement. We aren't sure how much control Geneva has over him and his force, but the rumbles we get are not promising."*

"Yeah, that's nothing new under the sun," Mac grumbled. *"Any idea how much real control he has?"*

I'eiBida gave a rueful ear twitch. "Sad to say, we aren't much good at spying on humans, other than by electronic means which produce only low grade intel, and the few operatives we develop tend not to last long. I'm afraid you will have to sound out the situation for yourself..."

§

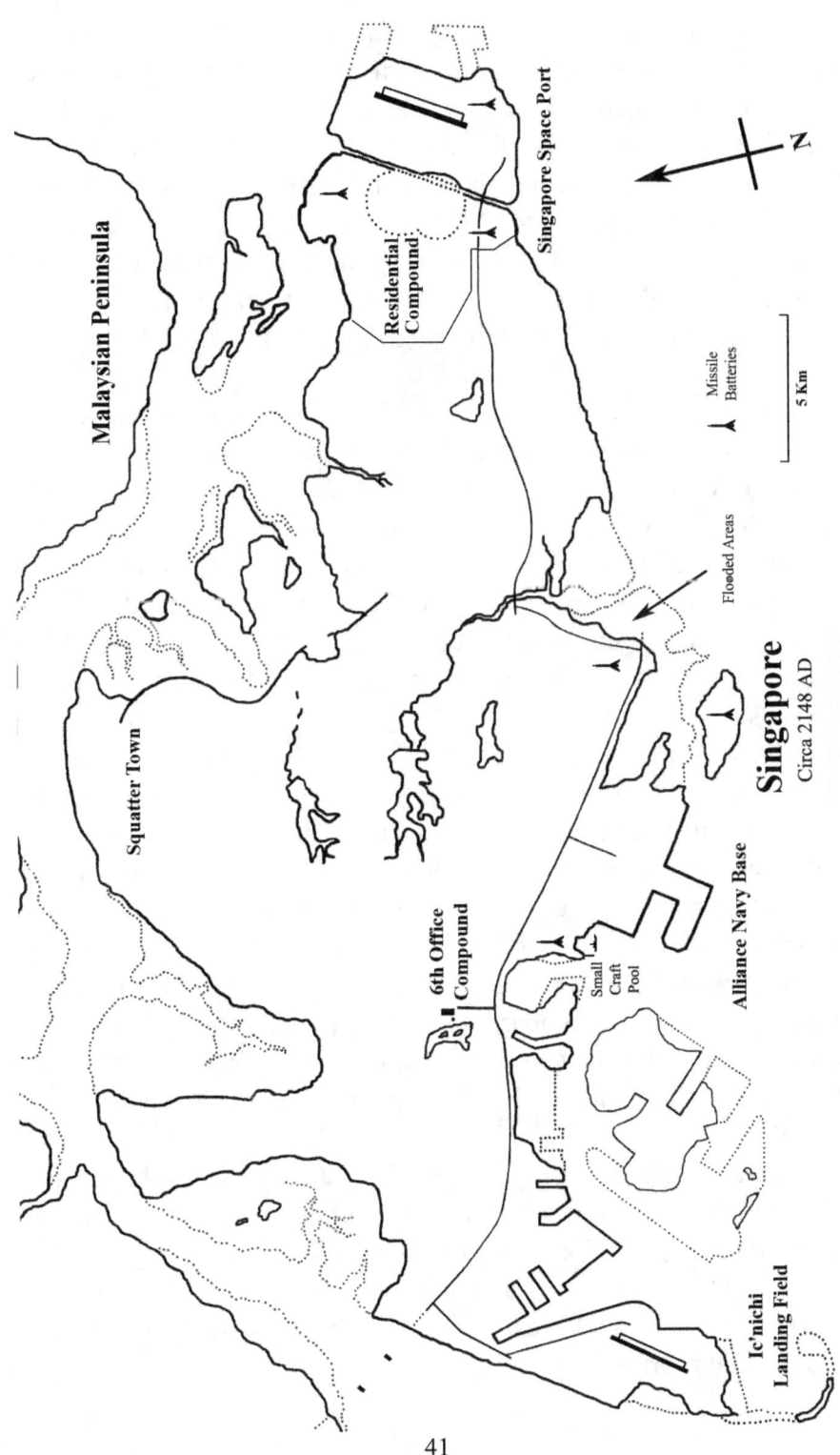

Singapore

Circa 2148 AD

41

...Leaving the spaceport, they paused at a security checkpoint where they were waved through with no more than a quick once-over, crossed a narrow channel, and wound their way around the vast shallow crater where the old International Airport once was. Mac used to see that crater through the window of his office back when he commanded Space Fleet: the sight of it always depressed him. Now it was a shallow, swampy lake which filled him with a sense of foreboding that this horror could happen again.

'Not on my watch,' he thought, grimly. *'Not twice. Not if I can stop it.'*

Right then he wanted to link up with I'eiBida in the worst way, but that would have to wait until he got past Colonel Alvarez and managed to gain some freedom of movement. *If* he managed to; *if* he didn't blow his cover and wind up in an interrogation cell. The thought chilled him; the next few hours would determine whether his mission would come to a sudden, messy end. He settled in the plush upholstery, stared at the bleak scenery, and tried not to think about the future while bitterly cursing all this damn-fool spy nonsense.

The spaceport was connected to the harbor and points west by the remnants of a four lane expressway built back when Singapore was a shining beacon of capitalism. It used to be lined by glittering skyscrapers; now there was nothing beyond the residential zone but scorched, wind-blown rubble. Space Fleet personnel in his day dubbed it 'The Highway To Hell'. That didn't say the half of it. The pavement was so broken up by weather and trucks and nuclear bombardment that it was little better than a gravel path. There were occasional smooth patches where the worst decay was plugged with asphalt, but it was slow, rough going.

There wasn't much traffic other than rare military vehicles, and a steady flow of flatbed semis hauling containers to and from the Ic'nichi landing field on the occasion when their transport came calling. The Navy base was faintly visible ahead to the left. The 6th Office compound was lost in the overcast, with the Ic'nichi landing field further on...

§

...""Why did they move your landing field down to the far end of the island?" he asked I'eiBida during another briefing.

"The official story was that they were running out of room at the spaceport. They gave us an abandoned military air strip so we could have more space for ourselves. That was five years ago. We pretended to go along because we wanted to avoid trouble, and because it gave us better security and room to expand our intelligence watching the spaceport and the 6th Office."

"A fine line of bullshit."

I'eiBida gave him a wry ear twitch. "We can see now that it was an early part of their effort to isolate us, but it played right into our hands...

§

...'We never learn, do we?' he thought, sadly.

The highway was even worse past the seaport entrance; desolate and deserted except for occasional flatbed semis. It was more than a hundred years since Singapore Island was devastated, and it was still an uninhabited wasteland except for the sparse Alliance presence.

A movement caught his eye: a slender, almost stunted dark-skinned Asian dressed in a simple pullover and armed with a crude machete, skulking amid the piled ruins, watching warily as they drove past...

§

"...The island is still deserted except for a few small settlements along the north shore known collectively as Squatter Town. The inhabitants are overflow from the Malaysian Peninsula, and a constant danger. Whatever happens, avoid the area at all cost."

"What will my chances be if I am forced to seek refuge there?"

I'eiBida gave him a long, searching look. "It might be a better option than falling into Alvarez's hands, if it comes to that, but not much better. It'll be quicker for you at least..."

§

...It was an old story, one dating from early in his former lifetime. Even as a young ordinary seaman, they warned him about any number of places which had descended into anarchy and tribal feudalism. The whole planet was like that during The Collapse. The devastation brought back memories.

They slowed and turned into a well paved side road leading to a large slab-fab office building set well back from the highway. The 6th Office compound was a six story rectangle of concrete tilt-up on the lowest floor, with glass and steel further up. This was the heart—if one could call it that—of the Purity Movement's Pretorian Guard. Here in this innocuous office block, the evil infesting mens' souls festered and plotted, sending out its plans and policies and orders with one goal in mind: to enslave the human race. The whole thing was perhaps a hundred meters wide and four times as long set in the middle of a parking lot with carefully tended grass further out. He glanced around cautiously, and noted there was no cover on the perimeter and clear fields of fire in all directions. The limo circled a driveway past the front of the building, and Mac got a glimpse of a smaller, squat building set along the far side of the main building: the secret laboratory. His objective.

The main entrance was up a broad flight of shallow stairs through wide glass doors into a two story lobby bare except for a security door to the left, a glassed in booth with two 'Tan Shirts' at the far end, and discreet gun slits all along the walls. Mac had no doubt that the glass was a lot tougher than it looked, and the lobby a tougher objective yet. The 'Tan Shirts' buzzed them through the inner door without waiting.

The two goons escorted him deep into the building, where they were intercepted by a familiar figure, who looked him over with some surprise and evident distaste. "Well, Krauss, interesting you should show up here. Had enough of the Lizards, have you?"

"Zey are all right, Volmer," Mac said, scornfully. "At least zey *nicht* stink like wallowing *schwine*."

Volmer was Alvarez's Aide: but unlike the Colonel, he was short and corpulent, his face blotched and sweaty, his uniform blouse studded with medals. Mac noted with distaste that he wore his braided Aide-de-Camp's aiguillette around his right shoulder—a distinction reserved for the Aides of national leaders. Either this was some calculated snub to the Alliance leadership, or Alvarez was getting ambitious. Hard to say which with this slovenly pig.

"Is that so?" Volmer gave him a venomous smile. "I am sure the Colonel will appreciate your *tolerant* attitude." This low-life was a player in the nastiest game of them all: someone to fear, not that Mac would give him the satisfaction. "I look forward to hearing your report, Krauss."

"You vill haff to ask zee Colonel for it, since I vill slit mine own throat before I report to *you!*"

Volmer gave him a poisonous glare. Ic'nichi Intel was right: the two of them were bitter rivals for Alvarez's favor, and since Volmer had all the morals of a Chicago drug dealer, he was a dangerous enemy. "Very well, Krauss," he snapped. "I will discuss it with the Colonel once he is through with you. It ought to make interesting reading."

Not that 'reporting to the Colonel' was all that simple around here. Mac wound up in an interrogation room with a plain wooden table, one chair, a blinding overhead light fixture, a large mirror on the side wall, and the two goons stationed on either side of the door. They glowered at him silently while a succession of intelligence types ran multiple identity checks and questioned him at length. The 'Tan Shirt' interrogators knew their stuff, and behind a facade of polite debriefing, they dug relentlessly into every detail of his cover story, and tried to trip him up on the smallest items. They dug far deeper into his cover story and his host's background then he was briefed on, in fact, so he was forced to improvise constantly. That added a new burden of made up facts to keep track of while worrying if his next utterance would blow his cover and end his mission. The worst of it were all the mannerisms of his host, not to mention that damned German accent. It took a real effort not to sound like *Herr Professor Schickelgruber*, the ludicrous Saturday morning cartoon Mad Scientist they used to imitate in grade school. The two goons hovered in the background all the while were an unspoken reminder of what would become of him if he tripped up.

It must have been early evening by time they gave up and left him and his two shadows alone. He sat at that table for perhaps half an hour pretending to be bored and annoyed while the two goons watched him silently. His nerves were raw, and he wanted a cig in the *worst* way, but sternly resisted temptation. If he started now, he would wind up chain-smoking, which wouldn't look good. It seemed like forever before the door opened abruptly, and the much-discussed Colonel Alvarez entered.

"Vell, hello, Colonel," Mac said with calculated insolence as he jerked a thumb at the two goons. "I see your hospitality iss ass fine ass always. It iss good to feel loved."

Colonel Alvarez was a bit shorter than Mac/Krauss, with an athletic build, a high forehead, and an elegant style which made the plain 'Tan Shirt' uniform seem classy: the very stereotype of a Junta Colonel which evoked a dozen bad memories from Mac's former life. He considered Mac with no favor. "Welcome home, Mister Krauss," he said at last. "I trust you are well?"

"Managing, I suppose."

Alvarez stood opposite him and studied him across the table like something unnatural. There was something in his eyes, and his look, and his tense posture that was...unsettling. "I must admit I am most curious about why you went missing," he said at last. "And why you turned up here on earth, of all places." His polite manner fooled no one: he wanted answers, and he wanted them now, and they better be good.

Mac dropped his insolence act and sat a bit straighter. "Zee Lizards vere on to me," he said, seriously. "Zey vere closing in und I couldn't get back to zee embassy, so I had to go to ground."

"And what put them on your scent, do you suppose?"

"I haff no idea. In fact, if I hadn't been alert, I might never haff seen zem. Zese weren't zee Inspectorate, they vere fleet Intelligence, zee 'Dark Grays'. Zey are *verdammtes gutes*, I can tell you."

"No doubt something to do with your recent success," Alvarez muttered. That caught Mac's attention, although he was careful not to show it. Then Alvarez drilled him with a hard look. "So why did you not use your escape route?"

For a fleeting instance, Mac almost panicked; he didn't know whether such a bolt-hole existed on d'enchia, or if this was a cunning trap. All he could do was hope for the best. "Zey vere too close to risk compromising our resources. Zee only thing I could do vas to go underground, und try to figure a vay to get back to zee embassy or to make contact. I vas lucky to evade zee dragnet und get away."

Alvarez pondered him for some time, and Mac took the occasion to revert to his insolent act. He slouched in the chair and ostensively lit up a desperately needed cig to the Colonel's annoyance while wondering if this mission was about to implode on him.

"Indeed?" Alvarez said at last. "And where did you go? Where did you hide for four months?"

Mac took a deep draw on his cig, which helped to settle his nerves a bit. "I happened to know vere zey keep a stock of human space rations und medical supplies for emergencies." They were back on the story line; good. "Zee warehouse had minimum security, so I vas able to break in mitout drawing attention."

Alvarez smiled; it wasn't a friendly smile. "Clever. And where is this warehouse, may I ask?"

Mac smiled at him in turn. "Zee last place zey vould think to look: right in zee main spaceport."

Alvarez chuckled. "Right in the middle of their fleet's main base? Most clever indeed. You never fail to amuse me, Mister Krauss." Then his tone turned hard. "But why did you remain there so long? And why did you leave?"

Mac took another draw on his cig, and made a show of contemplating the swirl of smoke. "I tried for zee longest time to contact zee embassy, but zee Lizards had communications sealed up air tight, und I vas hard pressed to get in und out of zee spaceport. Ass to why I left, something must have tipped zem off. I vas there four months when zey showed up in force one night. I bugged out of zere und took zee only escape I could find: I flagged down a shuttle about to take off, und hitched a ride home."

"That was most fortunate," Alvarez said, judiciously.

"*Ja!* I vas getting sick to *death* of space rations!"

Alvarez chuckled again, and again it was not a friendly gesture. "Your dedication and sacrifice for the cause are most worthy, Mister Krauss!" He stood in silence pondering Mac for some time, clearly deciding whether he would leave this room alive. "So, what are we to do with you, now that you have been compromised?" he asked at last.

Mac ground out his cig on the floor with vast relief, and sat up in his chair. "Zee ugly I vas getting on zee ship iss zat vee are looking at war mit zee Lizards. I vant some of zat." What he really wanted was to remain here at Singapore for as long as possible, and hopefully Alvarez would be his meal ticket.

"It would seem, indeed," Alvarez mused. "And your experience with covert operations on d'enchia will prove valuable. I daresay we can find good use for you, Mister Krauss." He mused further. "So for now, let us put you up in temporary facilities here. At the rate things are progressing, I suspect we will find useful employment for you shortly."

Unspoken, but plain, was that Alvarez wanted to keep him under his thumb for as long as possible. Men like him never trusted anyone despite Mac's story, which seemed to be holding for the moment. Normally that would be worrisome, but Mac was pleased with this break.

§

Alvarez lead him out of the security zone and down the building's main hallway with the two goons trailing silently behind. "I daresay we shall soon put you to good use, Mister Krauss," he said as they passed another security checkpoint. "Aside from an extensive debriefing on conditions on d'enchia, I think you will be valuable in organizing and training our Fifth Column for the Chamber Of Ancients action."

That wasn't comforting. "So vee are committed to war, zen?"

"Indeed we shall have our war with the Lizards, but not for a while yet; not until everything is ready with the fleet and here at home." Alvarez gave him a smile which was utterly devoid of humanity.

That was not good either. "How soon do you expect to begin, *mein herr?*"

Alvarez frowned, and regarded him coldly. "It will be a while yet." He clearly didn't like being questioned, and didn't trust even his best operative. "There are...developments...pending both in Geneva and on d'enchia which will require some time yet. Rest assured when the time comes, we will solve the Lizard problem once and for all."

Coming from Alvarez, that was disturbing news. "I suppose vee vill destroy their fleet?"

That seemed to stir Alvarez to life. "*Si*. But we will also destroy them! Once we have enough high yield nuclear weapons, we will neutralize their government with a preemptive covert action, then devastate their home world in a sudden raid. After that, we will hunt down any survivors of their fleet, and take over their colonies as well." His eyes lit up with a feverish gleam as he contemplated the havoc he would unleash. "It will be swift and complete. We anticipate a campaign of no more than a year, and the Lizard question will be solved once and for all."

In fact, this was alarming. Mac tried to dig for more while not arousing the Colonel's obvious paranoia. "Perhaps I am dense, *Herr* Colonel, but don't vee vant to keep zee Lizards around? Weakened, of course; weak enough zat zey don't pose a real threat, but one vee can still use to keep up zee proper martial spirit, you might say."

Alvarez smiled, with his lips, anyway; the rest of his face was a stone mask. "You have a fair grasp of geopolitics, Mister Krauss, but you overlooked the subtle details. The Lizards are a useful threat for as long as we wish them to be. Our propaganda can keep them alive and dangerous long after they are reduced to savagery, or eliminated altogether. So why risk an unfortunate situation when a more complete solution is within our grasp?"

Something in his eyes and his cool words sent a chill down Mac's spine. "*Ja*, vell, you haff me zere, *Herr* Colonel."

"And your recent *acquisition* will no doubt speed the process along. A fine bit of luck, no?"

Mac backpedaled fast to avoid another possible trap. "It iss hard for me to say. Zee problem mit *feld operat* iss zat vee never know how valuable something vill turn out."

Alvarez chuckled, gloating in his one-up. "Oh, your success was *most* significant. Perhaps you would care to see the results of your great coup?"

Mac eyed him curiously, wondering what this new development portended. "I vould indeed, mit your permission. So vat iss progress on zat?"

"I think you will be impressed."

§

Alvarez led him to a security door off the main hallway where the 'Tan Shirt' on duty gave him a rigid salute and buzzed them in post-haste. Beyond the door, a broad ramp descended, ran underground for a way, then climbed to another security door guarded by two more 'Tan Shirts' in an enclosed booth. Once buzzed in through a small lock, a corridor ran off to the right for about twenty meters before entering a large, brightly lit room. Mac's excitement rose as he realized Alvarez was leading him into the secret laboratory he hoped to penetrate. It could mean only one thing: his former self lead the plot to copy the recording. That would have huge implications back on d'enchia, and could make this operation much easier.

The corridor ended at another security door which opened into a large room. "This is the data processing center." Alvarez waved grandly to a bank of computers monitored by several civilian technicians. "Here is where we duplicated the Lizards' mind recording and programming methods based on the information you provided. As soon as we eliminate a last few technical problems, we can begin the conversion process."

Mac looked back and forth, taking in the layout and estimating what it would take to wreck the place. It was brightly lit, with the antiseptic sterility of computer centers anywhere. The technicians watched curiously or went about their duties while a third 'Tan Shirt' watched in the background. It wouldn't be easy to break in here, or to effectively wreck it if he could.

"So, you *nicht* have zee duplicate MacKenna yet, *Herr* Colonel?"

Alvarez gave him a chilly look and an equally chilly smile. "All in good time, Mister Krauss. All in good time."

50

Another security door lead to a broad corridor of tan painted cinder blocks lined in turn with steel doors. The overhead fixtures gave the place a chill, sterile feel. By each door there was a blank video screen and a display of lights that looked like medical monitors, all silent and dark.

"This is the processing section," Alvarez said with a sweeping gesture along the corridor. "This is where you will change the course of history, and insure us *permanent* supremacy."

The end of the corridor was sealed by another security door which opened onto a narrow corridor. One wall was more cinder blocks; the other a blank wall of sheet steel with a row of doors stretching to the end. Alvarez used his key card to open the first, and gestured Mac in with a flourish.

"Behold your great triumph, Mister Krauss: Admiral Brian Adelbard MacKenna!"

She was young, early twenties at best; slender and dark complected, with flowing black hair and delicate features contorted by misery and fear. She was dressed in a dirty prison fatigue, and lay in a fetal curl on the bunk. She turned her head to look at them when they entered, and her eyes were haunted by madness.

Mac was stunned, and had to say *something* to cover his shock and dismay. "I...don't follow vat you're doing, *Herr* Colonel." He turned and gave Alvarez a confused look, trying urgently to hold onto his cover. "*Zis* iss Admiral MacKenna?"

"One and the same."

Mac studied her in consternation. The look she gave him in turn was one part burning hatred, one part cold iron: that look convinced him his counterpart was hidden—trapped—in this unlikely vessel.

"She iss hardly going to command zee respect of zee troops. You vill vant someone better *equipped* to inspire zee men."

Alvarez laughed: he did that a lot, it seemed, and it didn't give him a jolly air; more like someone riding on the edge of hysteria. "Ah, Mister Krauss, your sense of humor is wicked! She is a test subject. As you reported, the process still needs refining; she is a handy political prisoner who is useful for perfecting the technique. Once we have it working, she will be *superseded*."

Mac saw her flinch, and had to fight to avoid showing any reaction himself. He knew full well what Alvarez meant by *'superseded'*.

"We are making steady progress isolating the functions which cause the rejection. In a few more months we will have the process perfected, and matters can proceed."

"You're dead meat, Alvarez!" she snarled. "I get the chance, and your ass is mine!"

"Which is why you will never have that chance," Alvarez said in smug satisfaction. "To the contrary, once you are no longer needed, I will allow my associates to dispose of you." Behind him in the corridor, his two goons stirred restlessly; Mac had a good idea of what Alvarez was talking about.

She flinched again, but her eyes smoldered. "Yeah? They're on my list too!" For all that she was a slip of a girl, her voice and mannerisms were disturbingly familiar.

Their eyes met briefly as Alvarez left and he followed. In spite of himself, Mac had to turn away.

*****

"Chapter Four"

Alvarez had him draw some clothing from their stores, put him up in 'guest quarters' on the sixth floor, and left him to his own devices. His new home was a basic apartment like you'd find in any workers' block anywhere in the world at one time; white painted walls, tile floor, a restroom with shower, and a window overlooking the central courtyard. Mac's first act was to luxuriate in the first long hot shower he'd had since his rebirth. It was sinfully indecent, and brought back memories of other times when he made do with a lick and a promise. There was no escaping his former life it seemed, but right then he felt too good to worry about it. When the hot water finally ran low, he toweled himself off, flopped on one of the twin beds, and contemplated his next move.

It seemed Alvarez bought his cover story—enough to quell his suspicion for the moment, anyway. That didn't mean that he, Mac, was out of danger, but it gave him some wiggle room. The next step was to make contact with I'eiBida at their landing field, which according to the original plan meant receiving some special communication gear through a series of safe drops over the next several days. But no plan survives contact with the enemy: he had some major strategic intel to report, and the memory of that young woman haunted him. This needed to go up the feeding chain in a hurry, which meant he needed to take chances. He stood by the window for a time, absently watching the lights across the courtyard go out by ones and twos, and brooded. He devoted his entire life to protecting humanity from the evil within, and now that evil festered anew in the Purity Movement, armed with some truly horrible technology which should never have been inflicted on this misbegotten Universe. The Ic'nichi intelligence reports were damning enough; the reality on the ground made the nightmare all too visceral.

His reflection showed faintly in the glass, and as he stared through it, the face of that frightened woman-child watched him in turn; solemnly, with big dark eyes begging silently for help she had no reason to believe would ever come. No, whatever doubts he held before, he would have no problem opposing these monsters.

But if he was going to make direct contact and have any hope of retaining his cover, he needed to move fast. He dressed, pulled on his shoes, grabbed his new jacket, stuck a pack of cigs in his pocket as an afterthought, and headed out.

Getting on and off the elevator meant passing through two security stations. Aside from signing through their checkpoints, the watch standers treated him as routine, which he made careful note of. As he went, he studied the hallway, memorizing every little detail for later use. The security watch at the laboratory door gave him a perfunctory nod and ignored him otherwise, which he also noted. Beyond the laboratory access, the hall turned left about a hundred meters further down and emptied into the lobby through another glass partition security door.

The end of the lobby, opposite the main entrance, was glassed off into a control booth for two 'Tan Shirt' security men. They buzzed him through the security door, and one of them came out to meet him. Another slack move.

"Can I help you, sir?"

Mac gave him a truculent look as he headed for the entry. "*Nein*."

"Where are you going, sir?"

"Out. I haff been cooped up in zat ship for too long. I am going out to get some air."

"Ah...sir, I will need the Colonel's permission..."

"If you wish to annoy him mit every little detail, zat iss your neck." Mac left before the man could decide what to do.

§

Outside, the low stair emptied onto the driveway as it looped back on itself. The night was cool and damp, with a half-moon peeking through a thinning cloud cover. The pavement was wet, and the air held a faint mist. Mac paused to size up the situation, then set off down the access road leading to the main highway. The access road wound along the shore of an old overgrown reservoir. Once past the manicured lawn, there were low mounds of weed-covered debris to either side where the wreckage was bulldozed. The night was utterly dark once he moved away from the building, and aside from a few faint lights from the harbor in

54

the distance he might have been the only human being on the planet. But he wasn't alone: he had never been alone in this place, back when he was alive. He hunched his shoulders and tugged his jacket tighter against a chill from no earthly weather. *They* called to him: the millions who died here. *They* watched from the shadows, silently blaming him as they had every right, silently damning him...

§

"...Con, sonar, still nothing, sir."

The glow was well beyond the horizon, but the dim red lights in the con were overwhelmed by the blinding glare that came through the periscope from above. He clicked a filter in place: the glow was still painfully bright. The light faded as he watched; faded and rose into the air, a vast white pall over the city they were guarding. As he watched in horror, another white light burst beyond the horizon, growing and rising like an obscene parody of dawn.

"Singapore, sir?" their Kiwi Number One asked.

'What a waste,' *he thought.* 'What a miserable, senseless waste.' *A third burst of light joined the prior two. His hands trembled.*

"Con, sonar. We're getting something now, sir."

"Oh, dear God..." Greg Baker, the Third Lieutenant— one of his—muttered. They could hear the rumble through the hull, from eighty klicks away.

'Thirty million defenseless refugees, for no good reason.' *It was sickening. A fourth burst of light appeared. Whoever was doing this intended to destroy all life on the island. Thirty million people...*

§

...He shook the stray thought off and moved on as he tried to shake off the guilt. He failed that day. They were tired, so he took the easy way out: moved the sub off shore—off station—so they could go deep and unwind for a while. Thirty million people died as a result. Right here where he was walking. He would *not* allow it to happen again.

§

55

The main highway was what remained of a four lane expressway after being nuked then left out in the weather for a century. He sized things up, then headed west over the broken, crumbled concrete, picking his way carefully around potholes and cracks where the pavement rippled under the nuclear concussion. As he walked, he thought feverishly about how he was going to do this. It was a good fifteen or sixteen klicks to the Ic'nichi base. He *must* have a ride; there was no way past it. He needed to connect with I'eiBida and get back before he was missed, which looked freakin' impossible unless he found some wheels...

...The ruins were bathed in faint light. He ducked behind a pile of rubble and watched as a truck came rumbling down the road. It was a flatbed semi hauling another container to the landing field. Just west of the 6th Office drive, the old highway was wrecked so thoroughly that they needed to build a bypass which swung south for a way. The corner was tight, and the truck braked sharply, and leaned over as it negotiated the turn. There was his ticket.

Once the truck was gone, he scuttled along the road, keeping a wary eye open, and went to ground beyond the turn. It wasn't long before another truck came around the corner behind him, slowing on the tight turn. When it came past, he was able to catch the rear of it. There were enough handholds on the container door latches that he was able to scramble up and lay flat on the roof.

§

Getting past the 'Tan Shirt' security on the landing field's main gate was no problem, since they gave the truck a perfunctory once-over and waved it in. Once past the gate, he clambered down from his perch and presented himself to the first gray uniform he came upon. Once that one got over his surprise, he escorted Mac at gunpoint to the guard room, where he was confronted by the Ic'nichi security elder.

Boss Security was a bulky mal wearing Fourth Degree Service Warden pips. A lowly Fourth Degree was lightweight for such a sensitive position, and he seemed alarmed to find a large human roaming the base at random. "Who are you, human? Why you come here?" Aside from being very junior, his language skills weren't the best. "What you do?"

"I am *Admiral* MacKenna, on a secret mission for 'Dark Grays' Intelligence." He gave him his best forbidding glare to keep him in his place. "I have urgent information to report, so I came in rather than wait for your contact. If Ki-Eldest I'eiBida is here, I need to see him, pronto."

That name-drop disconcerted the Elder and his Worthy, and his late captor was dispatched with a hurry-up message. I'eiBida and B'monTrea arrived soon thereafter.

"Brian? Thank the *Ancestors* you are safe!"

Mac disregarded Boss Security's surly look, and settled wearily on the corner of his desk. "It went smooth enough."

"How you get in here, human?" This goy didn't know when to quit, it seemed.

"That's *Admiral* to you," Mac snapped. "I hitched a ride on the top of a truck, if you *must* know." Ic'nichi body language is different from human, but his embarrassment was obvious.

"Relax, D'remNek," I'eiBida told him, with a bemused glance at Mac. "The Admiral goes far beyond your usual security threat."

"Yeah," Mac grumbled. "You know all that bad karma you built up? I'm it."

I'eiBida sagged a bit, and gave him a forced grin. "You must have had it easier than I did. You would not *believe* how C'traBenla knotted my tail when I told her I was coming here."

"War is hell." Right then, he was so relieved to be there in some illusion of safety that he actually chuckled at the memory of I'eiBida's temperamental bondmate.

"So why did you come in, Brian? Have you been compromised?"

"Not yet. At least I don't think so, but if I'm to maintain cover, I can't hang around for long." He sat up and looked I'eiBida in the eye. "I have some major intel to report, so I had to take the chance and come in."

"I'm anxious to hear what you have. Come and meet the rest."

He led Mac down the hall to the Intelligence circle with D'remNek grumbling along behind, and sent runners to fetch the higher-ups. The Intel circle was large and well equipped, with television and teletype monitors, a bay of communications gear around a plotting table, and several well laid out work stations. That would follow since this nominally diplomatic outpost was ideally sited to monitor both Space Fleet and the 6th Office.

The Intel watch was large even this late, and gathered around curiously. "I suppose introductions are in order." I'eiBida pointed out his key people. "Second Degree T'thReptn leads our intelligence circle here in Singapore. You may rely on him; I picked him personally for this post right before I retired." The fact that he was only a Second Degree after five years here said something about 'Dark Grays' politics back home. For all that, he was alert and reserved; Mac took a liking to him right off.

"And Fourth Degree D'remNek you've already met."

Mac shrugged. "I've had the pleasure."

The runner returned with a new Ic'nichi dressed in ordinary. "And this is Arbiter C'broVbron, the base diplomatic Eldest," I'eiBida introduced her. She looked him over as I'eiBida explained the situation and didn't say anything, but she didn't seem thrilled with all this sneakery.

"So what have you learned, sir?" T'thReptn asked. *His* Swiss was excellent.

Time to get back to matters at hand. "Your Intel people were right: they are definitely planning for war against you. Alvarez outlined a lightning campaign to reduce d'enchia to ruins, then follow up with a sweep of your fleet and your colonies. Their goal is to eliminate your people as a possible threat, and later expand into your stellar sphere."

I'eiBida's ears wilted. "How long do we have?"

"He didn't say, but two key factors are the production of nuclear weapons and consolidating his power here on earth."

I'eiBida glanced at T'thReptn, who got his people busy digging through their files. Points for him in Mac's book.

"It turns out my former self was the one who scarfed the recording. Who he had contact with might help you track down the turned operative in the Staff."

I'eiBida nodded at that. "Yes, it should. We haven't found him yet, but we've eliminated a lot of possibilities. We'll find him eventually."

"Keep at it. You don't need a snake in the grass right where he can do the worst, not with war brewing."

C'broVbron shook her head in obvious dismay. "How bad do you think it will be?"

"As our old friend Alvarez put it, 'Our propaganda will make the Lizards a useful threat long after we have reduced them to savagery, or eliminated them altogether'."

I'eiBida blanched. "Are you sure they plan to go that far?"

"Count on it. Alvarez also mentioned a preemptive move to neutralize the Chamber Of Ancients. He didn't say how, but I suspect it'll be some sort of Fifth Column action from the diplomatic compound."

That produced a stir in the room. "Great," I'eiBida said. "We need to alert Intel right away. Thank you, Brian."

"You'll get my bill."

"This is incredible," C'broVbron said in alarm. "How can any one human exercise so much authority he wasn't given?"

"Alvarez is a genuine Hitler wannabe, and its clear he packs some major weight," Mac told her. "I take this seriously; you should, too."

"Its worse than we thought," B'monTrea muttered. The Intel staffers stirred uneasily, and kept digging in their files.

"So...do they have another MacKenna, sir?" B'monTrea asked.

"Sort of. Alvarez showed me the project in person. They have a test subject they've been using to perfect the process."

"So they aren't as far along as we feared, then."

"We have to get her out of there."

"Her?" I'eiBida considered him doubtfully.

"She's a young woman; hell, she's just a girl. They're erasing and refilling her mind like a disposable data chip, and she's on the ragged edge of insanity because of it."

I'eiBida blanched again. "Ancestors!"

"We have to get her out. She's an innocent victim, and she can give us a lot of info on their project if we can bring her away safely."

"That's...not in the mission parameters..." B'monTrea said, doubtfully.

59

"Missions change."

"Is not for you to say, human!" D'remNek snapped.

I'eiBida beat Mac to the draw. "That will do, Fourth! Return to your duties!" D'remNek wilted and withdrew, grumbling to himself. At that he was lucky: Mac had a *whole lot* of pent-up ass-chewing in him just *waiting* for some unlucky winner to push him once too often.

"I know she's not one of your people, but what she's going through must be unspeakable," Mac said emphatically. "We *must* help her."

I'eiBida tried to reason with him. "Brian, I'm sorry, but we have to think of the mission first. This is too critical to the future of both races to allow us to be distracted by the fate of one individual."

"Innocents suffer in wartime, Admiral," C'broVbron said, sadly. "Her fate is tragic, but the fate of billions hangs in the balance. You need to focus on the mission."

"There's no way I can destroy that place on my own: it's too big, and there are too many people around. Our only chance is to get her out of there, and use the intel she can provide to pressure the Alliance. Threaten them with preemptive war unless they agree to the supervised destruction of that laboratory."

"But..."

"I'eiBida, trust me. I know something about destroying defended positions, and this is a non-starter." Mac crossed his arms and gave them all his most forbidding frown. "I'm going to get her out of there. You know its the right thing to do. Help me or not as you choose."

"Our Ancestors will curse us for this," I'eiBida muttered. "All right, Brian. We will help you to rescue her if at all possible."

"But..."

"We must trust the Admiral's judgement concerning human matters." C'broVbron subsided reluctantly. "And he is right that she could offer some useful intelligence."

"But what can we do, sir?" B'monTrea asked.

I'eiBida considered for a moment. "Call S'deMnveb in."

§

60

They were soon joined by a pair of 'Dark Grays' with unfamiliar uniform tabs. "This is Second Degree S'deMnveb and his Worthy," I'eiBida said. "They command our best section of Special Service defenders."

"I have studied your record, sir," S'deMnveb said somberly. "Its an honor to meet you at last."

"Let's reserve judgment on that," Mac told him, then confronted I'eiBida. "So what's with the *sturmcommandoes*?"

"A last minute change on my part. This situation is so critical that I decided to set up as many options as possible."

"We had this discussion back on d'enchia. Any direct act by your forces could trigger the war we hope to avoid. A raid would be a last desperate resort."

"Agreed, Brian. But if we are to destroy the recording, we may have to turn to that last resort."

"One person can only do so much, sir," B'monTrea said. "Even if you can find the recording, we may have to destroy that laboratory ourselves if your idea of pressuring the Alliance fails. You'll need a long tail to do all that."

"Time is not on our side, Brian. Pressuring the Alliance may not work, in which case we will have to do it at whatever cost."

"And there may be no other way to get her out of there, sir," T'thReptn added.

Mac hated being pinned down by subordinates, but they were right. "Yeah." He turned to S'deMnveb. "Well, right now we need your input. Let's see what our options are." He described the problem quickly, and started to draw a sketch map of the laboratory interior before T'thReptn produced a copy of the blueprints. "Um...thanks.

S'deMnveb and his Worthy studied the floor plan carefully. "That is a tough objective, sir," he said at last. "I don't see any way to infiltrate, and I'm not sure we have the strength for an assault."

"Certainly not against the main building," I'eiBida said. "We might be able to storm the lab, but it would take a finesse move."

"One we want to avoid if at all possible," Mac reminded them. He examined the floor plan carefully. "I don't see any doors or windows."

"There aren't any, nor ventilators, either, sir," T'thReptn said. "The only access is through the underground passage from the main building." He dug through a thick file folder, and extracted several orbital photos of the building under construction. The work site was covered by a huge tent, but infrared photos gave hints of what the canvas tried to hide. The access tunnel came out of the main building just West of the front entrance, ran about a hundred meters, and came up in the center of the lab, exactly as Mac remembered.

"As you can see, the only way in or out is through the main building, sir. I can't imagine any excuse you can use which will get them to let you walk out with her."

"It may take a direct attack," C'broVbron said reluctantly. "But we're trying to avoid a war, not start one."

"That's not something any of us want," I'eiBida told her.

Mac leaned on the table and tried to fight off his weariness and fugue while he pondered the floor plan. I'eiBida was right: he couldn't risk war over the fate of one person, no matter how horrible her fate was. He wondered to himself what he hoped to accomplish; if he'd learned anything in his bloody lifetime, it was to pick his fights carefully. This looked hopeless; hell, it *was* hopeless. But those dark, solemn eyes haunted him, and he was nothing if not stubborn. If ingenuity was his strong suit, then this was the perfect spot for a wild-ass unorthodox move.

"There is one possibility," he said at last. "I go in there with an explosive charge, and blow a hole in the wall for us to escape."

"Brian, this is *er'trxxda*. You could never smuggle an explosive in there."

"I'm Alvarez's fair-haired boy, remember? Plus I made the whole thing possible by that recording. Their security is slack, more than I would have expected. They likely won't ask too many questions if I want to go in and gloat over my crowning success."

"Even so, how could you smuggle explosives in there?"

S'deMnveb's ears perked up. "We have some special munitions, sir, including a light shaped charge no larger than a human fist especially designed for demolitions in close areas. It should blow a hole large enough for him to crawl through."

B'monTrea picked up on his enthusiasm. "It would be a quick stealth raid, sir, ideal for the Admiral as an infiltrator."

"And if we can get her out, she could give us the critical intel we need to pressure the Alliance, sir," T'thReptn added. "The Admiral's proposal is our best chance, and this is key to that."

"I...don't like it," I'eiBida said, reluctantly, then turned to him. "What do you think, Brian?"

Mac was thinking this was Ivy-League dumb-ass, even if it was his idea to start with, but it would forestall S'deMnveb and his Specials, and those dark eyes were in the background, pleading silently for help.

"Let's get moving. I'm due back."

§

"You have everything you need?" I'eiBida asked as they headed for the warehouse area.

"Yeah." The explosive charge, a half sphere the size of an orange, was tucked into an interior pocket along with a set of human wire cutters someone found for him. "Except for some common sense, maybe."

I'eiBida gave that a nervous chuckle. "Some old human saying about more balls than brains, I believe?"

"You got *that* right."

It was sprinkling when they came out of the Admin building, and the area was shrouded by a thin ground fog. A row of cylindrical warehouses across the main road were silhouetted by the landing field lights beyond. The area was dark otherwise, except for a row of street lamps set low to illuminate the pavement in Ic'nichi fashion. Another truck ground by on its way to the warehouses, but the area was deserted otherwise.

"Our intel people gave me a rough initial report," I'eiBida said. "Based on known weapons production and the rate of new ship construction, it looks like we have less than a year."

"That would figure," Mac grumbled. That was fast work on T'thReptn's part. For all that he was a youngster, he was on the ball; only to be expected from someone I'eiBida hand picked. "By then Alvarez will have his MacKenna, and will have neutralized most of his competition."

63

I'eiBida took his sleeve as he turned to go. "Brian, are you sure about this? You're taking a terrible chance. She is only one person, and when you think of how many will die if we fail..."

"You didn't see her," Mac told him, gently. "You didn't see the look in her eyes."

I'eiBida's ears wilted. "Good luck, Brian," he said, softly. "For both of you."

§

A shuttle was standing on the tarmac next to one of the warehouses while a row of fork lifts dug its contents out. A row of tractor-trailers were backed up to the freight docks along side. The hour was early, the first faint traces of dawn in the Eastern sky, and the driver of one truck was in a hurry to finish this last run and go off duty. No sooner was the container sealed and the paperwork signed by the Lizard in charge, then he gunned his bulky rig around out of its narrow slot between two other trucks, and...

...an Ic'nichi utility vehicle came around the corner of the offices and cut right in front of him. He slammed on his brakes and swerved, narrowly missing the interloper, then narrowly avoiding the wall. As soon as he got his rig under control, he leaned out his door and yelled some choice human curses at the other driver. That one waved to him happily and drove off. The human driver sent an angry glare after him, so didn't notice when a shadowy figure jumped from the roof to the top of his container.

§

The ride back was routine, if anything about this mess could be considered 'routine'. The temperature was dropping, and his thin windbreaker wasn't much use. He huddled in a knot and tried to keep warm while wondering what came next. As sorely tempted as he was to rush to her rescue, he knew that was impossible. It was nearly dawn: they would need the cover of darkness to make their escape. He also needed food and rest, and could hardly pull this off while the laboratory was busy. As much as he wanted to help her, she would just have to hang on until tomorrow night.

His thoughts were interrupted when a military police vehicle sped past in the opposite direction with its lights flashing. That didn't look good. Best efforts notwithstanding, his journey lasted far longer than he intended. Likely he was missed by now, and the search was on. He worried about whether he should ditch the explosive and wire cutter rather than risk being searched when he returned, but decided not to. Odds were he would not be able to leave the building casually again, and it was unlikely he could find them if he simply dropped them in the dark. No, he paid his nickel and had to ride this one to the end of the line.

The truck was nearing the bypass, and he could just make out the driveway to the 6th Office compound ahead when they braked to an abrupt halt.

"Have you seen anyone on the road?" a voice demanded. "A large man in a blue windbreaker?"

The driver mumbled something inaudible.

"Well if you do see anyone, report him at once."

More mumbled words, and the truck lurched into motion. The hunt for him was definitely on, and he needed to come up with an idea fast. He scrambled as far forward as he could on the container roof, and pressed himself flat. A quick look back, and he saw the roadblock manned by a half-dozen 'Tan Shirts', who watched the truck go, but thankfully didn't see him.

Through the curve and back on the highway, and the 6th Office compound was coming up on his left. He could make out another roadblock in the gloom ahead, but by great fortune, there was no force covering the driveway entrance proper. Time to get off while the truck was slowed.

He hit the ground hard, rolled, then scrambled to his feet and scuttled into the weeds beside the road. Once gone to ground, he watched and listened anxiously as the truck moved off and silence returned. The world was empty but for the creaking of insects and the distant sound of the waves on the shore, and the silent damnation of those who lay unburied for a century around him.

There was a rattle of falling rocks, and faint voices from across the road. A foot patrol was coming toward him. He looked around frantically, then scuttled away from the road, keeping carefully out of sight, and made for the waterfront some two hundred meters distant. It was rough going over the piled wreckage, but it gave him good cover...

...perhaps *too* good cover: he spotted another patrol to the west just in time to avoid them. He fell back a way, and waited until they passed him in an open search line, then swung wide to pass behind them.

The waterfront used to be an anchorage formed by dredging out a shallow coastal inlet. The Singaporeans enclosed it to form a sheltered lagoon, lined it with concrete piers, and packed the surrounding area with godowns and large cranes. All that remained now was the crumbled remnants of the seawall and the submerged hulk of a ship capsized by the force of the blast which swept everything else away. The sheltered lagoon had been reclaimed by the sea, and was now a shallow bay. The Alliance Navy base was visible off to the southeast, with an unfamiliar anti-aircraft missile battery on the shore opposite.

No time for rubbernecking: Mac selected as comfortable a spot as could be found in this desolation, settled against a pile of rubble under an overhanging slab of concrete, pulled his windbreaker tight, and tugged his cap down over his eyes. It wasn't the best illusion, but it was all he could come up with on the spur of the moment.

He sat there for some time and fought against his rising fear as he waited for the patrols to find him. For all his war experience, or perhaps because of it, he was as mortal and fallible as the next guy. This was a desperate move which could easily go against him if Alvarez's paranoia was aroused. He tugged his windbreaker tighter and debated with himself whether this was taking one too many chances; whether he should cut and run back to the Ic'nichi base and get safely off this hell-world. They had the critical information they needed, and Alvarez could be dealt with by any number of ways.

He stared, unseeing, at the lights of the Navy base in the distance. He couldn't do it. Those dark eyes were faintly reflected in the mist and in the choppy water, her thin face outlined by the glow of the distant lights. She needed his help. He was her only chance. He couldn't walk away while there was any hope of saving her.

"Mister Krauss?"

"Hmph?" It was a patrol, spread out to surround him with their weapons at the ready. It seemed he actually did nod off for a bit. He jumped, startled out of a half doze, and looked at them in genuine confusion. *"Ja?"*

"The Colonel sent us to find you, sir."

He stared at them stupidly for a moment. "Vat time iss it?"

"Nearly dawn, sir."

"Leiber Gott," he muttered as he struggled to his feet.

§

All the fuss and feathers made his return easier, since he wasn't sure how he would have smuggled the wire cutters past the metal detectors at the main entrance. The patrol's hardware sent the detector into hysterics until the watch hastily shut it off. Colonel Alvarez was waiting in the lobby when the patrol returned with their prize, and it didn't take a genius to see that he was seriously put out by all this.

"I...must apologize, *Herr* Colonel," Mac said, awkwardly. "I went out for some air, und fell asleep."

"So I understand, *Mister* Krauss." Alvarez eyed him coldly. "I *trust* you had a pleasant nap?"

"Nein...actually I did not. Mit your permission, I vill return to my quarters."

Alvarez studied him with obvious displeasure for a long moment. "Very well, Mister Krauss. But please do not leave the building in the future unless someone goes with you."

"Jawhol, Herr Colonel." It seemed this was one chance that paid off; he would avoid any further by not leaving unless someone went along, as Alvarez ordered. In fact, that was exactly what he planned to do.

*****

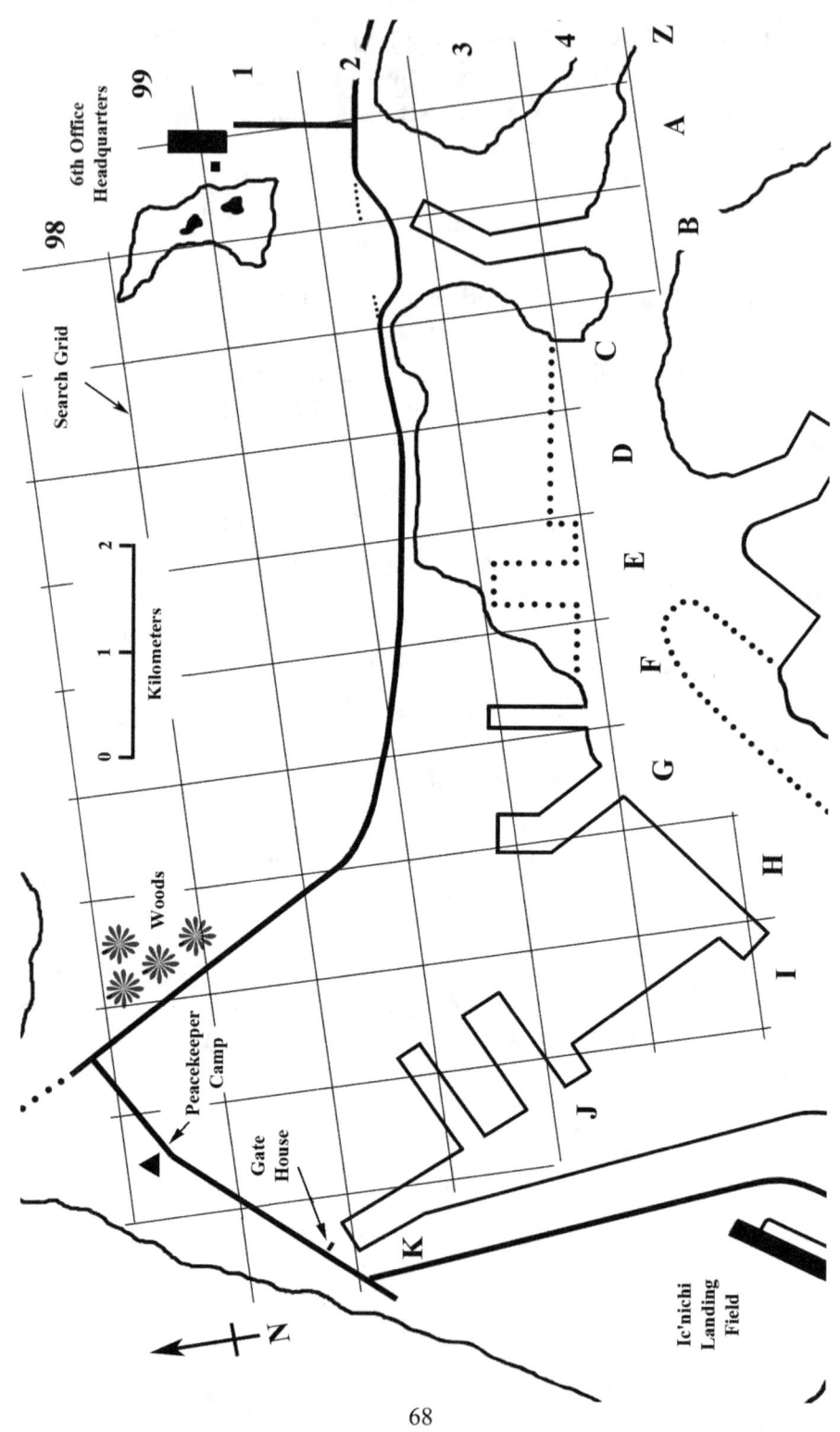

6th Office
Headquarters

99

98

Search Grid

1

2

3

4

Z

A

B

C

D

E

F

G

H

I

J

K

Kilometers

0   1   2

Woods

Peacekeeper
Camp

Gate
House

Ic'nichi
Landing
Field

N

"Chapter Five"

Like all office buildings, the 6th Office administrative complex was effectively abandoned by 18:00 hours. There were the twenty-four hour watches in the intelligence center and at communications of course, as well as the security, but most of the drones left in a herd well before dinner time. Mac waited nervously in his quarters, fiddling with the explosive charge while watching the clock twitch ahead one more minute, then another, then the next... For all his experience, it was a long time since he was low enough on the totem pole to go on tactical missions, and he was no cardboard superhero. He knew better than to be cavalier about it.

He finally forced himself to put the explosive away before he accidentally blew himself up, and lay on the bed chain-smoking and going over the mission in his mind. There were two crisis points: if he couldn't bluff his way into the laboratory, he'd have to fight his way in if he was close to the goal, or retreat. Either way would probably involve violence. He could depend on his size and strength for the initial surprise, but he would have to grab a weapon as soon as he could. Either way, the odds on success, not to mention survival, would be substantially lowered.

The second crisis point was if he made it in, but couldn't blow an exit. If that happened, they'd be trapped. His only option then would be to kill her, then do as much damage as possible before he was overwhelmed. The thought pained him, but it would be more merciful for her that way.

It was 21:00 almost before he realized it. His window of opportunity was closing: they'd be suspicious if he wanted to see her in the dead of night. He stubbed out his cig, and headed out.

§

The watch stander at the tunnel entrance security desk gave him distrustful look when he showed up. "Can I help you, sir?" That was not an invitation.

"I am heading out on a new assignment in zee morning, so I thought I vould take another look at our prize." Mac gestured at the glass and metal security door. "Zat vas quite a coup. It iss not every day vee bring a military hero back from zee dead, *ja?*"

69

The security man was unimpressed. "I'll need clearance from Colonel Alvarez, sir."

"I asked him earlier, und he said it vas all right." He gave the man an intimidating frown when he seemed unconvinced. "Of course, you could call him at home to get confirmation, not zat I would vant to be zee one who woke him out of a sound sleep."

The man hesitated: there are official and unofficial ranks in any military, and dictatorships tend to favor the unofficial. He was known to be Alvarez' favorite, and not someone to antagonize in general. Before the guard could decide what to do, Mac picked up the phone and offered it to him. He looked at it with something akin to dread, and waffled under the implied threat.

"Very well, sir, if the Colonel gave you clearance."

He reached down, pushed the button, and passed the buck. The door buzzed; Mac gave him a contemptuous look and entered without a further word.   That incident confirmed his earlier suspicion: the 6th Office was so obsessed with security that, paradoxically, they felt their own security was so tight that they slacked off without realizing it.   Human nature triumphed once again. Hopefully their slackness would hold up for a few minutes longer.

§

The other end of the access tunnel was guarded by two 'Tan Shirts' wearing the elite 'Executive Service' collar trim.   The security door buzzed as he approached: he got past the first guard, so they weren't too concerned.   One of them came out of the reinforced control booth when he entered; more lax security.

"Can I help you, sir?" That wasn't an invitation, either.

"Zee Colonel asked me to check up on our test subject. He wanted me to be sure everything iss in order."

The man's reaction was a mix of disapproval at his second-guessing them, and worry over what his visit might imply. "Very well, sir. You know the way to the cell block?"

"*Ja.*" Mac waited a moment, then stuck out his palm. "Your key card?"   The guard looked him over doubtfully, then surrendered his magnetic key.

§

70

She lay curled up on the cot staring at the wall when he entered, and gave him a wary, frightened look. There was a moment of painful silence as they stared at each other, then, "Wolf, seven-three-two," he said, cautiously.

Her eyes widened in surprise, and she sat up. "Tiger Lilly, six-two-nine," she answered. "Who are you?"

"I'm another copy of you, Admiral MacKenna. I've come to get you out of here."

"Yeah, right," she said, scornfully. "This is another one of Alvarez's tricks, but I'm not about to bite. I didn't just fall off the turnip truck, you know."

"I'm real enough; an authentic Fairy Godmother come to sprinkle you with Pixie dust so you can walk through walls."

She clearly didn't buy that one. "So what's your game? Lead me on, and then lower the boom to break my spirit? You'll have to do better, Bubba."

Mac was starting to lose patience with her, not that he could blame her for her paranoia. "Believe it or not, I'm the real deal, and this isn't the time for guessing games. You need to get on the stick if you want out of here, 'cause I'm your only chance."

"Yeah? All right, tough guy, prove it. What was Hythe-Morrison's nickname? The one you always kept to yourself?"

"Jeeves The Butler."

She wilted, and stared at him doubtfully. The look in her eyes said she wanted desperately to believe, but didn't dare risk it. "What the *hell* is going on here?" she demanded at last in a shaky voice. "How did I get in this body?"

Mac checked the hallway, then carefully moved forward to block the camera over the door so her reactions couldn't be seen. "Our Ic'nichi friends copied our memories shortly before we died some forty years ago. The humans pirated a copy of that recording, which they used to activate you. The Ic'nichi activated me to counterbalance you."

She sagged on the cot in dismay. "*Son* of a friggin' goddamned *bitch*," she muttered. "If this don't beat all." She gave him a bleak look. "Those damned Anti-techs were right; we can't be trusted with technology."

"That's not the issue right now. We need to get out of here in a hurry before they become suspicious."

"I'm all for that, but how?"

"Our friends sent along a little present." He hefted the shaped charge. "We'll make a grand exit, then head cross country for the Ic'nichi landing field. You up to it?"

She stood up eagerly, just coming to his shoulder. "I'll crawl if I have to. Anything's better than this."

"You got that right." He gestured at the camera. "This'll draw attention, so we'll have to move fast."

"Do it, mister." In spite of himself, Mac responded to her ring of authority.

He eased out into the block and looked around: hers was the first of a dozen cells along one wall. He blocked the cell door open with a convenient trash can, then handed her the access card as he returned to the cell. "Get down to the last cell in this row, quickly!" She sprinted past him as he peeled the paper off the sticky pad, shoved it against the wall about half way up, pulled the timing ring, and retreated after her, snagging the trash can as he went. She huddled against the wall at the far end of the cell block, trembling. The door was already open, so he herded her inside and jammed it with the trash can. "All right, here we go!"

There was a sudden rush of footsteps, and the cell block door opened just as the charge went off. The explosion was stunning: it knocked them off their feet, and left them shaken for a moment with their ears ringing from the concussion. The cell door flew open in the shock wave, and almost slammed shut again before he jammed his leg in it to keep it from closing. He pulled himself together, grabbed her arm, and dragged her out of the cell and down the block. Two guards—what was left of them—lay sprawled in the doorway; caught by the explosion as they rushed in. The third lay on the floor, stunned, but still alive. Mac pocketed his automatic pistol, then gave him a calculated kick to the temple. He gasped, and quit moving.

"Let's go!"

The cell door was partly ripped loose, and the steel wall bulged. The hinges were jammed, but Mac managed to pull it clear enough for them to shimmy past. The hole blown in the cell wall was just above ground level, and just large enough for him to squeeze through, which was a huge relief. He hefted her by main force and shoved her through the hole, then clambered up on the overturned cot frame and struggled through.

§

The air outside was chilly and bracingly fresh. The drizzle ended, and the broken cloud cover gave them glimpses of a half moon. After the close confines of her cell, the sense of freedom made them giddy. There was a siren squealing in the distance. Mac shook off the distraction and glanced around nervously, but there was no one in sight. "Let's move. No time."

They ran for the fence, Mac watching their flanks for any sign of pursuit. It wouldn't take long for Alvarez's goons to figure out what happened and come looking, and they needed to be long gone by then. Like all chain link fences, the perimeter's fatal weakness was the wire ties which held the mesh to the posts. Mac lead her along the fence until they came to a splice point, then fished the wire cutters out of his pocket. They were too small for this sort of work, but by worrying the wire back and forth, he was able to twist them loose one by one until there was a gap at the bottom.

"You first." He hauled one corner back by main strength, and watched nervously for any sign of intruders as she dropped flat and wiggled through the opening. Then she held the mesh back while he struggled through. His belt snagged on the mesh, and he fought down a moment of panic as he struggled to free himself.

"Move!" she hissed as she yanked him free from the snag.

Once on his feet again, he got his bearings quickly while recalling the details of the map. There were flashlights coming along the side of the main building in the distance. They couldn't head south for the main road without being seen, not that that was a clever idea to begin with. "All right, we head north to circle the lake, then due west."

The old reservoir west of them was rank and overgrown, more a muddy swamp than a real lake, but they still had to move several hundred meters north to skirt the end of it. The ground was rough and uneven; formerly a workers' apartment district, now nothing but low mounds of debris hidden by rank weeds. These ruins covered most of Singapore, and while it was slow going, there were worse areas ahead of them.

"God, I'm glad to get out of there," she grumbled as he helped her over a rough spot. "I always hated spooks." She gave him an angry look. "Now its personal. I've got dibs on Alvarez. He owes me, big time."

"That bastard's got it coming," Mac said, evenly. "Just make it slow for him."

"You better believe it!" Despite the venom in her voice, she was trembling.

§

Colonel Alvarez lived twenty minutes away from the 6th Office compound; he was there fifteen minutes after receiving the call from the Security Duty Officer, with Volmer on his heels. Everyone in sight kept a nervous low profile as he stormed in, and the sight of the ruined cell block and the bloodstained tarp filling the narrow corridor drove him right to the edge.

"You let some *Puker* saboteur bring *explosives* into my laboratory?" he yelled at the Duty Officer in a spittle-spewing rage. "You let them steal my test subject! What kind of security are you running here?"

"We tried to stop him, sir..."

"THEY tried to stop him!" Alvarez gestured wildly at the covered corpses. "THEY did their duty! *Why aren't YOU laying there with them?*"

"It was *Herr* Krauss, sir." The Duty Officer held out a video print with a shaking hand. "He snuck in before we realized..."

Alvarez turned on him in fury. "Krauss! What garbage are you drooling, you fool?" He snatched the print and eyed it, then wilted.

"H-he told the front gate watch-stander that he had your permission..."

"And that bastard believed him? Arrest him! He'll learn the meaning of discipline before I'm done with him!" Alvarez paused to catch his breath, his eyes burning, his whole body trembling in rage, then looked at the photo again. "How did he get through the inner door?"

74

"We don't know, sir." The Duty Officer pointed to the covered corpses with a shaky gesture. "I assume he told them the same story."

"Fools! Arrest them! All of them!"

"They're...dead, sir."

"Traitorous swine!" Alvarez kicked the nearest corpse at random. "Then arrest their families! They *will* *not* escape my justice!"

"B-but sir..."

"OUT! ALL OF YOU!" Alvarez screamed. The Duty Officer beat a hasty retreat. "You haven't heard the end of this!"

After a moment, Volmer dared speak up. "Ah...they couldn't have gone far, sir. Should we go after them?"

Alvarez thought about that as he fought to calm his heavy breathing and his trembling rage. "There is only one place they can go." He turned on Volmer, who drew back in fear. "But am I to trust these fools again? *I think not!* Call the Navy base! Issue a Case Black alert for infiltrators between here and the Lizard base. I want *every one* of our people out there pronto!"

"Yes, Colonel!" Volmer saluted and ran.

§

They'd been on the run maybe an hour, and were circling around to the west along the shore when Mac spotted lights in the distance. "Convoy." They took cover behind some brush, and watched as a seemingly endless stream of vehicles came rolling up the road from the harbor. Some of them turned into the 6th Office drive while the rest continued westward.

"It looks like the hunt is on. That was a fast response."

"Checkpoint." She pointed off to the right where a group of vehicles had pulled off the road nearly due south of them, ideally positioned to cover the opposite shore of the reservoir.

"They'll send out search parties, too."

"We can still clear them if we circle wide." She pointed off due west, across the ruins.

Mac stood and peered off into the darkness; there was precious little to see. "We pretty much have to. Are you up to it?"

She gave him a bleak, angry look. "I have to be."

75

"Right. I don't much care for the neighborhood, so let's get a move-on."

"Don't be afraid," she mumbled as she followed him. "We'll be all right if we keep moving."

§

I'eiBida was holding vigil in the security Elder's grotto for over a day with no more than brief, troubled naps on a human couch in the guard room. He struggled to consciousness when B'monTrea shook his shoulder urgently. "The humans are on full security alert, sir. It looks like the 'Tan Shirts' are deploying their mobile assets between here and the 6th Office compound."

I'eiBida greeted that news with enthusiasm. "Excellent! Then Brian got in and got her out."

"All to the good, sir, but they have a long way to go, and from the extent of the human radio traffic, it looks like they are conducting a massive sweep of the ruins."

"If I know Brian MacKenna, they'll have a merry tail chase trying to catch them," I'eiBida said as they headed for the Intel circle.

§

The ground west of the reservoir was even worse, if possible. From the look of things, the area was partly sheltered by a low rise which gave enough protection to leave piles and mounds of rubble, rather than it being pulverized and blown away by the thermonuclear shock waves. It was slow, treacherous going in the dark.

"Ow! *Maldita sea*," she muttered when she turned an ankle in a grass covered pothole.

"Are you all right?"

She gave him a weary look. "About as much as I can be, considering."

Clambering through these ruins in the dark was no joy. Mac was weary and sore, and a bad scrape on his left leg where the cell door slammed him bothered him. She didn't complain about her injuries, but she was limping slightly, and was having trouble keeping up. What was worse, the weather was turning down again. High clouds rolling in from the east blocked the moonlight, which made finding their way a lot harder. Still, they struggled along partly out of fear, and partly from dogged determination.

"Damn, I'm gonna be sore in the morning," he grumbled after slipping on some loose debris for the umpteenth time.

"We can turn back if you prefer," she snapped.

"Not a chance." He glanced back at her. "Are you managing?"

"Just don't stand in my road, mister."

A familiar whistling sound came faintly from the northeast. "Chopper," Mac hissed. They went to ground, and watched as a military hovercraft moved slowly south. It wasn't showing any lights, which made it hard to see.

"Air cover. *No ayudará a.*" Mac caught the sudden change in her voice; she didn't sound so hard-boiled now.

They watched as it hovered in the distance, and its searchlight lit up the ground below. There was movement on the ground, and faint figures appeared, combing the ruins. "Search party." Mac pointed them out.

"That is not good." She was trembling.

"We're still ahead of them."

After a couple minutes, the light went out, and the hovercraft moved on. "Okay, let's burn rubber." Mac helped her to her feet and set out again with her trailing in the path he made.

"Hell of a deal," she grumbled as they moved on.

They headed west again, keeping a wary eye on the hovercraft as it drifted south until it was lost in the distance. They kept up a slow but steady pace, working carefully through the ruins to avoid injuring themselves on unseen obstacles in the dark.

"I'm dead?" she asked plaintively after a bit. "We're...dead?"

He looked at her again, his own sense of unease rekindled as he thought about that. "So they tell me."

"It's been forty years?" Now that the immediate threat had receded, she was having a hard time coming to terms with it. "I remember a sharp pain, in my head..."

"We had a massive stroke."

"Death by natural causes. Who'd have thunk it for me? Us?" She seemed bemused, as well she should be considering their war record. "We sure beat the odds, didn't we?"

He paused and turned to her. "It isn't over yet. We're still alive, like it or not."

She wilted. "Why'd this have to happen? I was safely dead and buried; couldn't they leave well enough alone?"

"I never asked for this either, but here we are, so we just have to make the best of it."

That made her angry. "God damned...*politicians*, always getting our sack in the wringer! Why we put up with it all our life is beyond me."

"It had to be done," Mac said, softly. "It was the times. You know how bad it was."

She was silent for a long moment, remembering. "Yeah. But we did our share, and then some. Why do we have to go through this all again? We ought to just up and quit."

Mac turned to her. "Aside from being impractical under the circumstances, we have to get her to safety."

She looked at him bleakly. "Damn you for being right."

"Likely. Can you manage?"

She wilted again, and gave him a plaintive sigh. "I am all right, *gracias*." Her voice was strangely different, softer and less focussed somehow.

"Okay, but watch your step. I can't carry you that far."

"You just worry about yourself, mister." *He* was back.

There was another checkpoint on the road south of them, and they skirted wide through the ruins to avoid it. They were passing through a shallow crater left by a nuclear air burst at the moment. The ground was smooth and fused; treacherous going, but at least there was hardly any rubble to trip over, and the crater hid them from the road.

"Can we trust the Ic'nichi?" she asked at last. "From what you say, they created this mess."

"Yeah, they did, and they're not happy with how their little shop project turned out."

"That's precious little reason to trust them."

He looked at her. "You remember a defender named I'eiBida?"

"I'eiBida?" She pondered for a moment. "Yeah. He was a junior officer attached to their embassy."

78

"He's a top-notch heavyweight now, barks with the big dogs. He's in personal charge of this fubar circus, and he's stared down all comers. I think we can trust him, at least."

She considered. "Well, that's something, anyway."

"Plus we have no other options. Our one chance is to get off planet, and they've got the only ride in this one-hearse town."

"Hell," she muttered. "They can fire me out of a cannon if it'd do the trick."

It began to sprinkle again. They moved on, picking their way through the scraggly weeds growing in the thin layer of wind-blown dust which accumulated in the crater over the last century. "Don't be afraid," she whispered. "We're ahead of the game. All we have to do is keep moving."

Mac heard, and wondered what that was about, but didn't say anything.

"We'll be all right," she said as they struggled up over the rim of the crater. "Just hang in there."

§

"WHERE *ARE* THEY?" Alvarez screamed at his people. The communication watch-standers cringed, and tried to look busy. A few of them knew from ugly experience what could happen when he got like this; the rest could figure it out easily enough. The communications center was wire taut with fear.

Their edgy silence didn't appease his rage. "Answer me!" He advanced on one of the technicians and kicked him, sending him sprawling over his console. "Where ARE they?"

"I don't know, sir!" The unfortunate man cringed and backed away along the line of consoles. "We're searching for them!"

"NOT GOOD ENOUGH!" Alvarez whipped him across the face with his swagger stick, leaving a nasty welt on his cheek. He cowered under the blow, then ran sobbing from the room. "Traitorous dog!" Alvarez yelled after him.

His focus broken, he stood in the center of the room, breathing hard, his eyes blazing, shaking with rage. "You will find them!" he yelled at the room at large. "You *will not* stop, you *will not* eat, you *will not* rest until they are brought to *ME!* And if *any* of you maggots fail in your duty, you will pay the *dearest* price!"

79

"Sir?"

Alvarez spun in place with his hand on his automatic. The rest of them flinched again.

"It's your call to Geneva, sir," Volmer said as he offered him the telephone.

"Right," he muttered as he grabbed the handset.

§

"Sir, here's the infrared photo from the courier." B'monTrea slapped the large scale print down on the table, and started pointing out heat traces. "There is a solid wall of human security out there, supported by aircraft and mobile units. Their chances of getting through aren't promising."

I'eiBida brooded as he considered the orbital photo. That terrain was rough, with little or no ground cover, which meant they faced slow going with a high risk of detection.

"Roust S'deMnveb and his Specials up. We may need them."

"Yes, sir!" B'monTrea left at a gallop.

"And someone get some *V'liz* going!" I'eiBida yelled after him. It was going to be a long night.

§

They'd been at it for hours—forever, it seemed. Mac paused to catch his breath and surveyed the darkness around them with a sense of atavistic dread. Back when he commanded Space Fleet, they used to refer to this as the 'Haunted Land'. No one ever came around here. There were still mildly radioactive spots a hundred years after the island was swept clean by a rain of thermonuclear fire. There was nothing worth salvaging, and the bones of millions who died that day lay just below the surface. The inhabitants of Squatter Town looked on this area with superstitious horror, and even the sophisticated Fleet officers viewed this area with foreboding. They were as alone as two human beings could be on this earth, except for the restless dead, and the memories.

"*Maldita se*," she gasped as she slipped on some loose gravel.

Mac's distraction was broken, and he turned to look at her. "How you doing?"

She gave him a frazzled sigh. "I am...managing. How much farther is it?"

He studied the dim terrain ahead of them with no joy. "We have a way to go yet."

The whole island used to be densely built up. The area they were traveling through was once a gritty industrial district of tattered sweatshops and godowns. All that remained now were crumbled lines of ancient concrete foundations rust-stained from rebar and sheet tin long corroded away, and half buried in rank weeds. It made for treacherous footing, and since the streets once wandered at random, it was easy to get turned around.

The highway was about two kilometers south of them, with another checkpoint right opposite. No doubt the patrols were a lot closer. The hovercraft they saw earlier was east of them, and they could hear the whine of a second one somewhere off to the northeast.

"Time to get a move-on."

"*Si*," she sighed, and followed him wearily.

§

"You sent for us, sir?" S'deMnveb said when he and his Worthy arrived.

"Yes." I'eiBida showed him the orbital photo. "Brian got the human prisoner out of the 6th Office compound, but they are being pursued. We may need your Specials to help them get through."

S'deMnveb studied the photo doubtfully. "We don't have the strength to fight that lot, sir, nor can we hold them off if we do get the humans back here. I urgently recommend against a direct confrontation."

"Quite right, but can we provide them with a diversion? Draw the humans off their trail?"

"We can. But first we need to know where they are, sir."

§

"Ooofff! Dammit!" Mac muttered as he slid down a mound of rubble. His trousers caught on something, ripping his pants leg, and leaving a long shallow cut in his thigh.

"Help me!" He turned in time to catch her as she half-fell-half-slid down the slope. As they were sorting themselves out, they noticed the small avalanche of bones shaken loose by their passing. Human bones.

"It's all right, Giselle," she muttered to herself as she stared. "We'll make it." She was trembling. "We're out of there, and we'll be at the Ic'nichi base in a little bit. They'll protect us."

Mac stopped and looked at her. "Did you say something?"

She eyed him cautiously. "Nothing."

"I've heard you muttering like that before. What is it?"

She stopped and looked at him anxiously, then her shoulders sagged. "There's something wrong with this mind transfer process, something they haven't worked out yet. She's still in there, in the back of our mind, still aware. She's afraid: I talk to her to help her cope."

That brought up what I'eiBida told him about the first time they reactivated him: the memory erasure was imperfect; she was trapped in her body as a helpless passenger.

"She's coming back, isn't she?"

She nodded. "Each time they erase us, she keeps growing back. She's weak at first, but she keeps getting stronger." She gave him a tense look. "And I keep getting weaker. My guess is if they'd leave us alone, I'll fade away eventually."

"I'eiBida said that happened the last time."

"*Last* time? How many of us have they made?"

"Just the one, I think."

She shook her head. "God, I hope I last long enough to kick somebody's ass."

"Take a *friggin'* number," he grumbled.

It was late. The search was closer than ever, and they had a long way to go. He turned and headed west with her trailing wearily in his footsteps. It was sprinkling again.

§

"I do not care how many men you need, or how long it takes," Alvarez told the 'Tan Shirt' field leaders in cold fury. "You will stay out there until you find them! And Heaven pity you all if they come back dead!"

The communication center was painfully silent but for the muted chatter coming over the radios. The technicians at their stations and the team running the improvised plot map hunched their shoulders in fear, and tried to look busy. The two team leads

82

fidgeted under the Colonel's icy glare. They were a prime pair of bullies who relished fear, and loved terrorizing hapless victims: they knew the real thing when they saw it, and were shaken. "We will find them, sir," one of them half-whimpered.

"Let us *hope* so." The look in his eyes made them shudder. "Get out there and push your men. Speed up your sweeps. Do not stop until you *find them!*"

"Yes, Colonel!" they snapped.

"I want them alive! Both of them!"

"Yes, Colonel!"

"Do not give me reason to doubt your devotion to the cause," he added as they turned to go.

Alvarez stood silently for a while after they left, staring at nothing, his rage simmering as he went over the situation in his mind. "The Lizards must know about the recording," he said to himself after a bit. He glanced at Volmer. "That is the only reason why Krauss would help her escape. That would explain where he got the explosives, and why they are headed for the Lizard base."

"But how could they know, sir?"

Alvarez pondered the map absently, fighting to hold off his fatigue, and to keep his rage in check. "I will ask Krauss when we meet him again."

"What if they make it to the Lizard base despite our best efforts, sir?"

"That would be *most* unfortunate." He brooded over the map for a while, not really seeing it except for the Ic'nichi landing field at the far Western end of the island. "Contact the Ministry in Geneva again," he said at last. "We need to make some preparations, just in case."

"Yes, Colonel!"

He gave Volmer an icy look. "I *trust* you appreciate how important it is to find them?"

Volmer was chilled by his tone, and the look in his eyes. "Yes, Colonel!" He was scared through and through; Alvarez was angry enough to turn even on him. He cursed Krauss under his breath as he hurried to the long distance telephone.

§

"I have the latest from the courier, sir," B'monTrea said as he laid an enhanced infrared photo on the Intel circle plotting table. The high resolution scan of the ruins to their east was impressive, for orbital night photography. I'eiBida grabbed a magnifying glass and pored over the photo, marking out hot spots with paper clips, erasers, coins, anything handy. It soon became clear the humans had a search pattern laid out along the road which was slowly expanding to both sides as they systematically swept the ruins.

"Impressive," he muttered. "They put together a solid search in remarkably short time."

"We've been monitoring their radio traffic, sir, and they haven't found anything yet," T'thReptn said. The Intel staff were on full alert, keeping a running update of human activity.

"Which means our friendlies are still beyond their search radius. We need to find them." I'eiBida shifted to the area north of the road, starting by a small lake near the 6th Office compound. "There!" he said after a bit, and pointed to an isolated pair of hot spots. "That has to be them."

B'monTrea examined the photo in turn. "The search is overtaking them, sir. We don't have much time to intervene."

I'eiBida turned to S'deMnveb. "Are your people ready?"

"Yes, sir."

"All right, gallop. And good luck."

*****

"Chapter Six"

Access to the Ic'nichi landing field was over the narrow neck of an artificial peninsula amid the ruins of what must have been a dismal ship-breaker's yard. The humans long ago seeded the ruins to either side of the road with sensors to guard against any Ic'nichi sneaking off the base, and the local Intel had long since charted their positions, and found a narrow gap they could exploit at need.

One of T'thReptn's operatives guided S'deMnveb's herd through the twisting passage a few at a time, pointing out unseen hazards at practically every step. It was well past midnight by the time they rallied beyond the perimeter in a sheltered area in the ruins, and S'deMnveb briefed the Hand Leads over their improvised map.

"All right, First Hand, move south of the road and try to divert the pursuers down toward the water. You should be able to tangle them up in those ruins along the shore." The ancient wreckage along the waterfront was a jumbled nightmare where whole echelons could hide.

"Second Hand, I want you to move through the center north of the road. Stay just above the human search line." They would have the most open country to cross and ran the greatest risk of being spotted, but it also gave them the best chance of intercepting the fugitives.

"Third Hand, move up past the Second and draw the humans off to the north and east." That put the four of them far out on the fringe where they would be a long way from help. "If you are spotted and can't make it back here, disperse into these hills," he indicated some high ground in the middle of the island, "and circle back along the coast once the search ends."

"The Fourth Hand will belly down in these woods." He indicated a small patch of scraggly trees, all that remained of a local park, just beyond a bend in the highway where it circled northwest toward a collapsed suspension bridge before cutting off to enter the Ic'nichi landing field. "This will be our base. We'll be in position to intercept the humans if they get this far, and to come to your help if any of you run into trouble."

85

The others absorbed this quietly. This was nothing new to any of them. For his part, S'deMnveb wasn't happy with the quick, patched-together plan, and how exposed the Third Hand would be in particular, but they had no real choice. They were well trained for this sort of thing; they could manage.

"Remember, our mission is to misdirect the search so the humans can reach safety. Don't engage the searchers if you can avoid it, use your communications only for emergencies, and don't let them get a look at you. Once they catch on to our plan, they'll ignore us and go after the humans, and we can't rule out the chance that they might take a few shots at us."

The conference broke up, and they hastily organized their gear, including the clumsy infrared-resistant cloaks intended to shield them from night vision gear. Within minutes, they moved out in four different directions.

§

"I *do not* care to hear your opinions, and I *will not* put up with your interference," Alvarez told the island Peacekeepers' Colonel sternly. "*We* have a security matter, *I* have the authority from Geneva, and *you* have your orders!" A new burst of squawking came over the line, but Alvarez cut him off peremptorily. "*ENOUGH!* You will have your *entire* command fully equipped and ready to deploy by dawn, or you will explain your *dereliction* to the Executive Committee!"

He slammed the phone down hard enough that it slid off onto the floor, and stood scowling at the duty section as they updated the search map. They nervously avoided his gaze as he fumed. The *nerve* of that peon! He barely contained his rage at a mere *bureaucrat* who dared dispute his authority while the others in the room tried to be inconspicuous, and pushed the search parties for results.

"Sir..."

"WHAT?!" He spun on Volmer, who trembled before his wrath as a mere *peon* should.

"The...ah...search parties are advancing rapidly, sir." The man couldn't look him in the eyes, he was so nervous. "We should overtake them shortly."

If he hoped to placate Alvarez, he was sorely disappointed. "And you expect me to be amused by this nonsense?" Alvarez roared. "Is this news? WHERE ARE THEY?"

"I...I..."

"I will tell you what is news! Either I have those two, alive and unharmed by dawn, or those search parties can not move rapidly enough to escape my justice!"

"Y-yes, sir..."

"Get out of my sight!" Volmer retreated hastily, cursing under his breath. "Tell them they have until dawn!" Alvarez yelled after him. Once Volmer was gone, he glared at the room in general, creating a gratifying wave of fear. "You will answer, Krauss," he muttered. His mind churned with the wrath awaiting his former protégé. "You *will* answer!" His attention went back to the huddled figures around him. "And you will answer too!" he screamed. "Onc of you will die this night if they are not found! Do *not* test me!"

§

Mac paused for a quick breather, and scanned the darkness around them to orient himself. The moon was gone behind the growing cloud cover, and visibility was damn-all amid the jumbled ruins. Vehicle lights were faintly visible in the distance to their south, so at least he knew which direction they were traveling, but he honestly wasn't sure where they were. Visibility wasn't much more than a hundred meters or so, and it would be all too easy to get turned around in this monotonous landscape...

"They are behind us!" Her panicked squeak brought him up short, and he strained his eyes to search the gloom behind them. Sure enough, there was movement. He couldn't make out any detail, but there were a half-dozen of them in a broad line: a squad, advancing in skirmish order.

"They must have followed us," he whispered. She had damned good eyesight, or maybe it was terror-induced hyper-alertness. In any case, they were closing steadily.

"What do we do?" she whimpered.

"We move. Fast."

§

"Something up ahead." One of the squad turned and pointed ahead into the gloom. The sergeant stopped and studied the darkness with his infrared binoculars. There: two blurry, vaguely humanoid hot spots about a hundred and fifty meters ahead and moving away rapidly.

"It's them!" Just as they faded into the landscape, he caught a momentary glimpse of a faint hot spot in the distance, but didn't think anything of it. "After them!"

§

The third Hand Lead was appalled at the sights around them: all his studies of human military history and their stellar bombs hadn't prepared him for this. 'This' was once a teeming nest with a population of millions: all that remained was crumpled refuse, and everywhere they stepped they uncovered human bones. He knew he would have nightmares about this for years to come.

"Something over there," their right flanker reported.

He shook off his sense of dread; they had a job to do. He paused and studied the area off their right with his night vision goggles. "It's a human patrol," he whispered to his people. "We'll circle around them and draw them north. Up tails, everyone; we have a long way to go." They gripped their gear tighter and slipped silently from one bit of cover to the next, working around the humans' flank.

§

They were pushing west as fast as they dared when Mac caught a faint movement out of the corner of his eye. "Shit!" He dove for cover, pulling her down next to him. "It's another patrol."

The new intruders were coming up from the south in a broad line. They were neatly boxed in between the two skirmish lines. Their only escape was to the north, but that would take them far off course with both squads in hot pursuit.

"Dammit," he muttered to himself as he tried to contain his rising panic and looked around desperately for an escape route.

"Steady, Giselle," she whimpered. She was trembling, with tears flowing down her cheeks. "Stay focussed. We'll get out of this."

§

"Do you see them?" the first squad leader called by his tactical link to his opposite in the other squad.

"I think we caught a glimpse of them," the message came back. *"We see you, so we should have them pinned between us."*

The two squads joined a few minutes later, with the platoon's lieutenant in tow. "*Maledizione,*" he muttered as he scanned the darkness. "Where are they?"

"We had them, sir," the first squad's sergeant protested. "They must have slipped past you."

The lieutenant gave him an angry look. "Or you missed them perhaps? That would not surprise me." Colonel Alvarez's wrath put everyone on edge, clear down to the field forces.

The sergeant was about to offer a stinging retort when his opposite from the other squad interrupted. "We need to call in for air support, *tenente.* They can't be far."

The lieutenant pondered for a moment, then reached for his radio. "*Si,* we will do that." Before he activated it, he gave the first squad leader an icy look. "Then we shall see who was derelict in his duties."

§

Mac eased carefully down until he lay flat behind some weeds with her trembling beside him. The two patrols were mingling not more than ten meters away, milling about at random as they waited for their leaders to make up their minds. All it would take was for one of them to idle over this way and it was all over. He felt her pressed up against his side, trembling in fear. He squeezed her hand to reassure her as his mind raced to find some angle they could use to get out of this. There was nothing. It was all up to the two squads of heavily armed Peacekeepers not ten paces away.

One of them drifted over to a bush not five paces to their left and paused to urinate. They waited anxiously until he finished, lit a cig, and drifted back to the squad. Another one, the officer, was talking on a hand radio: they would have more company soon.

§

"We think they may have split up, and are proceeding separately, sir," the lieutenant reported. *"Thus far we've only had glimpses of them, and they are very good at evading us."*

89

Alvarez pondered that suspiciously: it sounded like a tactic Krauss would employ, but he wouldn't credit the girl with such coolness or stamina. Still, it was the best lead to turn up yet, and two full squads would soon overtake them no matter how much Krauss squirmed. "I *trust* you understand the importance of taking both of them alive?"

"*Si, Colonel.*" The lieutenant's fear came clearly over the transmission.

Alvarez dropped the radio hand piece and brooded over this new development, then glanced at Volmer. "Get them some air support."

"Yes, Colonel."

Alvarez headed for the wardroom for a cup of coffee while Volmer eagerly lit a fire under the Peacekeeper air liaison. Air support was no simple task: there were just four hovercraft on the island, two of which were down for refueling, and far too many patrols who needed air cover. They had a fine balancing act on their hands. But for all that, Volmer was pleased with himself and about as happy as could be. He would soon be rid of his arch-rival once and for all. Air support done, he called the garage to have a vehicle standing by; he fully intended to be there when Krauss was taken down.

§

"The air support will be here in a moment," the lieutenant said. "Once we have some light, we will find them." The issue night vision goggles they carried weren't the best; Peacekeepers avoided them whenever they could because they caused headaches.

They were interrupted by what sounded like a small avalanche of loose wreckage to their right. "*Verdamme!*" the second squad sergeant muttered. "They slipped around our flank!"

"You heard the man," the lieutenant said with a gesture largely off to their right. "We have them! After them before they get away."

"But what about the air support, sir?"

"They can catch up. Move out." The two squads spread out and resumed their sweep north.

§

"Damn," Mac muttered. "They're moving off." That was a vast relief, and he sent a fervent prayer of thanks to whatever Gods Of War were watching over them.

"¡*Agradecer al cielo para!*" she said as she struggled to her knees. "We must get out of here."

"Stay put!" he hissed as he pushed her back down. They waited in nervous silence until the patrols faded into the gloom. "Right," he said at last. "Let's get the hell out-a here." They crept south a short way at a crouch, then began picking their way west again.

§

"Nothing yet?"

T'verTra set his umpteenth bowl of *V'liz* aside and stared wearily at the large map on the Intel circle plotting table. "Nothing yet, sir." He looked at I'eiBida and sighed. "This is going to go bad, sir. We'll be lucky if we don't wind up in a major battle out there."

I'eiBida frowned at the thought. "We can only hope for the best, Third." He pondered the map himself, wishing fervently for a bowl of *V'liz,* as if he hadn't drunk enough to sour his stomach already. "It all depends on Brian now."

"Ancestors help them," T'verTra sighed.

"Ancestors help us all, including the humans."

§

The second Hand was spread out in a broad front to intercept the human fugitives, but this was rough country. The night was thick under the spreading overcast, and it was slow going at best. The Hand Lead was on the right flank of his line, searching his front and flank, pausing to use his infrared goggles now and then. Nothing. The faint mist quickened into a steady drizzle; he pulled his camouflage cape tighter against the chill, squinted into the gloom to check his footing, and moved forward again.

"Something," his number two hissed.

Surprised, the Lead looked again, then hefted his infrared goggles. There were several faint heat traces in the distance. "*l'cc'vn!*" he grumbled. The humans had snuck up on them.

§

91

They'd been on the move for several hours trying to keep ahead of the search which was pushing them steadily off course to the north.   Finally her strength gave out, and she slumped on a crumbled foundation and rubbed one leg, which had a couple nasty scrapes on it. His own strength was waning, so he turned back and settled by her.

"Are you all right?"

She gave him a weary look.   "I am not used to this sort of thing. I need a bit of rest."

Mac noted her choice of phrasing, and her broken Swiss, which didn't reassure him. He turned a wary eye to the south, looking for any sign of movement.   In this dark, amid this broken clutter, a search party could easily slip up on them. They weren't all that far away as is.

"We can't stay here long."

"A few minutes more, please."

She was obviously on her last legs, and her trembling grew more uncontrollable as he watched.   "We don't have the luxury. They're getting closer. Can you make it?"

That galvanized her, and she turned to him with features contorted with fear and anger. "I *have* to make it! People have to know what is going on in that *mal lugar*! I have to warn them!"

"About the mind transfer? You don't need to worry about us. We'd never help those bastards. Turning out more of us would be the worst mistake they could make."

"I know. He told me." She hesitated and clutched herself in a forlorn gesture, her brief flash of rage evaporated.   "But it is far worse than than you know."

Mac paused and looked at her, wondering what could be worse than what Alvarez was already up to.

"...I..." She shuddered, almost a sob of anguish, and clutched herself tighter. "E-every time they erased us...I would grow back. I would...remember what happened before." She was trembling now.   "I heard them talking..."   She sobbed, on the verge of breaking down. "We have to warn the people!"

He urgently gestured to her to lower her voice.

§

"I thought I heard voices over there, sergeant." The 'Tan Shirt' on lead scout told his squad leader as he pointed off to their left. The sergeant scanned the darkness for several seconds, but could see nothing. Still, their company commander was pressing them for results, and the rumors about the Colonel's present state would scare anyone.

"*Da*. We check it out." The squad shifted alignment as he called for air support. That way was as good as any in this desolate wasteland, and no one wanted to earn Alvarez's wrath by missing something.

§

"It's a search party." The second Hand Lead pointed off to their right where the faint heat blooms in the distance resolved into several armed figures in his infrared goggles. "They will walk right into us!" He glanced around frantically, but there was no real cover, and it was too late to avoid them. "Prepare for action!" he hissed. The Hand went to ground and spread out to form a fighting line.

§

"Do you see it?" she sobbed. "Alvarez is a monster!" She lost it then, and broke down crying on his shoulder.

Mac *could* see it, clearly, and the implications set his stomach churning. Of all the horrors he witnessed in his former life, this one set a whole new skin-crawling standard. All of a sudden this was far bigger than their two lives; big enough to justify an interstellar war. They *had* to get through.

"Look, I..." A faint sound came to him, snapping him out of his weary haze. "...chopper!" Instinct took over, and he dove for cover without waiting to see where the intruder was, dragging her with him.

§

"We may have something about a hundred meters to our northwest," the sergeant reported to their air support.

"*...Copy, Mobile Twelve...*" the pilot's voice came faintly over his earphones. The sergeant could just make out the dim shape of the hovercraft off to their east as it changed course.

§

"*Esto es malo*," she whimpered. "They will see us!"

"Shit," Mac muttered. It looked like the jig was up: a squad was advancing a hundred meters distant, and a hovercraft was heading in. They had perhaps a minute to come up with a righteously slick maneuver if they were to get out of this one.

§

The first Hand came out of the tangled ruins of the ship-breaker's yard and picked up a broad open road running east. "We're way behind," the Lead snapped. "Move!" The four of them broke into a fast trot, intervals wide, everyone alert for any sign of danger while the Lead grumbled to himself about the delay. As they came out of the major ruins into more open country, he spotted lights on the highway to their left.

"Checkpoint." He gestured to the left. "Swing over that way, and we'll start the show." The Hand took a side street leading off to the northeast.

§

"Spread out," the 'Tan Shirt' squad leader said to his men. "They may be armed, so go in carefully. We want them alive."

The squad divided into their two-man teams and spread out while the hovercraft waited. Once deployed, they advanced in skirmish order, weapons at the ready.

§

"The humans are getting close," The second Hand Lead whispered. That was hardly necessary as his people were fully deployed behind what cover they could find, and waited anxiously for what would happen next. There was no way to avoid the confrontation they all feared. The Lead worked the charging slide on his machine pistol to chamber the first round, and squeezed the hand grip tighter, unlocking the safety...

His second raised his grenade launcher...

The other two raised their weapons...

§

Mac turned to her urgently with the only option he could think of. "Look: you go to ground; find the best cover you can and *stay* there. I'm going to make a break for it to try and draw them away to the north. Once you're clear, head for the Ic'nichi base."

94

"They will kill you!" she whimpered.

"Yeah, some days just suck. But you wouldn't *believe* the medical coverage I carry."

She clung to his arm convulsively. "*Please* do not leave me!"

"This is your one chance," he said, sternly. She was losing it, which would get them killed unless she snapped out of it fast. "I'm expendable, I'll draw them off. You have to get through and tell the Ic'nichi."

She was shaking so hard that he needed to hold her up. "I...I *cannot!*" she sobbed. "P-please..."

The hovercraft passed overhead low enough that they were buffeted by its downdraft. They broke off arguing and dove for cover as it circled back toward them.

§

Two klicks due south of the search party, the platoon's headquarters section manned one of the many road blocks strung along the highway. They were all alert to any sign of movement, and they were all anxious to be the one to report something to Colonel Alvarez, *especially* with the mood he was in.

The platoon sergeant sat in their command vehicle parked by the road, taking full advantage of his lordly rank to keep out of the drizzle while monitoring radio traffic. He was chilled, bone weary, and about fed up: headquarters needed to get their collective heads out of their asses, and get this search *over* with. He gazed into the night to their north, where the rest of the platoon was sweeping the ruins. The whole damned island was a vast graveyard of unburied dead, and being out here at night, in this weather, raised everyones' hackles. So many ghosts; so many restless, unburied souls; millions of them. It gave him the creeps every time they drove through this area. That bastard Alvarez scared him white, which made duty in this Godforsaken hole all the worse...

Heads turned as they heard a faint 'POP' to their south. "What?" the sergeant wondered. There was a second 'POP'.

"That was gunfire!" his driver said.

The sergeant's frustrations were forgotten as he realized to his dismay that the entire platoon was scattered north of the road. If the fugitives were *south* of them, and Alvarez found out...

He grabbed the vehicle's radio mike. "Checkpoint Six to Lieutenant Vagoiovich! We have shots fired to our south, sir, somewhere around the western edge of grid Golf-Two!"

§

"They're leaving," Mac said in surprise. Sure enough, the hovercraft continued turning away to the south, and the patrol was falling back at a clumsy double-time. "Right. Let's go." He dragged her trembling form to her feet, turned and headed west...caught a furtive movement out of the corner of his eye, halted in mid-step, and dove behind a bush, dragging her down beside him.

"What is it?" she whispered.

"Something moving over there." He pointed to their northwest.

"¿Más soldados?"

"Sssshhh!"

§

"Right, here they come!" The first hand Lead jumped down from the rubble pile where he was watching the distant hovercraft. "Split up and rally a hundred paces down toward the water."

They covered themselves with their cloaks and sprinted southeast, burrowing into the jumbled ruins as the hovercraft came swooping in. By time it arrived, they were effectively invisible, ready to stage another scene to draw them further away.

§

"They're withdrawing?" The Second Hand Lead watched in confusion as the human squad and their hovercraft receding into the gloom. "What are they up to?"

"Good riddance," someone muttered. The Lead didn't answer, but he shared the sentiment since it meant they wouldn't fight an outnumbered battle after all. He released the safety on his weapon with a fervent prayer of thanks to his Ancestors.

"Should we go after them?" another ranker asked.

The Lead watched for a long moment, his confusion heightened as he considered the unexpected human move. "They may have spotted the fugitives. We'll circle to the east to get between them and the 6th Office base. If they are caught, we will be in position to rescue them."

His people headed out in an open skirmish line, moving stealthily from bush to rock, pushing northeast to circle the search party in response to their sudden change of course. They were too preoccupied to notice the large human crouching in the bush a hundred paces distant.

"This should do," the Lead said at last. "We need to gallop." They dispersed, swing south, and picked up the pace to overtake the retreating humans.

§

"Do you see anything?" she whispered.

Mac didn't answer for several minutes as he searched the dark nervously. "Um...no," he said at last. "False alarm. Still, let's be careful, hmmm?"

He crawled southwest for some distance on hands and knees, watching in all directions while she crept along behind him. After a couple hundred meters, he helped her to her feet, and they headed unsteadily west.

§

The tension in the operations room of the 6th Office compound was thick enough to slice like steak. Colonel Alvarez' mood was deteriorating steadily as the hours passed and one rumor after another failed to produce results. At the moment there were no less than five separate leads being pursued by those 'Tan Shirt' bunglers, and his temper was climbing with each negative report.

"Where are they?" he wondered. One line of pencil marks caught his eye. "What of that group to the north?"

The replacement Duty Officer studied the pencil marks in confusion, then hastily examined the communication log on his clip board. "Part of Group Two, sir. Their latest report puts their quarry leaving grid Delta Ninety-Nine northbound, sir."

"I can see it." The Duty Officer cringed as Alvarez glared at him, then went back to pondering the map and the row of penciled-in sightings. "They're heading for Squatter Town," he said at last. "They picked up a band of locals. Get those fools turned back west, and *find them!*"

"Yes, sir!"

§

"The latest recon photo, sir," B'monTrea said as he laid their newest on the plotting table. I'eiBida ordered the courier to send high resolution infrared photos with each orbital pass, regardless of whether the communication traffic might arouse the humans' suspicion. T'verTra took personal charge of it, and began updating their plot almost before the photo settled.

"They've made some progress," I'eiBida said as he examined the thermal image.

"Yes, sir, but they're not going as fast as before." B'monTrea pointed to a larger hot spot to the northeast. "And that aircraft has changed course." From the distance it traveled since the last sighting, it was moving fast. "They seem to be redeploying."

"Hmmm, not good. They must have detected something."

The two hot spots were making good time, but the hour was late, the weather turning down, and the worst part of their journey was still ahead of them. The spread of hot spots marking their pursuers were overtaking them, and the aircraft was closing fast.

"They're through S'deMnveb's screen," T'verTra said, pointing to a group of four hot spots slightly to their southeast.

I'eiBida chuckled. "I told you Brian MacKenna was a slippery *riv'Agna.*"

"He needs to be. Should we contact S'deMnveb and have him intercept them, sir?"

"That's taking a risk, sir," B'monTrea cautioned. "No doubt the humans are listening to every thing we transmit; even a coded message will alert them to something."

"They'll need to link up with S'deMnveb in order to infiltrate through the perimeter, sir," T'verTra said. "And with that aircraft coming in, they can't stay out there much longer."

I'eiBida hesitated. "Good point." He pondered the photo for a bit, then turned to the communication console.

§

They came out of the ruins and picked up the highway about eight klicks west of the 6th Office headquarters near a sweeping bend in the road. By then, she was staggering with fatigue. "Is it much further?" she asked plaintively as she sagged against the stump of a telephone pole.

He hushed her with an urgent gesture as he looked around for any sign of pursuit. The only sign of activity was well to the east, and there were no sounds other than the chirping of insects, the furtive scramble of some small animal in the undergrowth, and a hovercraft drifting west in the distance. They seemed to be focussing on a spot off to their southeast, but the hovercraft northwest of them had changed course, and was headed west again. At the rate it was moving, it would be there soon.

"How does it look?" she asked plaintively.

"I think we lost them for now, but we don't have much time." He considered her with some misgiving. "How you doing?"

She was trembling, her arms wrapped around her to ward off the damp chill. The steady drizzle was turning into light rain, and she wasn't dressed for this weather. "I am running out of steam fast. Is it much further?"

Mac tried to recall the details of the map he reviewed all too briefly yesterday. "We've come about half-way, best guess."

"I am not sure I can make it without some rest."

"Dammit, we may have to go to ground," he muttered. The night was chill and damp, with occasional light mist, but the sky behind them showed the first faint traces of dawn. She was battered and soaked to the skin, and had gone all night with no food or rest. Even he was feeling it; she was staggering, in no shape to continue, and the morning light would make it too risky to attempt the last part of their journey in any case. "We need to find cover somewhere up ahead, and wait for tomorrow night."

She looked at him anxiously for a long moment, then studied the ruins ahead of them. The ancient shipyard beyond the road was a jungle of twisted girders and pipes half buried in the mounded rubble. "Can we risk it?" she asked. "That will give them all day to search for us."

"No choice. They'll spot us easy in the daylight. We have to risk the delay."

"I am sorry," she mumbled.

"Don't blame yourself," he said, gently. "You made damn fine progress getting this far. Let's find a spot to hunker down, and you can get some rest."

She seemed to change before his eyes. "There's no time for it." She struggled to her feet. "They'll keep widening their search, so we have to keep moving." Her MacKenna persona had clearly taken charge, and while she was still trembling and rocky on her feet, she seemed determined to push on.

Inwardly, he wondered if she could go the rest of the way. They couldn't stay on the road: that would be easier, but the highway was crawling with vehicle patrols. They needed to cross the road and head off southwest through the ruins. That would reduce the risk of being spotted, but this Universe being what it was, it would be the worst part yet.

"Can you do it? You look about used up."

"I have to try," she sighed. "But she doesn't have much left."

They were suddenly bathed in faint light. A truck rounded the turn behind them, and was bearing down on them. "That's our ride," Mac said as he grabbed her arm. "Fight me. Put up a struggle." She put up a convincing one as he waved the truck to a halt, dragged her to one side, and shoved her against the fender.

"What you got there?" the driver demanded.

"I am Krauss, 6th Office. I caught this infiltrator, and I need a lift to the guard room at the Lizard base."

The driver punched his truck into park and climbed down. He was about average height and build, and his scruffy appearance and cowboy boots said volumes about what became of Peacekeeper standards over the years.

"That a fact?" He looked her over with obvious contempt as she cringed. "Likely come from Squatter Town, lookin' t' steal anythin' not nailed t' the floor." He considered her for another moment, then turned to Mac. "Is that what all the fuss is about? There's checkpoints all along the highway all of a sudden."

"We are conducting a security sweep of these ruins. There have been too many incidents lately."

"Well, good hunting." He looked her over again, and his thoughts were plain. "She ain't half bad lookin', for all that she's a skinny 'un. What-say we have us a little party before you turn her in? She'd be a nice change of pace. We know how t' deal with the likes of this in Texas..."

As soon as his back was turned, Mac threw a savage right at his neck with every bit of strength he could muster. The blow landed with an ugly *SNAP!*, and the driver collapsed in a heap. She dropped to her knees, and checked him for a pulse. "A perfect hangman's fracture," she said with a shaky voice. "That's a handy trick."

"Yeah." Mac was bemused by his strength. He'd never backed down from a fight, but it was never as easy as this. Perhaps there were advantages to being a hulking brute after all. And as distasteful as it was, in that creep's case, it felt *good*.

He looked around for a likely hiding place, then grabbed the driver's ankles and dragged him off into the ruins for fifty meters or so, and left him in a shallow ditch behind a crumbling wall.

"All right, let's go," he said when he returned. She climbed into the helper's seat while he peeled off his outer shirt after a moment's calculation, and grabbed the driver's cap where it lay in the road.

It was a lot more than forty years since he drove a truck, but military vehicles never really change. The controls were clustered on a touch panel, but it didn't take long to figure out the essentials. Thankfully they still used a steering wheel and floor pedals.

"Okay" He donned the driver's cap, and gave her a reassuring look. "You hunker down in the foot well there, and I'll slip us past the checkpoint."

"Good luck," she muttered as she squeezed down below the seat.

§

"Any sight of them?" S'deMnveb demanded when the two perimeter scouts he sent out returned.

"Nothing yet, sir," the Lead reported. "One of the aircraft is headed this way. They'll be here soon."

S'deMnveb muttered a venomous curse. "What's taking them so long?"

"Humans don't move as fast as we do, sir, and that's rough country out there."

"Yes. I need you to..." His ear plug com link buzzed, interrupting them. "...S'deMnveb here."

101

"The humans are in your area, Second," I'eiBida's voice came through faint and tinny. "They already slipped past your eastern element, and they've reached the road about four hundred paces southeast of you."

"What...?" S'deMnveb looked around in confusion, dismayed that their quarry had infiltrated past his best people, and were all but under foot. "Sir, are you..."

"Truck!" one of the lookouts hissed. They went to ground as another truck rolled by. S'deMnveb noticed the driver was dressed in a white undershirt, but didn't think anything of it.

"We'll find them, sir," he said once the truck was gone.

"Good luck with that."

§

"Checkpoint coming up." Mac eased off on the throttle and gingerly touched the brakes, slowing the heavy semi as they drew up to the main gate of the Ic'nichi landing field. "Get down and stay quiet."

She squeezed further into the foot well as he pulled up to the gate, where they were met by a burly sergeant in 'Tan Shirt' fatigues carrying a clipboard.

"Vehicle number?" he demanded.

"It's right there on the hood, sarge." Mac gestured at the stencil on the fender. The sergeant gave him a chilly glare, then wrote the number down while Mac glanced around to take in the surroundings. The 'Tan Shirt' outpost was on full alert, most of the half-dozen patrolling around his rig with machine pistols at the ready while their squad leader made a military pain in the ass of himself. On the other side of the gate, not ten paces and a lifetime of forlorn hope away, two Ic'nichi defenders huddled under a wooden awning and watched the scene idly.

"Haff you seen anything unusual this trip?" the sergeant demanded when he was through.

"Yeah, there's all kinds of checkpoints and patrols clear back down to the harbor. What's going on?"

"A security matter." His tone said it wouldn't be wise to press him for details.

Mac shrugged. "You say so."

102

"So vere iss Willis?"

"He got elected to Parliament," Mac grumbled. "They're starting to relieve some of the drivers," he added when the sergeant frowned. "He's taking a few hours off."

"Hmph. Und vere iss your uniform jacket?"

"Back at the base. A bunch of us got shanghaied on pretty short notice." Mac kept his foot hovering over the accelerator as he prayed the sergeant would buy that one; this was hardly shirt-sleeve weather. He managed a quick glance at the two Ic'nichi: they would probably be useless in their surprise if he had to rush the gate.

The sergeant gave him a contemptuous look. "Vell, pick it up ven you return. You are out of uniform." He pulled a form off the clip board and thrust it at Mac, who took it with an inward sigh of relief. "You vill report to warehouse C for a load of office supplies."

"It's a living." Mac gave him a wave which wasn't *quite* a 'Seig Heil', and gunned the big rig forward past the two bemused Ic'nichi watch-standers.

*****

"Chapter Seven"

"Brian!" I'eiBida was ecstatic when they were brought to the guardroom. "Thank the *Ancestors* you..." He trailed off in mid sentence when he saw his counterpart, and stared at her in disbelief. "This...is the other you?" he mumbled at last.

"I'eiBida?" She looked at him in equal amazement. "You've changed."

"So have you. Um...what can you tell us about your hostess?"

She shook off her bemusement. "Her name is Giselle, twenty years old, Spanish. She's a sweet, innocent kid who thought that waving picket signs and chanting slogans ever mattered in this world. She was a first year med student at Barcelona when she got caught up in an anti-government demonstration. Hundreds of them were rounded up for subversive activities. Alvarez picked her as a test subject for their mind transfer program."

"Ah...why her in particular?"

She wilted a bit, and gave him an uneasy look. "She's mixed race: Spanish and Arabic. The Purity Movement has this *thing* about race mixing, so they marked her to be used up in their experiments." It felt strange listening to her describe herself like she was speaking of someone else.

I'eiBida sighed. "I have never understood why you humans hate each other so much, and it seems worse than ever; far more so then when I retired."

"That's the way things are these days. The Purity Movement has no room for Sausages, so she's expendable..." She gasped for breath, and mumbled, "*Dios nos perdone por lo que nos hemos convertido en.*" She struggled to fight back her tears, then went on. "She...is expendable for the 'greater glory' of mankind."

Mac watched her in concern for a moment, wondering if she was finally coming unglued, then turned to I'eiBida. "And it gets better. It's like I reported earlier: the implant isn't holding. They've been erasing her mind over and over trying to find something which will make it stick, and she keeps coming back, like I did when you activated me before."

I'eiBida's ears wilted. "How...extensive is her recovery?"

104

"I...he...is pretty far gone." Her voice was tight and thin, right on the edge. "Each time they erase us, I recover faster. I'd say we're about equal right now, and she's gaining strength steadily." She was trembling by that point.

I'eiBida shook his head in dismay. "This is terrible!"

"And I saved the best for last," Mac added, grimly. I'eiBida looked at him in foreboding. "That place is a production facility. They have a dozen holding cells, and at least that many processing rooms. From what she told me on the way here, it's designed to turn out mind erasures in mass, and the whole thing is set to go as soon as they whip the rejection problem."

"*Es horrible...tanta maldad*," she whimpered.

"I...don't understand..." I'eiBida said, uneasily. "Why make so many copies?"

"Not copies; replacements. They created that place to process political enemies, to turn them into zombies."

"Ancestors!" I'eiBida gasped.

"That's the 'political development' Alvarez spoke of. He only needs to convert a few dozen key people to seize effective control of the Purity Movement. That would go unnoticed if he focusses on the key back room players rather than taking actual Alliance leadership. Once he is the power behind the throne, he will have effective control of the Alliance, enough to start his war, anyway. The complete in-depth control can come later as he consolidates his position."

She sobbed in anguish, seeming to shrink as she curled her arms around herself in a defensive posture.

I'eiBida stared at Mac in dismay. "This...is monstrous," he whispered at last.

"Yeah, and that ain't the start of it. He can systematically process anyone who gets in his way, which means he can choke off any dissent, or crush any resistance before it can get started. Without an effective resistance, the Purity Movement will be eternal."

"Dear Ancestors...we may have destroyed your civilization!"

"Yeah, well, it won't be the first time. The question is, what do we do now?"

"You have to stop him!" Giselle implored them in tears. "That is all that matters. Alvarez is a monster!"

"That's why we're here." I'eiBida watched her in concern for a moment, then turned to Mac. "Did you find the recording?"

"No. I didn't have a chance to search the place. There is sure to be a copy in the laboratory computer center, but where any master copy might be is unknown."

"Great. After your escape, you won't be able to go back in. I hope pressuring the Alliance works; it's all we have now."

Giselle sagged against the desk, trembling and sobbing convulsively. I'eiBida eyed her in confusion. "What's wrong...sit down!" He took her hand to steady her as her knees gave way while B'monTrea grabbed a chair and shoved it under her. By then she was shaking so badly that she collapsed into it, all but falling on the floor. "What is it?" I'eiBida turned from her to Mac. "What's wrong with her?"

"S-she...I'm...losing control..." she whimpered. "...she's too frightened...c-coord...ination..." The tears flowed freely as she broke down and cried like a lost child.

"I saw this earlier, on our way here," Mac said to I'eiBida as he comforted her. "She tends to freeze up in a crisis. She must be strong enough that her emotions can overwhelm the implant now that it's weakened."

"She fights him? Why?"

"She's not fighting him. Look at her: she's no match for our memories, and she's certainly no soldier. She panics when the stress is on, and her fear locks them up."

"I'm not sure...but she seems to be hysterical."

"What do you expect after what she went through?"

Giselle regained some self control by then, and sat staring at the wall, trembling and wringing her hands, tears streaking the dust on her face.

"It's easy to be brave when you're standing in the plaza of your university with thousands of people around you," Mac said, grimly. "When you're locked in a cell facing inhuman monsters—that's another story. I'm surprised she held together as well as she has thus far."

"I-it...was damn...close..." She rocked back and forth, arms wrapped tightly around her middle, tears flowing down her cheeks.

"Are you all right?" I'eiBida asked.

"No. I will manage." She looked at him with her face contorted with fear and anguish. "Y-you have...to do s-something. You created this mess. You have to stop them."

"We will." I'eiBida was shaken. They all were.

"N-now if you will excuse me, I...need time...the s-shakes."

"Yes, of course." I'eiBida tried to comfort her. "B'monTrea, find her a quiet place to lay down, and see if you can find some human food for her."

"Yes, sir." B'monTrea took over and gently guided her to the couch I'eiBida had occupied for three days.

§

"You humans never fail to amaze me," I'eiBida said, hollowly, as they made their way to the Intel circle. "Just when I think I've seen it all, you manage to come up with some new horror."

"Yeah, we have a gift," Mac grumbled. "So how does this affect your threat assessment?"

I'eiBida paused, and vented a weary sigh. "This is bad; very bad. From what you say, Alvarez will soon be in effective control of the Alliance. I'm afraid I must advise the Staff to prepare for immediate preemptive war."

"You're not giving up, are you?"

I'eiBida stood looking off at nothing. "I can't afford to give up," he said, softly. "But I can't afford to have any hope, either. This...is going to be horrible." He shook his head in despair. "All that effort...all those years of diplomacy..."

"You can't fold now. If there is *any* chance of choking this war in its cradle, its here, now, with us."

"You're right, Brian. I just hope my Ancestors will provide me with a clue, because I am at a loss."

There was an ugly silence as they absorbed that, then Mac said, "Look, whatever happens, get her out of this. Get her back to d'enchia, and do what you can for her."

I'eiBida looked at him with haunted eyes. "I will, Brian."

§

S'deMnveb and his people made it back just before dawn, looking weary and a bit disgusted. "My congratulations, sir," he said, curtly. "Did you get her out?"

"Yeah." Mac was too distracted by Giselle's revelations to take exception to his tone.

Giselle was resting on the guardroom couch, staring at the wall when they came to see her. She was calm again, except for the stricken look in her eyes.

"So you are Admiral MacKenna?" S'deMnveb asked when they were introduced.

"It would seem." She sat up. "But he is...quiet now. I have always been fascinated by your people, but I have never met your soldiers before. What branch are you?"

"We are the Special Service defenders, who apparently can be sent chasing our own tails at whim."

She didn't like his tone either; her persona changed sharply. "So what's your problem, mister?"

"I'm afraid you humiliated poor S'deMnveb," I'eiBida said. "The Specials are specifically trained in human tactics, and you two ran their tails off."

"Yeah?" She stood up, standing slightly taller than S'deMnveb. "And we didn't even realize we did it at the time. You need to go over your field manuals."

I'eiBida intervened to cool the rising tone. "Brian, you know any battlefield situation is a matter of chance. The Specials are our elite, and S'deMnveb's herd is among the best. You got lucky, is all."

She eyed the two of them, then wilted. "Yeah. You're right. Sorry."

S'deMnveb gave that a sour grunt of laughter. "Actually, sir, I suppose I can take it as a mark of distinction." He offered I'eiBida a wry ear twitch. "I can now claim I was defeated in action by Admiral MacKenna himself. Two of him, in fact. That ought to be worth a small medallion on my *t'plk'asira*."

"You know, it might at that," B'monTrea said once he left.

"Hmph."

§

108

Some time later, after a hasty debriefing and some hot food, Mac found her laying on the guardroom couch, staring at the wall. She sat up when he came in, and looked at him somberly. "Thank you for getting me out of there."

"Happy to oblige, but it's not over yet. We still have to eliminate the recording and get off planet."

"The odds are not good. He...told me enough to get an idea of what you will be up against."

"He's right. We'll just have to wedge it somehow."

She watched him for a bit with a haunted look. "At least...if the worst happens, I will die free." The *emptiness* in her eyes was chilling. "Promise me you will not let those *hombres malvados* have me again."

He nodded. "I hope we can get you out of this altogether; get you back to d'enchia where they can help you."

She sighed. "*Si*, thank you." She clutched herself and withdrew into a tight knot, staring at nothing. "It was... They are *los Diablos!* I...was so afraid...all the time...I died, again and again...e-every time they...gave me those *injections*... A-and there were those *memories*..." She shuddered, and wiped her eyes. "In my mind...all the time...so much violence...so much pain...s-so much death..."

"Look, don't think about it. Those memories are too painful for you. Give it time, and the implant will fade away."

"You are kind." She shook her head sadly, and stared at the floor. "So much evil," she mumbled. "Sometimes I am ashamed to be human."

"We're a messed-up lot. But don't you worry; the Ic'nichi are good folks, and they'll help you get rid of the implant."

"If we get to d'enchia."

"Yeah. If we get to d'enchia." There was a heavy silence as she stared at nothing. Mac decided to change the subject. "So...what's it like, being a girl?"

"Watch it, sailor!" The sudden change startled him. "Remember who you're dealing with here!"

"No, hey." He held up his hands in a pacifying gesture and retreated from her sudden outburst. "I was just asking."

She considered him angrily, then sagged. "Sorry. It's not easy, the way men look at me...I've come close to being raped more than once." She shuddered. "God, they made me feel icky. I think the only thing which saved me was they're terrified of Alvarez. And the monthly periods..." She gave him a bleak look. "We always underestimate women. They're a lot tougher than they seem."

"They'd have to be to put up with our shit."

She answered with a derisive snort. "You got *that* right." She looked him over, then asked, "So what's it like being a hulking great brute?"

Mac paused to reflect on that, unconsciously flexing his shoulder muscles. "It feels good, real good."

"Yeah? Well don't snag your cape on the flagpole when you leap over them tall buildings."

"I'll try not to," he grumbled.

She seemed to collapse in on herself again, and turned away. "I am sorry...that...was him...I really am grateful." She sagged back onto the couch in a fetal curl, and stared at nothing. Mac left her there without further comment.

§

"The aerial search has found nothing," Alvarez yelled. "NOTHING!"

The two 'Tan Shirt' section leaders cowered under his tirade. "We are still searching for them, sir..."

"And finding *nothing!* There is not enough cover to hide them from a determined air search in broad daylight, so I can only *assume* they slipped through your nets!"

"I don't see how, sir..."

Alvarez glared at him. "You don't see how? What I do not see is what *good* you are to me!"

That shook them both. Word of the fate of the last person Alvarez had no use for—the luckless Duty Officer in the laboratory—had spread far and wide. The two sadistic bullies, and Volmer too, were getting a taste of their own medicine.

"But where could they be, sir?" Volmer asked.

Alvarez turned on him. "It is obvious; they slipped past these *tontos miserables*, and reached the Lizard base!"

"But how? Krauss is good, but not that good, and he had the girl to slow him down." It was no longer '*Herr* Krauss': Alvarez's fair-haired boy had fallen from grace, and those remaining were all too happy to join the chorus howling for his blood.

That brought Alvarez down a notch or two. "The girl. She has the memories of MacKenna! He is a survivor if ever there was one, and he must have had the Lizards' help, too. It is no wonder they eluded these miserable *chapuceros*."

"So they're at the landing field."

"You never fail to impress me, Volmer! OF COURSE they are at the landing field! Now we shall have to go and get them."

"What about these two, Colonel?" As scared as he was by Alvarez's present state, Volmer never hesitated to deal out possible competition when the chance arose.

Colonel Alvarez considered the two 'Tan Shirts' in icy silence. "Today is your lucky day," he said at last in a chilling undertone. "I still have need of you, which shows my poverty for all the world to see." The two wilted in relief. "Get out!" They got, in unseemly haste. "Do not fail me again!" Alvarez called after them.

§

I'eiBida shook him out of a dead sleep a few hours later. "We have a situation, Brian."

"Wha? What time is it?"

"Mid-afternoon. The 'Tan Shirts' have ended their search, and troops are moving up from the harbor. I don't like the look of it."

The base Intelligence circle was jumping, with the full Intel compliment busy monitoring radio traffic and plotting positions on the large scale map of Singapore. Mac snagged a rice cake and some coffee—taken from the human stores outbound for the embassy on d'enchia—and studied the map as the plotters shifted the markers representing various human units in response to the latest direct observations and radio intercepts.

"We are picking up a lot of radio and telephone traffic between Colonel Alvarez and the Peacekeeper garrison, sir," T'thReptn said. "It seems Geneva gave command authority on the island to Alvarez, and the garrison Elder is not happy about it. They're having a huge argument about troop movements."

S'deMnveb came over to join them. "Alvarez seems to have the longer tail for now, sir. They are moving most of their available Peacekeeper units toward us." He turned and pointed out several markers arrayed in a broad arc on the map. "The 'Tan Shirts' are making up units too."

"That's not looking good." Mac pondered their deployment, and wasn't pleased. "They're moving to box us in. Analysis: what are they up to?"

"He is going to attack us," Giselle said from the doorway. They turned to her in surprise. "He must realize we got through their net, and this is the only place we could go. He will come looking for us soon."

"Yeah, makes sense. He's desperate enough to do anything to protect his little secret."

"He wouldn't," I'eiBida said, uncertainly. "His superiors in Geneva would never approve such a provocative act."

"He is paranoid and power-obsessed, and the 6th Office is a law unto themselves," she said, firmly. "There is nothing that *Diablo* will not do to recapture me."

B'monTrea stared at her in confusion. "How could you know?"

"She doesn't need to read your intel files," Mac said. "It's obvious just from talking to him. The guy's a nut-job, and her escape must have driven him over the edge."

"And they have been renegades for some time now," she added. "Geneva's control over them has been slipping, and this could be the breaking point." She preempted T'thReptn's objection. "I have been part of the protest movement since the start. We know Alvarez all too well from bitter experience. Trust me: he is coming."

Mac considered her in surprised approval for a bit, then turned to the assembled leadership gathered around the Intel plot table. "What's their strength?"

"Roughly four hundred, backed up with limited air and mechanized," I'eiBida said.

"And we can expect them to bring up a few light naval units if they do attack us, sir," T'thReptn added.

"Against what?"

"Less than forty all told, with light weapons."

"Forty?" Mac was stunned by that bit of news, and turned on I'eiBida. "Is that it? What about all the chaos in Malaysia you briefed me on? Forty isn't enough to mount an effective perimeter guard on an area this large!"

I'eiBida was put out by the thought. "And half of those are S'deMnveb and his Specials. The normal garrison here is D'remNek's section."

"We've had to call the humans for backup more than once, sir," T'thReptn said.

"We are in big shit." Mac shook his head in dismay. "What the hell happened? You need a full echelon here at least."

"The Alliance wouldn't authorize a larger contingent despite repeated requests," I'eiBida grumbled. "That goes for Admin and Support as well. This facility is badly understaffed all round."

"Which means they'll steam-roller us. You can't offer more than nominal resistance."

"Wonderful," I'eiBida muttered. "This could set off the war."

"The Alliance officials in Geneva must know that, sir," B'MonTrea said. "They wouldn't risk war over a minor incident."

"He must have come up with some story for them," Giselle said. "Something big enough to get their approval, however reluctant. In any case, he has a track record of doing what he pleases *a pesar de las protestas de* Geneva."

"So this is an unofficial action?" C'broVbron asked.

She turned to the Arbiter. "'Official' is what Alvarez *says* is official around here."

I'eiBida sighed. "Be that as it may, I cannot allow this facility to be attacked with impunity. We will defend it by any means necessary regardless of cost."

"We don't have the strength to stop them, sir," S'deMnveb said. "Even with my Specials, they will overrun our defenses."

"And with the 'Tan Shirts', a lot of us will be killed in the process," T'thReptn added.

"And they would be the lucky ones," Mac said, grimly. "But your people are right; you don't have nearly the strength to hold that lot off."

"We...have a tactical nuclear device on the transport," I'eiBida said, carefully. "We can launch a preemptive strike against the 6th Office compound."

Mac blanched, and gave him a hard look. "I'eiBida, you nuke this island, and you'll start something which will never end. We can't use nukes, no matter what."

"If war comes, we can strike a blow against the real enemy, sir." S'deMnveb tapped the image of the 6th Office compound on the latest orbital photo.

"Likely true. But trust me: you don't want that."

"It would also panic the common people," Giselle said in alarm. "We have an unholy fear of *armas atómicas*; it would give the Purity Movement all the excuse they need, and the public will support them eagerly."

"You are right, Brian." I'eiBida sighed in frustration.

"Yeah, dammit." It galled him to realize their efforts so far only made things worse. *'God, not another war,'* he thought. *'Haven't I done enough?'*

"So what can we do, sir?" T'thReptn asked.

"We have no choice." I'eiBida turned to the leadership. "We must evacuate to the supply ship and make a run for it. We can better afford to lose this outpost than to offer a futile defense which would raise tensions to the bursting point."

"But how can the ship escape the human orbital defenses, sir?"

I'eiBida glanced speculatively at Mac. "I'm betting the human Space Fleet won't be as trigger-happy as the 'Tan Shirts', plus both ships and the shuttles were recently refitted with a whole suite of defensive systems." Several sets of eye ridges went up at that. "If we can get a running head start, we might get clear." He turned to Arbiter C'broVbron. "How many people do we have here?"

"I cannot authorize abandoning this facility without the approval of the Arbiter in Geneva," C'broVbron said in alarm.

"There's no time for that, nor can we risk a communications breach. I am declaring a state of emergency under the authority of the Most Ancient himself, and assuming command here." That was a lie, but none of them had the means to check his story. "How many do we have to evacuate?"

"There are...one hundred and eighteen of us here all told," C'broVbron said, reluctantly. "Plus sixteen in transit, the Specials, the ship's crew, and a few odd tails."

"So, something like two hundred by time you count everyone."

"Can the ship hold so many, sir?" B'monTrea asked.

"It'll have to."

"They'll need an ears-up, sir," S'deMnveb said. "And they'll need to off load most of their cargo and take on extra consumables. That will take time."

"The ship is mostly loaded with supplies for the human diplomatic compound on d'enchia, sir," T'thReptn added. "It will take as much as two hands of days to offload it all."

"Hmmm...yes. And we won't want everyone to disappear at once anyway, so send a couple hands worth up on the next several shuttles to help with the unloading, and keep the rest out in public where the humans can see them. We'll need the defender detail and the Specials to secure the base in any event."

"I doubt Alvarez will give us that much time, sir."

"You need to draw them off, like before," Giselle said.

"How?" Mac pulled himself out of his funk; they had a situation, and he had to get to work, like it or not.

She gave him a pointed look. "They are after me, and presumably Alvarez wants you in the worst way as well. You need to slip out again and set up a ruckus somewhere else. Alvarez will assume wherever you show up, she won't be far away. That should draw them off on a wild goose chase which you can drag out for some time if you keep moving."

"One human against the entire island garrison?" I'eiBida was appalled. "Even he can't manage that!"

"He doesn't have to *defeat* them, dammit!" she snapped. "He just has to keep them jumping in circles, which one man can do *if* he keeps his wits about him."

"But..."

"It's our only hope."

"I'm afraid she's right, sir," B'monTrea said.

I'eiBida looked at Mac doubtfully. "Brian is too valuable to risk like that."

"Yeah? Well 'George' is busy, so he'll have to do his own dirty work for once."

I'eiBida turned back to her in confusion. "George?"

"Old human saying."

"You either fish or cut bait, Bubba," she said scornfully. "I'm in no physical condition for this, so it's up to you—*if* you aren't some big-talk commando." Mac fumed at her jibe, giving her his most forbidding glare, which she returned unflinching.

I'eiBida considered the two of them locked in an unspoken battle of wills. It was hard to say that either was winning. "Do you think they will chase wild gooses, Brian?"

Mac was seriously not thrilled with the idea, but he had to admit that she—or he—pegged it square.   "There are no guarantees," he said reluctantly. "But it should buy you some time. Every second counts, so you'll need to use the time to your best advantage."

"And don't get clever about it," she said.   "Just abandon everything, scramble for the lifeboats, and hope for the best."

I'eiBida pondered the matter for a long moment, and he wasn't happy. "Assuming you get out and can draw them off, how will you get back? This island is effectively mobilized, and once they think you're out there, they will lock the perimeter down tight to keep you out."

That was the brass ring of this whole deal, and at first blush, it didn't look promising. Right then, as much as he hated the thought of getting caught up in another war, he was even more appalled at this hare-brained stunt. If history was any guide—and he had a lot of history—this would be no picnic. "I'll have to fake something, I guess."

*****

"Chapter Eight"

Not being a complete fool, Mac knew to tank up on a good hot meal before heading out on what promised to be several days of unpleasant adventure. While I'eiBida put together the mission details, the Ic'nichi kitchen staff raided the human food stocks in the warehouses, and came up with a thick slab of canned ham, powdered mashed potatoes, canned green beans, and lots of strong black coffee. He was in the cafeteria wolfing it all down and trying not to think about the future when Giselle came in. She hesitated as she stood in front of him, then, "Hello."

Mac was working on a piece of ham, so he nodded to her.

"Do you mind if I join you?" she asked, diffidently.

He considered her, then nodded to the seat opposite. She settled awkwardly on the backwards-shaped Ic'nichi chair, and said, "I am sorry about carlier. That was him speaking."

He paused to swallow. "s'all right; that's just how we are." He offered a little smile. "I'll admit it was a bit of a shock to be on the receiving end of myself."

She gave him a wain smile in turn. "Argued with yourself and lost?"

He had to chuckle at her barb. "So to speak."

She was silent for a bit, staring hungrily at his plate. "Um...would you mind?"

There was a skillet with another helping by his elbow, but he shoved it toward her without a second thought. She didn't bother hunting for utensils, but grabbed the ham and attacked it. "I could never eat while I was in that place," she explained between bites. "I was too miserable and scared to be hungry. I only ate because those...*monstruos malas*...would force-feed me if I did not." She tackled the string beans, popping them one by one like finger food.

Mac took stock of her obvious hunger, and how thin she was, and made a mental note to tell I'eiBida to be sure she had plenty to eat on the trip to d'enchia. "Look, don't dwell on it. You're out of there, so let it go."

"Let it go?" She looked into his eyes solemnly. "If it was only so easy."

117

"The pain fades in time, I know."

Her thin shoulders sagged. "In time..."

"I asked I'eiBida to get you back to d'enchia; you'll be safe there. They'll help you. You should go up to the ship as soon as possible."

"Thank you, but I will stay for now." Her dark eyes met his. "They may need my help, the memories I carry. I will do what I can."

"This isn't your fight."

"This is everyone's fight. I am part of the protest movement; I have to do my share." She gave him a wain smile. "We Sausages must stick together, no?"

"Don't call yourself that."

"But it is true; I am a Sausage." She reflected for a few seconds, then, "I never really thought about my ancestry until those *diablos* came; now I wear it as a badge of pride." She gave him a look of bitter defiance. "I am Sausage, and proud of it!"

Mac felt a bit embarrassed that this innocent slip of a girl could show more resolve than he felt—but she wasn't innocent: no one who goes through what she endured was innocent any longer. "There's hope for us yet," he muttered.

Her eyes dropped, and she stared at nothing. "Is there? For any of us?" She looked at him again. "What about you? Will you be safe out there?"

He put down his fork. "I'm a soldier; we have to take our chances." She nodded, and turned away.

They ate silently for a bit, each lost in their own thoughts. She was right, he realized: this was everyone's fight, him included. As much as he resented being brought back from the dead and press-ganged into this, his skills could make a big difference in this war. And it was a war; he was under no delusions about it. Not all wars are fought with guns and bombs. If those caught up in it are lucky, the fight takes place discreetly, out of sight, with only those responsible having to face the music. I'eiBida had it right all along: he could make the difference between a covert action and genocide on a planetary scale. Put it that way, his course was clear —if he was to live with his conscience.

118

"It has to be done," he said to himself, then glanced at Giselle, who eyed at him curiously. "This mission: I'll buy the time to evacuate, if I can." They sat looking at each other, neither speaking of the risks he was about to take, but both of them fully aware of how slim his chances were. "The danger goes with the territory. The greater good is what matters; that's what a soldier's job is all about."

She nodded solemnly, and went back to eating.

§

"There is just one way you can leave here unobserved," I'eiBida said as they headed for the armory. "You can't go out on the top of a truck again; they're being searched too closely. You will need to go out in a container."

"Right," Mac grunted. "So how do I get out of it?"

"I hope S'deMnveb can help us with that."

S'deMnveb could, in fact. "We can cut a hole in the floor of the container, sir." He hefted a small reel of thick, putty-like thermacord. "If we can get into the container unnoticed, it will only take a moment."

"How soon can you have it done?"

"I'll get on it right away, sir. We should have it finished shortly."

"Good work, Second." I'eiBida turned to Mac. "We also have a few odd tools which you might find useful, Brian." I'eiBida handed him the pair of wire cutters he used earlier, and a genuine Swiss army knife.

"Thanks." Mac played with the knife, bemused by this artifact from his childhood, then slipped it in his pocket.

T'thReptn appeared just then, and I'eiBida turned to him. "You have that com gear?"

"Yes, sir." T'thReptn handed Mac a palm-sized device which could fit over a telephone mouthpiece. "This is a voice scrambler designed for your telephones. We have tapped into the island's phone system. Use this to call from any telephone; the scrambled transmission will be picked up automatically."

Mac examined the gismo curiously. "How do I hear you back?"

119

"It handles encoding in both directions. Use it to send us progress reports, or to call for help if needed. If you absolutely must, remove the scrambler and we can speak in the clear, but any listeners will be able to overhear it."

"And they will be sure to be listening," I'eiBida added.

"They will be able to trace your call, so keep your reports brief, or leave the area at once if you are on for any length of time."

"Right." Secretly, Mac was grateful for this lifeline, however tenuous. None of them were under any delusions about sending a rescue mission if he was cornered.

"Brian, always precede any message with the code word *'Adelbard',"* I'eiBida said. "If you don't, we will assume you have been compromised, and will order the unit to self-destruct."

"Wonderful." Mac examined the vocoder again gingerly. "So this thing might blow my head off?"

T'thReptn gave him a peeved look. "Microcircuitry, *sir*; we'll simply dump the power supply through the chip and fry it."

"Oh."

§

Another truck was backed up to a warehouse door, and had just been cleared of its load of dry goods bound for d'enchia, when the driver was accosted by the Ic'nichi dock supervisor. "You come fix papers," he said with a peremptory gesture to the dock office.

"Kay-*Rist!*" the driver grumbled. "What is it now?" He had been driving back and forth all day, and was tired, stiff, and bone weary. The one thing he didn't need right then was paperwork hassles; *especially* Lizard paperwork, which put human bureaucrats to shame. "All right, Godzilla," he sighed in exasperation. "Damned waste of trees." On top of *everything* else, it was raining again.

No sooner was he gone than a Hand of S'deMnveb's people dressed in ordinary set to work loading the container with pallet loads of office furniture bound for the embassy in Geneva. Once they filled it far enough to clear the back of the tractor unit, one of them laid a loop of thermacord on the steel deck while the others kept a discreet watch. Across the parking lot, an Ic'nichi load lifter slammed an empty trash container against the side of the building, the dull BOOM! muffling the thermacord as it burned a neat hole in the container's deck. The loading resumed, and the Specials carefully formed an open cavity around the hole which would be buried deep inside the final load. The smoke was long cleared, and the load-out well along by time the human driver could get away from the 'Godzilla' and return to his rig.

Mac and I'eiBida watched the loading from an out of the way spot while the Specials kept an eye on the area. "Points for your people," Mac said with an approving nod.

"We call them the Specials for good reason."

"It's time, sir," S'deMnveb called to them. The trailer was nearly full.

"Right." Mac turned to I'eiBida again. "How long do you need for the evacuation?"

"As long as you can give us, Brian. We'll need to clear most of the cargo off the ship to have enough room. If we're to do that discreetly, it will take time; the more time you give us, the better."

"Days? Weeks?"

"Three or four days, if at all possible."

"I make enough stink, I can buy you that much."

"Keep in regular touch." I'eiBida gestured to the vocoder. "We will aim our final evacuation for early morning, just before dawn. Check in at dawn and twilight daily. We'll give you an ears-up as far ahead as possible."

"And if I can't make it back?"

I'eiBida studied him somberly. "Then we go without you," he said at last. "In that case, try to reach the embassy in Geneva."

"Okay." His chances of making it off this island and half way around the world with every law enforcement agency ever spawned on his tail were somewhere between 'Nada' and 'You're kidding, right?'.

"I only hope Alvarez will hold off long enough for you to do some good," I'eiBida said, grimly. "Otherwise this whole trip will be for nothing."

"Yeah. If he doesn't get a move-on, he'll have to wait for morning."

§

121

"More supplies are being delivered to the Peacekeeper units now, Colonel," the new Duty Officer reported.

"About blessed well time," Alvarez grumbled.

He was in a foul mood at all the delays, not that it should be a surprise with how the Alliance deliberately starved the regulars these last few years. There were only two line companies available to guard this island and its key facilities, in fact, so he needed to borrow the Military Police unit from the harbor to give him anything like enough strength. The spaceport's Admiral flat refused to give him the other MP unit, siting the many threats of this lawless region, and the garrison's Colonel begrudged him a handful of engineers and transport. As annoying as that pompous *cochine* was, Alvarez couldn't blame him. By forming every available 'Tan Shirt' into two platoons, he had enough to do the job.

"So, I assume they are ready?"

"They are still short of ammunition, sir. It will take several more hours to bring up their stocks."

Alvarez turned on him. "Ammunition? What have you been hauling in those trucks?"

The Duty Officer fidgeted nervously. "Ah...food, sir, and tents. It's raining out there, and they need..."

"Food? Tents? *Are you trying to sabotage us?*"

The man flinched under his icy glare. "It's the Quartermasters, sir...that's standard priority for sending troops into the field."

"Standard priority?" Alvarez was incensed at their stupidity. "You tell those hyenas that *MY* priority is the *ONLY* priority! From now on they will ship *nothing but ammunition*, and they better deliver it quickly or they will soon be shipping brimstone in Hell!"

The Duty Officer was trembling by then; he heard the stories about Alvarez, and he could see they were all true. "Yes, sir! What about the forward units, sir?"

"It is too late to attack now thanks to those *traitors*. Tell the troops I want them ready to march by dawn. Ammunition or no, they will march!" The Duty Officer saluted and beat a hasty retreat. "And impress upon them how *significant* that deadline is!" Alvarez yelled after him.

§

The rain let up momentarily, although his breath steamed from the chill as Mac walked across the parking lot with his shoulders hunched and his hands in his pockets. There was foul weather coming in; it was nearly twilight, but the cloud cover was so thick that it seemed like night. The dim late afternoon light cast no shadows and glistened dully on the wet pavement, giving the world a surreal look. Idle raindrops brushed his face, putting him in a melancholy mood.

The driver of his truck was arguing with 'Godzilla' again, so no one noticed as he walked down the off side and slipped underneath the trailer. The hole in the floor was a snug fit, and the open space inside was barely large enough for him to lie curled up. The burned out metal plate was duct-taped to two pieces of wood, and it took some doing to wrestle it around in the cramped space and drop it into the opening. That done, he listened carefully to the faint sounds from outside, alert for any hint that his actions were noticed.

The rear doors slammed shut a short while later, and the tractor roared to life. The brakes hissed, and they started moving. "Damn-fool way to make a living," he grumbled to himself as he settled in for the ride.

The truck ground to a halt a few minutes later, and he heard faint voices. The main gate: the 'Tan Shirt' security team searched all around the truck carefully while the sergeant questioned the driver. Mac listened anxiously, and cursed himself for not thinking to take the pistol he liberated from the 6th Office security guard. There were faint voices outside, and something banged on the side of the container, about scaring him out of his skin. More voices as he waited in agony, then the truck started up again. He was finally able to breathe.

§

Giselle was sitting in an out of the way corner of the Intel circle nibbling some dried fruit when I'eiBida came by a short time later. "He is gone?" she asked.

"Yes."

"*Vaya con Dios, mi héroe.*" She was silent for a moment, then, "What are our chances?"

123

"That's hard to say." He thought about it, then added, "If he can stall Alvarez off for the next several days, we can get everyone onto the transport. From there it's a matter of evading the orbital defenses and getting away."

"And if he cannot?"

I'eiBida didn't answer. He didn't need to. The look in her eyes said she already knew. He watched her for a time trying to judge her strength. He met petite humans before, but she seemed more like a hatchling than a mature fem. Her weary, haunted expression said volumes about what she endured at the hands of those monsters. He pitied her, and wondered idly if she was considered beautiful.

"Can I count on you?" he asked, gently. "We need all the help we can get, and with Brian gone, you are our only source of human strategic thinking."

"I...will try," she said uncertainly. "He is pretty weak. I can still hear him and pass along his advice, but I am not a soldier. Not like him." She clutched herself, her earlier bravado faded. "I do not know how well I can do at this."

"Just do the best you can; that's all any of us can do. And weak or not, Admiral MacKenna is a formidable military asset. Anything you have to offer will help."

"I...hope he will be all right, the big goy."

I'eiBida almost offered her some reassuring platitude, but it just didn't seem right. "So do I."

§

Aboard the transport, Ship's Eldest A'vberBenn stared at the brief update from I'eiBida which came up on the latest shuttle, and muttered a venomous curse. "This is *er'trxxda!*"

"Sir?" His Second, seated at the galley table going over the loading manifest while nursing yet another squeeze bulb of *V'liz,* looked up in surprise.

"They're going to evacuate Singapore!"

"Why?"

"According to this, the *cc'v'renk humans* might attack them at any moment. They want us to offload *all* the cargo, and make preparations for something like two hundred evacuees."

"They can't be serious! Where will we put them all?"

A'vberBenn wadded the offending message up and threw it across the room. It bounced off the microwave, and began ricocheting slowly around the open galley space. "They warned me something like this might happen. It looks like the war may finally be on." He ducked the wad of paper, and turned to his Second. "As to where we'll put them, I'll save the crude suggestions for later. Call the departments together. We've got the biggest tail knot *ever* to untangle!"

§

"We've pulled all the ammunition we have together, sir," S'deMnveb reported when I'eiBida came by the armory later that evening. "Even with the security stockpile, it isn't much."

I'eiBida pondered the munitions piled on the armory work table with no joy. "What about your explosives?"

"We're rigging various traps with it, sir. Even so, it won't be enough to stop the humans. It might slow them, or push them into choke points where we can bring our firepower to bear."

"It still won't be enough." The armory was little more than a large closet with a shelf unit on one side, and a work table opposite with a section's maintenance kit. The shelves weren't overloaded.

"No, sir," S'deMnveb said. "But it's all we have." There was an uncomfortable silence between them, then he added, "Honestly sir...it seems hopeless. Perhaps we should cut our losses. Evacuate the human fem to the ship, and offer no resistance when the humans come. They won't have reason to slaughter us then."

I'eiBida understood how he felt, having seen the humans in battle more than once, and decided it wouldn't be right to knot his tail for that moment of weakness. "Have you ever heard of the Pagans, Second?" he said, softly.

S'deMnveb seemed a bit confused. "No, sir."

"They were an ancient human Mysticism. One of their strongest beliefs was that their Ancestors would judge them on their courage in battle. They would fight savagely to the bitter end, even when they knew they would be defeated." S'deMnveb was a bit dismayed. "That belief still permeates their military thinking, which is part of why they are so dangerous," I'eiBida went on.

125

"We can do no less. With the diplomatic situation what it is, this place is untenable. Our objective is to stall for time until we can evacuate the civilians, and *hope* a shuttle will be there for us when the Peacekeepers come. We must be prepared for sacrifices if need be, which is why we are called Defenders Of The Nest."

"I understand, sir," S'deMnveb said, solemnly.

I'eiBida gave him a reassuring ear twitch. "Just do the best you can, Second. No one could ask anything more."

§

The road leading east from the landing field was little better than a potholed gravel path, and the semi trailer's springs were woefully lacking. It made for a rough, uncomfortable ride, and the constant worry that the heavy load of furniture might shift and bury him. Still, he was on his way, and at this pace, the twenty-five klicks or so to the harbor shouldn't take more than an hour. It would be sheer dumb luck if the 'Tan Shirts' found his hideaway, so barring accidents he was safe enough for now. The real challenge would start once he got there.

He was beginning to think he had it whipped when the truck lurched to another abrupt stop. He listened carefully, wondering what was happening. As the truck's motor dropped to idle, he could hear the rumble of diesel engines and the clatter of treads. His first thought was that it was a tank, and he fought down the impulse to panic. His situation was hopeless if the Peacekeepers had surrounded the truck with armor... The clatter paused, and the diesel revved again accompanied by a steady *'beep...beep...beep'*. Earth moving equipment: he breathed a sigh of relief. They were repairing the highway.

"God, I'm getting too old for this," he grumbled as he settled in his cramped hideaway.

§

"I sincerely hope for your sake that you have progress to report," Alvarez snarled when the Duty Officer came in answer to his summons.

The man was shaken and pallid, and turned even whiter under the Colonel's tirade. "I am sorry, sir. There has been another problem..."

126

Alvarez advanced on him in fury, and slashed the Duty Officer's face with his swagger stick. "Problems! Do I care for your problems?"

The man recoiled under the blow and retreated. "But...they couldn't help it, sir!"

"Those *tontos miserables* saw fit to disregard my orders?"

"No, sir! The rain washed out part of the highway! The traffic is backed up while the engineers work to repair it!"

Alvarez reined in his temper once again, which was more difficult than *ever*. "Then I *suggest* you get out there, personally! and make sure they get the job done *immediately!*"

§

"This is impossible," the Ship's Third complained. "We don't have nearly the room for upwards of two hundred people."

"We'll have to stack them like pallets," The Eldest said. "Where we'll find hammocks for that many I can't imagine."

"The worst of it will be logistics," Second said. "We will need food and water for at least twenty-four days, and we have nowhere near that many endurance rations."

Third grunted in disgust. "The worst of it will be oxygen and sewage. We have nowhere *near* enough of the former, and we'll have far too much of the latter by time we reach home." That produced a grim silence. Without oxygen the whole effort was futile, and they all knew there were no oxygen reserves at Singapore.

"We have to get some from the humans," Second said.

"But...if we are at war with them..."

"*As far as we know* we're not at war with them, *yet*," The Eldest said. He turned to the Third, who normally handled shipboard logistics. "Tell the humans we lost our reserve due to a system leak, and pray to our Ancestors they will give us a fresh supply. If they do, cram every drop of liquid oxygen you can on board."

"Yes, Eldest."

"But first calculate if it will be enough," the Second said. "Otherwise we will have to call off the evacuation."

"Yes, sir."

§

Mac was awakened from a troubled nap when the truck lurched into motion. He listened carefully, and could still hear the clatter of an earth mover, and shouted voices. The truck crawled ahead, slipping and rocking on the uneven surface. He lifted the burnt-out plate carefully, and saw that they were driving over mesh panels laid over soft earth, no doubt just installed by the engineers, fitfully lit by spotlights and vehicle headlights. Watery mud oozed through the mesh, and the truck's tires sank almost to the hubs. It kept moving while he held his breath, but barely.

"Shit," he grumbled, and replaced the plate.

§

"The highway has been patched, sir," the Duty Officer reported. "The supply trucks are starting to move again."

Alvarez gave him an icy look tinged with madness. "You will live another day." The man saluted and retreated.

"I understand the traffic is still backed up, sir," Volmer said once he was gone. "At this rate, the forward units won't be fully supplied until morning at the earliest, thanks to those Peacekeeper fools." He cowered as Alvarez glared at him. "I have given westbound traffic absolute priority, sir."

Alvarez glowered at him, breathing hard, his eyes burning with barely suppressed rage. "We will not be able to attack before morning at the earliest."

"I-I'm afraid not, sir."

Alvarez's rage overflowed. He grabbed the plot table with both hands, and heaved it over on its back, scattering papers, coffee mugs, and people in all directions. "DAMN YOU ALL!" he screamed. He stood trembling and breathing hard, his features a mask of demonic rage, until the outburst passed. "Very well," he shouted at last. "Since none of you can follow simple orders, we will delay the attack until dawn. But then *someone* will die! Whether it is *you* or the Lizards—or both!—depends on what happens tomorrow!"

He stalked out of the room, and the terrified staffers began to pull themselves together while Volmer watched from a corner, thinking to his dismay once again that he served a raving madman.

§

128

Finally the truck slowed, and Mac could feel it cornering. A moment later it ground to a halt, and there were muffled voices. The truck lurched into motion again, and crawled slowly forward. The rough highway gave way to smooth pavement. Mac felt the change, and figured he must have arrived at the harbor. The truck drove slowly for some time, making random turns and stops until it ground to a halt again. A few minutes later the engine revved, and the truck crept forward a short distance. A few minutes after that, it did it again. Shortly thereafter it happened again while Mac wondered what the hell was going on.

The tension finally got to be too much: he wrestled the metal plug out of the way and poked his head out for a look. The truck was standing in a line next to a wall of stacked containers. There was the roar of a heavy engine, and two sets of wheels on tall columns drove past: a straddle crane. They were about to off-load his container and add it to the stacks waiting to load onto a ship. He had to bail out now before he was sealed in. Another look around, he wiggled out through the narrow hole and hovered under the truck to see if anyone was watching. Nothing. It took a bit of effort to straighten up after his cramped ride, but it felt so *damned* good to be out of that potential coffin.

A bit of bright yellow in the distance caught his eye: a plastic safety helmet left unattended by one of the dock workers. Mac took another cautious look, then idled over to the helmet, lifted it and the metal lunchbox next to it, and headed for the shadows.

§

Alvarez continued his slow burn as the hours crawled past at the 6th Office communications center. Everyone else kept a low profile; people avoided his gaze and kept busy; the relief personnel were as tardy as they dared, and the relieved shift left as fast as they discreetly could. In his present state, no one was safe, and dark new rumors of his insane rage were already making the rounds. He stalked back and forth around the map table, snarling at anyone at random and demanding ever more impossible performance. The first Sumatra squall of what promised to be a long bout of foul weather was moving off shore, but it left devastation in its wake, which didn't help his mood either.

Out west, the two Peacekeeper companies cowered under their blown-down tents and plastic tarps, trying to keep warm with small fires and meager rations, and wondered why they endured like this. Even their 'Tan Shirt' overseers admitted to themselves that the Peacekeepers would be useless until they could dry out and have a hot meal. There was also the question of ammunition, of which they had but a few clips each. How soon proper supply would come, or how they could attack without was beyond them.

That question also vexed Alvarez. His patience ran out early the next morning, and he summoned Volmer. "Well?" He gave Volmer a look which threatened to sink the island under his feet. "Are my orders *finally* being carried out?"

Fortunately, Volmer had a crumb of good news for him, which probably saved his life. "Yes, sir. The forward units are receiving ammunition now." He didn't dare mention that it was a single light truckload of rifle ammo—in boxes, which needed to be put in clips before it could be used. All common sense notwithstanding, the clips were not included. Despite their danger, the base Quartermasters were an abysmal lot, and the island's sole transport company was preoccupied—illogically, but no one told them otherwise—with hauling containers between the Ic'nichi landing field and the harbor. Volmer at least had the wit not to annoy Alvarez with such petty details.

"Very well then." Alvarez glowered at him for a long moment. "I am gratified that people around here *finally* take my wishes to heart. We will attack at first light."

"Yes, Colonel!"

Alvarez gave him an icy glare, and headed for the wardroom. As soon as he was gone, Volmer was on the phone badgering the Quartermasters to get *moving*. It was going to be a long night.

§

Mac wandered around the harbor at random for the next couple of hours sizing up the area. The plastic helmet and lunch box together with his bulky build seemed to be his free pass; no one questioned what looked like any another dock worker on his way to somewhere. Still, he kept moving, always careful to set a steady pace which didn't linger while not attracting attention.

The place was busy. Two ships were tied to the piers while a third was anchored off shore waiting its turn. That was freakin' huge traffic by what he remembered. As fast as the trucks were loaded, they moved out only to be replaced by new arrivals. Most of what was being unloaded was in containers, so he couldn't tell what it was, but there were several containers marked off with yellow tape: secure cargo. Military equipment.

After a while he settled on a pile of pallets and checked out the lunch box while scoping the area. Dinner was two stale ham sandwiches and a plastic bag of cookies. He sat munching absently and watched the action around him. A steady stream of containers was being loaded onto the waiting flat bed trucks, while other containers were moved from the stacks to shipboard.

Beyond that was a row of light patrol craft tied to another dock. The Alliance Navy needed precious few capital units since no one had the strength to present them with a main force challenge, but there were swarms of these small craft to deal with the near anarchy lingering in places like Southeast Asia.

While he ate, Mac reviewed his strategy. Looking at it from Alvarez's point of view, assuming they hadn't gone to the Ic'nichi landing field, the obvious move was to get off the island either by air or sea. An airplane is a lot faster, but there was little chance of hiding in one. Unless there was a smaller aircraft they could steal at the spaceport, a ship was their only alternative. And it was an attractive alternative because they would have a far better chance of stowing away on a large cargo liner undetected. Yes, the fugitives' first choice would be here in the harbor, so this was where he needed to start his show.

His thoughts were disrupted when two MPs—the first he'd seen, they being part of the handful held back from Alvarez—came cruising by and slowed to check him out. He carefully kept his cool, and looked back at them like his life was so dull that even a passing cop car was entertaining while reminding himself that the secret to successful infiltration was to look bored. He finished his sandwich with a flourish, and raised the lunch box as a casual salute. They were spread thin, and had a lot to do. They considered him for a moment longer, then moved on.

The night was getting cold, and that close run-in reminded him he needed to bunker down for the night. But first he needed to call in an update. Back on his feet, and he headed down the road after the MPs along the row of buildings. A little further on, he came to an ordinary door into a warehouse office. He looked around cautiously, but saw nothing; no movement; no sound but for the spattering rain. He gave the door a solid heave with his shoulder, and it popped open.

Inside was a small reception area, with warehouse shelving visible through an inner doorway. There was a phone on the receptionist's counter, and its reassuring hum sounded like a chorus of angels. He slapped the vocoder over the mouthpiece and hit a button at random.

"This is *'Adelbard'*. I've reached the harbor. Going to ground for the night."

There were flashing lights in the distance: as thin as they were spread, harbor security reacted damned fast. He didn't wait for a reply, but hung up, put the vocoder in his pocket, and headed for the rear of the building. He noticed stacks of military field ration cases as he passed through the warehouse proper, and paused to grab some before ducking out through a rear door.

*****

"Chapter Nine"

"What do you think, sir?"

I'eiBida, B'monTrea, and S'deMnveb were standing on the roof of a warehouse overlooking the base entrance to size up the tactical situation. The morning was chill and wet, and the night's storms had given way to light mist and occasional showers. In the distance, where the entrance road turned onto the old highway, they could just make out the improvised camp of one of the Peacekeeper units. They were finally stirring from under their plastic and canvas tarps, milling about in loose knots as they slowly worked their way into some resemblance of a battle formation. Even from here, their low morale and lack of training were obvious, but there were an awful lot of them, supported by a hand's worth of light armored vehicles. They wouldn't mill around aimlessly forever.

I'eiBida sighed, and glanced at S'deMnveb. "As knotted tails go, this one is Righteous."

Hopeless would be a better term. According to the latest from Intel, the humans had deployed some three hundred Peacekeepers backed up by light armor and a hand of tactical aircraft, with two units totaling about one hundred 'Tan Shirts' parked further back along the highway. The Peacekeepers were second rate troops by all accounts, with poor training and morale, and outdated equipment, but once they got rolling, sheer inertia would carry them over the Ic'nichi defenses.

Against that, they had S'deMnveb and his Specials, D'remNek's 'Dark Grays' Service Wardens (who were good, but not that good), two warehouse volunteers—a retired 'Green-And-Red' and another 'Blue-And-Brown' hastily and irregularly sworn into the 'Dark Grays', plus B'monTrea and himself. Forty all told: armed with light weapons and limited ammunition against ten times their number of human troops. The rest of the staff—busy with the evacuation—were useless for this. I'eiBida was forced to turn away a hand or more of volunteers; few Ic'nichi realized what fighting the humans could be like, and their one hope if the evacuation failed was their non-combatant status.

133

"It's a sad thing," I'eiBida said philosophically as he watched the distant encampment. "The Peacekeepers were once an elite force; it's a shame they've come to this."

"The name doesn't really apply any more, either," B'monTrea grumbled.

The latest intel gleaned off the newscasts included a sickening massacre of a village in central Africa which was leveled by air strikes while a brigade of Peacekeepers stood by and watched. Further afield, there was a report of rioters in central China being bloodily suppressed with gunfire. And that was just what the Purity Movement allowed to be seen; they all knew there was much more which was never reported. No, the name didn't fit.

"Our one chance is to hold them at the gate, sir."

"Hmph. And what is the chance of that?"

S'deMnveb's ears twitched nervously, but he didn't answer. The answer was plain for all to see.

The entrance to the Ic'nichi base was on the narrow neck of a peninsula separated from the main island by a dredged estuary formerly lined with docks and ship ways. The neck of land was only a few hundred paces wide, but the far shore was a jungle of industrial wreckage; ideal sniper and heavy weapons territory. If they watched carefully, they could catch occasional glimpses of human observers in the ruins across the waterway. They maintained a low profile, but they were definitely out there. All common sense said there were heavy weapons out there as well.

What was worse than the overwhelming numbers was the Ic'nichi couldn't dig in because they needed to keep up appearances. According to their plan, the base's four load lifters would be rushed to the front at the first sign of trouble, and set to erecting barriers with whatever was at hand. There were also improvised strong points tucked out of human sight in some of the buildings, but they wouldn't have the time or resources to do much. If—when—the attack came, the bottleneck wouldn't last long. After that they'd be urban fighting in an open area where any resistance could be easily outflanked.

"We'll have to do the best we can, I guess."

"Is there any change in our plan, sir?" As if it mattered.

I'eiBida considered the area from their rooftop vantage point. "No. All we can do is buy time." He turned to B'monTrea. "Spread the word: when the fighting starts, anyone not directly involved is to drop everything and head for the landing field. If there's a shuttle on the ground, or if one can come in, we'll hold the humans off as long as we can so as many can be evacuated as possible."

"And if no shuttles are available, sir?"

"Then it's a convenient place to surrender. In either case, we'll end our resistance before we get to the loading area. Hopefully that will prevent a slaughter of the noncombatants."

"Yes, sir." There was a brief silence, then, "How long do we have, sir?"

"They probably won't come right away, otherwise they would have halted the deliveries," B'monTrea said.

"Good point," S'deMnveb muttered.

The steady parade of trucks had continued through the night and into the morning despite the rising tensions. As they watched, another one pulled through the gate and headed to the warehouse area, its headlights reflecting off the wet pavement and its passing marked with the hiss of tires in the runoff. The main gate 'Tan Shirt' guard detail hid in their duty shack about a hundred paces distant, ducking out only to check trucks through before retreating to the warmth of a smoking oil heater. It didn't make sense under the circumstances. The whole scene was hardly warlike, but then humans could be baffling at times.

I'eiBida sighed again. "Ancestors alone know. I don't see why they haven't already attacked." There was a brooding silence as they pondered their likely future. "Is anyone keeping track of the humans?" he asked as an outbound truck drove by.

"Sir?"

"We need to keep a count of how many humans go in and out. We don't want any infiltrators getting in to hit us in our rear when the fighting starts."

"It might be wise to search the area too, sir," B'monTrea said.

"Yes, good point."

§

Giselle was waiting for them when they returned into the Intel circle. She had hung around the circle since the mission started, subsisting on brief naps in a chair in an out of the way corner, and whatever human food the base personnel could scrounge for her. "How does it look?" she asked.

I'eiBida considered her, then said, gently, "It doesn't look good. I want you to go up on the next shuttle. I promised Brian I would get you out of here, and that's your best bet right now."

She eyed him somberly. "No. You need me here."

"But..."

She overrode his objection. "You need his skills. He is pretty far gone, but we can still help."

"She makes a good point, sir," B'monTrea said.

I'eiBida gave him a hard look, then turned to her. "Our defenses won't last long, and there's no guarantee any of us will escape once the fighting starts."

She clutched herself in the humans' nervous posture, trembling ever so slightly as she stared at nothing for a bit. "I know," she said at last. "But he was right, the big goy: waving picket signs never did a bit of good. I have to do *something*, and right now his skills are needed here." She gave him a woefully defiant look. "So I am staying."

"Thank you," I'eiBida said at last. "Well, since you're here, do you have any suggestions?"

She drifted over to the table where the tactical map was being updated again. It didn't take a military genius to see that their situation was desperate.

"You sent out some scouts?" She pointed to two blue push pins flanking the Peacekeeper unit on the access road.

"Yes, a Hand of them."

She pondered the map for a moment. "They will not be able to get back here when the fighting starts. Tell them that when the time comes, they should regroup and hit the humans from behind. A steady string of sabotage and hit-and-run raids will distract them." She looked at S'deMnveb, who seemed disturbed by the idea of a fourth of his people being trapped behind an oncoming human attack. "It may buy us some time."

I'eiBida exchanged looks with S'deMnveb, then turned to her. "Yes, excellent. Thank you." They focussed on the tactical map while the rest of the Intel staff went about their business with a subdued hum of scratchy radio transmissions, quiet voices, and office equipment. She drifted aimlessly away, and wound up by the window staring at the sky. The clouds were heavier and darker, and the rain was picking up again. It was a chilling, dismal sight which fitted the black depression in her mood perfectly; the whole world was crying for the fate of mankind. She thought about him, her unlikely knight in shining armor, and wondered idly how he was doing and whether she would ever see him again.

'You need to rest, Giselle.' She twitched when the voice in her head spoke. *'You can get so tired that you start making mistakes if you don't pace yourself.'*

"Please leave me alone," she muttered.

'This is important. We're in a bad situation; we need to stay alert.' She had endured these whispered conversations through the endless months of her captivity; having the ghost of a dead man in her head filled her with dread, and the *memories* this one bore left her shaken with horror. She had to wonder at times if she was *poseído por el diablo.* The unseen but very real aura of death and destruction behind that voice made it seem all too likely. *His* mere presence filled her with dread, both from her nightmare experiences in that *place*, and the all too graphic nightmares of *his* past. She shuddered as if enduring a painful blow every time *he* spoke to her.

'You need a hot meal, then get some sleep.'

"All right," she muttered. "Just leave me alone." *He* was right, though. She really did need some sleep.

'That was some good advice you gave them,' *he* said as the presence faded.

§

"*Where* are those munitions?" Alvarez demanded for the umpteenth time. "Can't you people do *anything* right?"

The Peacekeeper liaison flinched under his tirade. "They have a partial issue now, and more is coming, sir. We are working as fast as we can..."

"If *this* is all the better you can do, then perhaps we should surrender to the Lizards now!"

"...but we are short of light trucks...we need to..."

"ENOUGH!" Alvarez roared. He got squarely in the liaison's face. "The attack will start in one hour. *ONE HOUR* whether they have adequate munitions or not!"

"Yes, sir!" The man retreated hastily after offering a sketchy salute.

"Do NOT fail me!" Alvarez shouted after him. He fumed while the liaison beat a fast retreat, then turned his wrath on the new Duty Officer. "For your sake, I *hope* you have no problems to report."

"Nothing of importance, sir." He man considered his daily report nervously. "There was a minor burglary at a warehouse down at the docks, but nothing significant was taken."

That would concern him solely because it was a security matter, and Alvarez was about to dismiss it before the thought started nagging at him. "What is in this warehouse?"

The Duty Officer consulted his clip board. "It's a low security zone, sir. All it contains are uniforms, personal stores, and rations for the Navy."

"Very...rations?"

"Yes, sir."

That sent a foreboding chill through Alvarez for some reason. "Rations?" he muttered.

"Will there be anything else, sir?"

Alvarez was preoccupied, and didn't answer for a moment, staring into the distance while he pondered that minor burglary. It was probably nothing...but then...rations...and uniforms... Finally he turned to the Duty Officer. "I want that building searched carefully. And search the grounds as well. I want to know if anything is amiss."

"Ah...yes, sir." The Duty Officer was perplexed, but knew better than to question the Colonel, especially after what became of his predecessor.

"Do you want to continue with the attack, sir?" Volmer asked. "They're about ready to kick off."

Alvarez brooded over that, and the mysterious minor burglary. It was probably nothing...but who would steal field rations...when the base cafeteria... He turned to Volmer. "The attack can be put off for a few hours. I want to see the results of that search first."

§

The Hand Lead shifted uncomfortably in his shallow hideout, and cursed the endless drizzle. At least the temperature was comfortable, but the constant rain got on their nerves and made their equipment harnesses chafe. He shifted slightly to be sure his silencer-equipped machine pistol was safely out of the damp, and tried to fight off the urge to fall asleep. It was his own stupid fault for being here; he had to volunteer not only for the 'Dark Grays' but for the Special Service as well. He shook off his momentary fit of pique with an ear twitch of annoyance. He was here because he was needed: he joined the 'Blue-And-Whites', and later the 'Dark Grays' to defend his people against whatever threats would endanger the nest. It was a proud tradition, and he was solemnly pleased to live up to it so well. Unfortunately, these aliens threw all the traditions out the window; upholding tradition could mean one wouldn't live to retire. He and his entire Hand—not to mention everyone back at the landing field—would likely be dead by nightfall. But no one lives forever, and if he had to go, he would prefer it this way. He was a hunter, a predator, which was rare among the people. Stalking the humans tested his skill and courage, and he was pleased by how well he and his Hand performed. And while the thought of the pending battle filled him with foreboding, he was ready to do his part for the nest...

"What are they up to?" his second, laying a body length away in his own shallow pit in the rubble, whispered.

That snapped him back to the here-and-now. The human Peacekeepers a hundred paces distant were congregating under their improvised tarp shelters again, and stoking up their cooking fires. As they watched, the humans stacked their weapons and broke out their personal gear. Soon there were metal cups warming over the fires everywhere they looked.

"Mid-meal?"

"Perhaps. It's a bit early for that."

139

But the longer they watched, the more obvious it was that the humans were boiling more of their coffee and trying to keep warm rather than preparing meals. A few nibbled what were probably ration bars, while others inhaled those burning leaf tubes which were so popular. Off in one corner, a couple humans were passing a plastic bottle back and forth.

"They don't seem very warlike," the second said.

"No, they don't." The Lead keyed his tactical circuit. "Third? Are you seeing this?"

"Yes," the answer came back from the other two who were deployed on the far side of the Peacekeeper encampment. *"It looks like they are settling down again."*

"The attack was called off?" the second wondered.

"It looks like." As they watched, one of the light armored vehicles drew off the road, its crew crawled out and joined one of the campfires.

"We better call this in." Maybe they would live to tomorrow after all.

§

"The humans have stopped their deployment, sir," T'thReptn reported when I'eiBida came to the Intel center in response to an urgent summons. "Our forward observers report the humans in the unit nearest us seem to have settled in again, and their communications volume has died down considerably. We aren't sure what the other two Peacekeeper units are doing, but communications have died down for them too."

"What do you make of it?"

"It looks like they are standing down from the impending attack, sir."

"What about the 'Tan Shirts'?"

"Their radio volume has increased sharply. We aren't sure what they're up to."

I'eiBida pondered the map with the latest human positions. It wasn't good. There was a lot of firepower out there. "Could they intend to throw the 'Tan Shirts' in instead?"

"That is not how they do things," Giselle said, doubtfully.

I'eiBida eyed her in surprise. "What are they up to?"

140

"I...do not know. Neither does he."

"We're also picking up greatly increased radio usage in the harbor area, sir."

I'eiBida jumped at that. "Whose radios? Base security?"

"Yes, sir. Them and the 6th Office, both. We are monitoring a lot more telephone traffic between the 6th Office compound and the harbor as well."

"Brian!" I'eiBida muttered.

§

The rain was picking up again, and the chill breeze off the ocean was freshening. As much as Mac hated to leave the cozy hideaway where he spent the night, the 'Tan Shirts' were getting too close for comfort. They received reinforcements in the last hour or so, and were going through the warehouse with a fine tooth comb. It wouldn't take them long to realize no one was there, and the search would probably spread out. He lay under the ventilator hood on a nearby roof, and watched their gyrations with grim amusement. His impromptu bread crumb trail stirred up some major poo-poo. But now they were there in earnest, and as he watched, a utility vehicle with a K-9 unit pulled into the parking lot below. Things were getting a little too warm hereabouts. Time to relocate.

But before he did that, he decided to enjoy another of the rations he grabbed earlier. They were similar to the zero-G rations Space Fleet used, but contained more variety including a candy bar and a disposable toothbrush. He crawled back under his ventilator, fished one out of the backpack he snagged, peeled it open, and waited absently for it to heat. While he waited, he pondered his next move. If he and Giselle were planning to escape by ship, they would need food, a few basic toiletries, blankets, perhaps a first aid kit, and some uniforms wouldn't hurt either... Yes, his logical move would be to hang around the warehouse area gathering supplies. That would be risky since there were only so many warehouses, and they would soon catch onto his pattern. Another raid or two, and he could expect them to start laying ambushes. This could get dicey before the day was out, but it would surely draw Alvarez's attention.

The aroma of his dinner caught his attention. Stroganoff noodles: not the greatest, but a welcome hot meal. He finished it quickly, and left the trash where it would be found.

§

"The humans have completed the oxygen transfer, sir," the Third reported. "I had to tell them we faced an emergency, but they did it."

"Thankfully they still cling to that custom," the ship's Eldest grumbled. Giving aid to a ship in distress was an old, old tradition still honored by both the Ic'nichi and human fleets. Orbit Dock fussed and argued, but they delivered. "What is our oxygen status now?"

"I filled the reserve liquid helium tank, as well as the number two liquid hydrogen tank with oxygen. It's still not what I would like, but we have enough to reach *b'vem'n'uii* Great Nest. We can off load most of our passengers there."

The Eldest wasn't thrilled, since it left them with little margin for fuel and for supercooling the mass polarizer, but he agreed it needed to be done. "Hopefully they have enough consumables to get us the rest of the way home." *b'vem'n'uii* Great Nest was a new colony not far from the frontier; they had precious little industrial development, and depended heavily on cargo runs from d'enchia. "Otherwise we could have to leave the ship in orbit and be stranded there for who knows how long."

"Yes, well, we have to get there first, sir. That will depend on whether we can fool the humans and pull off this evacuation."

The Eldest twitched his ears in dismay. "And we complain that freight service is boring!"

§

Another shuttle touched down and taxied awkwardly to the warehouse at the end of the row where a herd of Ic'nichi waited to unload it. This lot proved to be canned human food; lots of it. The shuttle was dangerously overloaded, in fact. The shuttle crew waited impatiently as the ground force worked, since they were boxed in by heavy cartons which filled every bit of the interior. The warehouse was all but emptied of its accumulated human cargo earlier, but now that self-same cargo had to be returned.

There was still a lot of cargo to be transferred, so they faced a long stiff gallop. The human drivers were kept strictly on their side of the warehouses so they wouldn't notice the familiar cases being passed from hand to hand by a volunteer conga line, and the dock supervisor was in his element harassing them about the paperwork. They were coming to heartily loathe 'Godzilla'.

As soon as the shuttle was empty, a herd of four Ic'nichi nonessentials, each clutching a single bag with a minimum of personal gear, slipped on board one by one amid the ground workers while the crew made quick toilet runs.

The shuttle took off two hours later. To all appearances it was routine, if one didn't look too closely. Despite their progress, there were still nearly a hundred tails waiting for room to evacuate.

§

Alvarez was growing more agitated as time went by, which made everyone in the communications center nervous. "Well?" he demanded of Volmer. "Is there any word from the harbor?"

"Only that the search continues, and they haven't found them yet, sir." Volmer had ridden them over the telephone all day hoping to be the bearer of glad tidings which, despite his threats and demands, they still hadn't delivered.

"Idiots!" Alvarez turned away, and fought to restrain his frustration. This was taking *forever!* He brooded over the lack of progress, but had to admit the 'Tan Shirts' were doing their best. He knew how much effort went into a thorough search, and how a skilled and wily operative like Krauss could avoid detection. No, this was not going to be fast or easy... His eye paused on the map marker representing one of the companies deployed for the attack on the Lizard base. "What about the Peacekeeper units?"

Thankfully, Volmer had some good news there. "They have received more ammunition, sir. They are about as ready to attack as can be expected."

"Indeed? How fortunate." He brooded over the map for a time, weighing his options and the numerous forces within the Purity Movement and elsewhere who were a threat to his ambitions. This needed to be settled, fast, one way or another...

§

It was getting late in the day before Mac got far enough away from the search area to break into a closed up garage. As he hoped, there was a convenient pry bar which he pocketed, and a telephone.

"This is *'Adelbard'*. Sorry about the delay in reporting; I've been busy." His voice came back through the vocoder sounding rich and vibrant due to the Ic'nichi's sound reproduction technology, no doubt. "I seem to be drawing attention from the 'Tan Shirts'. There are patrols and K9 units searching the area. I'm doing all right. Is there any word on the evacuation?"

He waited for over a minute before he got a reply. "Hello, Brian. Things are quiet, so everyone is busy with the evacuation except for the duty watch."

That was a bit of a surprise. "Hello, Giselle. Are you doing alright?"

"About as well as I can, considering. How are you?"

"Managing. I appear to be making an impression. What's the situation there?"

"The Peacekeepers seem to have settled down for now. The evacuation is going steadily...and your...counterpart said to cut the chatter and keep these messages short so they cannot trace you."

"Yeah?" Mac was a bit annoyed by that. The one thing he *didn't* need was being nagged, especially by himself. "Tell him he's a right-angled hard-ass from way back, and needs to take his laxatives."

There was a brief pause, then, "He said you are a sorry excuse for a Superhero."

"Yeah, well, he got that right anyway."

"Is there anything else, Brian?"

"I guess not. I'm continuing at this end. Good luck to you. *'Adelbard'* out."

§

"*Buena suerte* to you, Brian," she muttered when the transmission cut off.

"He seems to be doing some good," T'thReptn said. The rest of the Intel watch stood silently at their stations, listening with rapt attention.

144

"It is not conclusive," Giselle said. "Alvarez can spare a few squads for a search. What we need is to shift Alvarez's focus away from us. He has not done that yet."

"Give him time," I'eiBida told her.

She gave him a weary look. "We do not have much to give."

"True enough." I'eiBida changed the subject. "You handled that well." She had insisted on acting as communication liaison, which I'eiBida agreed to partly to keep her alter ego in the herd, and partly to give her something useful to do.

She shrugged. "At least I can be helpful."

The Intel staff got back to work, and she drifted over to the window and absently watched the rain trickling down the glass. The passing vehicle lights sparkled with rainbow highlights. She always loved the rain; now the cool draft coming off the glass chilled her soul. Would she ever enjoy the rain again she wondered? Would she ever know any happiness after...with what the world was coming to?

'You'll be all right in the long run, Giselle.'

She didn't answer, didn't even flinch from the dark aura surrounding that voice. She was too weary of life to be afraid any longer, which was good since the chances were they would all die within the next few hours. She would, at any rate; she was determined never to let Alvarez get his hooks into her again, and had been steeling herself over the last day for what she knew she must do.

'Once I fade away, you'll be free again.'

"Free?" she mumbled. "What is free? Can I ever be what I once was? Can I ever go back to being a student nurse? We are all going to die, anyway."

'You don't know that.' She didn't answer. *'The Ic'nichi are good people; they'll help you start over.'*

"*La mañana gloriosa.*" She bowed her head under the weight of her despair. "I long for it with all my soul."

'All fine and good, but right now we have a situation, so you need to stay focussed.'

She sighed with genuine weariness. "Do you never get tired of this life? It is always duty with you."

145

'Always,' he snapped. *'And speaking of life, you need to shape up if you want to live through this.'*

"He was right: you do need to take your laxatives."

That brought the echo of a chuckle. *'Likely.'*

§

Word came up from the harbor in the late afternoon. "They found a carton of rations broken open, sir," the Base Security liaison reported to the Colonel. "They can't tell if anything else was taken."

Alvarez mused on that bit of news. "And no sign of the intruders?"

"Nothing, sir," the liaison said, diffidently. "But they found a couple of empty ration packs on a nearby roof. They searched the general area, and found another building broken into as well."

"Indeed?" Alvarez pondered that while Volmer watched expectantly. "Very well. Search the area thoroughly, and keep me informed of any developments."

"Yes, sir!"

"Is it Krauss, sir?" Volmer asked once Alvarez hung up.

Alvarez ignored him, staring at nothing while he worked the puzzle in his mind. It couldn't be Krauss, could it? What could he stand to gain in the harbor? He was obviously working for the Lizards...but why didn't he head to their landing field like he, Alvarez, anticipated? Their only chance was to get off planet before the search could be organized, and those Space Fleet pukers couldn't be trusted to prevent the supply ship from leaving without good reason. Perhaps he knew better than to try outrunning the search? He was stuck with her...she was hardly fit enough...or was this some sort of misdirection...

"Perhaps," he muttered absently.

Perhaps he was hoping to find a boat. He might plan to reach the Lizard base by water...or escape by ship?

"What about the attack, sir?"

Or perhaps...he didn't intend to get off planet after all? Could he expect to escape to the mainland, perhaps with the aid of Puker spies? To what end? Who would protect them from the 6th Office? Certainly not the Sausages... The Purity Movement!

That sent a chill through him. With her at large...revealing the mind process to the world...to his political enemies... The danger filled him with foreboding. It was a brilliant strategy; neat, discreet, and damning...exactly the sort of finesse move Krauss could come up with. And Alvarez wouldn't put it past the Lizards to let the Purity Movement do their dirty work for them.

"Sir?"

In a way, he was impressed by his former pupil's cunning. This was a new high in misdirection, in deception. Let him, Alvarez, embarrass himself with a misplaced attack on the Lizards creating a massive diplomatic crisis while Krauss slipped away with the evidence his enemies needed to move against him.

"Colonel?"

The real enemy was at the western end of the island, wherever Krauss and the girl may be. But attacking them would play into their hands if Krauss slipped away in the confusion. First things first: deal with Krauss, then with his masters. And if anything, it would be better to wait until morning; so many things could go wrong in a night attack, and there was no sense in giving Krauss an opening if he *was* there.

His thoughts were drawn back to Volmer. He favored his lackey with an annoyed frown, carefully masking his near panic. "Maintain the hold for now. We will see what develops in the harbor before making any final decisions."

The Lizards could wait while the harbor was secured.

*****

"Chapter Ten"

By late afternoon the 'Tan Shirts' were getting thick on the ground, backed up by more MP vehicle patrols. Mac spent most of the day on another warehouse roof where he could keep an eye on things, and he was beginning to worry about all the activity.

"Looks like you stirred up a shit storm, boy," he muttered as another patrol drove past. It was good in a way, since he was there to get Alvarez's undies in a bunch, but he was all too aware that he was a long way from any safe haven, out here all by his lonely, and that getting caught was not a viable option.

"Damn-fool way to make a living," he grumbled for the umpteenth time. The weather was turning down again; despite being several hours to sunset, the light was already fading under the cloud cover, and a steady rain was falling. Despite his temporary shelter, he was cold and wet, and the few field rations he found earlier were gone. He made a mental note to see if he could find a waterproof tarp on his next 'shopping expedition', which would have to be that night.

There were voices, so he risked another quick peek. A 'Tan Shirt' K-9 unit was working the grounds around the next building over while several more with drawn weapons covered the entrances on all sides. He had to move soon, and now that dark was settling in he could risk going out in the open. He needed to freshen his bread crumb trail in any case.

Access to the warehouse roof was by a steel ladder up the far side of the building. He was just about down when, as luck would have it, a 'Tan Shirt' came around the corner not more than twenty meters away. They stared at each other in surprise for several seconds before the 'Tan Shirt' drew his automatic and yelled, "You there! Halt!"

Mac cursed a blue streak and he scuttled down the last dozen steps. The 'Tan Shirt' was on him by then, grabbed his arm, and shoved him up against the building. Mac bounced off the wall, knocked the pistol out of his hand, and waded in with a roundhouse left. The 'Tan Shirt' fell back in surprise, then piled on with their favored tactics of billy club and fists, and got in a couple good punches before Mac reacted with a mix of school yard brawling and his Fleet Featherweight Boxing Champ skills from another lifetime. He couldn't linger; this guy had to go down fast before backup arrived. He blocked a vicious swing with the club at his head, and waded in with a repetition to the gut which drove the 'Tan Shirt' back gasping for breath.

They circled each other warily, the 'Tan Shirt' stunned at meeting forceful resistance, then he lost his temper and charged. Too bad for him. Mac fended off another swing of the club, caught his opponent in a head lock, and *heaved*. There was an ugly *SNAP*, and the 'Tan Shirt' went limp, almost dragging Mac down with him as he collapsed.

Mac cursed his luck as he ran. The one thing he didn't need was to make this hunt *too* personal. The 'Tan Shirts' would redouble their efforts now, putting just that much more pressure on him. If anything good came of it, he thought ruefully, at least Alvarez would be focussed squarely on the harbor from now on.

§

"One of my men was killed, sir," the 'Tan Shirt' team leader reported a short while later.

That caught Alvarez completely off guard, inspiring a wave of panic. "What? Killed? How?"

"His neck was snapped clean, sir."

Alvarez fought to recover his composure. "It's him," he said, firmly. "He *is* there. Seal the area air tight, and turn over every stone until you find them!"

"Yes, sir!"

"And do not forget I want them *alive!* Him in particular!"

"Yes, sir!" Resentfully.

Alvarez hung up the phone, and stood pondering the new development. This confirmed his earlier suspicion: Krauss evaded the search by doing the last thing anyone would have expected; running *away* from the only shelter on the island. As he fought his rising panic, he realized it was exactly the sort of finesse move Krauss would come up with. But what was he up to? His one hope now was to continue his shell-game until he could get off the island, and that meant he needed to connect with someone who could provide transportation. There had to be someone on this island who could provide help, that much was plain. But if not the Lizards, then *who?* Sausage conspirators? His political enemies? That sent another flush of panic through him: if they knew of his plans, and were moving against him...

He reminded himself desperately that his network of informants within the Movement would have sniffed it out in time. So if not the Movement, then *who?* The Sausages weren't that well organized—were they? The Lizard embassy in Geneva? Perhaps. They had the incentive, and their forward base here in Singapore, and they certainly wouldn't care who got hurt. So many threats! What mattered was that whoever Krauss served, *they* had the means to turn his most loyal operative—as impossible as it seemed —provide him the intel and resources, and a way to get her out. What else could they do?

"Is it Krauss, sir?" Volmer asked.

"Brilliant, Krauss," he muttered. There *were* Puker traitors right here in Singapore; among the military contractors no doubt. Who knew how wide-spread *that* conspiracy was? For all he knew, it might reach as far as Geneva, with the Sausages trying to curry favor from his enemies, or cooperating with the Lizards. *They* would be waiting to smuggle the two onto a ship, in which case Krauss's gambit wasn't so desperate after all.

"Sir?"

He fought to get his paranoia under control, to quell his panic. If there were enemies in Singapore—and there were *always* enemies—then his answer was to hunt them down and destroy them. "*They* are there." He turned to Volmer with a ferrel gleam in his eyes. "Planning to escape by ship."

"But...can we be sure?"

"Only he has the strength and skill to take down one of those 'Tan Shirt' thugs. He will remain in the area until he can make connections with whoever is helping them." He brooded over the tactical map laid out on the conference table. "Suspend the attack. Leave the Peacekeepers in place, and transfer our assets to the harbor area. No ships will leave the harbor until they are found!"

§

B'monTrea shook I'eiBida out of an all too brief and troubled nap a few hours later. "Sir, the 'Tan Shirt' units are withdrawing."

I'eiBida eyed him in confusion, then struggled to his feet with a weary groan. "Where are they going?"

"They seem to be convoying back toward the harbor, sir."

The Intel staff were busy updating the tactical map when they arrived. Giselle was there, looking frazzled and exhausted from her long vigil, but clearly determined to follow the latest developments.

"The Peacekeeper units are still where they stopped, and are showing a marked decrease in activity, sir," T'thReptn told him. "The 'Tan Shirt' units are retreating in mass to the harbor."

"What changed?" I'eiBida studied the positions with a sense of foreboding. "Radio traffic?" he asked at last.

"There was a brief flurry of transmissions to the Peacekeeper units a short while ago, but that has mostly ended. Radio traffic in the harbor is increasing."

"Who's radio traffic? The 'Tan Shirts'?"

"Yes, sir, and the base Military Police."

I'eiBida nodded absently. "He did it," he muttered to himself. "Brian pulled them away."

"Do not relax your guard, *mi amigo*," Giselle said. "We are not safe yet."

"The pressure is off for now, at least."

"Alvarez has not given up on us. He still plans to attack, probably after he has captured Brian in the harbor."

T'thReptn considered her doubtfully. "That doesn't make sense. He must know such an act could trigger a war they aren't ready for."

She gave him an impatient look. "Neither are you. And he does not care for the consequences."

"But...how could you be sure of that?"

"We in the resistance have struggled against Alvarez for a long time. One learns ones' enemy fast, or one dies. He is mad, and the escape must have driven him into a rage. He is fixated on capturing me, which means once he realizes I am not out there he will attack; it is just a question of when."

T'thReptn and S'deMnveb exchanged worried looks. "It makes sense," S'deMnveb said.

"But how could you know?" T'thReptn asked. "You were only a minor member of the resistance."

She gave him a solemn look. "True. But I had many good friends there, including some who understood Alvarez's madness." She gave T'thReptn a quirky smile. "One nice thing about being a medical student is there were several doctors in our group, including psychiatrists. We talked about the 6th Office a lot. Knowledge is our one real asset, so we spread any news or information as far as possible."

T'thReptn's ears shot up. "That...is where the rumors came from!" He turned to I'eiBida and exclaimed, "We first learned about Alvarez's condition through whispers on the internet!"

She smiled, which seemed to light up her features. "Professor Juan-Pierre will be pleased to hear that." Then her smile faded. "If he is still alive."

§

Another shuttle loaded with canned goods touched down, and the three crew slumped into exhausted sleep at their stations as soon as it stopped on the loading apron. The ground crew were equally tired, and it took some time to excavate the pallets, passing cases of cans hand to hand, before the load lifters could get in and start pulling the main cargo out. The ground Lead rousted the crew as soon as they could exit the flight deck, and sent them to the dining circle for a hot meal.

The pilot turned his snout to the heavens as they walked, reveling in the light mist. "Ancestors," he groaned. "It *is* real."

The cargo specialist gave him a sardonic tail twitch. "No, sir, this is all a bad dream."

"I hope so!"

"I hope I wake up soon, safe in my bed on d'enchia with a passionate *tra'taj*," the co-pilot grumbled as they limped toward the dining circle. What they really needed was sleep, but at the rate the shuttle was being off-loaded, they would do well to get a quick bite and a hefty bowl of *V'liz*.

§

At about that time, Volmer came to Alvarez with some intel from the spaceport flight control. "The Lizard shuttle flights are continuing round the clock, sir, and the pace has quickened. They are up to something."

"*Of course* they are up to something!" Alvarez snarled. "They are Lizards! What do you expect?"

"But...their crews must be on the verge of exhaustion, sir. They wouldn't push this hard, in this weather, without a good reason."

"What do I care for their reasons?" Alvarez roared. "They are *Lizards!* Not even Sausages!"

Volmer backtracked carefully, trying to avoid agitating the Colonel any further and steer him back on topic. "They *are* the enemy, sir, and we know they helped Krauss steal the test subject. We should shut down their flight operations..."

"Fool! We have more urgent matters to deal with! We will deal with the Lizards in good time, never you doubt it for an instant!" It was clear that Alvarez was beyond reason. "First we will track the traitors in the harbor down, and *then* we will *crush* the Lizards!" He twisted his swagger stick with so much rage that it snapped in his hands. "They will learn not to tamper with us! They will learn to *fear* us!"

Volmer accepted it philosophically, as one must in dealing with the Colonel's rages; he cut his losses and got out of there.

§

The rain let up some time earlier, but Mac was soaked to the skin, chilled, and hungry enough that his strength was slipping. This always being on the run, always on guard for any ambush or chance encounter was wearing him down, and he was beginning to realize his new body's stamina was something he couldn't entirely depend on.

He spent most of the afternoon getting as far as possible from the unfortunate run-in with the 'Tan Shirt'. It didn't take a military genius to know they'd be righteously pissed after one of theirs was killed. In fact, the body was discovered almost at once: the 'Tan Shirts' evidently weren't used to being on the receiving end, and Mac paused to enjoy their panic and wetness and running in circles from a discreet distance before slipping away.

153

But that was then; now it was fully dark, and the rain was picking up again. Mac squatted in the narrow gap between a warehouse wall and a stack of pallets, thankful for the temporary shelter of a truck dock awning. As tempting as the spot was, it wouldn't do to hunker down here, and he still needed to promote some rations if at all possible. He ate the last of the rations that morning, and the chill and exertion were getting to him, which meant one more break-in that night. He sat for some time idly watching the rain and wondering what to do. He needed another food warehouse, but the one he broke into earlier was the center of an ever-widening search. No, that was out. Could he risk going to the base commissary? Even if they didn't have his picture posted everywhere and armed guards on every food source (which was how he'd handle it), he had no money. Perhaps he could...

...There was a grinding noise somewhere close, and a heavy motor kicked on. He struggled down in his hiding place as a light truck pulled around the far corner of a nearby building and drove away. Once it was gone, he slowly relaxed, and breathed a weary sigh of relief.

"This is getting to you, Bubba," he muttered. Quiet returned, except for the wind and the eternal damned rain. He sat and watched for a while longer until he was convinced no one was in the area, then struggled to his feet. One thing he learned in his former life was to get an unpleasant task over with, rather than sit around avoiding the inevitable. He paused at the corner of the building, and looked all around for any sign of activity. There was nothing but the steady rain shimmering in the glow of the occasional street lamps.

He noticed a piece of paper laying in the road where it fell off the truck. Some instinct made him risk scuttling out into the street to grab it and beat a hasty retreat. The chance proved well worth it: a commissary requisition form for frozen food.

The building the truck came from was another warehouse, this one made of cement blocks. As he scouted the corner, he saw a large refrigeration unit next to the building: frozen stores all right; meat. He had no idea what he would do with a frozen side of beef, but right then he didn't care. The front of the building was a row of dock doors and an office at the far end. He circled the other way, and wound up in an alley behind the building. It was mostly a smooth blank wall, but there were a few windows at the far end next to another street door.

The view through the windows showed ceiling high shelves piled with cardboard boxes and heavy sacks. The light inside was dim, but he couldn't see anyone. He searched the alley again for any sign of trouble, then hefted his stolen pry bar and carefully break the glass in one window. The latch was stiff, but he managed to pry it open, and slipped in.

Inside was chilly but blessedly dry. Mac listened for a long moment for any sign of activity, but there was nothing. He sized up the situation, and decided since he was here, he should take the opportunity to call the landing field. Things were closing down fast, and he needed to know how much longer I'eiBida needed. In any event he was going a bit stir-crazy, and craved the sound of a friendly human voice like a sinner craves salvation. From what he could see, most of the warehouse was a row of large drive-in freezers, while the area he was in held canned food. There was no one in sight, so he started down one of the aisles between two rows of shelves toward the distant lights of the office. The aisle ended in an open area fronting the office. Mac hesitated, wondering whether all the lights in the office meant someone was still here after loading that truck...

"*Aandacht! Iemand is er!*"

...It was an ambush! There was a scramble of boots, and Mac ducked behind the end of a shelf row as a mixed lot of two Peacekeeper MPs and two 'Tan Shirts' came around a nearby corner. He went to ground and peered cautiously through one of the stacks as they halted nearby.

"You sure, Heinz?" one of the MPs asked doubtfully.

"*Ja! Ik hoorde...*I heard him!"

"*Das tun wird!*" one of the 'Tan Shirts' said impatiently. "Spread out in pairs, und remember, *Der Oberst* vants zem alive!"

Mac retreated hastily as the two MPs started down one row and the two 'Tan Shirts' drew tasers and headed in his direction. He ducked into a side aisle just as they appeared at the end of the row.

"You sure about this?" one mumbled. "This fellow is dangerous."

"Do you vant to explain to *Der Oberst* zat vee allowed zose Sausages to catch him?" the other asked impatiently. "He ist here somewhere. Vee find him!"

They came on cautiously side by side down the wide aisle, tasers at the ready. Mac faded back into the shadows and looked around for a line of retreat. There was nothing; he was in a cul-de-sac between two rows of shelving, and would have to fight his way out. Those tasers were not promising; they wouldn't hesitate to use them at close quarters, and having been hit with one in the past, he knew he couldn't afford to let them get off a shot. The two reached the cul-de-sac...

...He waded in and threw a savage right at the first, who turned toward him just in time to take it on his chin. He went down; Mac grabbed his taser and fired at the other, catching him in the side. He went down in turn with a strangling whine as Mac leapt past him and took off down the row. There was an incoherent shout from behind him, followed by a shot. The bullet buried itself in a cardboard case as the two MPs responded with shouts of their own.

As he reached the end of the row, he noticed a pallet-load of canned hams. Without pausing or thinking about it, he grabbed a couple and scuttled toward the rear of the building, trying to keep out of sight as the MPs searched through the stacks with their flashlights. A tense moment to size up the pursuit, and he ducked through the rear door, and sprinted down the alley.

The area swarmed with MPs and 'Tan Shirts' in a matter of minutes. None of them noticed a burly figure crouched beside a loading dock in the distance watching them.

§

"I am sorry, sir," the 'Tan Shirt' platoon leader reported to Alvarez some time later. "They cornered him, but he overpowered two of our men. The MPs were useless, of course."

"Four armed men, and he got away?"

"He's a hulking brute, sir! My men never saw what hit them."

Alvarez fought down his rage by main strength. "And what are you doing now?"

"I have a perimeter set up, and we are combing the area."

"Very well." It wasn't very well, but there was nothing Alvarez could do about it at the moment. Volmer watched nervously from the background, knowing as he did what his dangerous calm meant. "This warehouse, what is in it?"

"Commissary stores, sir."

"Commissary stores? Food? Did he acquire any?"

The 'Tan Shirt' leader sounded even more nervous. "We don't know, sir."

"Very well. Continue your search, and keep me informed." Alvarez hung up without waiting for a reply, and stared into the distance as he pondered his next step. Finally his gaze shifted to Volmer. "Arrest them. All four of them. And the platoon leader too. I have had *enough* of their excuses!"

"Yes, Colonel!" Volmer saluted and scuttled for the phone in the next room, thankful they, not he, would bear the Colonel's wrath.

§

"Ic'nichi shuttle flight 285 to Singapore control, request clearance for landing at our base."

The latest shuttle flight sagged through the cloud cover with its turbines idling, following an imaginary line in the inertial navigator as they fumbled their way toward the landing field. There wasn't a blessed *thing* visible out there between the night and the miserable weather, and the crew were on edge from fatigue and the flying conditions.

It was nearly three minutes, and the shuttle was painfully close to having to abort, before they got a reply. "Singapore, shuttle 285. You are clear to land at your base. Weather is full overcast and rain, visibility is 3000 meters, with turbulence at 1500 meters. Pick up your ground control on your regular frequency."

The co-pilot sighed. "Shuttle 285 acknowledge." The delayed response was part of the ongoing harassment by Singapore ground control, who weren't so overburdened that they couldn't find time to come up with petty *x'mnnb'* to annoy them.

"Miserable planet," the pilot grumbled.

"They deserve it."

If anything, the weather was worse than ever, with another line of squalls coming in off the South China Sea. The two pilots had been on flight duty for over a day with short breaks for food and one brief nap which only made them more groggy. They were fighting exhaustion.

The co-pilot changed frequencies. "Shuttle 285 to ground control, now on final approach."

The answer came back immediately. "Ground control to 285, you are clear to land. Ground conditions are light and variable winds, visibility under 1000 lengths. Be advised we have rain, and the runway is slippery."

"285 acknowledge." Like they needed to be told *that*.

The pilot in particular was fighting to stay awake and cursing himself for ever volunteering for this mission. Keep your tail down: the first thing they teach new recruits. Pity he didn't remember such a wise admonition back on d'enchia. He scanned his instruments, trying to focus through his fatigue headache. They were losing altitude steadily, and should break out of the cloud cover soon. A gust of wind shook the shuttle, and rain spattered the windshield. "Flaps," he mumbled.

"Flaps down," the co-pilot said. They could hear the grinding noise of the flaps extending over the whine of the engines.

The wind buffeted them again, and there was the sharp patter of hail. These were *Ancestorless* flying conditions, and they were badly overloaded. The pilot gave vent to another curse, wishing he was a commercial pilot back home on a regular schedule which avoided bad weather. He swore to himself that if he got through this alive he would resign from the fleet and start hitting the recruiters.

"Thrust reversers."

The co-pilot threw a switch on the central console. "Armed. Speed is good. Angle is good."

Yes, he would do it the pilot swore to himself. Experienced shuttle pilots had no trouble finding good employment; no more dangerous landings in primitive conditions at some colony or here on this *Ancestorless* alien world. He promised himself that each time they left d'enchia.

"Descent and speed are in the groove,"

The pilot was too tired to answer. They broke through the last low-hanging clouds, and the lights of the runway were visible just ahead. The pilot eased his throttles and lifted the nose further...

"Shuttle!" their ground control radio crackled. *"Your landing gear isn't down!"*

"p'quas'tka!" the pilot yelled as he hauled back on his control column and hit the throttles. The overloaded shuttle continued to sink, hovering on the ragged edge of a stall until he recovered from his panic and eased the nose down. They gained airspeed bit by agonizing bit, and managed to level out about a hundred lengths above the runway. By then, he was so shaken that the co-pilot needed to bring the shuttle around for another approach.

§

"That was close," I'eiBida said to B'monTrea after he interviewed the flight crew.

"Too close, sir. Those three are exhausted. They can't keep up this pace of flight operations, especially in this weather."

I'eiBida gave him a frustrated ear twitch. "No, they can't."

The crew were too shaken by their near disaster to be any more use anyway. The two pilots and the cargo specialist were sprawled on the hard seat cushions in the dining circle, too dejected to eat despite I'eiBida's reassurance that they wouldn't be taken to task for their near mishap. What almost happened was a sobering wake-up call to all of them: if a shuttle smeared itself all over the runway, it would not only cost the crew their lives and fatally restrict the evacuation, but it would also give the humans an excuse to come snooping around.

"Send these three over to the transient quarters for some sleep," I'eiBida said, reluctantly. "Contact the ship and have them suspend flight operations until the other crews can get some sleep too."

"You're delaying the evacuation, sir?"

"There's no choice. We'll just have to hope for the best. In any event, I want the crew of the last shuttle to be ears-up in case we have to make a fighting retreat."

B'monTrea made a sour snout. "Yes, sir."

§

159

Mac crouched behind a dumpster as an MP patrol drove past, then sagged against it with a shaky sigh. "This is too much like honest work," he muttered. He was still hungry, soaked, and chilled to the bone, and painfully aware that he was losing his edge. He needed to hunker down for some sleep, and eat some of the ham he liberated earlier. He was also way overdue to call in, although after that last near miss, he wasn't looking forward to it.

There were several large metal structures nearby, probably machine shops or assembly buildings. He saw precious few people during the day other than security patrols, so he could go to ground somewhere around here. He considered the building next to him, a multistory metal cube sitting in the middle of a yard littered with vehicles and piles of junk. Getting in would not be fun.

He hefted the two hams and decided he couldn't lug them around any further, so he stuffed one into his jacket and hid the other under the dumpster. With luck, he could recover it later. He clambered over the chain link fence and headed for a nearby metal door, but hesitated when he reached for the knob. Some sixth sense warned him this was too easy. By all reason, there should be security watches in every building by now. Who might be waiting right inside? Still, it was as good a bet as any, so he scanned the building for some other access. There were no windows. He was about to give up when he spotted an unlikely way in.

First he had to climb up a ladder on some sort of piping tower. The next step was a doozy: crawling along a narrow catwalk suspended four stories above the pavement to reach the building. The pipe vanished through the wall. The hatch next to it was locked, and the pipe access was too narrow for him to squeeze through. There was a ventilator grill near by, but it would be suicide to try for it. He was about to retreat when something caught his eye: a steady stream of headlights entering the main gate in the distance.

"Shit," he muttered. That was *just* what he needed.

He studied the pipe access, and realized the cheap galvanized sheet tin was half rusted out. He tugged on an edge experimentally, then peeled the tin back until the hole was big enough to shimmy through.

Inside, he found himself on a narrow catwalk high above a cavernous, dimly lit space; a massive garage for some sort of heavy vehicles parked bumper to bumper below. It wasn't easy to make out detail, but it seemed like the place was deserted. The catwalk led him across the building to a ladder which finally left him hiding behind a portable air compressor. After listening for several minutes, he crept down an open corridor along the wall. A glassed-in modular office appeared out of the gloom. He crept up to it, and peeked through the window. A phone sat on the desk...

...There were voices in the dark ahead. He ducked between two vehicles and listened anxiously. They came again; he couldn't make out what they said, but they didn't sound like a search party. As tempted as he was to leave well enough be, he had to know who was out there, so he crept forward from one truck to the next, hyperalert for any danger. His journey took him clear to the far end of the building where a faint light glowed.

Two MPs, a hastily assigned security detail, sat close to an electric heater near the door. He realized to his dismay that he almost tried that door earlier. He would have stumbled right into their arms. If they were a security detail, they didn't show much enthusiasm for the job. One was wrapped in a canvas tarp while the other hunched near the heater, chugged on a bottle, then passed it to his comrade. They both were cold and forlorn, and probably wouldn't stir from their camp without good reason. Mac retreated, happy to let them be.

Thankfully the door office was unlocked. He looked around again, then slipped in and hunkered down behind a filing cabinet. There was enough cord so he could pull the phone down with him.

"This is *Adelbard*. I've gone to ground for the moment."

There was a brief pause, then Giselle answered. "*Hola*, Brian. Are you all right?" She sounded weary and tense.

"I'm managing for now. I killed a 'Tan Shirt' earlier, and it looks like they're pissed about it. I also had a run-in with four of them later. They lived."

There was a brief, awkward silence. "That...would explain why they are redeploying. Alvarez ordered the 'Tan Shirts' to the harbor in force."

There was a sound somewhere to his left; faint voices arguing about something. "Yeah, I've got the Shit-Hurt Express coming in," he whispered. "Reinforcements are pouring into the harbor area. It looks like I've been a little *too* successful, so I'm going to lay low for now." As an afterthought, he added, "I might be kind of erratic on my contacts for a while."

"Please be careful, Brian."

"Speaking of which, why are you still here? You should be up on the ship by now."

"I stayed to help. His skills are needed." She sounded calm but resolute, perhaps even defiant.

"This is not the time for heroics. You need to get out of there before the roof caves in."

"I will leave when I am no longer needed, not before." Definitely defiant now.

Then I'eiBida was on the phone. "Brian, are you safe for now?"

"Not hardly, but I'll manage. How goes the evacuation?"

"I suspended it for a few hours to give the flight crews some rest. We need a few more days. The Peacekeeper units appear to have settled down for now, but they are still in position, and can strike on short notice."

"Figures. I want you to put her on the first shuttle. That is no place for her to be."

I'eiBida chuckled. "Brian, you should know better by now than to argue with yourself; you keep losing."

"Yeah. Tell me about it."

"I will take care of her, Brian."

"Thanks." He paused to suppress a yawn. "Look, I'm tuckered out, so I'm gonna grab some shut-eye. I'll call you in the morning."

"Good night, Brian."

He pocketed the scrambler and peeked through the office window: no sign of activity. He made his way back up to the catwalk, and settled between a large blower and the wall. He recalled the ham he scrounged earlier, and dug it out of his jacket. Thankfully they still included pull tab openers; the lid came off with a faint hiss, and he dug in with a will. He felt better once it was gone. He lay there for some time, wondering about tomorrow; about whether the Ic'nichi could escape; about whether he would live to see it. There were no answers. All he could do was keep on keeping on and hope for the best, like he did so many times in his former life.

His grim determination rose through the fatigue and funk, and he banished those defeatist emotions with a muttered curse. There was a job to do; an urgent one; those people at the landing field depended on him for their survival, and by God he would deliver. He never did know when to quit; couldn't, really. He would do his duty come hell or high water, and there was plenty of both to be had. He could only hope he'd live to see it over, like he did so many times in his former life.

He curled up in a knot and tried to go to sleep, but his thoughts drifted. The Ic'nichi...T'thReptn...S'deMnveb...his old friend I'eiBida...and *her*...depended on him. He needed to buy time, more than ever with the evacuation temporary suspended. He couldn't let them down, not and live with his conscience.

"My own damn fault," he grumbled as his memories drifted back to Cleveland and that tough young punk. Could he have had any idea what he was getting into?

The air was filled with the soft drumming of rain on the roof. He stared restlessly into the dark, hearing the wind and rain without listening until he drifted off into a troubled sleep.

*****

"Chapter Eleven"

The next day was even worse, if possible. The 'Tan Shirts' received massive reinforcements during the night, and it was like Times Square around there. It gave him a grim sense of satisfaction, since it seemed his diversion was working, but now Alvarez was seriously on his case. Not good.

He ducked behind the corner of a building for the umpteenth time to avoid another vehicle patrol. When it was gone, he leaned against the building with a shaky sigh, tried to wipe the rain out of his eyes, and wondered what to do next. His heart was racing, and his hands trembled. He never really did get used to this; not in seventy-five years of military service. He was still human—in principle, anyway—and feared injury and death as much as the next man.

'A hero is a fool looking for attention,' he reminded himself of one of his favorite sayings. He was no cardboard Superman, although he wasn't sure about being a fool at the moment.

They had a systematic pattern going which was squeezing his range of action narrower and narrower. He couldn't duck the patrols forever even with the steady rain which came in during the night, and he certainly couldn't fight his way out if they cornered him. If one of the patrols didn't get him, they would eventually drive him out into the open near the perimeter fence where the guard towers were no doubt fully alerted.

"'bout wore out my welcome, I guess," he grumbled.

There was movement in the mists to his right, and he ducked around the corner again as another patrol appeared down the street. This wasn't working. He looked around nervously, then cut across the side street and into an alley between two warehouses.

Another vehicle patrol passed the far end of the alley; he ducked into a doorway and watched anxiously until he decided they hadn't spotted him. He remained in the shelter of that doorway for a moment trying to calm himself and decide what to do next. He obviously had to get the *hell* out of Dodge—but first he needed to check in to let them know of his move, especially as his morning report was overdue.

The door was steel, dead bolted, but the window next to it had a tilt-out section to provide ventilation. He hefted his pry bar, carefully knocked the glass out, and slithered through the shallow opening.

Inside it was warmer and blessedly dry. He gave the area a split-second look: there were row after row of ceiling-high metal shelves filled with machine parts and coils of electrical wire. This part of the base was dead storage in his day, and evidently still was: there would be precious few people around unless they had to draw materials for a shipboard repair project. He listened carefully, and there was nothing but the rain drumming on the metal roof at first. Then he heard a faint voice. He crept carefully down the corridor trying to stay in the shadows until he reached the end of the first shelf row. A short distance away, next to the front entrance, two Navy ratings sat in a glassed-in enclosure near a small heater, passing a bottle back and forth. He watched until he was sure they didn't show any initiative, then headed the other way looking for a phone. There was nothing but endless shelf rows and a small fork lift parked in a corner. He kept moving, looking frantically, but the warehouse seemed to stretch on forever. How long did he have before someone reacted to the silent alarm? Just as he was about to give up the search and get out of there, he came to a loading door with a work station and a phone. The dial tone sounded like an angelic chorus.

"This is *'Adelbard'*. Things are getting too hot in the harbor, so I am going to relocate. Out."

He slammed the phone down, pocketed the vocoder, and headed for the door as a siren started braying in the distance. *Damn*, they reacted fast!

§

Everyone in the Intel circle, and Giselle in particular, were stunned by the abrupt cut-off. "That does not sound good," she muttered.

"The 'Tan Shirts' must be ramping up the pressure." I'eiBida turned to T'thReptn. "Perhaps we should recall him."

"It may be too late for that," Giselle said. "They will expect him to try to get back here."

T'thReptn nodded. "She's right, sir. His only chance is to move away from here; it's the last thing they would expect." They got into a huddle to consider options, leaving Giselle to stare absently at the large plot map for a bit before she drifted away.

'Don't fret, Giselle. He knows his stuff.'

She sighed wearily. "Please leave me alone."

'I'm sorry, Giselle, but we have to stay focussed on the situation for now. I won't be around for that much longer.'

She didn't reply, and sprawled on the backward Ic'nichi chair and hugging the back rest.

'You are doing a good job of advising them.' The voice in her mind was fainter than ever, fading in and out. *'You seem to have a knack for tactics.'*

"Something I learned from you," she mumbled. "I am turning into a raving militarist."

'I'm just doing my job, Giselle.' The voice seemed hurt.

She knew that wasn't fair. "Sorry."

§

The supply ship's Second rode the elevator wearily up to the galley deck where A'vberBenn was relaxing with a squeeze bulb of *V'liz*. "We have the latest shuttle loaded, sir. The other one will be docking before the watch change."

"How are we doing?" A'vberBenn asked.

"About half of the upper deck is cleared, sir, but the lower hold is still a mess since I've been sorting out food stocks to provide for the trip back."

A'vberBenn nodded approval. "I just hope we're wasting all this effort."

"I am worried about the shuttle crews. They haven't had nearly enough rest, and the weather is putting them under a lot of strain."

"We all need rest, Second. The crews are good; they can manage." Ic'nichi shuttle crews were trained to land on limited facilities—often a cleared open field—when supplying the colonies; earth embassy service with its traffic control and concrete runway was usually thought of as a plump assignment. Usually. "I'm sure your cargo handlers are every bit as tired and sore, too. The topside people certainly are."

166

The Second made a sour snout. "Especially our volunteers, sir, Ancestors bless them. If we weren't abandoning all that cargo, I swear I would break down crying for all the damage they cause. And we've had several minor injuries as well."

The Eldest snorted. "So our physich hasn't escaped the call of duty either, I see." As much as the ten volunteers from ground-side tried, they were not trained in zero-G cargo handling, which was an engraved invitation to mashed hands, pinched tails, and worse. All things considered, they had gotten off lightly thus far.

The Second helped himself to a longed-for bulb of *V'liz*, then said, "I was wondering about these crates marked 'machine tools'. They weigh a lot; we'd have to limit our shuttle loads to move them. Do you want to send them down now, or hold them for later?"

A'vberBenn mused on that for a bit. "Mmmm...no, let's hang onto them. We won't be able to off-load everything, so focus on getting as much cubic out as you can."

"Perhaps we should save the heavy things and jettison them when we make our run, sir. Items that massive will make a fine screen against any pursuers."

A'vberBenn chuckled. "They would at that."

§

Back on earth, the weather was turning steadily worse as a series of squalls came sweeping in off the South China Sea. The steady rain drenched the Peacekeepers huddled around their fires along the access road, and the Hand of Specials assigned to watch them fared no better. The Third Hand was deployed in pairs on either side of the Peacekeeper encampment at the moment, with the Lead and his second less than a hundred paces from the humans' perimeter. There were plenty of places to hide amid the ruins, but they had no protection against being spotted from the air except their thermal cloaks. At least the humans weren't flying recon missions, which was one small comfort. The steady chill rain didn't help things either, and their cloaks were precious little good against that. At least the humans showed even less inclination to run patrols than their air support did, for which all four of them were grateful.

The Lead idly watched the humans some hundred paces distant, and cursed the miserable weather. What was worst about this place was the unspeakable aura of *death* which permeated the whole island. According to their briefings, the humans slaughtered *millions* of their own kind here. The very concept boggled the mind. There were human bones *everywhere.* As a devout Ancestor mystic, the very thought laid his ears back in atavistic dread.

"The humans can keep this planet," his second grumbled. No doubt he felt much the same. They all did.

"Why would they want to?"

"They're all *er'trxxda,* the lot of them."

"You would be too if you were hatched here."

'Lead?' the call came in over the tactical frequency from the two on the far side of the human encampment. *'It looks like the humans are settling in. Several of them are setting up the large tents they took down earlier.'*

The Lead used his thermal optics, which were needed to see movement through the steady downpour. "Hmph. Good eyesight, that." He keyed the tactical frequency. "We see it. Keep alert for any other signs of the like."

'Understood.'

"They must have received orders to put the attack off," his second said.

"But not to cancel it and go home." He thought about it, then keyed his command frequency. "I suppose I should call in a lack-of-progress report."

§

"It looks like they called the attack off, sir," B'monTrea said as they digested the latest word from their scouts.

"It's on hold for now, anyway." I'eiBida brooded over the map, sizing up the situation again, and trying to understand the thinking of an *er'trxxda* human. What was Alvarez up to? Which way would he jump next? Privately, I'eiBida had to admit that he was completely at a loss: humans were hard enough to understand; a human madman even moreso.

"Alvarez must have told them to stand by while he pursues the sightings at the harbor, sir," T'thReptn said.

168

"Yes, but it won't last." I'eiBida glanced at Giselle, who by now had a place at the plot table with them. "Will it?"

"No. He will see through the deception eventually; we need to be gone by then."

"That won't be easy," T'thReptn grumbled. "This weather is making a fine mess of flight operations."

I'eiBida turned to Giselle. "How much longer do we have?"

"There is no way to say." She thought about it for a bit. "Alvarez is known to obsess on things; as long as he thinks we are out there, it will hold his focus."

"So Brian is the key."

"*Si*. But once Alvarez sees through his game, he will start to obsess about *this* place. We must complete the evacuation before that happens. Once he realizes we made a fool of him, his reaction will be *rápida y terrible*."

"If I know Brian, he will keep Alvarez fixated for some time yet." He glanced at T'thReptn. "Keep your ears up, and let me know promptly of any changes." With that, he headed for the door intending to grab a nap if at all possible.

"What do you plan to do about the recording?"

I'eiBida looked at Giselle in surprise. "Honestly, I don't see what we can do now. We'll be lucky to pull off this evacuation."

"So you are giving up? You are going to fight the war you came here to prevent?"

"What can we do?" I'eiBida asked in exasperation. "Brian was our only covert resource, and a direct attack is out of the question with the island mobilized."

"You must do something! The big goy said you came here to prevent a war. He said we could trust you. You cannot give up now, not when so many lives are at stake!"

That hit I'eiBida hard, especially as he was already tail-knotted over their failure to neutralize the recording. This was a winner-take-all situation: saving their test subject wasn't enough. He cursed himself silently for letting Brian's demand to save her get in the way of the greater good...which brought on a sense of shame that he would even *think* of dooming this helpless young fem to that horror.

"Honestly..." He looked to B'monTrea and T'thReptn for moral support; they watched the tense scene silently. "...I don't know what we *can* do...but you're right, we have to do something."

"Sir..."

He spun on T'thReptn. "This isn't over yet. We have to destroy the recording if at all possible."

"But how?"

I'eiBida hesitated, and his tail sagged. "I am open to suggestions."

"Sir..."

"Give it your best thought, all of you." He retreated then, embarrassed to be so lacking in ideas, and for his vacillation over her.

§

"Well..." T'thReptn said once he was gone. "You heard the order. Everyone give it your best thought." The Intel herd went reluctantly back to their duties as Giselle drifted over to the window again, and stood watching the rain.

'I don't know what they can do either, but you did the right thing by insisting they keep after it,' the voice whispered.

"You are not the only one with a stake in this," she sighed.

§

A phone call came into Intel that afternoon. "We found some humans hiding in a warehouse, sir," D'remNek reported.

I'eiBida exchanged dismayed looks with T'thReptn. "Right. Hang onto them, I'll be right there." They headed out at the gallop.

There were six of them, all dressed in Peacekeeper utilities, guarded by a pair of D'remNek's security with machine pistols when I'eiBida and T'thReptn arrived.

"Our two volunteers found them and called us, sir." D'remNek seemed a bit put out that the two civilians had done his job.

"Did they?" I'eiBida considered their two ex-defenders, who seemed inordinately pleased with themselves, and decided he would recommend D'remNek for a less sensitive assignment as his next duty posting. "Have you questioned them?"

"Not as yet, sir." D'remNek turned to them and demanded in his broken Swiss, "Who are you? Why you here?"

They looked back and forth doubtfully, then one said, "We're deserters, sir. We've come to ask for political asylum."

"Are you now?" D'remNek studied them for a moment. "Why you not come to me? Why you hide?"

"Ah...we weren't sure what to do, what with the rumors about an attack, sir." From his look and tone, the human seemed to have been caught a bit off guard.

"A likely story," T'thReptn said to I'eiBida.

"Can't say I'm impressed," I'eiBida muttered in turn.

They drifted over to examine the humans' hideout, which took some doing as they had to climb up on a mountain of cargo. A large stock of miscellaneous freight bound for d'enchia had collected in an out-of-the-way corner of the warehouse where it waited for available shuttle space. The humans wrestled various bales and boxes aside to create a hollow area against the back wall large enough for them to lay down. The only access was by clambering over the stacked cargo.

"No rations," T'thReptn commented. "Just a little water." A couple of empty water bottles and a few discarded human field ration packs were the only evidence of their occupation. "No sign of waste, either. They haven't been here long."

"So I see." I'eiBida was impressed by how on-the-trail T'thReptn was; that overdue promotion would soon be corrected.

"That was a well laid hideout," I'eiBida said to their 'Blue-And-Brown' after they climbed down again. "What gave them away?"

He grinned broadly, and offered an amused tail twitch. "They must have underestimated our sense of smell, sir. That human odor is hard to mistake."

Now that he thought about it, I'eiBida could detect the faint odor of unwashed humans. "Indeed. "Good work, that."

"We'll be sure to air the place out, sir."

"What do you make of it, sir?" T'thReptn asked.

I'eiBida considered them skeptically. Their story could be true if Peacekeeper morale was as bad as all the signs said it was. But it was too pat; something about it was off. He pondered the six, and began to notice small details which told a very different story. Their uniforms were all new; recent issue at best, with none of the mismatched items typical of Peacekeeper dress these days. They all had a clean cut, athletic look which shouted 'Tan Shirts', as well. Two had fur stubble on their snouts, while the other four were still clean shaven. Their head fur was neatly trimmed, and while it was hard to read human body language, their postures made them seem alert and confident—hardly military dregs prone to go chasing their own tails. And their hideout was ambitious for demoralized deserters.

"They must have infiltrated the last couple of days," I'eiBida said at last. "Some last-moment move by Alvarez, no doubt."

"That's how the 'Tan Shirts' operate, sir," T'thReptn said, angrily. "*No doubt* they planned to sabotage our defenses when the attack comes." The sensitive Ic'nichi noses had prevented a potential disaster.

"So what do we do with them, sir?" D'remNek asked.

I'eiBida sighed. "We maintain appearances for now." He turned to their two volunteers. "Search the area thoroughly. They will have smuggled in weapons and communication gear at the least, and explosives as well." He didn't plan to leave such a critical matter to their security lead.

"Yes, sir!" The two set to work enthusiastically.

§

The 'Tan Shirt' sergeant on the gate hunched his field jacket against the damp chill as he enjoyed a cig. The awning of their guard shack allowed him to smoke in peace without leaving an oder for that pain-in-the-ass *leutnant* to raise a fuss over. Things were quiet for now: a truck went in just a few minutes ago, which assured him a few more minutes of solitude before the next arrived. A dozen meters away, two Lizards huddled under their own awning looking no more comfortable than he was, not that he cared.

He took another drag, and eyed the pouring rain with no pleasure. His squad had just come on duty, and they would all be soaked to the bone by time their relief arrived. He *wished* Command would get the attack on the Lizards under way so he and his men could be assigned to some other duty, but who knew *when* that would happen.

He was surprised when a parade of four armed defenders escorting six humans appeared out of the gloom. When they were close enough to see through the driving rain, he saw the mens' hands were bound with disposable binders. *"Vas is los?"* he demanded when they reached the duty shack.

"Good day, Sergeant," D'remNek said, crisply. "The humans hide in our warehouse. They say to be deserters, so we turn them to you."

The Sergeant looked them over with no pleasure. None of them seemed nervous or afraid, as he would expect. If anything, they seemed more put out by being drenched in the downpour than anything else. It didn't take a genius to recognize 'Tan Shirt' agitators when he saw them.

"Indeed?" he grunted. *"Danke.* Vee vill see zat zey answer for zer crimes *properly."*

Now they seemed nervous.

§

"Who were they?" Giselle asked when they returned to the Intel Circle.

"Some 'Tan Shirt' infiltrators," I'eiBida said. "We're searching the area now to be sure there are no more of them."

She nodded. *"Si*, that is how they operate. It confirms that they plan to attack regardless of whether we are captured some where else. Alvarez will not call it off now, having gone this far."

"Well, that's hardly a surprise," I'eiBida grumbled. "At least our tails won't be in danger while we're fighting."

She gave him a worried look. "Perhaps: but be sure to search thoroughly. Did they have a radio?"

"We didn't find any." He thought about the incident, and realized there were too many things missing from that picture. "They didn't have weapons either. I ordered a search of the warehouse."

Giselle gave him a tense look. "Could they have informed Alvarez of the evacuation?"

I'eiBida considered glumly. "Probably not. He would have reacted by now."

She clutched herself nervously. "Then we were lucky."

I'eiBida nodded. "Any word from Brian while we were gone?"

"No, *nada*. I hope he will be safe."

"He is cunning and elusive; with a bit of luck he can hitch a ride on another truck out of there."

She leaned against the plot table and stared at the wall in exhaustion. "He will need more than luck with all the checkpoints and patrols. And where can he go?"

"Back here, hopefully. But knowing him as I do, I wouldn't count on it."

§

The weather was getting worse. The dirty clouds scudding in from the east were so low that they barely cleared the masts and cranes in the port. The steady drizzle was turning into a genuine downpour, and the waves pounding the shore said that worse weather was on its way in from the South China Sea.

Mac hunched his jacket against the chill, crouched at the entrance to a drain pipe leading under the perimeter fence, and studied the area carefully. The drainage channel he followed had taken him to the edge of the Navy base, and he now needed to find a way out of this box. There was a guard tower some two hundred meters to his right, and the missile battery he saw earlier was a few hundred meters further along. A gravel road ran along the fence, with vehicle patrols passing every few minutes. This was not a place to get careless, although the rain hid him from view, hopefully.

His objective was another two hundred meters ahead, down by the shore; the vague bulk of a metal building picked out with faint lights shrouded by the thin fog. He could smell the tang of the nearby ocean—hell, he could *hear* it. He couldn't see what he was after, but this was where he remembered it: they *had* to be there, or he'd be in a fix.

Lights played along the fence, and the faint rumble of a vehicle sent him scuttling into the drainage pipe, where he lay shivering in the steady torrent of runoff as another patrol drove slowly by. They were more aggressive than ever: dogs, search squads, and random patrols combing the area relentlessly. He'd clearly worn out his welcome in these parts.

The patrol reached the metal building, turned, and vanished inland. No sense in putting this off any longer. He struggled out of the pipe and worked his way along the fence, keeping low to avoid being seen by the guard tower. The building, when he finally reached it, was a dilapidated utility shed with a walkway of salvaged brick around it. Weeds grew up between the bricks, and the building foundation sprouted patchy mold. Mac went to ground again and listened carefully. There was faint music from inside, and an occasional mumbled voice. A thin stream of oil smoke came from a tin chimney. This was a good night to hunker down by the stove and enjoy a few stiff drinks, knowing that the officers wouldn't venture out in this muck.

Satisfied for the moment, Mac worked his way around the building...barely avoided tripping over some junk...and finally reached the sea. The building faced the old breakwater which now served as a jetty. On the wall next to the door was a faded sign:

Small Craft Pool

An improvised rock berm enclosed a small harbor, which sheltered the prize he sought: a half-dozen assorted harbor craft tied up to the jetty.

There was the clump of boots on gravel, and he ducked down behind the raised jetty as two figures emerged from the mist around the far corner of the building. They paused at the door and vanished inside, to be greeted by raised voices. He waited anxiously until they seemed to settle down, then turned his attention to matters at hand.

There was a small utility tug, an ancient motorboat half flooded and unserviceable, a small barge loaded with buoys and other navigation aids, and the real prize: a neat motor whale boat tied up at the end of the row.

Lights showing past the end of the building caught his eye: another patrol was coming along the fence. Only this time they stopped near his drainage culvert, and flashlights appeared in the gloom. He must have been spotted by the guard tower after all. No more options. He crept along the wall, ducked low to avoid a misted-over window, worrying all the while that someone might come through the door. There were raised voices inside: he froze for an instant, then scuttled along to where the whale boat was moored. The mooring line came free, he jumped awkwardly into the boat, and shoved off from the jetty with one foot. When he hit the starter, the motor sounded like a cement mixer. He hurriedly throttled back, popped the clutch, and backed out of the anchorage; praying all the while that the voices in the building wouldn't hear. The flashlights were investigating the culvert. The chop set the boat to rocking as he cleared the anchorage, and he was forced to hold onto the gunwale to steady himself. The wind kicked up, spattering him with renewed rain. This was no night to go out to sea in an open craft, especially one with a clattering valve. He turned the boat and headed out to open water.

§

"We have a report of a man matching Krauss's description down near the waterfront, sir," Volmer reported. "By time security arrived, he was gone."

"What is he up to?" Alvarez mused. In an odd way, he was pleased by his former pupil's cunning and illusiveness. Krauss was making this a fine chase; Alvarez's rage had almost vanished as he was caught up in the thrill of the hunt. But all chases must come to an end, and he, Alvarez, had hard questions to be answered. "Where exactly was he on the waterfront?"

Volmer studied the report, then turned to the tactical map, now heavily marked with penciled updates. "Right in here, sir. Near the fence." He pointed to a spot on the edge of the Navy base not far from the 6th Office compound.

Alvarez examined the map at length. "Curious. He can't expect to sneak them aboard a ship now. Is he trying to escape..." A map notation caught his eye. "...small craft pool?" Something was wrong here: he recalled all too well how slippery Krauss could be. He turned eagerly to Volmer. "Find out who is in charge down there! Make sure nothing is missing!"

"Yes, sir!"

This was proving a fine chase indeed.

§

Another shuttle landed late that afternoon, this one loaded with electrical materials for a new telephone system at the human embassy, and a load of assorted holiday gifts and toys. When the crew were excavated from their cramped control deck, they headed in for some hot food. I'eiBida intercepted them in the cafeteria.

"How is the weather affecting your flight operations?"

The pilot stared stupidly at him, then said, "We can manage on instruments, sir."

"The ship is over half empty with this lot, sir," his co-pilot added. "Another three days ought to do it."

"If you last that long." Both of them were wilted with fatigue. "You need some rest, and a hot meal."

"The shuttle needs servicing too, sir," the cargo specialist said. "They aren't supposed to be pushed this hard without running safety checks on the reactors."

"And servicing the hydraulics, too," the co-pilot grumbled.

As much as he hated it, as dire as their situation was, I'eiBida didn't want a shuttle crash with the unwelcome attention it would draw from the humans. "When you get back to your ship, tell your Eldest to give the shuttle section a full watch of down time. They can service the shuttles, and *you* can get some sleep."

The pilot didn't answer; he stared at nothing and nodded.

§

"The yard attendant reported that they are missing a motor whaleboat, sir!" Volmer told Alvarez a few hours later.

"Of course they are," Alvarez said, fatalistically. *'Clever, Krauss,'* he thought. *'Very clever. Your friends have failed you, hmmm? Too bad.'* His Puker contacts must have been scared off by the heightened security sweeps, wisely for them. Now Krauss and the girl were stranded, and he was trying desperately to improvise. *'Run, Krauss,'* he thought, smugly. *'You have been lucky thus far, but this time your luck has run out.'*

"We'll find him, sir! Don't you worry!"

Alvarez turned on him severely. "*I* am not the one who should worry!"

That brought Volmer down hard. "Where can he go, sir?" he asked, nervously. "Should we alert the Navy to send out patrols?"

Alvarez ignored him as he pondered the situation. It was raining solidly now as another Sumatra squall swept over the island. A boat that small couldn't venture out in the open ocean in this weather. Krauss's best bet was to work his way along the shore either to the Lizard base or around the eastern end of the island to the Malaysian mainland...but that would be foolish. They wouldn't last long in those pirate-infested coastal towns. They would make short work of him, but her...Krauss knew better, no matter how desperate he was. His only other option would be to dare the open ocean to try for the northern coast of Australia...

"They are headed for the Lizard base," he said to Volmer. "Alert the Navy to send some patrol craft down that way, and order the Peacekeepers to make ready for the attack on the Lizards."

*****

"Chapter Twelve"

It was still raining early the next morning, and the Hand assigned to watch the Peacekeepers camped on the road were wet and miserable. It was all part of the game here on earth, it seemed, and the Hand Lead endured it with stoic resignation. At least the Specials brought along camouflage tarps to shelter under this time. Right then he was scanning the human camp a hundred lengths distant, where the Peacekeepers were more active than ever. "What do you think?" he asked his number two.

"They are definitely preparing for battle."

The Lead went back to studying the human camp through his optics, and wasn't happy. However lacking they may be, there were an awful lot of them, and he could see several heavy weapons: some hand carried, some vehicle mounted. They went about their preparations with little obvious enthusiasm, but it was clear that once they got moving, it would be ugly.

"How soon will they pull us back?" number two grumbled.

"It better be soon." The Lead watched the human activity for a while longer. "Time to call in," he said at last.

§

T'thReptn called an emergency meeting of the advising circle a short time later. "The Peacekeepers are stirring again," he announced. "Radio communications are picking up, and our scouts report more activity in their camps."

"What about the 'Tan Shirts'?" I'eiBida demanded.

"The search in the harbor seems to be winding down, sir. According to radio intercept analysis, at least some of the 'Tan Shirts' are being pulled out."

"Are they reconstituting their attack units?"

T'thReptn hesitated. "It's hard to say, sir, but that's the only thing which makes sense. If so, they must be headed back to the 6th Office compound."

"Great," B'monTrea muttered. "What went wrong?"

I'eiBida fumed over the map as the latest intel was posted. "It looks like Brian's game has run its course."

"Could they have caught him?"

"There may simply be no fresh sightings of him since he called last, sir. He said he was relocating."

"Hmph. But where?"

"Alvarez may have decided he came back here, sir," S'deMnveb said. "So he may have decided to go ahead with the attack on that basis."

"Unintended consequences." I'eiBida's tail lashed, and his ears folded back in agitation. "Brian's move may have sent Alvarez the wrong signals."

There was an ugly silence as the circle pondered that, then T'thReptn asked, "How soon will they come, sir?"

I'eiBida turned to Giselle, who gave him a nervous look. "They can come at any time," she said.

"Their supply situation still isn't great, according to our radio intercepts and traffic count," T'thReptn objected.

She seemed to twitch all over, and her mood changed in an instant. "Do they train you to be clueless, or is that a natural skill?" she snapped. "They're cannon fodder; they don't need supplies. They'll roll over your defenses by sheer numbers." She faltered for a bit, and the fire animating her seemed to wain, then, "Overrunning this place will take time, and they will want to finish before dark. They will come by noon."

I'eiBida turned to Arbiter C'broVbron. "How many are left to evacuate?"

"Aside from the defenders, we have fifty left to go," she said.

"And four hours at best." I'eiBida pondered the map as he ran through the problem in his mind. "How soon will the next shuttle arrive?"

"Within the hour."

"And the other one?"

"At best, probably about 10.0."

I'eiBida sighed, and wondered to himself what Brian would do in this situation, or if there was anything any of them could do. "All right, get as many of the noncombatants on the next shuttle as you can, then have them suspend the unloading and send the next one down empty for the rest of them. I want the one after that on the ground, empty, ready to take off by 11.4."

The advising circle broke up and went about their various duties, leaving I'eiBida alone with Giselle. "This is going to be a shambles," he muttered in despair.

"*No se preocupe, mi amigo,*" she said, softly. "He told me to say all battles are a shambles. You are doing fine."

"Thank you."

She shuddered, and withdrew into herself a bit, her inner passenger receding into the background again. "I was too hard on T'thReptn."

I'eiBida looked at her. "Not really. We just don't think like you humans do. I fought our mindset all through my career, even among those of us with personal experience with your kind." He gave her a wry ear twitch. "Your killer instincts take getting used to."

"*Dios, tienes ese derecho,*" she sighed. "Still, he is too good to be a Third. He deserves a promotion."

"He'll get it."

§

Eldest A'vberBenn came tearing down from the command circle via the hand holds rather than waiting for the elevator. "They're stepping up the evacuation!" he told the Fourth when he reached the equipment bay five decks below. "It looks like the humans are finally attacking. The next shuttle is bringing most of the remaining non-combatants, and we're to send this one down empty."

"But it's almost loaded!" the Fourth complained.

"There's nothing for it; you'll have to off-load again."

"That will take too long. They'll have better luck unloading it down there."

A'vberBenn took an exasperated look around the cramped equipment bay and the mix of cargo handlers and ground-side volunteers who were paused in mid-act to witness the tense confrontation. "*I'cc'vn!* Send it down, then, and move the last of the cargo from the upper hold to the lower; perhaps we can get it cleared at least." The upper cargo bay was only about two-thirds cleared, while the lower was still chaotic as they tried to sort out food which could be kept for the trip home.

181

"Wonderful! It's not like we have anything better to do!"

"Put a knot in it!" A'vberBenn snarled. "Blame the humans; it's not like we have any choice."

"But where can we put them, sir?" They had nearly half the ground staff aboard, and aside from a couple hands of volunteers working cargo, the upper decks were already crowded.

A'vberBenn gave him a dismayed ear twitch. "I have no idea. We'll have to manage as best we can."

"Yes, sir. We'll do our best."

§

It was mid morning, and about as light as it was going to get, but the rain coming down in buckets both obstructed Mac's view of the shore and hid him from sight. He eased the boat's throttle forward, and set course to follow the shore just far enough off so it was a vague shadow to his left. The whale boat fought its way through the heavy chop, kicking like that mechanical bull he was fool enough to try back when he was a Midshipman. The surf slopped over the bow, adding to the hands-width of water already sloshing around in the bilge, but he was too preoccupied to start bailing again. He was somewhere off the spaceport—had sheered off hastily to avoid running ashore right by one of the missile batteries—but he couldn't say just exactly *where* he was. In addition to being spotted from land, there was the risk of encountering a patrol boat, so he needed to locate himself, get ashore, and find cover.

He was distracted by a rising roar, and an orbital shuttle passed ahead, a vague shadow in the cloud cover. "All right," he muttered. He knew where he was now, and steered toward the shore. Sure enough, the breakwater curved away ahead to form the entrance to the narrow channel separating the base from the rest of Singapore. The Singaporeans had built up a shallow area east of the old International airport for their major air force base, and for some reason left a narrow channel across the width of the peninsula. The old airport was devastated in the attack, and when Space Fleet set up shop here, they built their base on the peninsula so they could fortify all around against the pirates who infested these waters. The channel was still fenced and patrolled, but the area behind it had become a dumping ground of odd junk, old vehicles, piles of durable materials, and a dogs' breakfast of dirty shop buildings and godowns. It was the perfect place to go to cover, if he could get past the guard towers.

Sure enough, no sooner did he turn into the channel than the rusty chain link fence became visible on his right, with a guard tower looming in the background. He throttled down to bare headway, and worked his way carefully along the jumbled rocks of the breakwater. It was high enough that he was invisible from the guard tower as long as he kept his head down. Lights showed in the gloom, and he shut his engine off hastily and dove for cover as a patrol drove past on the service road.

He hesitated for a long moment after they were gone, honestly afraid to continue. He'd been lucky thus far, but luck has a way of shafting one just when needed the most. He studied the low embankment and the fence with no enthusiasm as he pondered his options. The evacuation must be well along by now; the smart move would be to turn the boat around and work his way west to the Ic'nichi landing field. The smart move...

"Hell of a way to make a living," he grumbled.

They seeded this whole area with pressure sensors back when he was in command here, and had probably added mines to the bargain since. He would have to hurry if he was to get through the fence before someone came to answer an alarm, but hurrying is the *last* thing one does in a potential minefield. Nothing for it, and the longer he sat there dithering, the greater the risk of being spotted. He ran the boat onto a narrow sand spit, scrambled up the rocky embankment, and 'made haste slowly' on hands and knees to the fence. It was only ten meters or so, but ten meters can be an awful long way in a minefield.

Once he made it, he dug out the wire cutters and tackled the fence binders. It seemed to take forever while he sweated every faint sound, but he finally had a corner of the mesh loose, and was able to crawl under. It was another eternal ten meters to the nearest pile of scrap lumber, and from there to the back of an ancient tin building.

§

183

"According to our scouts, the humans don't seem in much of a hurry," T'thReptn said when they gathered in the Intel circle for their midday briefing. "Not that I blame them; it's pouring out there." The humans, by the staff's latest estimate, would be ready to move within the hour.

"Should I recall the scouts, sir?" S'deMnveb was obviously thinking they would be stranded out there if the attack came, but they would have to wait until dark to return safely.

I'eiBida considered. "Yes, have them move back, but tell them not to risk exposure unless the attack starts."

"The humans will be in a foul mood when they come, sir," D'remNek said. "They don't like being cold and wet."

I'eiBida gave him an annoyed look for quoting the textbook *he* wrote to him.

"We have a report of two light patrol craft leaving the Navy base, sir." T'thReptn was reading a report just handed him. "One is coming along the coast, but the other put out to sea. They may be circling that group of islands." He referred to a formerly built up area once part of the seaport which was wiped clean in the nuclear attack, and was since mostly reclaimed to the sea.

"They may be maneuvering to come up on our western flank." S'deMnveb traced a route on the map circling the abandoned island and the tip of the peninsula to come up the river bordering the western shore.

"Yes..." I'eiBida muttered.

One of the Intel staffers shoved another report at T'thReptn. "It's confirmed. Our remote sensors show the 'Tan Shirts' reforming near the 6th Office. The attack will come soon."

"They'll roll right over us, and the Peacekeepers will come in to finish us off, sir," D'remNek added.

"No." Giselle was listening again. "The 'Tan Shirts' are political troops. They will let the Peacekeepers take the beating, then they will march in to claim the victory."

D'remNek looked at her doubtfully, then turned to I'eiBida. "She's right," I'eiBida said. "They won't get their pretty pink hands dirty unless its to mop up what's left after the regulars do the bleeding."

"That will make it even worse," she added. "They are *soldados de la tormenta*, not disciplined like regulars."

D'remNek paled. "You think they would...?"

"*Si*. Their kind usually do, and they answer to Alvarez."

"Why haven't they attacked thus far?" Arbiter C'broVbron asked. "It's not like Alvarez has any scruples about it."

"No, but he doesn't have complete control over the 6th Office yet," I'eiBida said. "He won't risk an open breach with us until he can be sure he can contain any backlash from Geneva."

"Not without a compelling excuse, sir," T'thReptn said.

"Or a compelling reason," Giselle said. "Such as if he thinks Brian is back here."

"So the human's deception is what kept them from attacking us so far?" C'broVbron asked.

"*Si*. But now it looks like that fell through, so we can expect trouble in short order."

"Will they still come by mid day?"

I'eiBida pondered the map as he went over the latest intel reports in his mind. Then he glanced at Giselle. "Probably not. At this rate, I'd say 13.00 at the earliest; more likely 14.00." She nodded solemnly in agreement.

"That's one small favor, at least."

"But we must make the most of it. Get the last civilians out on this shuttle, and have the defenders take their place to keep the humans from noticing."

"It was loaded, sir."

"Huh?"

"This shuttle, it came down fully loaded."

"*p'quas'tka!*" I'eiBida slapped his tail against the map table legs in disgust. "Get it unloaded, then, at the gallop!"

"That will wear our people down, sir," D'remNek said.

"There's nothing for it, and the fight won't last long when it comes anyway."

"Sir?" One of the Service Wardens came trotting in and offered a hasty tail wave. "We found something in the human cargo. You might want to take a look, sir."

§

185

Their two volunteers were waiting for them in the same warehouse where the infiltrators were captured earlier. There was a pallet of wooden crates marked 'Machine Tools', one of which was broken open, revealing a light machine gun.

"I've handled cargo here for two years, sir," their 'Blue-And-Brown' said. "There have been several of these lots sent to d'enchia lately, and it struck me as suspicious."

"Those few infiltrators couldn't use all this firepower, sir," D'remNek said, doubtfully.

"Smuggling weapons to the human diplomatic compound, I see." I'eiBida nodded thoughtfully, then glanced at the two volunteers. "Brian warned us they were planning something on d'enchia. Good work, that."

"*hro'n'nad!*" B'monTrea grumbled. "What can they expect to accomplish with this *x'mnnb'*?"

"You're dealing with racially tinged paranoia," I'eiBida admonished him. "Don't look for rational explanations."

"It seems we have four of these, plus some ammunition, sir," one of the volunteers said.

"Those will make a big difference," B'monTrea added, hopefully.

"Right. Some good news, for once." I'eiBida turned to the dock workers. "Get these uncrated and assembled as fast as you can, and get them to D'remNek's people. And keep it *quiet*; we don't want the humans to notice."

"Yes, *sir!*" Their two volunteers turned to with enthusiasm.

§

It was actually more than an hour before someone came to investigate Mac's hole in the fence. A utility vehicle with four Military Police materialized out of the gloom, and they spread out to search the fence line. It seemed there were no mines after all, since once they spotted the whaleboat, they swarmed all over it.

Mac was watching from the upper floor of a nearby tin storeroom, and nodded to himself as reinforcements arrived a short while later. The game was on again. He headed out before they could get a search organized.

§

186

"The Peacekeepers received their last allotment of munitions a little while ago, sir," Volmer reported to Alvarez as he brooded over the map in the communication center while his two goons waited silently in the background.

Alvarez gave him a smoldering glare. "It took them long enough!" It wasn't the Quartermasters' fault their few trucks were kept busy hauling 'Tan Shirts' back and forth on a days-long wild goose chase, not that anyone was about to say so to the Colonel. "It takes those fools *forever* to do anything, to say nothing of getting it right!"

"Not to mention they burned up a large part of their fuel reserve with all this wasted motion, sir." Planting suspicion was second nature to Volmer, and right then he was anxious that the Colonel aim his distemper at innocent strangers. "However, the Peacekeepers can move whenever you please, sir, now that they are fully supplied."

"They *will* move whenever I please whether they have ammunition or not!"

"Ah...presumably so, sir."

But Alvarez ignored him, as he was obsessing over Krauss and the girl. "We will find them!" He hammered his fist on the table, causing those nearby to twitch nervously. "We will hunt them down wherever they hide! Them, and the traitors who helped them, and the Lizards who subverted my best agent!" He was trembling in fury, his eyes glowing feverishly. "We will destroy them all!"

"Your orders, sir?"

Alvarez fought to contain the rage which had him gasping and trembling while Volmer tried not to cringe under his gaze. It took some doing, but he managed to calm himself enough to think rationally. "Krauss and the girl must have made it to the Lizard base by boat; it is the only place he can go. Tell the Peacekeepers to launch their attack, and have our forces ready to swoop in and collect the two fugitives." He brooded for a bit, then turned to Volmer again. "Arrest one of the Quartermasters at random, and ship him off to the camps. Tell the rest they are lucky not to go with him, *this time!* They will learn to do their jobs *properly!*"

"Yes, Colonel!" Volmer saluted and scuttled away, thankful his wrath was pointed elsewhere. In his present state, no one was safe.

§

The rain had dwindled to a light sprinkle at the moment, and Mac managed to work his way around the south side of the base to a clutter of storehouses and semi-abandoned buildings. He took shelter under a rusted awning and kept a wary eye out as he contemplated his next move. The base MPs were busy, their patrols driving every which way like they were trying to cover as much area as possible, rather than make a concentrated search. Thus far he hadn't seen any 'Tan Shirts'. It looked like the boat sighting stirred some interest, but experience told him he needed to be a bit more obvious to get Alvarez really focussed in his direction. After thinking about it for a bit, another building break-in seemed in order. He should call in, anyway.

The building was a nondescript cinder block cube with large industrial windows and roll up doors onto the dock where he stood. He peered carefully through the windows, but saw nothing other than some dusty machinery, work benches, and parts bins. A telephone on a desk along the far wall caught his eye.

The simple wooden door was no problem. The phone gave him a dial tone, so he slipped the vocoder in place and hit a button. "This is *Adelbard*. I've reached the spaceport, and have gone to ground for the moment."

"*Hola*, Brian. You are in the spaceport? It is good to hear from you. We were afraid they caught you."

"Hello Giselle. Sorry I've been out of touch. Things were getting too hairy in the harbor, so I relocated. How's everything?"

"Alvarez is massing his forces; it looks like he will attack us soon."

"Dammit," he grumbled.

"We think he misinterpreted your disappearance, that you might have come back here. You must get his attention again, and quickly."

That was the *last* thing they needed; Mac was chagrined to think he might have royally screwed the pooch for all of them. "Right. I'll see what I can do. How long do we have?"

"The best estimate is only a few hours."

"Hmmm, guess I'll have to get crude. I'm on it."

"Good luck, Brian."

§

"The spaceport?" I'eiBida stared at her, bemused, after she reported Mac's latest. "I should know better than to think Brian would grab his own tail at a time like this."

"It may not help," she said. "Alvarez must think he returned here, which would be the sensible thing to do."

"I just hope Brian can distract him soon, otherwise it will all be for nothing."

§

Mac pocketed the vocoder and stood pondering his options for a long moment. His seaborne shift was backfiring, which put him in an uncomfortable spot. He couldn't play cat-and-mouse any more, but at the same time he couldn't risk a direct confrontation which could lead to a hot pursuit...

...he noticed a shelf loaded with cans of oil and cleaning solvents...and an acetylene welding rig nearby...

§

The building was well ablaze when the base fire units arrived. It didn't take them long to notice the kicked-in door he carefully left open. The MPs were there in force by time they had the fire out, and as Mac watched from a distance, they soon had search parties on the move.

§

Mid morning, and another Sumatra squall swept across the island soaking Peacekeepers and defenders with fine impartiality. The temperature, which hovered uncertainly since dawn, began dropping again; the wind picked up, and the cloud cover was dark and ugly.

The first sign of trouble was when the trucks from the harbor stopped coming. Remote sensors showed the last few parked beside the road or turning back. At the same time, the Peacekeepers had finally struck camp, and were in battle formation, ready to move. Both sides could read the signals, and neither were happy.

There were still several dozen human drivers waiting at the warehouses to have their rigs unloaded and refilled. Tentative plans were made to round them up before the fighting started, but as time passed they drove away one by one. D'remNek's defenders watched and waited.

§

It was nearly noon before the next shuttle arrived, and ground to a halt under a sullen sky. All across the landing field, Ic'nichi staffers started drifting toward the tarmac by ones and twos, moving with studied nonchalance as some of D'remNek's and S'deMnveb's people dressed in ordinary took their places right under the humans' snouts. The office staff, already reduced to a single Hand of volunteers, were sent away; as were most of T'thReptn's Intel staff. Arbiter C'broVbron, who was seriously unhappy about all this, put up a bold front by calling the Harbormaster to complain about the supposed traffic hangup. Aside from a lone banqueter who remained to keep the defenders supplied with hot *V'liz*, all base activities ground to a halt.

It took a human hour to get as many as they could aboard, and the shuttle took off—again as calculated a display of boring routine as they could manage. The few remaining civilians tried to keep up appearances, and wondered about Alvarez's next move, and worried. D'remNek's positions were already prepared, including the four captured machine guns, but aside from the watch detail on the gate, and an observation post on the Admin roof, and the Hand of Specials out in the ruins watching the Peacekeepers, their lines were vacant as the defenders focussed on other things.

The waiting continued.

§

The Hand Lead watching the Peacekeeper camp on the road was not happy. The Hand was reunited after being partly pulled back so they were now in a loose line between the Peacekeepers and the landing field, hidden under their camouflage tarps. His big fear was the humans would roll over them once they did advance; he spent the last hour or so pondering how they could manage a fighting skirmish retreat against that much firepower.

"I don't like it," he grumbled.

"No one said you had to," his second replied. "How soon will they recall us?"

"It better be quick."

"There is no chance we can infiltrate through their lines to reach the field with them nipping at our tails," the fourth muttered.

"Don't knot your tail over it," the Lead snapped, although he had to admit to himself the fellow was right. He could only hope the rest of the Specials would take out the 'Tan Shirt' gate watch before his people were pinned between them and the Peacekeepers. He went back to scanning the human position with his optics. They were in full combat gear, forming up into attack elements behind their two armored cars. This was an *Ancestorless* mess; they could come at any time.

§

The other shuttle came drifting in by mid-afternoon, and the remaining ground staff boarded with feverish haste. By that point, the tension had risen to where some were physically ill from worry. The damp mist left over from the latest Sumatra squall didn't help either. Everyone was overheated, agitated, and worn out. Tempers flared, and minor accidents took their toll while the evacuees waited and worried.

Out on the perimeter, a thin screen of defenders kept watch and added to their positions as best they could with the materials at hand. Everyone knew it wouldn't make a difference when the humans came, but they couldn't sit still and do nothing. A round of *V'liz* stew appeared, which was a welcome release from the tension. They all knew it was the last hot meal they would likely see.

§

"Our forward observer post reports the Peacekeepers are moving up, sir," D'remNek reported a short time later. "It looks like they are finally coming."

"How soon will the shuttle be cleared?" T'thReptn asked.

"They're close to finished now, sir."

I'eiBida sighed. "Very well. Call the scouts in, and prepare your defenses." D'remNek gave him a tail wave, grabbed his machine pistol and munitions pack from a nearby chair, and left.

I'eiBida stared at the map on the plot table for a moment, then looked at Giselle. "Time is up. The attack will start soon. You need to get to the shuttle."

"I am sorry."

"Thank you. We'll do our best, but this won't last long."

She withdrew into herself a bit, staring into the distance. "*Buena fortuna*," she muttered at last, and turned to the exit. I'eiBida watched her go, then vented his angst in a string of human expletives which would have stirred the soul of any old time Sergeant Major.

"True enough, sir," T'thReptn said when he wound down. He glanced at the mere handful of his people who remained. "Are you going to send that shuttle away now, sir?" he asked softly.

I'eiBida scowled at him. "We have to; there are too many remaining for all to crowd into it, so we'll need another run."

"Yes, sir. The other shuttle is on its way now."

I'eiBida fumed as he studied the map. "Hopefully they'll have time to get here before the fighting starts. You and your people get to the landing field."

"Yes, sir."

T'thReptn gathered his people and sent them on their way, each toting a cardboard box of key intelligence files he had saved from the general destruction. I'eiBida looked at him in surprise after the others left. "You're staying?"

"Yes, sir," T'thReptn said, evenly. "You still need someone who knows snout from tail around here." He drifted back to the map table while I'eiBida contemplated him, and decided if any of them lived through this, he would see T'thReptn got a double promotion.

§

"Colonel?" Volmer interrupted Alvarez's much-needed nap; not a smart move normally. "We have a report of a motor whaleboat found on the coast by the spaceport, sir."

"What?" Alvarez blinked in confusion as he tried to absorb this latest turnabout. "The spaceport?"

"Yes, sir. They also found a hole cut in the perimeter fence. They're searching the area now."

192

"They damned well *better* be," Alvarez snapped as he struggled to his feet and tried to change mental gears from his obsession with the two fugitives. "Do they know what that is about?"

"It must be Krauss, sir. The Navy reported their ship saw nothing along the coast, and the boat is the same type as the one stolen from the harbor."

The Colonel's eyes lit up with a predatory glow. "Perhaps it is. We shall soon find out."

His first act was to send a hurry-up call to spaceport security, who tried to sluff him off with vague generalities and the usual platitudes, which was exactly the *wrong* thing for someone reporting to Alvarez.

"What is this garbage you hand me?" he roared. "There are two dangerous fugitives loose in your territory, and you give me nonsense?"

"We don't know that, sir. It could very well be scavengers from Squatter Town..."

"Do you think I am a *peon* you can dismiss with some fantasy? This is an urgent security matter, and you *dare* patronize *me?*"

"I can assure you, Colonel, we are doing our best..."

"You can assure me of nothing! NOTHING!"

"But Colonel..."

His protest was cut short. "Colonel? Lindemann, sir, 'Tan Shirt' spaceport security. I have my men conducting a systematic sweep radiating from the point of entry, sir. We will find the intruders."

"At least *someone* knows his duty! What have you learned thus far?"

"We confirmed the boat was stolen from the harbor. Beyond that we have nothing solid, but we think it ties in with the fire, sir, possibly a diversionary tactic."

"*Fire?* What fire?"

"An arson fire in a machine shop on the other side of the base, sir. The building was broken into and torched. If Krauss is here, the fire must have been set by his contacts to pull us off his trail."

"Yes, it must be! Krauss is a clever bastard, and this fits his pattern thus far. We have him now!"

"We're putting together a search of the entire base, sir."

"You better! I want them both alive! ALIVE! DO YOU HEAR ME?"

"Understood, sir!"

"And start a systematic hunt for the saboteurs, too. We *will not* tolerate Puker terrorists in our most important military base! Arrest anyone who looks the least bit suspicious."

"Yes, sir. Can you send reinforcements? I only have my element, and we know we can't count on these *Peacekeepers*, so I need to replace them as soon as we can." There was a squawk of protest in the background.

"You will have all the help you need! Promptly!"

"Thank you, sir. We'll press the search with everything at our disposal."

"Do not stop until you find them!" Alvarez yelled. "And tell that Peacekeeper *tonto* he works for you now, and if he causes *any* trouble, arrest *him!*"

He slammed the phone down so hard that it bounced and fell on the floor. He ignored it, and started pacing back and forth, cursing in frustration. That...damned...Peacekeeper! This was their Admiral's doing, no doubt. He would have him and his flunky both in the camps if Krauss managed to get away. Gradually his temper cooled, and he started to think the matter over, which left him perplexed.

What was Krauss up to? It didn't make sense: if his contacts in the harbor failed him, why not head for the Lizard base since he was working for them? What could he hope to find at the spaceport? Help from Space Fleet? They wouldn't dare! Additional Puker contacts...?

Then another possibility stopped him in his tracks. "An *airplane?*" he said in dismay. That sent a chill down his spine; an airplane would get them off the island, possibly to their Puker allies...or to his enemies in Geneva... Whatever Krauss originally intended, it was their only hope now...but Krauss didn't know how to fly...

"Get MacKenna's dossier!" he snapped at Volmer. "I need to know if he ever flew an airplane!"

"Sir?"

"The woman, you idiot! She has the memories of a seasoned combat veteran! I need to know if he ever flew an aircraft!"

A couple of staffers pawed through the stacked files on the table, and quickly brought the thick folder to him. "What about the attack on the Lizard base, sir?" Volmer asked diffidently as he flipped through the file.

Alvarez paused. He should go ahead and eliminate them on general principle... But Geneva would raise hell if he started a war without adequate reasons... His hold on the 6th Office wasn't as complete as he would like yet... The war preparations weren't complete... There were traitors to dig out in the harbor, and perhaps in the spaceport as well... If this crisis was past, perhaps it was better to wait until the process could be perfected...

"Call it off for now until we know what is happening in the spaceport. Get those ships over there and set up a blockade. Transfer our forces to aid in the search, and put the Peacekeepers on standby."

Volmer saluted and turned to, clearly disappointed that the crisis was averted for the moment. In a way, Alvarez was as well, and he promised himself he would find or fabricate justification as soon as matters at hand were dealt with. But for now he would need time to go through this file.

*****

"Chapter Thirteen"

"I don't understand, sir," T'thReptn said as they puzzled over the latest intel reports. With his staff in orbit or on their way there, he was working feverishly to monitor human communications and the network of remote sensors in an effort to keep up with developments. His efforts uncovered something unexpected. "The Peacekeepers have halted again, and those two patrol boats are headed east. And now we're picking up major radio traffic from the spaceport."

I'eiBida laughed out loud. "It's Brian! He knotted Alvarez's tail once again!"

§

Giselle waited on the tarmac wrapped in a bath towel to ward off the steady drizzle as the latest shuttle was hastily prepared for the trip into orbit. The crew arranged various pads and improvised safety harness while the passengers waited stoically. There was no panic, despite the tension in the air, and no more than a subdued chatter which seemed more like grumbling than any real alarm. She had never met an Ic'nichi before coming here, and the more she got to know them, the more impressed she was.

'If only we could be like them,' she thought.

'They're good people,' the voice in her head said. *'Life would be a whole lot simpler for everyone if we were.'*

For once she and the voice agreed. *'It will be a terrible shame if we destroy them.'*

'Yeah. We can only hope for the best.'

'Will there be a war?' she asked as she watched the first Ic'nichi boarding.

'Yes.'

That was a chilling thought. *'Will they survive?'*

'Probably. Hopefully. I just hope their culture survives as well. The dead are not the only casualties of war.'

"*Tan tristemente cierto,*" she sighed.

She watched as the last two dozen or so civilians, including the Arbiter and her Aide, queued up to board the shuttle one by one, each carrying nothing but a small bag or pillow case with a few

196

essentials. A defender detail appeared, and passed a few more paperboard boxes through the hatch; more official documents. The boarding continued unabated.

'Refugees,' the voice whispered with a sense of bitterness. 'God, so many refugees. It never ends.' The echos were tinged with a sense of despair and revulsion.

"It never will, *mi amigo*," she muttered.

'No, it never will. Life is a fools' errand on good days.'

She answered with a bitter sigh, and joined the line of Ic'nichi ground staff as they crowded aboard.

The shuttle was soon packed. Someone offered her a floatation device to sit on, and she managed a spot in one corner of the cavernous cargo bay amid the horizontal bodies, buckled a strap around her waist, and tried to make herself comfortable. The last one entered, the cargo specialist pulled the hatch shut and dogged it, and the engines started.

'God, it grinds me,' the voice whispered. 'Sometimes there's no choice but to run, but even when it makes sense, it feels wrong.'

'It feels like defeat,' she thought. It did.

She felt a sense of growing respect. 'Yes, that's it exactly. It's like we lost something important, something worth fighting for.'

The engines pitched up, and the shuttle rocked gently as it started to taxi. The crowd around them were silent, lost in their own thoughts.

'I hope we can come back some day.'

'All refugees do. They always have. Honestly, your odds on returning aren't good.'

She reflected bitterly, and wondered about her family and her many friends from the University. How many were refugees? How many were fugitives? How many were still alive?

'Trust me, Giselle, brooding over their fate just makes it worse. I hate to think of the friends and family, my old comrades—hell, even the country I was born into—which vanished into the past.'

'I cannot help but worry, and pray.'

'Sometimes prayer is all we have. There are things in life we have no control over.'

'It is so wrong...'

Their debate was interrupted by a brief burst of alien chatter over the intercom. Those around her stirred in response, and a faint murmur of conversation rose.

"What did he say?" she asked someone.

The clerical she spoke to looked at her in confusion, then answered in his broken Swiss. "He say...humans stop...no attack."

Her eyes widened in surprise. She muttered a quick "*Gracias*", unhooked her harness, struggled to her feet, and fought her way to the entry hatch. "Let me out!" she demanded. "I need to get out."

The cargo specialist studied her in surprise. "Why?"

"I am staying. Please open the door."

"You stay?" The specialist was confounded.

"They need me here! Let me out! Please!"

He hesitated in confusion, then used the intercom to alert the pilot. The heavy shuttle ground to a halt, and the specialist undid the hatch. A moment later she was standing on the runway, blinded by the spray whipped up by the engines and deafened by their noise. The hatch shut behind her, leaving her grimly alone.

'You're going back,' the voice whispered without surprise as she headed to the warehouses.

"*Si*. There are things in life we have no control over, but they are still worth fighting for."

§

"What...?" I'eiBida looked at her in confusion when she turned up in the Intelligence circle. "Why are you still here? You were supposed to be on that last shuttle."

"Word came the attack was halted."

"Even so, you are still in danger."

"You need me. You need his skills." She leaned on the plot table and crossed her arms, clearly claiming her place in their command circle, and contemplated him and T'thReptn as equals. "As long as I can do some good, I will remain."

"Thank you," I'eiBida mumbled at last.

"What is the situation?"

"The Peacekeepers parked on the road are returning to their camp." T'thReptn outlined the situation on the map. "The 'Tan Shirts' and some light naval units are converging on the spaceport, and we're picking up a lot of radio traffic from spaceport security. It looks like Brian managed to pull them away again."

"That is good. I have faith in him."

"I *wish* they would make up their minds," I'eiBida grumbled. "This on-again-off-again war is getting tedious."

"Be careful what you wish for, *mi amigo extraterrestre*," she said. "You may wind up with 'on-again', which we will all regret."

I'eiBida stared at her, bemused, then chuckled. "You are right; no sensible person wishes for war."

"Alvarez does."

"No, he wishes for power. He'll resort to war if he has to, but what he wants is victory, not war itself."

She brooded on that, then nodded. "You may understand us better than you think."

§

One can only be rained on for so long until it no longer matters. Mac was soaked to the skin, chilled, and weary from hunger, but right then he hardly noticed or cared. He spent much of the day working his way back west and then north along the canal to the spaceport's main warehouse district, ducking patrols and avoiding random encounters with base personnel.

The building he was aiming for—if memory served—would solve his most pressing logistical problem: food. This whole section had been torn down since his day and rebuilt on a grander scale, but the numbering system appeared to be the same as he remembered. He hovered at the end of an alley between two warehouses, and looked up and down the street for any sign of movement. There was nothing except a duce-and-a-half being loaded several buildings down, but they were too far away to notice him.

Now or never. He strolled casually up the street, stopped at the street door, and listened carefully. No sound from inside. The door was a simple wooden affair, and rather run down at that. It was hard to imagine anyone willingly stealing zero-G rations, so from long tradition Facility Management didn't lift a finger to do anything more than strictly required. In fact, the door was unlocked when he tried it. They forgot to activate the alarm, too.

199

The front desk gave way to a short corridor lined with offices, which gave way in turn to the warehouse proper. He listened carefully, but no one was there, the workers here having gone home a short time earlier at the end of their shift. And his persistence was rewarded: this turned out to be the *El Dorado* of zero-G space rations—shelves as far as he could see crammed floor to ceiling with *cases* of the dull gray packets. Mac hunted around eagerly until he found an empty burlap sack, and began filling it with the slender mylar bags. He learned his lesson in the harbor; odds were he couldn't come back here, so he would stockpile enough to keep him going for several days...

"Halt!"

Mac flinched, and looked up the aisle at the 'Tan Shirt' covering him with his automatic. A quick glance the other way revealed a second 'Tan Shirt' also with drawn pistol. Then he realized to his dismay the door and alarm should have warned him of an ambush; instead of keeping on his toes, he'd walked right into it.

"We thought you'd show up here," the first gloated. "Now we have you."

Mac tried bluffing. "Of course I'd show up here. I work here, and you don't have Jack."

"Where is the other one?" the second demanded.

"What other one?"

"The girl you helped escape from the 6th Office compound! Where is she?"

"I don't know what you're talking about. I'm a civilian contract worker. I'm doing inventory..."

"No nonsense, you!" The first fished out a set of hand cuffs. "Up against the wall. The Colonel will be pleased to see you!"

"Oh, for crying out loud!" Mac eyed the two warily as he tried to spot some opening. They had him cold, so he turned, carefully put the sack on the shelf next to him, and leaned up against the unit with his hands at shoulder height. Despite his pretend exasperation, he was on the edge of panic; once they cuffed him, it was all over. He had seconds left to come up with something against two armed and wary men...

...The 'Tan Shirt' grabbed his wrist with one hand...and had a set of cuffs in the other...which meant he had holstered his weapon... Without thinking, Mac twisted loose from his grip, pivoted, and kneed him savagely in the groin. He grunted and went down, and Mac was already swinging his sack at the other, who instinctively raised both hands to ward off the blow. He never saw the kick to his groin which curled him up on the floor, or the second kick to his face, driving his skill into his brain.

The other one lay on his side clutching himself. When he saw what happened to his partner, he tried to fumble his automatic off the floor where he dropped it. Mac kicked it away, and stomped on his face. He let out a gurgling cry, and went still.

He hovered between them for an agonizing moment, watching for any sign of movement, and the nearby doorway for any sign of other intruders. At long last he let out a shaky sigh, and collapsed to sit between the two bodies. "Damn," he muttered in dismay. The whole fight lasted about five seconds, and went entirely on instinct. Now that it was over, he realized how close it was, and how blind instinct was all which saved him. It shook him: not that he felt any remorse for them, but killing two men wasn't easy.

But this was not the time or place to feel sorry for himself. Those two would be missed soon, and when they were discovered, there would be a righteous shit storm. He struggled to his feet, collected his sack, and headed for the rear of the building. As an afterthought, he collected their pistols and added them to the sack.

§

The first shuttle to arrive since the evacuation was halted brought a mere three hands' worth of volunteers, barely enough to get the base back up to a minimal operating level. Half of those were some of T'thReptn's key Intel staffers.

"Things in orbit are near chaos, sir," one of them reported. "The ship's Eldest is biting his own tail, he's so upset. It will take them the rest of the day to get things sorted out and the off-loading resumed. In the mean time, people are standing on each other's tails. He said he will have to send some down again just so they will have room to work. If it weren't for being in zero-G, they wouldn't be able to get everyone on board at all."

201

I'eiBida sighed. "At least he won't have to maneuver under those conditions. How much longer to complete the off-load?"

"Their Third said it would take another two days, sir. Assuming the flight crews can hold up."

"They have to; we're right on the edge."

A telephone buzzed, and one of the staffers answered it. "The gate reports the trucks are starting to arrive again, sir."

"Good," I'eiBida said. "That's a positive sign."

"I don't understand, sir," D'remNek complained. "Since they stopped because of the pending attack, and might still attack us, why start the deliveries again?"

"Never underestimate the power of bureaucratic inertia, my friend," T'thReptn told him.

§

It wasn't more than half an hour after the two bodies were discovered before their 'Tan Shirt' squad was joined by no less than Colonel Alvarez's personal Aide, Volmer. Even the Purity Movement's elite Security Directorate feared him, and the 'Tan Shirts' knew his showing up meant grief for them all.

"Everything is in order, sir." The squad leader saluted hastily and tried to hide his nervousness.

Volmer gave him a look of pure ice. "So, you have captured the culprits and wrapped the case up neatly, then?"

"Ah..." The leader wilted under his cool look. "No, sir."

"Then everything is *not* in order, your claims notwithstanding." He dismissed the man's sputtered protest. "No more than I expected from *amateurs*. The Colonel is *most* displeased with this pathetic display. Since you cannot capture a single unarmed man without losses, he sent me here to find new motivation for you." He considered the rest of the squad with no favor. They had good reason to be nervous; Volmer's personal four-man escort were the most ruthless, brutal, hand picked assassins in the 'Tan Shirts'.

"It seems you are unable to discipline your members to such a degree that *some* of you fail in your duty," Volmer said to the squad leader, coldly. "The deaths of these two are no more than they deserve, but they reveal a deeper failing which *cannot* and *will not* be tolerated." He gave them a chilling glare which was one part

202

righteous wrath and one part sadistic bloodlust. "From now on, if *any* member of *any* squad fails in his duties, that entire squad will pay the price!" He turned and whipped the tarp off the two bodies, revealing their gruesome remains. "Discipline! You *will* find them, and you *will* capture them! *Alive! Anyone* who fails will pay the *ultimate* price." He dropped the tarp, and gave them another contemptuous once-over. "I *trust* you understand the *importance* of finding the two fugitives, and returning them alive and well to the Colonel?"

The four assault-rifle-toting psychopaths with their distinctive white neckerchiefs around him made his meaning clear.

§

Are you *insane?*" the Admiral demanded. The fleet leadership were gathered in his office, and they were not happy with Volmer's latest bright idea. "This will wreck havoc with our operations!"

"We are pursuing two dangerous fugitives who were last reported somewhere on this base," Volmer said, coldly. "Their capture has absolute priority."

"You mean some poor bastards who ran afoul of your precious Movement!" Flight Ops yelled. "We have people in orbit who need food and supplies!"

"They can manage for the time being," Volmer snarled. "And I will *require* the assistance of your security people...*unless* you would prefer that I inform the Colonel of your non-cooperation in an urgent security matter?"

"I won't give you the satisfaction," the Admiral said, bitterly. He was a hard-case in the Fleet's cherished MacKenna tradition, but he knew better than to push his luck with the 6th Office, even with the solid backing of Space Fleet.

"But sir..."

"Let this jackal have his search. And you," the Admiral pointed to the fleet security chief. "Give him your full cooperation. The sooner he finishes, the sooner we'll be rid of him, and we can get back to work."

Flight Ops and Security were not happy, but surrendered to the inevitable. "Yes, sir."

§

The ship's Second came up to the galley from the cargo levels in a state of near despair. "How goes it?" A'vberBenn asked as he passed over a squeeze bulb of *V'liz*.

"It's like herding hatchlings down there." He didn't bother to strap himself to one of the seat cushions, but floated listlessly in mid air and considered the squeeze bulb, but didn't have the stomach for more *V'liz* at the moment. "The food supplies are sorted out, and the upper deck is mostly cleared. The lower deck and equipment bay are still a shambles, though."

"How are your volunteers working out?"

The Second uttered a scathing vulgarity. "I haven't seen such a collective tail knot since my days as an apprentice." He contemplated the squeeze bulb, then chucked it at the disposal chute. It missed, bounced off, and vanished through the elevator shaft to the quarters deck below. "It's a wonder we haven't had more injuries then we already suffered."

"We have no choice. Things down there in Singapore can't last much longer."

Since the evacuation scare yesterday—was it yesterday?—the cargo handlers had worked flat-out, knowing time was not on their side. The volunteers from ground-side were all that kept the exhausted cargo section going, but at a price of a steady run of mashed hands and pinched tails.

"They stand on each others' tails down there," the Second grumbled. "Most of them are more trouble then they're worth."

"They're what we have to work with. Ears up; this won't last much longer."

"It can't. I just hope my Ancestors will forgive the way the safety regs are being bent."

There was a dull echoing boom from somewhere below. A moment later the intercom lit up. "Physich to the lower cargo bay!" A moment later the lights sputtered and went out, followed by a call of, "Damage control detail to the lower cargo bay, at the gallop!"

"Great," the Second muttered as he pushed off for the elevator. "What now?"

§

Mac hunkered down at an upper floor window of a store house and munched a zero-G ration while checking the scene spread out below. The spaceport was a lot busier than the harbor, which made his lot that much more difficult. Most of the base was wide open space around the runway and taxi ways, while the rest was constantly busy. The hangers were turning shuttles around as fast as they could be serviced and refueled. The assembly areas were bustling as elements of new ships were prepared, while the supply depots fed a steady stream of raw materials and consumables up to orbit for the fleet. There were vehicles everywhere; trucks, busses, or MP patrols; and he could see at least two checkpoints as well. It would be hard to move in these areas by night, and all but impossible by day without taking enormous risks. That meant he was pretty well restricted to the fringe of the spaceport, the older areas in particular; outdated facilities from his time here. It didn't give him a lot of room to maneuver.

"Damn-fool got your sack in a vise, boy," he mumbled.

It took him some time to notice it, as the movement was scattered at first. When he first caught it, he studied the row of assembly shops across the road, confused. The big doors in one building were being shut, stranding the hull section they were about to wheel out. Everywhere he looked, trucks were being parked and doors shut, and a steady stream of figures poured out of the buildings and boarded shuttle busses and trucks under the watchful eyes of armed 'Tan Shirts'.

"Shit," he muttered when he figured it out.

He waited until the store house was evacuated and locked, then crept cautiously down from the loft in search of a phone.

"This is *Adelbard*. I've got some special news to report."

Giselle answered almost at once. "*Hola*, Brian, are you safe?"

Mac glanced around nervously, wondering how long he had before the 'Tan Shirts' turned up. "For now, but this place is being shut down all of a sudden. There's hardly anyone left other than security types, and it looks like shuttle operations are suspended."

There was a brief pause, then, "We have seen that too. There have been no shuttle flights for the last hour, and the base traffic control is off the air. Do you know what is happening?"

Mac nodded. "Yeah, I killed two more of them a little while ago; they jumped me, and I had to take them down. It really hit the fan around here soon thereafter. They're shutting the place down to reduce my freedom of movement. It'll be a whole lot easier for them to spot me now."

§

"I ordered flight operations suspended, and everyone confined to quarters except for the security troops," Volmer reported to Alvarez by telephone. "I've also stepped up the security sweeps. Without protective cover, Krauss will be a lot easier to spot."

"I see. I assume you are receiving the full cooperation of Space Fleet?"

"The Admiral and his Chief of Operations objected strenuously, sir. Their behavior is further reason to doubt their loyalty, the Flag Ops in particular." Like all survivors in the Purity Movement, Volmer never missed a chance to blacken a possible threat, or to sew Red Herrings wherever he could.

"Indeed?" Alvarez said, coolly. "We shall have to keep that in mind." Volmer smiled to himself at the thought. "How long do you expect flight operations to be suspended?"

"As long as it takes, sir."

"Very well."

"Should I order the flight control to suspend the Lizards' shuttle flights too, sir?"

Alvarez mused. "I wonder..."

"They've made far more flights than usual this last couple of days. They are up to something."

But by then Alvarez was obsessed with supposed Puker agents infesting the island. "No doubt, but we will allow their pretense for now. You focus on securing the renegades and our two test subjects."

"But..."

"You have your instructions! As for the Lizards, once we attack their base, I will order the fleet to destroy the transport, and the courier as well. Let them run for now; the trap is already set."

"Yes, Colonel."

§

"So what do we do, sir?" T'thReptn asked after they listened to the intercepted phone conversation a second time.

"It's not like it's any surprise," I'eiBida said, grimly. Mac's recent call put them on alert, and close monitoring of their phone taps paid off.

"If Space Fleet is waiting for us, we don't have a hope, sir. There is no chance that we can shoot our way out of their defense zone with our ships' limited armament."

I'eiBida sighed, and his ears twitched in agitation. "We have to come up with something, but what we can do is beyond me."

"Do you have any more of these recordings?" Giselle asked. She had listened to the recorded conversation with grim attention.

"Days' worth," T'thReptn muttered.

"They might be our answer. Where are they?"

T'thReptn gave a startled twitch, studied her in confusion, then turned to one of his people. "What did you do with those telephone intercepts?"

That one held up a plastic bin he was just heading out the door with. "I'm getting ready to destroy them, sir."

"No! We need them!" Giselle took the bin filled with disposable data chips and put it on the map table between them. "I think we can put a wrench in Alvarez's plans."

§

Another shuttle touched down late in the evening, and the weary ground herd stirred themselves once again. Eldest A'vberBenn had sent down some thirty of the hasty evacuees, not always willingly on their part, just so they could have room to work. That got the stream of cargo flowing, and the ground staff turned to once more. When the flight crew were excavated, the pilot reported to I'eiBida in the Intel circle.

"They've more or less got things sorted out, sir. We should be back up to speed shortly."

I'eiBida stared numbly at the floor while he absorbed that through his fatigue. "How much longer?"

"My guess is we can start evacuations again in the morning, sir. We need another twenty shuttle loads, minimum, to have room for everyone."

207

"Can your crews manage?"

The pilot was wilted with fatigue, but was game enough. "We'll make do, sir."

It took I'eiBida a moment to grasp that through his own fatigue, then he nodded, dismissing him.

Giselle was sleeping on a bed pad dragged into the Intel circle and plopped on an unused desk. I'eiBida noticed she was watching him. "Is there trouble?" she asked.

"Ah...just routine. The off-load is taking time."

She sat up, then climbed stiffly off the desk. "Is everything stable otherwise?"

"Yes. There's been no sign of movement from the Peacekeepers, and radio intercepts indicate a continuing search at the spaceport."

She smiled. "*Muy bien*. Brian is keeping them at bay."

I'eiBida noted the warmth in her tone. "I'm sure he will be all right. He is very good at this sort of thing. He will make it back here in time."

She wilted slightly, and gave him a worried look. "We can only pray for his safety."

"Isn't that uncomfortable?" He gestured at the desk where she was sleeping. "You can use the transient quarters if you prefer. You don't need to be here all the time."

She stretched and rubbed her aching lower back. "I am needed here." She glanced at the thin bed pad. "And that is Paradise compared to some places I have slept lately." She stretched again, with a huge, unladylike yawn. "I have work to do."

§

It was late, perhaps midnight, although Mac's watch had stopped. A new line of Sumatra squalls was coming in, and the temperature was dropping steadily. Mac huddled behind a parked trailer while the latest MP patrol drove slowly by. He was bone weary, the sack of zero-G rations weighed him down, and the endless strain was getting to him. The patrol vanished in the distance, and he tried to relax. "Shit, this is gettin' old," he grumbled. Time to call it a day...but first he had to call in and see how much longer this circus would last.

He was back in the older part of the base where most of the buildings were either disused or dead storage; the trailer he hid behind had a flat tire. The building was one of the slab-fab tilt-ups built during his time in command here, and was now corroded and rust-streaked. He worked his way down the alley between it and the next building until he found a window. The panes were wire impregnated safety glass, but it crumbled under his steady effort with the pry bar, and he was finally able to pull it loose.

This was another dead storage facility, with shelves full of pipe fittings and racks with steel and copper tubing. The dust was thick, and the air had a close, musty smell. He hunted around in the dark until he found an office with a phone which worked, put the scrambler in place, and hit a number at random.

"This is *Adelbard*. Sorry I'm so late calling in. I've had a busy little day."

The response came back instantly. "*Ola*, Brian. *¿Cómo estás?*"

"Hi, Giselle. Managing, I guess." He was surprised by how good it felt to hear her voice. "How's it doing there?"

"The Peacekeepers have quieted down for now, and *los diablos*...the 'Tan Shirts', have gone to the spaceport. It looks like your deception is working."

Mac nodded to himself at that. "Good. It'd be a shame to burn a hole in a perfectly good container for nothing."

"You sound tired, Brian."

"I'm managing. It's hectic out here." He thought about it for a moment, then said, "The search is getting really serious. I'm not sure how much longer I can manage."

§

In the Intel circle, I'eiBida took the phone from her. "You've taken enough risks, Brian. Come back to the base."

There was a moment's hesitation. "How is the evacuation doing?" The voice on the line sounded weary.

"We're moving again," I'eiBida said, carefully. "It goes along as well as can be expected."

"But you still need more time, don't you?"

"Another day, at least. Perhaps two."

There was another pause. "Then I need to stay out here and keep them looking the wrong way. Alvarez will roll over you once his attack gets going. A hasty evacuation under fire could turn into a disaster."

I'eiBida gave Giselle a glum look. "As you think best, Brian. But please be careful. I have promises to fulfill."

§

Mac wondered about that before remembering I'eiBida had promised his future would be secure; as if anyone could uphold *that* promise, especially to him. "Well that's one I hope to collect on, but I won't hold you to it."

"Good luck, Brian."

"Thanks. I'll try to be more regular on my reports. This is *Adelbard*, signing off."

He pocketed the scrambler, hefted his sack, and headed wearily for the broken window. As he walked, he cursed himself for his uncompromising sense of duty. This wasn't the first time he saddled up and marched out to meet certain death against a superior enemy; not by a long shot. A man's luck only goes so far, and he brooded over whether his was about to run out. Lord knew he'd abused the odds often enough, and got away with it far more than half the human race did in his day.

He paused at the window, and looked around carefully. There was no sign of activity, and the rain was starting to come down in force. He hesitated, wondering if he could get away with spending the night here where he could at least be dry. No, the patrols were too thorough, and he couldn't risk being cornered. He sighed in exasperation, crawled through the broken window, and crouched in the alley as he searched for intruders. Nothing.

His odds weren't good. Most likely he would be cornered and gunned down, and having been shot more than once, he was not eager to repeat the experience. But his being out here was buying the Ic'nichi time to evacuate, to save a couple hundred-odd lives, including Giselle.

The rain picked up, reducing visibility to a few hundred meters. He had no real idea of where to go next, but he knew he couldn't stay here. He headed north down the alley.

He thought about Giselle, and had to admit he was fond of her, not that he would ever... He admired her spirit and the tremendous reserves of strength she must have to carry her through her recent ordeal. Hopefully I'eiBida would get her back to d'enchia and safety; if nothing else, he did that much good in this life.

He came to the end of the alley, and looked around. No sign of traffic. He scuttled across the road and down the next alley. In the distance ahead was a scrap pile of old lumber where he could burrow in for the night.

The scrap pile yielded several large pieces of plywood, an old door, and some heavy plastic tarps which he used to patch together a more or less drip-proof burrow while keeping a wary eye for intruding patrols. Finally, with one last look around, he snuggled down under one of the tarps and tried to relax with one of the zero-G rations. Tomorrow would be another day, and could take care of itself.

He lay there for a long time listening to the rain and feeling like the last human in the Universe, like he had on so many nights in the past. The rain picked up some more. His thoughts drifted back over the years to family, friends, old comrades, to the places and things of his life—like that scrappy seventeen year old kid in the Cleveland Naval Reserve Center—all vanished into the mists of time. He felt lost; soulless; the wakeful dead doomed never to rest; like on so many nights in the past.

It didn't do any good to worry about it. He had a job to do, to protect all those people back at the landing field, and he knew deep down inside that if given the chance, he would do it all over again. This was his destiny, his karma, and there was no sense pretending otherwise. It helped in a way. Death comes to everyone, and if he was going to lose this new life, at least he would make this death mean something. That's what duty is really about, when you think of it.

*****

"Chapter Fourteen"

Morning brought renewed tantrums from Colonel Alvarez, and Volmer hastened to share the joy with the 'Tan Shirt' rankers and anyone else who got in his way. "It is *obvious* that your efforts are not producing the desired results," he told the search leaders. "This slackness *will not* do, so the time has come to change tactics."

"So what do you *suggest?*" the fleet's chief of Security said. His tone, and the conspicuously absent 'sir' made his feelings plain.

Volmer gave him an icy glare. "What I *suggest* is that we quit playing cops-and-robbers, and get serious about your duties!" He turned to a large map of the base pinned to one wall of the security office. "Note how this is mostly open space where no one can hide." He gestured to the runway and hardstands which took up most of the area. "These in turn are surrounded by a ring of buildings where the fugitives are hiding. Your present methods of random patrols and hitting likely targets is not working, so we will try a new strategy. First we shall withdraw all the patrols..."

"Even the regular security patrols?" the base MP leader interrupted.

Volmer gave him a chill look. "Yes, *even* the regular patrols. That will lull them into a false sense of security. We will then line everyone up from the outer fence to the edge of the tarmac, and sweep around the base in both directions, turning over every pebble and blade of grass until we find them!"

The base MP commander exchanged dubious looks with his boss, the chief of Security. That one shook his head ever so slightly. The MP commander took his hint, and said nothing. The meeting broke up, and they went their respective ways.

§

"I don't like this, sir," Security said when he came to update the Admiral a short while later. "The 6th Office is up to something, and I don't buy their story about these fugitives."

"No one asked your opinion, mister." Then the Admiral reined in his increasingly worn temper. "We don't get an opinion with those swine."

212

Security let that outburst roll off, since he knew it wasn't directed at him. "There's something going on here, sir. This story of theirs: someone *actually* sprung a prisoner from the 6th Office compound? They've been chasing them all over the island for days without luck? And now they're on *this* base and we haven't seen any sign of them? It doesn't add up."

The Admiral considered him uncertainly. "There's the fire, the fence, the break-ins..."

"Hints and clues, sir. Someone's leaving a trail of bread crumbs for some unknown reason. They could just as easily be the work of their operatives."

The Admiral brooded on that. "Yeah...they could..."

Security held down his nervousness and pressed on; he was taking a chance bringing this wild tale to the Admiral, who had little patience with fools. "And the Ic'nichi are up to something, too, sir. They've been pushing their shuttle crews relentlessly day and night, even in this weather. They must be staggering from fatigue."

There was an uncomfortable silence broken only by the ticking of the antique clock on the Admiral's desk, and the soft patter of rain on the window as they pondered the implications. "What do you make of it?".

Security took a deep breath to steady himself; this story was getting wilder by the minute, and he urgently wanted to convince his superior. "I think the Ic'nichi figure Alvarez plans to move against them, and they are evacuating, sir. That outpost is untenable; they must be abandoning it rather than risk a confrontation."

"Those Peacekeeper units..."

"Yes, sir. They must know that much force will overwhelm them, so they're getting out while they still can."

"But why?" The Admiral was genuinely perplexed, and beginning to worry. "Why attack them? And why the security sweeps out there in the ruins, and in the harbor? And what are the 'Tan Shirts' up to here?"

"Unknown, sir. But seeing it's Alvarez, we need to take this seriously."

The Admiral greeted that with a contemptuous snort. "*That's* hardly news, mister." They considered each other uncertainly, then, "You think there's more to this than the Ic'nichi, don't you?"

Greatly daring, Security said, "I think it's a ruse, sir. Even Alvarez wouldn't risk starting a war with the Ic'nichi."

"So? What are they up to, then?"

"We're the only force on this planet which has resisted the Purity Movement thus far, sir."

The Admiral gave him a chilly look. "Say what's on your mind."

Time to go for broke. "Our Peacekeeper company is camped out there at the far end of the island, and the base is crawling with 'Tan Shirts'. Everyone has been sent home, and my remaining MPs aren't strong enough to resist a concerted attack, especially if they've already saturated the base. They could be using whatever's going on to move against us, sir."

"They wouldn't dare!"

"We control the nuclear arsenal, sir."

That statement electrified the air in the Admiral's office. The fleet's nuclear arsenal was a blunt instrument at best, and one neither of them could seriously consider using against earthly targets...but Alvarez...

Security pressed the point. "Space Fleet is the only voice still able to speak out against the Purity Movement, sir. They control Parliament, the courts, and the media, and have neutralized the Peacekeepers and the Navy; silencing us will go a long way to securing their power. And if Alvarez controls the strategic defenses..."

That made a grim sort of sense. They were both thinking the same thing: maybe Alvarez was working for the Purity Movement, or maybe he was plotting to set himself up as an independent power; nothing could be presumed with that crazy bastard. Either way it did not bode well for the Fleet, or for a future with the strategic arsenal in their hands.

"But can you be sure of this?" the Admiral asked at last.

"No, sir. But with Alvarez, can we take the chance?"

§

I'eiBida came back from a quick meal, and noticed T'thReptn, Giselle, and a couple of his technicians hard at work. T'thReptn came over to update him. "We should be done by dusk, sir. Her idea is ingenious, I must say. I never would have thought of it."

"Will it work?"

T'thReptn pondered that. "Hard to say, sir. I don't think it would fool one of us, but with Alvarez..." He paused and glanced at Giselle, who was listening to a recorded conversation with a set of earphones adapted for her. "We really need to put more emphasis on human psychology in Intelligence work, sir."

"Perhaps we should. These humans are slippery *riv'Agna* at best." I'eiBida sighed, and watched Giselle for some time. "I only hope she can get us past Space Fleet." He regarded T'thReptn soberly. "Otherwise your revelation will come to nothing."

§

Mac was working his way north again. He was weary, and the endless chill drizzle was getting on his nerves. "Damn-fool way to make a living," he grumbled as he paused to check out a cross street: nothing. For that matter he hadn't seen any sign of the search for some time, and wondered about that vaguely. He scuttled across and down the next alley. Maybe he should contact I'eiBida to see how they were doing. Lord knew he couldn't keep this up much longer, and now that he thought about it, he wasn't sure how to get back to the landing field. The wind came up, sending a shiver through him. Poor food, lack of sleep, and the constant pressure were getting to him. Yes, he should check in to see how they were doing. Maybe it was time for him to start looking for an escape route. Things were bollixed enough around here that he could probably leave now, and Alvarez would spend *at least* another day chasing his own tail...

He turned a corner without thinking...and ducked back hastily. A squad of 'Tan Shirts' were standing not twenty meters away talking among themselves. As Mac ducked, they broke up, and one of them headed his way. The 'Tan Shirts' were thugs, untrained in police methods and lacking a policeman's schooled observation habits: the man missed sight of him completely. Mac looked around frantically, but there was no time to reach cover.

215

The 'Tan Shirt' came around the corner, walked straight into a brutal right to the jaw, and sagged against the wall, spitting blood and fighting to hold onto consciousness. Mac followed up fast with a left jab to his kidney, which curled him over, then a savage clout behind his ear which laid him out cold. There was a shout, and footsteps in the distance, so he took off running. A bullet whizzed past his ear as he turned the next corner, so he came up short, fished the automatic pistol out of his pocket, and emptied the clip blindly around the corner to force them to ground. He didn't wait to see if he hit anything; he ran for all he was worth.

§

"We almost had him, Colonel," Volmer assured Alvarez when he called for the umpteenth time. "He's a slippery weasel, but our methods are getting results."

"The only *result* which matters is Krauss and the girl in chains at my feet!"

"I'm pushing our people hard, sir..."

"*Not good enough!*" Alvarez roared. "Push them harder!"

"Yes, sir!" Volmer was worried by the Colonel's state of mind.

"How do I impress on you how critical this is? Borneo is a fitting answer to *any* failure. You do *not* wish to fail in this matter, Volmer!"

"I'm on it, Colonel!"

"Do *not* fail me, Volmer! My patience is at an end!"

Volmer hung up and headed back to the search line, cursing under his breath and genuinely afraid for his life. Borneo was all to near over the horizon for all of them, and he *sincerely* didn't want to have his wrath focussed his way.

§

"You were warned that further failure is not tolerable," he told the 'Tan Shirt' squad a few minutes later. They were in a rough line against the wall of a warehouse with Volmer's four bodyguards covering them. "And still you do not take your duties *seriously*."

"We almost had him, sir..." the squad leader protested.

"No more excuses! You are a sorry excuse for a 'Tan Shirt'! Your whole squad are sorry excuses, which shows what a poor job you've done in motivating and disciplining them!"

216

"Sir..."

"ENOUGH!"

The man lapsed into nervous silence; leaving no sound but the gentle patter of the rain.

Volmer stood in front of them for a long moment, uncertain what to do next, but painfully aware that he needed to do *something*, fast. Even with Krauss out of the picture, he was vulnerable. There was just one loyalty—to Alvarez—and that loyalty was strictly one way. Everyone in the 6th Office, including him, existed at the Colonel's pleasure, and failure was *never* an option. Fear—of the camps, of Borneo, of the antiseptic, soundproofed cells in the compound basement—undermined Volmer's common sense...while his urgent need for a scapegoat...stoked his sadistic instinct...pushing him closer...and closer...to a fateful decision...

"Since we still need you, pathetic excuses though you are, you will *not* all be sent to the camps," he announced. There was a stir in the squad; a mixture of relief and worry over what alternative he had in mind. "Instead, *two of you* will be chosen for *immediate* execution as an example to the rest." There was renewed tension as the 'Tan Shirts' realized they weren't out of danger yet.

"This is the standard for now on." Volmer swaggered down the squad line, slapping his riding crop on one chubby thigh for emphasis. "*Each time* a squad fails in their duty, they will execute two of their own until *discipline* is restored..." He turned to face the ranks with a sadistic gleam in his eyes. "...or until the state of their *discipline* is no longer relevant. Starting right now."

The silence which followed was painful. The only sound was the soft patter of the rain, and the *SLAP, SLAP* of his riding crop as he strolled down the line, looking each one over carefully. Their tense, neutral expressions inflamed his cruel ego. They feared him! His breath quickened, and a shiver ran down his spine as they tensed before him, and sagged ever so slightly as he passed. He may be a toady for a dangerous psychopath, but by God, he was Colonel Alvarez's right hand man; the Voice of Alvarez; Agent of His will. Krauss was out of the picture: that gave him *power*...power over them...over their lives...

"You..." He paused and tapped one man at random with his swagger stick. That one emitted a low groan and sagged in a shivering heap as his squad mates watched in dismay.

This was more like it! He turned his back on the condemned man and strutted down the line, daring each of them in turn to protest. His mind burned with feverish righteousness, the cadence of his swagger stick became erratic as his hands trembled. They were *afraid* of him! They were wire tense, sweating; unable to meet his gaze, afraid of his four enforcers, afraid to resist, afraid to run, paralyzed like mice. They *needed* discipline, and he would *teach* them discipline! They would not fail the Colonel again, and he, Volmer, would be there to deliver Krauss and the girl to the fate they so *richly* deserved...

He stopped in front of one surly ranker, and looked him over with sadistic glee; high on the tension, the fear... But something was off, jarring his evil mood: the man met his gaze with mute defiance and contempt. "...and you," he said, slapping the man's chest with his stick.

That one uttered a venomous curse, drew his automatic, and shot Volmer, setting off a wild free-for-all. When the smoke cleared, Volmer was down with a bullet in his side, two of his elite security goons were dead and a third gravely wounded, and the 'Tan Shirt' squad was wiped out.

§

Mac was about a klick away at the moment, and hesitated to listen to what sounded like a major fire fight somewhere to the south. "Damn," he muttered when the firing ended abruptly. He went to ground behind a dumpster as an MP vehicle screamed past with its lights blazing, then looked around nervously, senses hyperalert, trying to determine what happened.

There was nothing: no sign of life. All he could hear was the gentle patter of the rain...another siren started up in the distance. Whatever happened, it was spreading rapidly. And whatever happened, it likely involved the 'Tan Shirts'...fighting the Fleet MPs? Civilians? Each other? There was no way to know except by going to look, which was the *last* thing he would consider doing. Not that it mattered. What *did* matter was that things were rapidly descending into chaos. One thing he could be sure of was some major shit would come down over this, and soon. Even if open combat didn't break out, everyone would be on a hair-trigger edge, and the search would be more relentless than ever. His chances, never that great, were dwindling fast.

"Time to get the hell out-a Dodge, boy," he muttered.

§

"Damn you, mister! This is unacceptable!" The Admiral was furious at the body count, and didn't care who knew it. "I want your people either disarmed or off my base, or both, now!"

"This is a state security matter," Alvarez told him, coldly. "You will accept what I tell you to accept, we will go where we please, and we shall be armed as *I* choose!" He arrived shortly after the shooting incident to take personal charge of the search, and he came backed up by half the security contingent from the 6th Office compound.

"Like hell! I won't have your trigger-happy thugs shooting up my base!" If Alvarez could be intimidating, the Admiral was from the Lone Star Republic, and could bark with the big dogs.

"This is your base *only* for now, and *only* on sufferance! We are dealing with an urgent security matter, and I *expect* and *will have* your complete cooperation!"

"You'll get what I give you!" the Admiral roared. He shook his fist in Alvarez's face. "I'm warning you, mister! If there's any more of your bullshit, you'll answer for it!"

Alvarez gave that a cool sneer. "*You* are warning *me? I* do not give warning, as you will discover if you interfere with the 6th Office any further!" He walked out without a backward glance, leaving the Admiral to fume.

"Orders, sir?" Security asked.

"Don't tempt me." The Admiral sank into his chair, and gave Security a stern look. "We're playing our own game from now on. 'Cooperate' with them any way you can to slow them down, and push your own search for these so-called fugitives. If you find them, keep it secret and sweat them for answers."

"Yes, sir!"

§

For his part, Colonel Alvarez was in such a rage that his two goons had to hurry to keep up as he stormed out of the Admin building. He finally came to a halt at his limousine standing at the curb, and struggled to contain the fury he would never let the Admiral and his lackeys see. He stood for a long time while his two goons waited impassively, his mind boiling as the world seemed to close in around him, his enemies smothering him.

It was clear they were plotting against him. How else could the girl have escaped? Krauss hadn't acted alone, that was certain. At a minimum there were Puker agents, Sausages all, no doubt; certainly supported by the Lizards, and it seemed by the Space Fleet as well. So many threats, so many shadows. He fought the urge to lash out at random: that would be playing their game. No, he must bide his time, ferret them out one by one until the entire plot was uncovered. Only *then* could he act! Until then he was vulnerable...alone...

And it wasn't bad enough that Krauss turned on him; now that ham-fisted idiot Volmer stirred up a *mutiny*, and got himself shot. He was in the base hospital under heavy guard, and according to the Fleet doctors, he would be out of commission for a month or more *just* when he was needed the most!

The rain was dwindling to a light sprinkle. The breeze was warmer, and the heavy cloud cover was thinning. Alvarez inhaled the fresh breeze deeply, and reveled in the cool raindrops on his face as he fought down the last of his rage. His fury subsided, replaced with a cold, calculating anger which bode ill for anyone who crossed his path. *Damn* the Admiral; his time would come. *Damn* those mutinous traitors, and Krauss, and the girl, and the Lizards, and most especially that idiot Volmer. Yes, especially Volmer, who should have handled those 'Tan Shirts' with more finesse. He would crush them! He would crush them all! The weaklings, the Pukers, the Fleet, the Lizards... It all went to prove that old truism that if he wanted *anything* done right, he would have to do it himself. He, Alvarez, would focus on the search for now, and on uncovering the rest of this conspiracy. He would decide later whether Volmer recovered from his wounds.

§

Mac ducked into an alley just as an MP vehicle came around the next corner. Cursing the ill luck, he threw himself flat in the hope he wouldn't be silhouetted against the background light, but the vehicle slowed as it passed, and there was the squeal of brakes as it moved out of view.

Not good! He scrambled to his feet and down the alley, skirting a pile of assorted trash and empty boxes. There was no way out. The rest of the alley was empty; if he ran, they'd spot him. He dove into the narrow gap between the wall and two empty steel drums just as the MPs entered the alley.

"Are you sure?" one asked after a long moment.

"I thought I saw movement."

Mac peered cautiously through a narrow gap partly covered by an empty cardboard box. The two MPs—one Oriental, the other a Hindu—stood with weapons ready, searching the gloom.

The Hindu glanced nervously at his partner. "Cover me."

He started forward, weapon leveled, searching the rubbish pile. Mac eased further into the narrow crevice, and carefully tugged another piece of cardboard around to cover his feet, trying not to make a sound. The MP passed him, and Mac froze as he stopped just beyond the two drums. It took all his strength to keep absolutely still. His back ached in his cramped position, and a piece of gravel was digging into his side. A spasm set his leg twitching: he tensed all over trying to keep his leg from shifting the drum it rested against. The MP searched the alley, head turning back and forth, seemingly for ever. All he had to do was look down, and Mac was a goner.

"See anything?" the Oriental asked.

"No, nothing." The Hindu looked around again. "I must be losing it." He turned and headed back to their vehicle. "We must move on. We don't want those *vidvesh* 'Tan Shirts' to score."

"*Hai*. Those *aburamushi* make me want to bathe."

The first gave that a sour laugh. "They are nothing compared to the smell the Admiral will make if they find those two first."

"*Hai*, the *gaijin*. Where could they be?"

"They are slippery *doaglaas*, that's for sure," the other grumbled. "We better get moving."

For a moment, Mac was tempted to surrender to them. They were clearly competing with the 6th Office to catch him, no doubt wondering what all the fuss was about. Perhaps if he explained the situation to their Admiral, and told him what he'd learned of Alvarez's plans, they might help him. They had no love for the 'Tan Shirts', that was plain. But then cold realism quashed the thought: they would never believe his wild story about being the reincarnated Admiral MacKenna in the body of Alvarez's top operative—hell, he found it hard to swallow himself—and even if they did, they wouldn't go against the Alliance and the Purity Movement.

'...don't count on them for help...' I'eiBida told him back during their briefings. '...few people on earth dare oppose the 6th Office these days...'

"Shit," he muttered as he watched the MPs return to their vehicle and drive away. He'd have to do this one himself.

§

It was a couple hours after the shooting before the MP patrols located two of their missing vehicles parked in front of an office block being used by the 'Tan Shirts' as their temporary command center. The four MPs from those vehicles were inside, disarmed and surrounded by 'Tan Shirts'. The MPs tried to retrieve their fellows, but were rebuffed by the squad leader in charge. Since the 'Tan Shirts' were there in force and clearly determined to hang on to the four, the MPs retreated, and came back later with their squad leader.

That one fared no better, and almost came to blows with the 'Tan Shirt' leader before being forced to retreat in turn. Next up was the commander of the base MP contingent, who came on like an angry bull dog. "What the hell are they doing here?" he demanded.

"Zey are being held for questioning ass material witnesses." The squad leader's tone made it clear that a mere Fleet Military Police commander dare not question his actions.

"Like hell, sir!" one of them objected. "We already gave our statements!"

"Silence!" the 'Tan Shirt' yelled.

222

"Besides, we hardly got there when they arrested us!"

"ENOUGH!" The 'Tan Shirt' cuffed the MP, almost setting off a riot. "You vill remain silent!"

"You touch him again, and I will *kill* you," the MP commander growled. The four MPs knew their boss's Gallic temper and his traditional contempt for all Teutons. He meant it, sincerely. They tensed for a confrontation which could end in bloodshed.

The 'Tan Shirt' squad leader stood right up to him. "You vill do nothing! This iss a security matter, und zese men are to be questioned. They vill leave *if und ven* vee say, not before!"

It was clear to the commander that this Teuton pig was simply throwing his weight around for no good reason except that this was how 'Tan Shirts' usually behaved. "This is *mearde!* You have no reason and *no authority* to hold my men!"

The 'Tan Shirt' gave him an icy look. "Reason or not, vee haff zee *authority* to hold who *ever* vee please, und vee do not answer to zee likes of *you!*" He drew his sidearm, and leveled it in the commander's face. "Now *get out* vile you still can!"

Boss MP didn't like it, but he was hopelessly outnumbered, so he withdrew.

"Zat showed zose Dominions dogs who iss in charge here," the squad leader announced loudly. His men grinned at the commander's discomfiture while the four MPs exchanged nervous looks. This wasn't over.

It wasn't. He returned a few minutes later with twenty of his men armed to the teeth. The 'Tan Shirt' leader looked at them in alarm as they burst in and drew down on his squad. "Vat do you think you are doing?"

"WE will question our people," the commander growled. "And *we* decide who has what authority around here! You four," he gestured peremptorily to his men. "Out." They grabbed their jackets and equipment belts, and scuttled for the door.

§

"Things are deteriorating fast, sir," Security complained to the Admiral a short time later. "Those bastards are running rough-shod over everyone in their path. There have been a couple more incidents, and the tension is thick out there."

"I'll bet that swine Alvarez is having a grand old time," the Admiral grumbled. "Those 'Tan Shirts' make me itch. I want to step on them *so* bad, but then I'd have to clean my boots."

"And there's even more of them now, sir. Practically every 'Tan Shirt' on the island is out there."

The Admiral considered him glumly. "What about that shooting? Have you learned who they were fighting?"

"They have the scene sealed up air tight, sir, but from what my first responders tell me, it looks like they did it to themselves."

"A *mutiny* in the 'Tan Shirts'?"

"Is it any wonder with that pack of thugs, sir?"

The Admiral sighed. "Not really. Good riddance." He studied his Security chief for a bit. "I don't suppose they'll be more careful in the future?"

"I doubt it, sir. If anything, they're getting worse. My MP commander reported that they tried to hold the four first responders, for *questioning*, so they said, and he had to go in there in force to spring them."

"What the *hell* did..."

The Admiral was interrupted when Colonel Alvarez burst in, followed by the protesting orderly. Alvarez was in such a cold fury that he seemed to radiate thunder and lightning. "Your Military Police commander threatened one of my squad leaders, and helped four detainees escape!"

That was all the Admiral needed; he sprang to his feet, leaned over his desk, and gave Alvarez both barrels. "You're damned *right* he did! And he has orders direct from me to do it again if you pull another stunt like that!"

Alvarez glared at him while Security scuttled out of the line of fire. "You clearly *do not* appreciate the seriousness of this, or how broad my authorities are, or how *little* you have to say in the matter!"

"I *appreciate* that your people are a bunch of dangerous *yahoos* who can't resist shooting at everything in sight! *Thankfully* it was just your people who were killed, and good riddance to them! But I WILL NOT RISK the lives of the people on this base because of your foul-ups!"

"That man is to be arrested for treason!"

"Like hell! You try it, and you'll have a war on your hands! Now GET OUT!"

Alvarez fumed, but withdrew.

"Damn." The Admiral was not happy as he sagged into his chair. "They're getting uppity."

"Things are coming to a head, sir. Those arrests could only be the beginning. If they are planning a takeover, it'll come soon."

"Yeah. And we're all on his list anyway." The Admiral brooded for a bit, then turned to his Security chief. "Enough of this bullshit. Whatever Alvarez is up to, I doubt he has Geneva's blessing." He shook his finger in Security's face. "You get over to the Peacekeeper armory and secure any spare gear you can find. Alert your reserves, pull your people out of the guard towers, and get your emergency procedures on line—*quietly!* And detail a hit squad for Alvarez. If he makes a move, we'll settle with him now, and argue it out with Geneva later."

Security gave him a crisp salute, clearly relieved to be taking action at last. "Yes, sir!"

§

Mac spent the last couple hours holed up in a quiet spot to ponder his options, which weren't comforting. As he feared, whatever that gunfight was about, it put everyone on edge. There were more 'Tan Shirts' than ever, and the base MPs were increasingly active, clearly wanting to catch him before Alvarez could. On top of that the base was deserted and locked down tight so he stood out like a sore thumb wherever he went. It didn't take a genius to see that his welcome was worn out, and he needed to get while he still could.

Assuming he still could: he not only had to get out of the spaceport, but clear across the island to the Ic'nichi landing field, some fifty klicks away. Going in another truck was out, since there was no traffic exiting the base. Same for going by sea: there were no small boats to be had, and a check of the coast showed several light naval units on blockade. The few aircraft on the flight line were under heavy guard, which didn't matter since he couldn't fly anyway.

No, his options were precious few. About the only thing he could think of was to steal a car, crash the main gate, and hope he could lose any pursuers in the ruins west of the 6th Office. It was a lousy deal, but he learned a lifetime ago that dithering and wishing something better would turn up was a bad move.

But even stealing a car would be a neat trick, since there were none to be had, what with the base locked down. At one point, he considered stealing one of the large utility vehicles he saw earlier, but such a lumbering beast could never outrun the pursuit. That brought up the notion of finding some truly hulking monster and using it to crush all the MP vehicles before taking off, but he dismissed that with a sneer at his own misplaced machismo. "You're too old to play Dukes Of Hazard, boy," he grumbled.

Still, he needed to do *something*, so he prowled the back alleys looking for any target of opportunity. It was nerve wracking, since the patrols were everywhere, but there was nothing for it. Moreover, he was exhausted after several days on the run; always cold, always wet, sleeping in snatches, eating what little he could find. At least the rain was letting up. He'd been through this too many times in his former life; troops would usually be pulled back for a break by now.

His wandering brought him out of an alley, and he spotted activity down the road. Several military vehicles were parked in front of an office block, and there were lights from inside. He went to ground and studied the situation. The fact that it was open despite the lockdown suggested it was important, which meant people in the area. There was no one in sight, although he caught the faint ring of a telephone. What really mattered, what distracted him in his weary state, was the half dozen vehicles parked in front. It was risky, but they were his ticket off base, back to the Ic'nichi landing field and safety. The mixture of desperation, exhaustion, and having no other good choices overrode his usual survival instinct. Sometimes you just have to hope for the best.

Another careful look all around: no one in sight. He crossed the street, and worked his way down the row of offices, trying to look natural while mentally tracking places he could duck into if someone suddenly appeared. The street was quiet. His heart was pounding from the tension. Hopefully he could find a vehicle with the keys left in the ignition...

He reached the first vehicle: no luck. He checked the second... The third...

A nearby door opened, and a 'Tan Shirt' came out. He was busy studying a piece of paper, and didn't notice Mac at first. Then he looked up and froze in surprise. "You!" he muttered, then fell back and reached for his sidearm. Mac didn't wait as he retreated to the door: he took off running, cursing under his breath as the 'Tan Shirt' yelled, "It's him! It's Krauss! He's out here!"

Of all the rotten luck! He'd stumbled right into the 'Tan Shirt' command center! He cut across the road, running blindly as the alarm spread behind him. There was a shot, and a bullet whizzed past his head. "Hold your fire!" someone yelled as he ducked back into the alley he came from.

He came out the far end, and looked around frantically. The main gate was a couple hundred meters away; there was nothing to be gained by going that way, but Mac was beyond caring. The lure was irresistible. There was a shout behind him, so he took off running as several 'Tan Shirts' came charging out of the alley. He was gasping, his heart pounding. The adrenalin rush took him, and time slowed as he seemed to float over the pavement. The gate was close now, the empty road beyond beckoning as the mob fell back behind him. There were two more 'Tan Shirts' on duty at the gate who watched curiously as he approached, then moved out to intercept him. He drew on every bit of his strength for another burst of speed. His only chance would be to plow through them without stopping...

A utility vehicle pulled in front of him and ground to a halt, cutting him off from the gate. Three 'Tan Shirts' piled out, and were joined by the two on the gate in hot pursuit as he turned and ran along the fence. Up ahead he spotted activity: the ready garage serving the main gate. The big doors were open. He cut right sharply as one of the 'Tan Shirts' made a flying tackle, just missing him. His last hope now was the chance of a vehicle sitting there ready to go. He ran faster, his lungs burning as the pursuit pounded after him.

Nothing! There were two vehicles in the garage, but one had its hood open, and the other was up on a jack for a tire change. He faltered...someone grabbed his shirt...he twisted loose, cut left, and bolted for the office door. Even as he ran, he knew it was over. There was no back way out of the building, and even if there was, they would run him down in minutes. Instinct took hold: he had to get to a phone and warn I'eiBida before they nailed him.

He hit the door and vaulted the parts counter in one swift move, grabbed a telephone sitting on the back counter, slapped the vocoder on it, and hit 'Zero'. "This is Adelbard! They're on to me! I'm compromised!"

"Run, Brian!" a faint voice came to him before the vocoder emitted a whiff of acrid smoke. The 'Tan Shirts' came crashing through the door, so he dropped the phone and ran down the hall and into the shop with them hot on his heels.

The shop was a jungle of vehicles, tool boxes, and snaking air hoses, made all the more treacherous by the oily concrete. Someone grabbed him from behind as he was held up by the clutter. He managed to wrestle free, barely avoided stumbling into the mechanic's pit, cut between two cars, and made a break for the street...

...a 'Tan Shirt' appeared in the open doorway ahead. Mac doubled back, vaulted over the car's hood, and ran along the back wall. The end came quickly, trapped in the far corner with his escape blocked by a tire changing machine. He searched for any escape route, no matter how narrow: there was nothing. He turned to attack; to break out if possible, force them to kill him if need be; but before he could spring, a gas grenade landed at his feet and exploded. He gasped one quick breath and shut his eyes tightly, then something hit him from behind, and he faded out.

*****

"Chapter Fifteen"

"Our radio intercepts confirm it, sir," T'thReptn told an increasingly anxious I'eiBida when the met in the Intel circle a short while later. "The 'Tan Shirt' patrols caught the human, and are still searching the spaceport. They must be looking for her."

"What about the Peacekeepers?" I'eiBida was in a foul mood, which made all of them nervous. "What are they doing?"

"They're holding position for now, sir."

"Which means we are still in danger," Giselle said in a brittle hush.

"They could simply be packing up their gear and waiting for transport," B'monTrea suggested.

"Always presume the worst when dealing with humans, First." She was on edge worrying about Brian, as they all were. "Especially when dealing with the likes of Alvarez!"

"Even if they have him, his strategy is still sound," T'thReptn said. "They will assume he and you were trying to escape by air, and that you are somewhere in the spaceport."

"They'll come as soon as Alvarez sorts things out. It won't take him long to realize I'm here, if he hasn't decided that already." She gave B'monTrea a bleak look. "And something you need to learn fast is that we humans aren't very good at turning off armies once they get started."

"And they are all too prone to start shooting anyway," I'eiBida added. "What do you recommend, Brian?" he asked Giselle.

She gave him a stern look; her inner persona brought to the fore by the tension of the moment. "Push the evacuation, hard. We're on the clock, and it's winding down fast. My guess is we need to evacuate tonight. And...and..." she seemed to shrink within herself as the forceful persona within receded. "He says...to keep an eye on those 'Tan Shirt' units: their movements will telegraph Alvarez's intentions."

There was an uncomfortable silence, then C'broVbron said, "We'll need at least a couple more days to complete unloading the transport."

"Time is up," she said. "Alvarez will be here by morning."

"We have no more options," I'eiBida said. "Staff analysis: can we evacuate tonight?"

"If we maintain our present shuttle schedule, we should be about eighty percent unloaded by dawn, sir," T'thReptn said. "It will be a tight squeeze, but we can do it."

"Right. What about consumables?"

"We've sent up as much water as we have containers for. It's not a lot, but it'll do. We have no reserves of oxygen here, but I checked with the ship's Eldest, and he said they have enough to get to *b'vem'n'uii* Great Nest colony, where we can pick up more. Food is mostly a matter of trading storage space for warm bodies. We'll have to ration, but we should have enough."

"Good. Everyone keep at it. Twist any tails you need to, and above all, be discreet!"

The meeting broke up as they drifted away to their respective duties until only I'eiBida, T'thReptn, and Giselle were left. "Third, I want you to push your assets to the limit to locate Brian," I'eiBida said. "Use every resource you have!"

"Sir?"

"I want to know where Brian is! Where did they take him? It may still be possible to rescue him." He cut off T'thReptn's protest. "Find him!" he snapped as he stalked out.

§

Giselle caught up with him in the hall. "Going after him could jeopardize everyone," she protested.

I'eiBida turned on her. "I owe him. We owe him. I won't leave him in Alvarez's clutches if there is any hope of saving him." She started to protest. "You would do the same; I know it as surely as I know Brian MacKenna!"

She faltered, then nodded. "You are right. I owe him, too."

I'eiBida wondered which of their composite personas said that, then decided it didn't matter. "We'll get him out if there is any possible way to do it." He considered her for a moment, then, "Your advice will be a big help."

She gave him an uncertain look. "I will do what I can."

"That's all any of us can do."

§

Coming to was not pleasant. Mac ached all over, especially his head, and his vision was blurry. It took him a moment to realize he was in one of the laboratory holding cells, kneeling on the floor with his wrists and ankles chained together, forcing him into a painful bent-backward position.

"Ah, Mister Krauss!" Colonel Alvarez stood in the open cell door with his two goons leaning against the far wall behind him, watching him hungrily. "It is good to see you once again. I trust you are well this evening?"

It took Mac a moment to pull his thoughts together. He looked around the cell to size up the situation, which was hopeless. In a way it was a relief, since his fate was settled. Then fear welled up in him, and he clamped down on it hard, determined not to give Alvarez the satisfaction of seeing him waver. He started to speak, hesitated, and slid into his Krauss persona since there was no telling what Alvarez might do if he learned who he was really dealing with. "It has been one of zose days, und you?"

Alvarez sighed. "I am most unhappy with a recent incident right here in the laboratory. To think our prime test subject could be spirited away by someone who brought explosives into this building! I have expressed my concern to our chief of security over this laxness, and he agreed such a failure is *most* regrettable." No doubt that chief of security was contemplating his failures somewhere in the Antarctic, if he was still alive.

"*Ja.*" Mac tried to show a bold front, not all together successfully. "I haff to tell you I am not impressed by your security, seeing ass this iss zee *security* agency."

"An embarrassment, true. One we will not suffer again." Mac caught a flicker of insane rage in Alvarez's eyes; it scared him. "Tragically, the only four witnesses were all killed. They were good men; I hated to lose them."

"Zat iss zee unfortunate part of zese things, I guess."

Alvarez studied him closely as his cold rage boiled closer to the surface. "True. Thankfully, the answer to this riddle did not die with them. It seems the perpetrator was caught on the security cameras."

Mac was silent, since there was nothing more to say.

231

"We must have a *long* discussion about this matter." The Colonel's rage was beginning to surface; his eyes blazed, and by now he was trembling and breathing hard. The two goons behind him were starting to heat up too. This was going to be ugly. "I wish to know why you turned on your kind, *Herr* Krauss, and where you have hidden the test subject."

"Sorry," Mac said in a final show of bravado. It was over: all that mattered now was to hold out for as long as possible to give I'eiBida and his people time. "Can't help you."

Alvarez gave him a cold smile. "Oh, I am sure you can." The smile vanished, and he gestured the two goons forward. "Let us begin, shall we?"

§

Security arrived at the Admiral's office at about that time with a hurry-up report on the arrest. "We think we know who they captured, sir. He matches the description of one Reinhardt Krauss, one of Alvarez's top operatives." He handed Krauss's security dossier to the Admiral, who studied it with distaste.

"Perhaps he's one of their fugitives after all?"

"Unlikely, sir. He's a top 6th Office fanatic, Alvarez's right hand man, especially with Volmer out of the picture."

"So you still don't buy their story?"

"No, sir. And there are too many other things going on, the Ic'nichi evacuation and all. I don't like the smell of it."

"That goy was a plant, you think?"

"Yes, sir."

"They're still sweeping the base, aren't they?"

"Yes, sir."

"Then whatever they're up to, they aren't finished yet."

"No, sir."

The Admiral glanced at the dossier, then handed it back with a sigh. "God, what a mess. All right, put your people on alert, *quietly*. Make sure they're well armed, and scrape up some sort of mobile reserve. We need to be able to respond NINS to any move they make."

"Yes, sir."

§

Late that evening, the Peacekeeper units started stirring, which brought a higher alert in the Ic'nichi landing field, and provoked another council of war in the Intel circle.

"Could Brian have broken already?" I'eibida asked Giselle. "Or are they going to attack regardless?"

She paused for a long moment, and brooded on that with a far away look as if she was listening to a voice only she could hear. "Unknown. He is not Superman...despite his war experience, he is as frail as any of us." She shuddered, and clutched her shoulders in a defensive posture. "He may have broken by now...or he may draw on his need to buy us as much time as possible. It is hard to say how much longer he will last."

"It would depend on how thoroughly they question him, wouldn't it?" Arbiter C'broVbron asked.

"They...are...good," she whimpered. There were tears, and she clutched herself tighter. "They are *maldita buena*...vicious animals. He will break sooner or later."

I'eiBida took a deep breath to steady himself. "Staff assessment?" he demanded of the people around him. "Do we stage a hasty evacuation now, or continue as planned?"

They looked at each other uncertainly. "We know the Peacekeepers' supply situation still isn't the best, and the 'Tan Shirts' are still in the spaceport, so I suspect they won't move before dawn at the earliest," T'thReptn said.

"We should continue the evacuation as planned, sir," B'monTrea said.

I'eiBida brooded for a bit. "Right," he said at last. He turned to Arbiter C'broVbron. "What progress on that?"

"One shuttle is being unloaded, and the other should start down soon. I'm worried about the shuttle crews: they've been going nonstop for over a day now. They need rest."

"They'll just have to hang on. Tank 'em up on *V'liz* and power bars. We have to go tonight before Brian breaks under interrogation, or Alvarez figures out he was deceived."

C'broVbron nodded uncomfortably. "The new arrivals have returned to the ship, and twenty of ours have left as well. At this rate, we could have the last out of here by dawn."

233

"And your deception?"

"My people are putting up a busy front, especially at the warehouses."

"My defenders are in the warehouses too, in ordinary, sir," D'remNek added. "Everyone is standing continuous watch until this is over."

"And communications security has been tightened, sir," T'thReptn said. "My people are maintaining a full security watch; if they start something, we'll have at least an hour's warning."

I'eiBida nodded thoughtfully. "Good. Keep the deceptions up even if you have to delay departures until after dark, but target the evacuation of the rear guard for dawn." That was duty attended to. "Now what about Brian? Any word on him?"

They exchanged dubious looks again. "Nothing, sir," T'thReptn said at last. "But it seems likely they would take him back to the 6th Office for interrogation."

"Probably." I'eiBida pondered the map as he went over the situation in his mind. The hard truth was difficult to swallow, but he couldn't deny it. "Which means he is out of our reach."

"We still have to neutralize the stolen recording," Giselle said. "We need to attack the 6th Office compound to make sure it is destroyed."

They all stared at her in confusion. "My force isn't strong enough to take the building," S'deMnveb objected with an agitated wave at the 6th Office compound on the map.

"Not that building. That one." She tapped the image of the smaller laboratory. "They will have everything in their secret laboratory. Eliminate it, and you will get their copy of the recording, too."

I'eiBida considered her curiously, wondering which of them was speaking. "How can you be sure of that?"

Giselle gave him an even look, although her fear was plain in her eyes. "Alvarez is setting himself up as *un empiror* within the 6th Office. The mind transfer process is his secret weapon: *mantendrá segura*...he will keep it safe where his competition cannot interfere. That is the most heavily guarded spot in the complex; that is where the recording is."

234

"It makes sense."   I'eiBida examined the building plan doubtfully.

"And this is our last chance to stop this before war breaks out. We have to destroy that *taller del Diablo* before this gets any worse."

"She's right," C'broVbron said.

S'deMnveb pondered the photo at length, his ears twitching doubtfully.   "If we each carried explosives..."   He confronted Giselle.   "But how we get in...sir?   Access is through main building; they must have firepower to stop us."

"That place is sure to be an armed camp," she said, unsteadily. "But while they have the means for a battle...they are not ready for it...especially late at night...   At best, they will need a minute or two to react.   He said...if you *sorpresa les*...hit them by surprise and move fast, you can get into the laboratory before they can bring their forces to bear. You can then hold them off long enough to set the charges and escape."

"Likely true, but how do we get in to start with?"

"Commandeer a truck, and use it to crash through the front entrance."   Giselle reached for the building's floor plan, and pointed out the location of the entry way and the reception guard room.   "That will take out the front security, and it is a quick jog down the hall to the tunnel entrance."

S'deMnveb grunted in surprise.   "Might work at that," he muttered.   "But who will drive it, sir?   We can't drive human vehicles."

She hesitated for a long moment. "I will, I guess."

B'monTrea pondered her doubtfully. "Are you able to do that? This calls for highly trained elite forces; it will be dangerous, and any breakdown in the plan could be disastrous."

"I..." She clutched herself nervously. "...I am all you have...I must do it."

"Giselle," I'eiBida said. "You were never meant for something like this. Even with the implant's help..."

She turned to him with tears rolling down her cheeks. "This is our last chance to stop this war!"   She was on the verge of hysterics. "I must do it! I must!"

There was a long tense silence as those gathered around the map table absorbed that. "How do we get out again?" S'deMnveb asked at last. "There are no exterior doors, and the raiders won't be going back the way they came."

She was trembling now. "He said...blow a hole in the wall. Use a second charge to blow open the fence."

"Good." S'deMnveb gave her an uneasy look. Her composite persona was unnerving to all of them. "But if we use the truck to crash the front entrance, how do we get back? Our raiders need to return to the landing field and evacuate on the shuttle before the humans can react. Jogging back here will take far too long."

"And the returning party will have to get through the Peacekeeper unit parked on the road," T'thReptn added. "The raiders' only hope is to crash through in another vehicle."

I'eiBida nodded. "We need a second truck."

"How do we get it to the attack site, sir?"

"We will have to tow it. See if the humans have any towing gear here."

"If we commandeer their trucks, we will have to secure all the human drivers," B'monTrea said. "We can't risk them raising the alarm."

"We'll need to secure the gate too, sir," S'deMnveb said. "We can't have them wondering why no more traffic is coming out."

"Yes." B'monTrea turned to him. "We'll need your people to help with that."

There was a tense silence as they pondered the plan. "What is our timing, sir?" S'deMnveb asked at last.

"We go tonight." I'eiBida pondered the building plan, then turned and considered the overall map of the island. As doubtful as he was about their plan, and Giselle's part in it, and the probable consequences, there was no other way to stop the Alliance—and save Brian. "Figure on the raiding party leaving after dark," he said at last, his ears sagged in near despair. "We'll hit them at midnight, and be back here before dawn."

"*Maldito,*" she mumbled, and sagged against the wall clutching herself in dismay as they broke up. I'eiBida knew how she felt.

§

The afternoon seemed to crawl by on hands and knees as they made final preparations. The weather decided to give them a break as the rain let up, and the overcast broke up into scattered clouds. The weather was still chill and damp, but at least their preparations went more smoothly.

Flight ops went more smoothly too, which was good since the shuttle crews were exhausted. The latest shuttle sat where it halted, its two pilots dozing on their crash couches while a herd of casuals hauled away loose cartons and boxes which filled every corner of the shuttle. A load lifter stood by until they finished, then moved in to heft pallet after pallet of human frozen food out and carry them to the warehouse.

Finally, 'Godzilla' came in to roust the crew. "You're unloaded," he told them. "Your return cargo is ten passengers and several cartons of drinking water."

The pilot shook off his drowsiness and looked at him blankly. "How much longer?"

"The last flight will be early in the morning." That was met with resigned curses. "When you get back to the ship, have the Eldest put on the reserve crew."

"We *are* the reserve crew," the co-pilot grumbled.

"Hmmm...all right. Tank up on *V'liz*; another half day will finish the job."

"I never thought I would be sick of the sight of *V'liz*," the pilot said once he was gone.

At the other end of the base, D'remNek's and S'deMnveb's defenders were discreetly working on the strong points in buildings facing the main gate, not that it would make much difference when the fight started. They were careful to remain out of sight of the humans watching from the nearby ruins.

§

"The 'Tan Shirts' have reconstituted their units, sir," T'thReptn told I'eiBida shortly before dusk. "And we're seeing more activity in the Peacekeeper units deployed around us."

I'eiBida nodded. "It's starting to come apart. Either Brian broke, or Alvarez decided to go ahead anyway. Either way, they'll come soon."

"How long do we have, sir?"

"Hard to say." I'eiBida turned and gave Giselle a pointed look. "Will they attack tonight?"

Giselle gave him a nervous glance in reply, then paused for a long moment as she listened to the inner voice again. "Morning, more likely. He said...night actions are *complicado*...the Peacekeepers are not *la élite eran una vez* these days...and Alvarez is not an experienced field officer. He will probably wait for sunrise."

"Can you be sure of that?"

"No." She shuddered. "But if he does attack tonight, we are *los muertos*."

I'eiBida pondered the map for a bit. "Recall the scouts," he said to S'deMnveb at last. He turned to D'remNek. "Are those four machine guns ready?"

"Yes, sir. They are assembled, and I've detailed one to each hand of my section to crew them."

"Good. Mass them where they can concentrate fire on the main gate. We will try to hold the humans with a concentrated barrage for as long as possible." He turned to T'thReptn. "Pass the word that the sound of those machine guns means everyone should drop what they're doing and head for the landing field at the gallop."

"Yes, sir!"

I'eiBida brooded over the map for a bit, noting the penciled-in Peacekeeper positions. There was an awful lot of human firepower out there, and the defenders' positions were pitifully few and small by comparison. Finally he turned to Giselle. "What do you think?"

She was trembling visibly, and her voice was thin and shaky. "He says that will buy you perhaps thirty minutes...perhaps an hour before they reach the runway...if you can offer a rear guard. You must use that time to the best of your ability." She shuddered, and turned away. "Excuse me, *por favor*, I must sit down."

"What about the raid, sir?" B'monTrea asked. "The Specials are a large part of what little defense we have. Do they still go even if the humans are about to attack?"

238

I'eiBida sighed. "Yes. Destroying the recording is vital, regardless of the risk. As long as there is any hope of getting there..." He glanced at S'deMnveb, who nodded reluctantly. "...The humans have their objectives, and we have ours."

"The transport may be less crowded than we thought," D'remNek muttered once she and I'eiBida left.

"Probably," T'thReptn muttered back.

§

"What do you think our chances are, sir?" S'deMnveb asked as they headed down the hall.

"I don't know. It depends on so many variables; how Space Fleet reacts, in particular."

"I meant in the raid, sir."

I'eiBida paused and looked at him soberly. "If our Ancestors are pleased with us, we might pull this off. As to how many we will lose..." He shook his head in despair.

There was an awkward silence, then, "With every respect, sir," S'deMnveb said, carefully. "You've never commanded in the field; not since your days at the embassy, at any rate. This raid will work. We'll have to move fast and strike hard, but if our Ancestors smile upon us, we'll get through it without losses. We'll destroy the recording."

I'eiBida considered him for a bit, then nodded. "It's not just for us; it's for the humans, too. We unleashed that horror on the Universe; we have to save them from themselves. How we can join the Ancestral Herd with that weighing us down is beyond me."

S'deMnveb gave him a skeptical ear twitch. "And the two humans, sir?"

I'eiBida took a deep breath to calm himself. "We owe them, her in particular. That is one ear debt I intend to pay."

S'deMnveb's snout showed disciplined disapproval. "With every respect sir, the humans are the enemy; potentially, and in this case in fact. I can't understand why you identify with them so closely."

"Attend to your duties, Second, and leave the 'why' for tails longer than yours to ponder!"

S'deMnveb snapped to attention. "Yes, sir!" He left quickly.

I'eiBida watched him go, then stood silently for some time pondering his troubled hearts. Everything was coming unglued; their attack was a hopeless gesture, and their chances of getting off this world alive were slim at best. He fought with the temptation to call S'deMnveb back, to tell him the attack was futile, and there was no sense in throwing away their lives... No, it needed to be done. He had learned enough from his old friend Brian MacKenna over the years to understand that S'deMnveb would have to be sacrificed for the greater good. Living with his part in it would be another matter.

"Ancestors save us," he muttered.

§

"ANSWER ME!" Alvarez backhanded Mac across his face, sending him sprawling on the cell floor. "The vocoder you carried proves you had help from the Lizards. Why did you join them?"

"*Swine...*" Mac mumbled, which was about all he could manage by then. Alvarez fumed at him, then retreated out of the cell while his two goons hauled Mac upright and set him on his knees again.

§

The latest Duty Officer was waiting in the corridor. "The 'Tan Shirt' units are ready, sir, and the Peacekeepers have been placed on standby. Shall I order the attack?"

He ignored the man as he fought to contain his rage both at the betrayal by his former pupil and the fools who violated his express orders. They were to locate and shadow Krauss; instead, the fools arrested him! Now any hope of uncovering the criminal network rested with breaking Krauss, which seemed unlikely. He swore venomously that those *tontos* would learn the meaning of obedience as they tried to pacify Borneo, where few men ever returned.

"Sir?"

Alvarez gave him a venomous look. "We will move at dawn, since it will take those fools that long to find their boots. In the mean time, we will learn where the test subject is, and those who are hiding her. When he talks, we will move against the conspirators and clean out the vipers' nest once and for all."

240

"But if she's at the Lizard base, she might escape into orbit..."

"Krauss evidently didn't reach there after all, so she could be anywhere."

"There has been no sign of her, sir."

"Of *course* not. She has *his* memories; there is a MacKenna on the loose, and you will not find her easily. Our only real hope, short of sheer luck, is him."

"But...a MacKenna? In *the spaceport?*"

That struck an ominous note with Alvarez, which brought him up short as he realized to his dismay that they caught the kitten, but the wildcat was still on the loose. A MacKenna...in the spaceport... Cold fear welled up in him. If Krauss and MacKenna were working *together*...were they really trying to escape? Or did they have some *other* goal in mind? Was this a move by Space Fleet? The Lizards were involved, certainly, but what was their part in this? All of a sudden a black chasm of uncertainty lay open before him, stroking his paranoia like never before. "Call off the attack! Send the 'Tan Shirts' back to the spaceport! Take *personal* charge, shut the spaceport down again, and make sure *nothing* goes wrong!"

"Yes, Colonel!" The Duty Officer scuttled away while Alvarez brooded: this was proving more of a challenge than he realized.

§

Mac clung to one thing through the pain and disorientation: he had to hang in for as long as possible to give I'eiBida time to finish the evacuation. More than that, he had to maintain persona. Right then they had a fragile equilibrium: a losing game, but a predictable one. If Alvarez caught onto his game, he would attack the landing field at once.

The two goons left and Alvarez returned. "Now, Krauss, we begin again. Where is the test subject?"

Mac caught the sudden change of topic through the haze of pain, and felt a feeble surge of hope. His strategy was still working; Alvarez was running scared. "*Schmutzige Hund...*" he mumbled.

Alvarez waded in and kicked him in his stomach, sending him sprawled on his back wheezing for air. *"You will tell me, Krauss!"*

241

"Verdammt...Sie..."

Alvarez kicked him viciously, then left the room while the goons hauled him up again. Mac had a hard time focussing on Alvarez when he returned.

§

I'eiBida paused to hit the restroom a little while later, and was surprised to find Giselle seated on an overturned trash can in front of the mirror cutting her flowing hair with a pair of shears, awkwardly, since Ic'nichi tools weren't designed for human hands. "What are you doing?"

She didn't pause in her efforts. "I am disguising myself. The gate guards would never believe a *chica* would be assigned to drive a truck."

"Um...good point." He watched, bemused, for a bit. "Was that his idea, or yours?"

She glanced at him. "His, but he is right. There is sure to be an all-points bulletin out on me, so I cannot go out there looking like I did."

She went back to work with the sheers until all that remained was a shaggy crew cut. "What do you think?" she asked as she considered herself in the restroom mirror.

"I'm not really the expert on human grooming," he said, doubtfully.

She made a disgusted face. "It does not quite do." While she didn't exactly look like a young girl any more, she hardly passed for a man, except perhaps for an effeminate sissy-boy. "This will never get us past the gate. Now what?" She pondered her image for a bit, then headed abruptly for the Security grotto with I'eiBida scrambling in pursuit.

"Do you have any rubber cement?" she demanded of a startled D'remNek.

"Rubber cement?"

"*Si*, rubber cement. You must have something like it."

"I know what she's looking for, Third." I'eiBida pulled the lower drawer on his desk out, and sorted through the oddments there until he came up with a small bottle. "Here. What do you need this for?"

242

She ignored his question. "Your copiers use powdered toner, ¿*si?*" She gestured at the copying machine.

"Um...I think so."

"I need that cartridge."

Without a further word, I'eiBida pulled the machine open and fiddled the bulky toner cartridge out. Giselle grabbed it and headed back to the restroom, where she broke it open on the edge of the sink. It was filed with powder, as expected, which splattered all over the place. She grabbed a wad of toilet paper, and began dabbing it on her chin and neck. Enough of it stuck to give her a convincing five o-clock shadow.

"God," she muttered at one point. "I'm putting on freakin' *makeup*." She shook her head in dismay. "What would mom think?"

"Which mom, Brian?" I'eiBida noted the change in her speech.

She gave him a sharp look. "Either one." She went back to dabbing her face, and finished up a short while later. Then she used some of the hair clippings to fashion a bushy handlebar mustache and an imperial with the rubber cement to bind clumps of hair in place. "There. I'll pass in the dark, at least." Her hands were shaking by then.

"You humans never fail to amaze me."

She looked at him evenly. "That just goes to show how little you know: sometimes we scare ourselves spitless."

I'eiBida chuckled. "True enough. I think you'll pull this off in style, Brian."

She gave him a derisive snort. "He said 'thank you'."

§

"Is that the last of them?" I'eiBida nodded discreetly to a human driver as he walked past, protesting futilely as he was herded along by two of D'remNek's people.

"Yes, sir." Their 'brown-and-green' said with a cynical chuckle. "I haven't felt so challenged since I played 'grab-my-tail' as a hatchling."

"The element of surprise is your best weapon."

"The 25th Maxim Of The Defenders." The 'brown-and-green' nodded. "They taught us well."

"They did indeed." I'eiBida gave him a stern look. "Remember well: you will need those skills soon."

'Godzilla' was in his element, and enjoyed every moment of their little deception as he summoned the human drivers to the office one by one while a screen of Specials surrounding the area to prevent any escapes slowly contracted. It was all handled so discreetly that none of them were aware of what was going on until they entered the warehouse, where a hand of D'remNek's defenders cornered them, and hustled them to the drivers' lounge.

"Good work," I'eiBida said to the two volunteers. "Keep them in by any means necessary. We can't afford them getting loose and raising the alarm."

"And if we have to shoot, sir?"

I'eiBida gave him a searching look. This one was in for over twelve years before leaving uniform; the steady look in his eye said he knew what needed to be done. "Do whatever you must. Just keep them contained."

"Yes, sir."

§

T'thReptn was bubbling with excitement when I'eiBida returned to the Intel circle. "The 'Tan Shirts' are headed back to the spaceport, sir!"

"What? Why?"

"Unknown, sir, but they're in a galloping hurry, and Alvarez is sending part of the security contingent from the 6th Office compound as well."

"Brian!" I'eiBida shouted in sheer joy. "He has Alvarez chasing wild gooses again."

"But what about the Peacekeepers?" Giselle asked.

T'thReptn was listening to the radio monitors. "Unknown, sir...but the radio traffic seems to be dying down..." He listened for several minutes more while I'eiBida, Giselle, and all the rest waited anxiously. "...I think the attack is off again, sir!"

I'eiBida sagged in sheer relief. "Then that must mean Brian is still alive."

"If the Peacekeepers have settled down again, it means the raiders have a better chance of getting through, sir."

I'eiBida's ears shot up. "And if part of the 6th Office security has gone to the spaceport..." He looked hopefully at Giselle and S'deMnveb. "...we might pull this off after all!"

§

It was well after dark by the time everything was completed. "It's time, sir," S'deMnveb said. "My herd and the security are ready."

I'eiBida examined the two trucks they commandeered, which were now coupled together. Some of S'deMnveb's people were in the container on the first trailer, while the rest were waiting at the gate, and the hand which were out as scouts earlier were waiting to be picked up on the highway beyond the Peacekeeper encampment.

"Alright, good luck." After a bit, he added, "Destroying their lab and the recording are essential: we'll wind up fighting a hundred Alvarez's otherwise."

"Yes, sir. What about the human?"

I'eiBida fought with his emotions for a long moment. "If you can rescue him—or put him out of his misery—do so; but don't throw lives away. He knew the risks. He'll understand."

"Yes, sir." S'deMnveb gave him a crisp tail wave, and joined his people in the container.

It was nearly midnight. The quarter moon gave just enough light to see by. Giselle leaned against the driver's side door, hands on her knees, staring at nothing. She ignored I'eiBida as he came over to offer a last bit of encouragement.

"Are you ready to go?"

"Huh?" She twitched as if surprised and looked at him.

"You all right?"

"*Si*. I was just...listening to him." She gave a deep sigh, and stood up. "I have studied the controls; I am pretty sure I can drive this thing."

"Have faith in yourself. You're smart enough to be a physich's assistant; driving a truck must be simple compared to that."

She gave him a wain smile. "But no one shoots at me while I am taking temperatures."

"Are you able do this?" he asked her softly.

She gave him an anxious look. "I have to be, I guess."

"How are you now? Between you and him?"

She shuddered. "I...have recovered enough that I am pretty much in control. I can still hear him and relay his words to you, but he is too weak to take over now. I will...have to do it all by myself."

"I'm sorry to put you through this. This is something you were never meant to do."

She shuddered, and rubbed her hands nervously on her trouser legs. "There was a lot of loose talk in the protest movement that it would come down to fighting some day. I never thought I would be part of it."

S'deMnveb came up again. "We're ready, sir."

I'eiBida nodded, then turned to Giselle. "Listen to what he tells you. He's a survivor, and he knows more about this sort of thing than all of us put together. Trust him: it's your best chance of getting through this."

She took a deep, shaky breath. "I will try." She looked at the truck towering over them, then at I'eiBida again. "*Puede la Virgen vigilar usted en sus viajes,*" she mumbled before she climbed into the cab.

I'eiBida wondered what she meant. "Good luck."

§

Despite the tension between the two races, shipments continued to flow in and out of the Ic'nichi landing field over the last several days. A steady stream of semi tractor-trailers loaded with huge cargo containers came through the gate about every fifteen minutes, so the latest departure didn't draw much attention until it ground to a halt by the guard shack. It was only then that the 'Tan Shirt' sergeant noticed the second rig following closely behind.

"Vat iss zis?" he demanded, with a wave at the second truck while several of his squad circled the assemblage to check it over.

"Breakdown." Giselle tried to keep her voice as deep as possible. "They told me to tow it back to the depot."

"I shoult be surprised," he grumbled. "You haff your movement order?"

Giselle glanced up the road ahead: no sign of oncoming traffic. "*Si*, right here." She reached down with one trembling hand for the fictional document, and 'accidentally' brushed against the truck's horn, which emitted a brief toot. That was the signal that she was safely out of the line of fire. The Special Service Worthy and a hand of their defenders took the place of the security watch during the last shift change: he drew his machine pistol, and shot the sergeant down with one quick burst. Not waiting for him to fall, he rushed the door to the operations shed while the others tackled the remaining 'Tan Shirts'. The shed was a long wooden box with a few desks, some odd bits of furniture, and no internal partitions other than a small toilet cabinet. There were five more 'Tan Shirts' on duty: two in the shed, three examining the truck. Most of them never realized what was happening, none of them got off a shot.

§

I'ciBida listened carefully for the sound of gunfire in the distance, which would mean the humans had not been surprised, and managed to get off some fire of their own. There was nothing: the silencer-equipped machine pistols the Specials used for covert work didn't carry this far, which meant gate security was neutralized, and the humans farther down the road were not alerted. A few endless minutes crawled by before the truck's engine revved as it pulled out.

"Good luck, Brian," he whispered.

*****

"Chapter Sixteen"

Giselle was shaking so hard after the shoot-out at the gate that she could hardly drive the huge truck. It was far worse than she had expected: one of the 'Tan Shirts' actually died right before her eyes, gunned down without warning and without a chance to defend himself as she watched in horror. She thought she knew what war was like, but she realized now how badly mistaken she was. Death was sudden and violent; and even though they were evil men, she still innocently believed they deserved a fair chance.

"*Esto es terrible*," she whimpered to herself. "*Esto es una locura.*"

'*It had to be done, Giselle.*' She flinched when the hated inner voice she'd endured all these months whispered in the back of her mind. '*It's sad, but that's the way of the world.*'

Despite the power steering, they wobbled all over the crumbled pavement. She could barely reach the foot pedals to begin with, and was more or less standing as she drove. The one thought foremost in her mind was how she could easily meet the same fate: gunned down without mercy, or worse, wounded and left to suffer and die. The gristly lessons from her nurse's schooling came back to her. There were *so* many ways the human body could be destroyed, *so* many ways to die in agony. She needed to lean against the steering wheel to steady herself.

"*Dios*, I must be crazy to do this," she whimpered.

'*Be strong, Giselle. We have to destroy that recording, and we have to destroy Alvarez.*'

"Why me?" Her tears made it hard to see where she was going, and her long suppressed panic was rising fast. "Just get out of my head and leave me alone!"

'*That will come soon enough. At the rate I'm fading, you won't have to endure this much longer. But for now, we have a job to do.*'

"I should just go back to the base. This is hopeless."

'*Do you really want someone else to go through what happened to you?*' She cringed at the thought. '*There won't be any rescue for the next victim. We have to prevent that next victim by helping to take Alvarez down while we can.*'

Strangely, that thought calmed her a bit, and helped stiffen her resolve, which needed reinforcement badly. "I...guess you are right." She suppressed a sob, and wiped her tears with one sleeve. "Why did this have to happen?"

'Trust me, everyone caught in the crossfire wonders why. Even I did at times.' She felt a fleeting moment of bitterness, then a flash of grim resolve. *'You were an unfortunate victim. It isn't right, but that's the way the world works. All we can do, the two of us, is fight back.'*

Put it that way, the voice was right. Her panic receded a bit more, replaced with a feeble but grim determination. She was the only one who could get the raiders to the laboratory and back. Without her, Alvarez would win, and humanity would be lost. Oddly, that weight rested easily on her shoulders: she was free to act, to strike back. She was taking the fight to the 6th Office, and despite her fear, she felt truly liberated for the first time.

'You'll have to carry the ball. I'm too weak now. Can we count on you, Giselle?'

"I...I will try..." She was startled when a pair of vehicle headlights hit her without warning. "*¡Dios mío!* We are trapped!"

'No, Giselle, it's the checkpoint, remember? Stop the truck and stay calm. We'll get through this.'

She managed to pull her wits together and hit the brakes. The heavy rig ground to a squealing halt, almost ramming the command vehicle parked by the road.

"Watch what you're doing!" someone yelled.

She sat frozen in fear as shadows stirred in the gloom. The vague figure of someone dressed in helmet and poncho moved toward the truck.

"What do we do?" she whimpered.

'Stay calm, Giselle.'

The guard's rifle was silhouetted against the headlights. Other figures stirred in the darkness. She was sure the mission was about to come to a tragic end. They would kill her...or worse, turn her over to Alvarez...she would be sent back to that living hell. The alien leader, I'eiBida, made her use the restroom before they started out; she was so terrified she would have wet herself otherwise.

249

"...n-no..." The dim figure was getting closer.

'Stay. Calm. Giselle.' The steel in that hidden voice frightened her more than the approaching guard, stunning her into immobility. Providentially, there was a sudden burst of rain accompanied by a chill breeze. The figure hesitated, then waved them through as he retreated to the warmth of the command vehicle.

'All right, go!'

Shaken out of her paralysis, she fumbled the foot throttle, and managed to keep the lumbering convoy steady as they crept ahead past the checkpoint and through the Peacekeeper encampment.

'Hmph,' the voice grumbled. *'No outlying pickets, no entrenchments, not even a standing guard other than that roadblock.'* Despite herself, she glanced left and right as he took in the scene. The Peacekeeper camp was a ragged hodge-podge of small tents and canvas tarps, with disconsolate knots of troopers huddled around their portable cook stoves. *'What a bunch of sad-sacks. I've seen better discipline in refugee camps. Their morale must be even worse than the Ic'nichi realize.'*

"Will that help our side?" she asked as the convoy left the Peacekeepers behind and headed for the highway interchange.

She got an impression of a weary sigh. *'Not really. Not enough to matter.'*

§

"Is the last of your equipment destroyed?" I'eiBida asked T'thReptn when he joined them on the flight line.

"Yes, sir. We smashed all the communication and coding gear, and the files are ready to torch as soon as you give the word."

I'eiBida nodded glumly. They wouldn't need their com gear again; either S'deMnveb would make it back—with or without Brian—or they wouldn't. There would be no rescue missions.

They stood in an open doorway to one of the warehouses and watched the ground crew taking a break after the last shuttle departed.

"We're going to have a war after all, aren't we, sir?" D'remNek asked.

I'eiBida sighed. "S'deMnveb may still influence that, but I would say it's highly likely."

250

They were interrupted by the other shuttle as it coasted in and touched down on the runway. It finally came trundling back along the taxi lane, and ground to a halt on the tarmac. The ground herd stirred as the turbines died.

"Let's hope this weather holds," B'monTrea grumbled. The rain which plagued them the last few days had let up for the time being. The work crews were soaked and chilled, and even the four of them were a bit soggy.

"If it lasts to dawn, it will help flight ops no end."

"Yes, sir."

Thankfully, the chill heightened the work herd's metabolisms; the unloading was going faster than ever despite everyones' exhaustion. With the humans secured, the load lifters simply stacked the pallets of human food and office equipment off to one side of the tarmac rather than lugging them back to the warehouse. But some were already paying the price in physical and mental collapse, as they all would later after—hopefully—this was over and they were safely on their way home.

"How much longer?" I'eiBida twitched an ear at the feverish activity.

T'thReptn watched the scene for a long moment. "I would say about an hour, sir."

I'eiBida paused to mentally translate to their time. "Right." He turned to D'remNek. "As soon as they are through unloading, make your final deployment for the rear guard, and get everyone else on this shuttle."

"Yes, sir!" D'remNek trotted away to join the herd moving the last loose boxes and bales.

"We might make it after all, if our Ancestors smile upon us," B'monTrea said.

"Perhaps they will," I'eiBida mused. "We still have to see how S'deMnveb manages."

"They're good, sir. They'll do the job." Unspoken, but hanging in the air between them like an ominous cloud, was how many they would lose, and whether Giselle would come back alive. I'eiBida agonized in suspense, and wondered how the humans endured this endless wait on the edge of pending battle.

"Have the shuttle crew tell the ship to send down the last shuttle empty." There was no time for brooding; they had a lot of work to do.

B'monTrea gave him a crisp tail wave. "Yes, sir!"

§

The night was abysmal under the cloud cover, and there were no lights for miles. The steady rain streaking the windshield made it all but impossible to see the highway. The weather was clearing back at the landing field, but the rain hadn't let up yet here ten kilometers away. Giselle's emotional state didn't help, either. She was no truck driver to begin with, and her tattered nerves made it all the harder to concentrate on the crumbled, semi-obscured highway as it wound through the endless ruins. If it weren't for the truck's powerful headlights, she would have been completely lost.

In a way, the task helped keep her mind off what lay ahead. For all that she knew what must be done, and her dogged intention to smite Alvarez, the pending battle left her feeling watery and on the edge of panic.

'This is where we stop, Giselle.'

Startled out of her distracted haze, she stomped on the brakes. The truck almost jackknifed as the tow behind rammed the rear bumper, bringing the convoy to another shuddering halt. Only after she managed to stop did she see the faint light amid the rubble. She would have missed it completely if it hadn't been for her unwelcome passenger. Four dim figures emerged from the ruins—the scout Hand—and headed aft.

'I know how you feel,' the voice said as she watched them climb into the container. *'Trust me: the waiting is the worst of it. Once the fight starts, you'll be too busy to be scared.'*

"That does *not* reassure me!"

That brought on a mental chuckle. *'I know. Don't sweat it.'*

They drove in silence for a while, picking their way carefully around potholes and piled ruins spilled on the road. Another truck passed them headed for the landing field, splashing water over their windshield. Ahead in the distance she could make out the lights of the 6th Office compound glowing against the moonless night. The sight filled her with foreboding.

"Why is there so much evil in the world?" Even the hated voice within her would be a comfort at the moment.

'God only knows.' There was a brooding silence, then, *'There are two kinds of evil people: the afraid, and the ambitious. The ones who are afraid are the worst. Frightened people do frightening things, and the ones in charge fear anything different; even their own shadows. They enable the ambitious bastards like Alvarez.'* A sense of bitter weariness swept over her. *'I've dealt with his kind so many times. They're why civilized countries keep people like me on the payroll.'*

"Why do people like you not stop them?"

'It's not so simple. I was born and raised an American: you know how they became right toward the end. We professionals were ashamed of what our country turned into, but what choice did we have? Mutiny? Should I have nuked Washington? Would it have made any difference? There was too much fear to eliminate them all. In any case, there were very real threats out there at the time, so we did bad things because we had no good choices.'

"You always have choices."

'No, not in wartime; not like now. War is a never-ending series of hard decisions made to cope with bad options. Nobody wins; you can only survive.' The sense of bitterness grew until it threatened to overwhelm her. *'We soldiers are martyrs; we bear the weight of mankind's sins.'*

"Dios," she muttered. "We cannot win, can we? Humanity, I mean."

A sense of resignation flowed through her. *'No, we can't, because the enemy is ourselves.'*

§

B'monTrea returned as the last shuttle taxied toward the runway. "All quiet at the main gate for now, sir. They secured another human truck."

"Thank you." I'eiBida watched as the shuttle turned at the end of the runway, then came roaring back, climbing smoothly into the night. He felt a pang of loss as it vanish into the scattered clouds.

D'remNek came trotting over. "The shuttle pilot said the last shuttle has started down, sir. They should be here in an hour."

253

"That's cutting it fine," B'monTrea said.

"But it will do." I'eiBida already missed T'thReptn, on his way into orbit with the last of the Intel staff. Of the one hundred and eighteen tails assigned here, only D'remNek's defenders and their two volunteers were left, along with B'monTrea and himself. S'deMnveb's Specials were an unknown just then, and they could only hope for the best. He turned to D'remNek. "Get your people to their positions."

"Yes, sir."

§

'All right, pull over here, Giselle.'

She brought the convoy to another ragged halt in the middle of the highway. "Why do we stop?" she asked.

'This is where we make our final deployment.' She was so distracted by driving and her barely suppressed fear that she didn't even notice they had arrived. The sight of the 6th Office compound off to her left sent a shudder through her.

'You need to go back and release S'deMnveb from the container.'

That jolted her out of her paralysis. She fumbled her way out of the cab and back to the rear of the first trailer, where it took some effort to unlatch the locking bars holding the container shut. The Specials came piling out, weapons at the ready, and spread out to form a hasty perimeter. After sorting themselves out, the went into a huddle for a quick final brief. Giselle stood haplessly nearby listening to their chattering, warbling speech, but couldn't make sense of any of it.

'The next part will be the most difficult,' the voice said. *'The best thing is to charge right in. We have the element of shock and surprise; keep moving, and this will be over before they can react.'*

"If you think that reassures me, you are mistaken."

'Have faith, Giselle.'

"F-faith is all I have." It was all fine and good to stand around a table moving push pins on a map; being one of those push pins about to go up against the core of the dreaded 6th Office in a blazing gun battle was something else entirely. "I do not know if I can do this."

'Every soldier feels like that, every time. You'll make it.'

It took a few minutes for the Ic'nichi to unhitch the second truck, and considerably more for her to turn the heavy rig around and park it on the shoulder. "We are running late," S'deMnveb said as the Specials piled back into the first truck's container.

She climbed reluctantly back into the cab with S'deMnveb scrunched awkwardly in the seat next to her with his machine pistol out the window. It took all her remaining courage to gun the truck ahead the last half kilometer to the entrance and turn onto the drive leading to the 6th Office compound. That was where her nerve failed and the truck drifted to a halt. She sat mesmerized by the lights ahead of her, her heart racing, her breath ragged, stomach knotted, bowls threatening to cut loose.

'You can do this, Giselle.' She flinched as the inner voice broke her distraction. *'The best way is to plow right in. Don't hesitate. It'll be all right if we keep moving.'*

"We must go, Admiral."

'Be strong, Giselle.'

"I...I-I can not..." S'deMnveb gave her an alarmed look.

'Yes, you can, Giselle. You can to do this. You have to. I'm too weak now.'

"P-please..."

'NOW, Giselle!'

With a cry of anguish, she floored the accelerator and hung on grimly as the truck surged ahead. Somehow she kept them on course as they hit the traffic circle, plowed over the curb and through some decorative bushes, narrowly missing the flagpole, and back onto the pavement without slowing. By then, they were moving so fast that the truck became briefly airborne as it bounced over the curb again, and climbed the four steps to the entrance. She hung frozen in fear as they swerved to one side, and S'deMnveb gave the steering wheel a sharp tug to keep them from plowing into the wall. The glass entrance shattered with a thunderous crash as the truck plowed through it, and Giselle got a brief glimpse of the two 'Tan Shirts' in the lobby watching in wide-eyed alarm before the truck smashed into their booth and ground to a shuddering halt.

Somehow—it was all a blur by then—Giselle found herself standing by the truck's open door, clinging desperately to the handle as her feet slipped on bloodstained glass shards while S'deMnveb raced back to release the Specials. The first one out of the container was the grenadier, who ran past her and lobbed a grenade which shattered the inner security door and sent her sprawling with a scream of terror. S'deMnveb yanked her to her feet, and guided her as they stumbled down the corridor after the rest of them. There was a burst of machine pistol fire followed by another grenade. By the time they reached the corner, the watch at the lab entrance was dead, and the rest were pouring through the shattered security door to the tunnel. There were shots from down the hall; several humans in the distance were running toward them.

"Run!" S'deMnveb yelled as he dragged her forward. They careened into the open doorway as one of the Specials hosed the oncoming 'Tan Shirts' then retreated after them. She almost lost her footing on the sloping ramp, but somehow stayed on her feet as they chased the herd of Specials through the tunnel.

"Security door!" someone yelled. Ahead of them, a heavy steel door was sliding down from the ceiling, threatening to trap them. The first defender dropped his satchel charges, tackled a metal trash can, and surged forward, sliding it in place just as the door came down. The trash can buckled under its weight, but slowed the door enough that they were able to squeeze themselves and their gear under it. Giselle faltered before the door; one of the defenders knocked her down, and another dragged her unresisting through the narrowing gap. The last one squeezed under and kicked the can away, just managing to avoid having his tail caught.

Meanwhile, the head of the assault raced up the far ramp with the grenadier in the lead. The security door ahead of them was just being opened by two 'Tan Shirts' responding to the alarm; one of the lead defenders shot them both, and they fell blocking the door open. The grenadier sent a round through the open door. The grenade punched the booth window, incinerating the two humans inside. His next shot took out the inner security door, and the rest of the force poured into the laboratory.

§

"You will answer me, Krauss," Alvarez said with chilling patience. "You know it's only a matter of time, so spare yourself any further pain."

Alvarez and his goons had worked on him for over twelve hours, taking turn-about when they tired. Mac didn't have the luxury: their methods were brutal; the questioning relentless.

"You betrayed your people," Alvarez said. "I know you helped her escape. You could only have done it with the aid of the Lizards." He belted Mac across his face with a heavy leather paddle. "I will know why, Krauss."

"Schweinhund," Mac mumbled.

Alvarez smacked him again.

"What are their plans? Who are your contacts here?"

"Verräterische...Hund..."

Alvarez waded in and kicked him squarely in his groin for the fifteenth or sixteenth time; Mac sagged to his side on the floor, wheezing and cursing faintly.

"You will tell the truth, Krauss. You know this. Trust me..." He was interrupted by the sound of an explosion followed by gunfire from down the hall, followed in turn by the security alarm. Alvarez jerked around at the sound, and peered curiously toward the hall doorway. *"¿Cuál es ése?"* he muttered as his two goons drew their pistols and went to investigate. There was more weapons fire, and a faint scream. "Check it out," he ordered.

§

The fight was short and savage. With half the duty watch down in the first instant, the remaining 'Tan Shirts' put up a spirited but uncoordinated defense while a dozen or so technicians scrambled for cover. The Specials advanced with the swift precision of elite troops, using every bit of cover, coordinating their suppression fire, always on the move as they swept through the laboratory. The 'Tan Shirts' put up a good fight, but they were no match for the Specials' skill and firepower.

§

The sound of weapons fire grew sustained; as incredible as it seemed, they could tell there was a major battle going on in the laboratory.

"They wouldn't..." Alvarez said in dismay.   It was inconceivable the Pukers would dare raise a hand against the 6th Office, certainly not without his network of informants learning of it. The Peacekeepers were the only ones, and their leadership was too thoroughly compromised...

Two 'Tan Shirts' came running in panicky haste. "The Lizards are attacking!" they yelled as they took cover behind the door to the cell block with their assault rifles at the ready.

"What?" Alvarez was flabbergasted. "Are you mad? You're lying!"

"No, sir!" one of them said. "It's a raid! All the rest are dead!" Even as he spoke, the last of the firing abruptly ended.

Mac stirred feebly where he lay on his side in the cell. His hope was kindled again as he listened to the gunfire and the 'Tan Shirts' panicky words, although he knew it was probably too late for him...

§

It wasn't long before the last 'Tan Shirt' was rooted out and killed. Giselle stared wide-eyed at the bloody corpse felled by a burst of automatic weapons fire, and she trembled so badly that she needed to lean against a desk to steady herself. She was stunned by the ferocity of the attack: the whole operation, from start to finish, took less than three minutes, and the place was a bloody shambles.

"Fourth Hand, on the entrance," S'deMnveb snapped. "They'll be here soon. Second Hand, get to work on breaching the wall. The rest, secure the prisoners." One Hand fell back to cover their rear, while a couple others set to work planting a satchel charge against the wall in the far corner. The rest corralled the dozen technicians, and herded them into another corner.

"One wounded," the Worthy reported. One of the Specials took a round in his left shoulder, and was cursing vividly in their language as one of his Hand tried to help him.

S'deMnveb considered him, then turned to Giselle. "I was told you are a physich?"

"Huh?" She was jolted out of her trance, and stared stupidly at him.

"You are a physich? A healer?"

"...I...I was a nursing student..."

"Can you help him?"

"But...I am not trained in your medicine!"

"You know how to treat wounds?"

"Y...yes..." She looked at the wounded Ic'nichi in dismay...and her training kicked in. "I will do what I can."

S'deMnveb left her to tend to the wound, marched over to where the civilians were herded, and grabbed one by his lapels, half-dragging him to his knees.

"Where is the human?"

The technician was stunned by the recent attack, and stared at him in numb confusion.

"They come, sir!" one of the door detail called.

"WHERE IS HE?" S'deMnveb shouted, and jammed his machine pistol in his face. "The one who was captured by the 'Tan Shirts', where is he?"

The technician was terrified, but finally realized what he wanted, and pointed to a security door across the room. "Back there! In the cells with Alvarez."

S'deMnveb snatched his magnetic key card and tossed it to his Worthy. "First Hand, find the human! Third Hand, secure these people, then get the charges set. Hurry!" His Worthy lead the first Hand through the door in skirmish order and down the corridor to the cells.

"Clear the blast!" one of the Specials shouted as they retreated from a smoking satchel charge braced against the wall by a heavy desk. The rest of them took cover where they could as the charge went off, throwing the desk across the room in a cloud of smoke and pulverized concrete, sending Giselle sprawling with a screech of terror.

"All right, let's get this done," S'deMnveb said as he helped her to her feet again. One Hand resumed their watch on the entrance while the rest turned to the grim task of killing the civilians.

"*What are you doing?*" Giselle cried. She was there in an instant, trying to get between the Ic'nichi and the technicians. "This is wrong!"

S'deMnveb didn't answer since there was nothing he could say. This was something so utterly *alien* to their military traditions as to be unthinkable, but it had to be done. These were the ones who made the mind transfer process go. They couldn't be allowed to interfere with the demolitions in any event. He dragged her reluctantly to one side, ignored her protests, and watched until the rest of them were dead.

"Get the charges rigged," he said when it was over. He left Giselle standing there aghast, and trotted down the corridor to the entrance, trying to shut the image out of his mind.

§

"You cowardly dogs!" Alvarez advanced on the two 'Tan Shirts', slashing one across his face with his riding crop. "Deserters! Get out there and fight!"

The two were hyper enough that they almost turned on him, but were stopped by his two goons who backed him up with leveled pistols. In any event they were more afraid of Alvarez than the Ic'nichi...

...The lights in the hall went out. They hesitated in confusion, and were cut down by a burst of machine pistol fire before they could raise their weapons. The two goons flattened themselves against the wall with their pistols at the ready, but an Ic'nichi burst through the open doorway, caught them by surprise, and dropped them with one long spray of fire which chewed up the wall behind them, and sent ricochets buzzing around the cell block.

Alvarez reached for his pistol, but another Ic'nichi came through the door and shot him before he could clear the holster. He collapsed against the wall, and slid to the floor in a heap with a gushing wound in his left kidney. The first Ic'nichi grabbed his pistol as the second helped Mac up.

"The keys...pocket!" he groaned with a nod toward Alvarez. The one who confiscated Alvarez's pistol rifled through his pockets, evoking a whimper of agony. "What's the situation?" Mac demanded as the last shackle came loose.

"We blow up the building," the Worthy said. His words were emphasized by an explosion which shook the room. "Hurry, they are coming. We go now."

"Right." Mac staggered to his feet with a gasp from the sharp pain in his abdomen. He steadied himself with one hand on the wall, scooped up one of the guard's assault rifles, and flipped the safety off.

"Why are you siding with them, Krauss?" Alvarez wheezed. He struggled to a sitting position with his hand pressed to his side to staunch the bleeding. "What made you turn against your own kind?"

Mac gave him a cold look. "Let's just say I don't like your style. And the name's not Krauss: it's MacKenna, Brian A, Admiral." He waited until Alvarez's eyes widened in surprised recognition, then shot him repeatedly in the groin. "That's for her." Alvarez curled up with a thin scream of agony, and lay on his side panting and shaking. With reasonable luck it would take him some time to die. "Damn, that felt good," Mac said to the Worthy. "Right, let's go."

§

"Where *are* they?" S'deMnveb muttered as he paced nervously back and forth. This was his first real battle against the humans; the laboratory was a shambles, and for all he could tell the mission was too. At least they had only one significant casualty thus far. Their shoulder wound was resting comfortably after being tended by Giselle while one Hand guarded the entrance, and the rest were busy rigging explosives. The real thorn in his foot was his Worthy and the Hand sent to rescue the human. Could they find him? Would they meet resistance? Would he be able to travel? Objectively, things were going well—thus far—but they were a long way from safety. His fears were understandably blown out of proportion...

Giselle was in his path, looking stricken. "Why did you kill them?" She gestured wildly at the heaped corpses of the lab technicians laying in the corner. "That was murder!"

It took him a moment to focus on her and shift mental gears to answer her in Swiss. "They made the mind transfer work. Without them, the Alliance can't backward engineer the process. They had to be destroyed if we are to succeed."

"But..."

"I do not enjoy killing," he ground out. "I am not human. I did what I must to protect my people!" She started to protest. "I did it for your people too. They were as much a threat to you humans as to us. You, of all people, must know that!" She watched him with stricken eyes, then nodded and turned away.

"They're lifting the security door, sir!" one of the people on the lab entrance called.

"Wonderful." S'deMnveb trotted down the narrow hall and looked through the security lock, getting a burst of automatic weapons fire for his trouble. *"l'cc'vn!"* He ducked back, narrowly missed by the spray. The heavy security door in the center of the tunnel was partly up, and the first 'Tan Shirt' security were crawling under it. "Hold them off!"

He and two of the Specials hosed machine pistol fire blindly down the passage, getting screams of agony and return fire.

"The last charges are set, sir," the second Hand Lead called.

S'deMnveb trotted back up the hall to the laboratory; the satchel charges were scattered everywhere, detonator cords strung in a web around the room. "Right. Get to work on the fence."

He headed back to the entry as the Hand Lead ducked out through the hole blasted in the outer wall in the far corner. More weapons fire came from down the tunnel; the Fourth Hand were in a brisk fire fight. A grenade explosion caught him by surprise, knocking him off his feet. He struggled up with an exasperated curse; they were all getting rattled.

"How does it look?" he asked the Lead.

The Lead threw a quick glance at him. "They are coming in..." There was another grenade explosion, and the Lead yelped in pain as a fragment nicked his cheek. "...they come in force, sir! We can't hold them any longer!"

Another weapons burst grew into a sustained barrage. The humans must be under the gate in force, and advancing behind a storm of firing. "Time to go! Shut the door!"

S'deMnveb and the Lead hesitated long enough to toss two grenades, then slammed the inner security door. The first humans appeared on the other side of the armored glass as S'deMnveb shot out the electronic lock, then hastily retreated.

"Now what, sir?" the Lead asked as the Hand assembled at the end of the tunnel.

S'deMnveb looked around frantically: the rest of them were gone, and for all he could tell, the explosives were ready to go. There was no time to second-guess his people. "Where is the First Hand?"

"They must have left, sir!"

He peeked down the hall: the humans were pounding on the security door, but they would need time to break through the tough safety glass.

"Set the detonator. We have to go."

§

Mac and the rescue party finally reached the laboratory after what seemed an eternity. He staggered into the room, holding desperately onto the frame, and fetched up against one of the desks, wincing at the pain in his abdomen. "I don't think I'm gonna make it," he said to the Worthy.

The laboratory was a shambles; bullet marks and blood spatters everywhere, floor littered with shell casings. There was a dead 'Tan Shirt' nearby, and a pile of corpses in the far corner. Mac nodded grimly: the technicians needed to die along with the recording if this was ever to be over. Satchel charges were scattered around on the computer banks and large pieces of scientific equipment, all linked together by detonator wires. The master timer stood on a desk, neat blue numerals clicking off one by one on its face.

"It's nearly done," he muttered to himself. He could take grim satisfaction in knowing I'eiBida's wild-ass scheme came off after all. Maybe, just maybe if there was any justice in this Universe, the death of Alvarez and his mind transfer project would defuse the war between earth and d'enchia. Pity he wouldn't live to see it.

They were distracted by the sound of weapons fire on the other side of the wall. Mac vaguely recalled the security entrance was over there. The firing was followed by heavy thuds: the 'Tan Shirts' were trying to break into the lab.

"What we do, human?" the Worthy demanded. "Can you gallop?"

There was a gaping hole blown in the wall, and Mac longed for it with all his soul. "Ah...no. Can't make it." The pain in his abdomen told him his running was over. He gave the Worthy a feeble smile. "Thanks for getting me out of there anyway."

There was more gunfire, and the crashing noise grew more insistent. Mac limped over and peeked down the hall: the security door was buckled and all but broken down. They would be through any second now. He threw another look at the master timer sitting on the desk. Several minutes remained.

"We can't let them retake this room," he said, calmly. "We have to hold them off for as long as we can."

The Worthy considered him for a long moment. The crashing noise was more insistent. Finally, he turned and chattered something at the others, who quietly took positions where they could cover the doorway.

'So this is how it ends,' Mac thought. *'This time, anyway.'* He felt strangely calm, almost resigned in the face of impending death. He'd faced death so many times before that it almost seemed like an old familiar friend. He glanced around at the Ic'nichi defenders waiting alert and steady for the pending battle, and nodded to himself in approval. This wasn't the first time he'd died, and odds were it wouldn't be the last. At least he was going out for a good reason and in good company.

There was another burst of fire from the hall. He worked the action on his assault rifle, and flipped the selector to full auto. There was one more heavy crash, and the door flew open. Time to pay his dues. "All right, Pilgrim," he shouted. "Bring your boots!" He stepped into the center of the hall, and hosed the full clip into the packed bodies spilling through the doorway.

*****

"Chapter Seventeen"

The blast which took out the perimeter fence was drowned out as the building exploded behind them. The Ic'nichi cringed under the falling debris as S'deMnveb looked on in horror. He was dismayed to learn the rescue party wasn't with the rest of the force outside: now his Worthy and an entire Hand of his best defenders as well as the human they were sent to rescue were dead.

"What now, sir?" one of the Leads asked.

"They run with their Ancestors," he said, harshly. This was not the time or place to grieve; they needed to gallop before the 'Tan Shirts' recovered their wits. He turned to the other human, the young fem, who was prone with her arms wrapped around her head. "Are you well, human?"

She looked up at him, and for a moment seemed paralyzed in confusion. "Ah....*si*."

"They are coming, sir!" There were flashlights moving along the building in the distance.

"Come, human. We must get out of here."

One fencepost was snapped off clean, and the chain link fabric shredded and thrown back, leaving a gap three body lengths wide. The surviving Specials surged through the gap in one common impulse, while S'deMnveb and the Third Hand Lead hauled Giselle to her feet and sent her stumbling after them.

They made about eight hundred meters over rough ground, and had just reached the paved driveway when the wounded defender began lagging behind. Finally, S'deMnveb grabbed his arm as he staggered to a halt. "We need to treat his injury." The shoulder wound was bleeding again.

Giselle shook off her funk and pushed S'deMnveb aside. "I can take care of him." She dropped to her knees by the wounded defender. "I need an aid kit."

S'deMnveb pulled the kit off his belt. "Please help him, but be quick."

It was hard to see anything in the pitch dark, but she managed by the faint light of the burning building in the distance. "Hurry!" S'deMnveb said. "They will be after us soon."

She ignored him, and grimly went about the task of wiping the blood away and binding his shoulder while the wounded defender managed to fumble a pain tab out of his own kit and inject himself. "That will do," she said at last.

"We must go, now." S'deMnveb helped her to her feet, and the two of them helped the wounded defender down the road as the rest of the Specials formed a rear guard.

§

The cell block was spared the worst of the multiple explosions which wrecked the rest of the laboratory. At the end of the cell row, Colonel Alvarez lay against the wall moaning and writhing in agony from his multiple gunshot wounds. Even the emergency lights were gone, and the air was thick with smoke and kicked up dust, but although he could see nothing, he could feel the sticky blood on his hands, and the steady warm trickle flowing onto the floor where he lay.

"Volmer..." he wheezed. "Volmer..." He listened as best he could through the ringing in his ears... "Volmer..." But then his paranoia claimed its final revenge...Volmer would take advantage of his condition...he, Alvarez, was close to death...Volmer would stand there, watching, gloating... "Where are you?" he cried out feebly for his two bodyguards; there was no answer, no sound except the distant crump of falling masonry. "Anyone!"

Fear and pain kindled his rage, and he swore venomously at all those who didn't respond. He would deal with them! He would hunt them down one by one no matter where they hid...he would bring them back here...to be his new test subjects! And once the transfer process was perfected...he would have his war against the Lizards! He would...he would... His thoughts blurred, then focussed: Krauss...was taken...by the Lizards...they changed him...turned him...with the recording... Krauss...Krauss hadn't betrayed him after all! He was still loyal...he would come soon. Alvarez felt a feeble flush of renewed hope through the pain in his abdomen. Krauss was still loyal!

But then, as consciousness faded, quenching his last feeble surge of anger, he knew the truth. Krauss was dead...changed into MacKenna... Krauss...Volmer...his two bodyguards...the 'Tan

266

Shirts'...they all failed him... He wheezed as his heart faltered, and whimpered in agony. In one last fleeting moment of sanity as his life ebbed, he realized it was over. His glorious visions of power had been crushed...by Admiral MacKenna...

...There was a sound...faint voices...a vague figure moved in the shadows and a flashlight blinded him, evoking genuine terror...was it Volmer? Krauss? Who? Who came to finish him... His thoughts faltered, the agony faded, and the darkness claimed him as his life drained away onto the dirty concrete floor.

§

It was a long, difficult gallop to where the second truck was parked by the road. They moved as fast as they could, stumbling through the darkness, driven by the knowledge that the humans would react soon, and they must be gone by then. Giselle came stumbling along behind, steadying the wounded defender and steadied by S'deMnveb in turn, gasping for air as she tried to keep pace with the Ic'nichi and fighting to keep her panic in check. By time they reached the highway, she was an emotional wreck. She stumbled to a halt, gasping for air and trembling so badly that she could hardly stand.

S'deMnveb eyed her in concern. "Are you well?"

"I...I...must rest," she gasped. "...too tired..."

"We can't stay long. Can you move?"

"I...ah..." She was confused, her snout contorted in fear.

"We must hurry!"

"We have been discovered," someone said in a hoarse whisper. Their truck was faintly visible ahead, illuminated by the lights of a Peacekeeper patrol vehicle. Two MPs had come by and chanced on their escape route while they were busy with the laboratory. They could make out the vague figures moving against the headlights. If those MPs decided to drive off with their truck, they would be stranded, and probably doomed.

"Great," one of the Leads muttered. "What do we do, sir?"

"Prepare for ambush!" S'deMnveb snapped. "Three vector wide approach, one Hand on each vector." The Specials prepped their weapons and scattered into the darkness.

§

The two MPs were confounded by their discovery, and were wandering around it trying to figure out what they had here. The cab door was open and the engine running, but there was no sign of the driver, and no sign of foul play. On top of which they were distracted and half-blinded by the light of the laboratory burning in the distance, so they were caught completely off guard when they were swarmed by a dozen Ic'nichi commandos packing serious hardware. The surprise was complete: they offered no resistance as they were disarmed.

The corporal was the first to recover his wits. "What are you doing?" he demanded.

One Lizard who seemed to be in charge snapped, "No questions!", then dragged him to the cab door by his arm, shoved a machine pistol in his ear, and added, "You drive, you live!"

"What?" He recoiled in panic from the weapon's muzzle.

"I can do it," a feminine voice said. That was when they realized a human was with them; the voice gave her away, and they realized she must be the escaped test subject.

The Lizard looked at her. "You are sick?"

"I...am afraid."

Another Lizard reappeared, and chattered something at the first. The container was open, and the rest of them were piling into the back.

"Can you manage?" the Lizard asked the human.

"I have to." She sounded so shaky that her chances didn't seem promising, not that either of the MPs offered to help. The Lizard turned to them and raised his machine pistol... "*¡No matarlos!*" she shouted. "Do not kill them!" ...the Lizard looked at her, seemingly uncertain what to do. "There is no need to hurt them."

The Lizard leader pondered them for an eternal moment, then left them in charge of two of his people and turned his attention to their vehicle; first ripping out the radio and confiscating their assault rifle, then putting a burst of machine pistol fire into the engine. The vehicle sputtered and died. Then Boss Lizard pointed the two MPs back up the road toward the burning building. "You run. Ten seconds." They nodded as one, and took off.

§

Somehow Giselle managed to get the heavy truck moving, and with S'deMnveb's help they went weaving down the ancient highway, seemingly hitting every pothole and washout along the way. "I m-must be insane!" she whimpered as tears flowed down her cheeks. "Why did I do this?"

S'deMnveb was scrunched awkwardly in the seat next to her with his machine pistol at the ready, and gave her a nervous glance. "You do well, human," he said. "You do good for someone with no experience." In fact she was trembling so hard he needed to grab the wheel with one hand to steady her.

"*¡Yo no soy un soldado!*"

'You're doing great, Giselle,' the voice whispered encouragement. *'It's always like this the first time. You're doing far better than any of us could have expected.'*

"What choice do I have?" she whimpered. "This is madness!"

'This is war; war is madness.'

The truck rumbled erratically through the night as she fought to contain her panic. She was painfully aware that all their lives depended on her, the weakest link in their entire force, which did her nerves no good. The burden of responsibility added angst to her terror, reducing her to a near basket case. Her arms began cramping from her death grip on the wheel; the truck wavered to one side, and S'deMnveb needed to steady her. "I can not do this..." she whimpered. For all her determination to do her part against the Purity Movement, this was far worse than she could have imagined.

"Be strong, human. We will soon be safe."

'Breathe slow and deep, Giselle; like they taught you in nursing school. We're on our time now. The mission is done, and all we're concerned with is getting away.'

She was already hyperventilating as the terrors of the recent battle came back to haunt her. "They...killed...all those p-people...back there..."

S'deMnveb gave her a guilty look. "We did what we had to."

'Their deaths will keep the mind transfer process from being reverse engineered,' the voice whispered. *'Millions of lives could be lost if that happens.'*

269

Somehow she realized he was right. As much as it went against everything she was raised to believe, some people *need* to die for the greater good. That brought home the true horror of the 6th Office and its evils like nothing before. She sobbed from sheer anguish, and her eyes clouded up with tears...

"Careful, human!" S'deMnveb grabbed the wheel to keep the truck out of the ditch.

"I...am sorry..." She wiped her eyes on one sleeve, and tried to focus on the road ahead. She was well past the edge, and was hanging on solely because she didn't dare succumb to panic.

'Put the fear out of your mind, Giselle. Deal with it later.'

"I am d-doing the...best I can." She was trembling from fatigue as much as fear by then, and managed to ease her death grip on the wheel. "How much further?"

'We'll be at the base...there's the exit!'

She slammed on the brakes, almost jackknifing the heavy rig on the treacherous pavement. They nearly overshot the off ramp leading to the Ic'nichi base, and would have plunged off the collapsed bridge up ahead if her unwelcome passenger hadn't been more alert than she was at the moment. She sat there for a minute or more, staring into the darkness ahead, trembling in barely contained terror. It took forever for her to calm her overwrought nerves enough to relax her grip and sag in the driver's seat. "I cannot do this," she sobbed.

"There is no one else," S'deMnveb said, gently.

"...I..."

"Can the one inside you take over?"

A faint sense of regret welled up beneath her distress. *'I can't, Giselle. I'm too weak.'*

"...he...no, he cannot..."

"Then we depend on you. We can't drive human vehicles."

"*Maldigo a todos,*" she muttered. "*Qué un lío.*"

Somehow she got the truck moving again, made a hard left, and skidded down the embankment to reach the exit ramp. The trailer almost rolled on the steep incline, but she managed to keep it steady. At the bottom of the ramp, she hesitated for a long moment to collect her nerve before turning onto the access road.

Ahead were the dim lights of the landing field, so close that she could almost reach out and touch them...but the lights of the Peacekeeper encampment were closer. The riskiest part of their journey lay dead ahead.

'Don't be afraid, Giselle. We'll do this just like last time. Stay calm, and we'll drift right on through, no sweat.'

S'deMnveb was hunched down in the foot well, nervously holding his machine pistol at the ready.

'You're doing fine, Giselle.'

She could see the lights of the camp clearly; the soft glow of lanterns in the tents, and a pitiful few camp fires where huddled Peacekeepers tried to stay warm. Figures moved in the shadows, and she made out the vague hulks of two armored cars parked by the road. She struggled to keep herself under control for a few more precious minutes...until they got past this last barrier...another half-klick...

As they pulled up to the checkpoint, a figure emerged from the gloom and waved for her to halt. *'Don't stop!'* the voice snapped. She instinctively gunned the truck. The figure jumped aside with an inarticulate yell as the truck roared into the camp, scattering people before it. There was a shot from behind them, then several more. An alarm was shrieking somewhere in the darkness.

She hunched over the steering wheel as S'deMnveb struggled up from his hiding place. A vague figure appeared in the far side window; someone clinging to the side mirror. S'deMnveb shot him, and he vanished. More shots rang out; the side window shattered, barely missing her head. "Faster, human!" he yelled.

"Oh, God! There is something..." A command vehicle swerved onto the road ahead with its headlights pointed straight at them.

'Floor it, Giselle!'

The windshield shattered as they were sprayed with machine gun fire. She ducked instinctively, whimpered, and jammed her foot down on the accelerator as S'deMnveb leaned out the open left side window and sprayed the shadowy figures around them. Another bullet ricocheted off the windshield frame, and punched through the roof as they hit the command vehicle head on. The heavy truck shuddered under the impact, almost careening out of control as the command vehicle was shoved aside. S'deMnveb grabbed the steering wheel with one hand to help steady her as he sprayed a full clip into the darkness ahead at random. There was a dull *THUD!*, and the truck swerved to the left as a tire blew out. She fought the wheel desperately as S'deMnveb emptied another clip into the darkness.

The next thing they knew, the firing faded, and the road ahead was clear. She got a quick glimpse of gun flashes in the rear view mirror before it was shattered.

"We have passed them," S'deMnveb told her.

Giselle didn't answer, but stared straight ahead through the shattered wind shield and held the steering wheel in a death grip. The engine sputtered, and warning lights glowed on the instrument panel. The truck rode hard and tended to pull to the left, forcing her to hold the wheel hard over. There was a hot smell of oil and brake shoes, and the road ahead was all but invisible because both headlights were shot out. The landing field was only another two kilometers ahead: she prayed the battered vehicle would hold together that long.

§

The truck was smoking and sputtering by time they reached the main gate to the landing field. The two watch standers barely had time to jump aside as the truck careened through the checkpoint, scraped along a line of parked trucks by the road, and finally ground to a halt as its motor died. I'eiBida was there, and caught Giselle as she tumbled out of the cab in such a panic that she could hardly stand. "Are you all right?"

She looked at him in glazed, wide-eyed terror, too shaken to speak. But this was no time for polite conversation: there was a burst of weapons fire from the main gate, and the two watch standers came galloping. "The humans are attacking!" one of them yelled as they charged past.

"Alvarez ordered his attack!" S'deMnveb said in dismay. Another burst of machine gun fire revealed a Peacekeeper utility vehicle approaching, backed up by a swarm of humans who fired as they came on.

"No, they're in hot pursuit!" I'eiBida snapped. The Peacekeepers reacted by blind instinct to the fiery passage of the raiding party, and came swarming after them as an enraged mob. "Deploy your force for a fighting retreat."

The Specials piled out of the container without waiting for orders, and set up a hot fire which was quickly supported by the four captured machine guns from their concealed positions. The human pursuers were forced to cover as the utility vehicle was riddled, and its crew abandoned it. The humans held on for a bit, then wavered and fell back under the barrage, but soon an armored car rolled forward, wading into the hail of bullets, and the attack resumed.

"Fall back on the left!" S'deMnveb yelled as their flank was turned. Whatever morale shortcomings the Peacekeepers had, they were trained combat troops, and they came on in force. The Ic'nichi were too few to cover the front they needed to hold, and the humans soon took to feinting and maneuvering to take advantage of any weak spot. As fast as S'deMnveb countered one advance, another spot was threatened; and once the humans took ground, it was impossible to recover it again.

"You can't hold for long!" I'eiBida yelled to him. "Don't try to make a stand!"

"We're taking fire from those ruins!" S'deMnveb yelled back. The narrow neck of the peninsula was flanked by an anchorage where merchant ships once tied up. The ruins on the far shore were infested with snipers who flanked their positions. One of D'remNek's machine guns changed front and started hosing the far shore, but it was a futile gesture.

"Stage a fighting retreat! Don't let them press you too closely! You'll need room to maneuver when you reach the runway!"

S'deMnveb lobbed a grenade at an advancing human, who went down. "Understood, sir!" They still had plenty of cover here in the admin and quarters area, but beyond the warehouses they needed to cross the broad open expanse of tarmac to reach the shuttle. If the humans were in hot pursuit, it could be a disaster. "We should retreat now to get the gallop on them!"

"Right!"

S'deMnveb grabbed their wounded Special, who was fighting one-handed as best he could. "Get to the shuttle! Tell them to be ready for us!" The wounded Special nodded, and took off. Then S'deMnveb was on his command circuit. "All Hands, fall back in skirmish order. Slow them as much as you can, but don't let them close on you."

There was a cry of agony over the storm of automatic weapons fire. "Casualty!" someone yelled. "One down!" One of the Specials was sprawled in a heap with a gushing wound in his neck, thrashing in pain.

"*I'cc'vn!*" S'deMnveb turned to help him, but Giselle was there first.

"I am a nurse." She hauled on one of the wounded Special's arms. "Hold them off, I will tend to him." S'deMnveb fell back and joined the rest in a rear guard as Giselle and I'eiBida half-dragged the wounded defender toward the buildings behind them.

They got maybe a hundred meters to the rear before his legs gave out, and Giselle steered them into temporary shelter behind a dumpster. "He needs help!" The neck wound was hideous, a ragged gash which cut deep into the muscles supporting the head, and severed a major artery. He was covered with blood, which seemed black under the dim street lights; the sight made I'eiBida queasy. She, however, was galvanized into action, tearing the field kit off the casualty's belt and attacking the neck wound, ignoring his thrashing tail pummeling her side.

"How is it?"

She gave him a worried look. "*Muy mal.* I am not trained on their anatomy..." She was interrupted by a spurt of blood, and went back to work, binding up the wound as best she could with the small roll of bandage in the kit. She gave him another harried look when it ran out. "That is all I can do. He needs more."

"We have to go anyway." D'remNek's defenders had abandoned the captured machine guns as their positions were compromised, and were galloping to the rear. "Help him up." They wrestled the wounded defender to his feet by main strength, and half-dragged-half-guided his faltering footsteps as they followed the retreating defenders.

S'deMnveb overtook them before they went another hundred meters. "You need to hurry, sir!" His Specials—what was left of them—moved quickly and carefully from one bit of cover to the next, firing as they went, always coordinating their movements so they maintained a steady harassing fire. But it was hardly enough to slow the oncoming humans, who were over their surprise at the stout resistance, and were pressing a determined attack supported by the armored car.

"Ancestors," I'eiBida muttered when they ducked a stray burst of fire. "I had no idea it would be *this* bad!"

"At least they don't have friggin' artillery!" she snapped.

They could hear the shuttle's idling turbines up ahead, but it was a long, long way to the end of the runway, and the wounded defender was slipping into unconsciousness. Try as they would, I'eiBida and Giselle could barely handle him between them. A short way down the road, they found a couple of D'remNek's defenders in a hasty position behind a traffic sign. "It's no good!" I'eiBida yelled to them. "Help us move him to the shuttle! The Specials will stand rear guard!"

The three of them lifted the semi-conscious Special by main force and trotted for the runway with Giselle running along side trying to contain the bleeding. The sound of weapons fire faded in the distance as they gained ground on S'deMnveb's rear guard, but stray bullets still whizzed past, or glanced off the pavement around them.

"He is in bad shape," Giselle said as she fought to contain the bleeding.

"He'll have to hang on for now," I'eiBida said.

A stray gust of wind brought some light rain, which cooled them and gave them renewed strength. There was an explosion somewhere behind them, and the crackle of weapons fire grew. "Mortars," I'eiBida grunted. Another explosion; they redoubled their effort as they galloped between two warehouses and onto the tarmac. The shuttle stood on the runway ahead, its engines whining. They all uttered fervent prayers of thanks as they staggered across the concrete toward their one hope of escape.

§

It seemed like forever before they staggered to a halt under the shuttle's wing next to the open hatch where D'remNek and a Hand of his people formed a loose perimeter, and eased the wounded Special down on the wet concrete. Giselle dropped to her knees beside him, still fighting the blood flow. "He must have help now!" she said.

"Let's have the aid kit!" I'eiBida yelled through the open hatch. The shuttle was already jammed with D'remNek's people and their two volunteers, but they managed to free the aid kit from its bulkhead niche and pass it hand over hand. She snatched it out of his hands, and dug through the contents in feverish haste, coming up with a roll of medical tape.

"Is there any blood plasma?" she asked as she worked.

"Ah...no...first aid kits don't have artificial blood."

She gave him a harassed glance. "He needs a transfusion. Is there an infusion kit?"

"I...ah...don't think so." I'eiBida was increasingly unsettled by the gore covering her arms.

She brushed back a lock of her hair, leaving a crimson streak on her forehead. "You must have something..."

They were interrupted by a stampede of approaching feet, and S'deMnveb's force materialized out of the gloom. "They're right behind us!" he yelled. "We have to go. Leave everything behind!" His defenders shucked their weapons and gear as they piled into the shuttle.

"Help me with this!" she snapped as she wound the tape frantically around the casualty's neck. Shaken out of his distraction, I'eiBida grabbed a roll of gauze and pitched in. Between them, they managed to reduce the blood flow to a trickle.

"We have to go, sir!" S'deMnveb yelled as the shuttle's turbines revved. The sound of gunfire was closer, and they could see weapon flashes in the distance.

"Party's over," I'eiBida said as he grabbed the casualty by his shoulders and lifted him by main strength. A random spray of bullets kicked up concrete chips around them as they dragged her patient toward the hatch. In their haste, they left the aid kit laying on the runway.

She and S'deMnveb were the last two to board the shuttle. As soon as he secured the hatch, he half-dragged her to an open spot in the jammed cargo bay where the wounded Ic'nichi lay in a spreading pool of blood. "Help him."

Giselle didn't say anything, but looked the casualty over, and nodded grimly.

§

Up forward, the control deck was cramped by the addition of a defense systems station and its operator, so there was barely enough room for I'eiBida to squeeze in behind the two pilots' crash couches. The last blue tell-tale on the engineering panel changed to yellow, indicating that the hatch was shut. "All right, start your takeoff procedure," he snapped to the pilots. "Exactly the same as you always do."

"Yes, sir." The co-pilot keyed his radio. "Ic'nichi shuttle flight three-one-three to Singapore control, requesting clearance for take off. Over."

Tracers zipped past the forward window, followed by a metallic thud as one round hit the hull. "*I'cc'vn*," the co-pilot muttered. All they could do was pray nothing critical was damaged, and that the pressure hull was intact. "What's keeping them?"

The delay seemed to drag on for ever, although it was probably a minute before Singapore control responded. *"Ah...Ic'nichi shuttle three-one-three, negative. You do not have clearance. Wait for further instructions. Over."*

"They suspect us," the pilot said. More tracers, and several hits, hopefully on the heavy ceramic heat shield.

"Do not acknowledge," I'eiBida said. "Take off."

"Yes, sir." The pilot punched his turbines to full power and hit the mass polarizer, and the shuttle surged down the runway. Within seconds, they were airborne, just clearing the fence along the beach. A quick look in the rear view camera showed human troops swarming across the runway below. "Shall I stay low to avoid their tracking, sir?" the pilot asked as they headed out over open water.

"No. Follow your standard flight path."

The pilots exchanged worried looks, and the lead pilot hauled back on his controls. The shuttle climbed sluggishly under their full load as they headed into orbit.

"They are tracking us," the defense technician said. "Regular traffic control radar so far."

"Remain on standby," I'eiBida said. "Keep your transponder active."

A moment later, the radio lit up. *"Singapore control to Ic'nichi shuttle. You do not have flight clearance! Return and land immediately! Over."*

"Sir?" the co-pilot asked.

"Let me handle it." I'eiBida grabbed his headset and donned it hastily. "Ic'nichi shuttle flight three-one-three to Singapore control, please repeat your last. We did not, repeat, did not copy your transmission. Over?"

The two pilots exchanged confused looks.

"Singapore control to Ic'nichi shuttle! Abort your takeoff! Return and land immediately, do you copy? Over!"

I'eiBida waited for several seconds, as long as he dared before responding. "Ah...we do not copy, Singapore Control. You gave us clearance for departure. Is there a problem? Please advise. Over?"

"They fired at us!" Defense said. "We have incoming."

I'eiBida scrunched around to see his view screen. Two white ropes of smoke were climbing toward them from the island, the image surrounded by fast-changing tracking data. "So much for playing innocent," he mumbled.

"Shall I go active, sir?"

"Not yet." I'eiBida studied the view screen intently. The two anti-aircraft missiles were gaining rapidly, and he knew they had plenty of range to intercept them. "Shut down your transponder. Go to maximum thrust, no evasive action."

S'deMnveb stuck his snout in through the narrow passageway from the cargo bay just then. I'eiBida spared him a quick glance. "The mission?"

"We destroyed the lab, sir."

"Brian?"

"I'm sorry, sir. We weren't able to rescue him. We lost my Worthy and a full Hand."

"Ancestors receive them," I'eiBida muttered.

"She was instrumental in achieving the mission, sir."

I'eiBida nodded. "Thank you for getting her back."

"The missiles are closing, sir!"

I'eiBida gave S'deMnveb a quick nod, and turned back to the battle at hand. Grieving would come later.

§

Giselle fought against the acceleration as the shuttle climbed, and *finally* got the bleeding to stop with the last of the tape. She knelt beside the unconscious form, watching anxiously for any sign of renewed flow. At long last she began to relax, which brought the night's traumatic events to mind. She looked at her bloody arms and tunic in dismay as the horrors of the past few hours came back to her. The deck shifted as the shuttle climbed and accelerated, tumbling her on her side. The defenders around her kept her from sliding aft, and someone pressed a cargo strap into her hands. She clung to it with a terrified grip as the shuttle gained speed. Shaken out of her bemused trance, she broke down and began sobbing uncontrollably.

'It's all right, Giselle,' the voice whispered to her. *'We're almost in the clear. Hang on there.'*

"W-we will dieeee!" she moaned.

'Not in front of the troops, Giselle! You have to set an example for them.' The Ic'nichi jammed flank to flank around her stirred uneasily.

"...I...I..."

'You can do it, Giselle. You're the leader. You owe it to them to stay calm.' Somehow that helped her contain her own panic. *'They're counting on you, Giselle.'*

"Human!" someone yelled. "He bleeds!" The casualty was thrashing feebly, and had torn the improvised bandage.

"Dammit!" she snarled. Her panic receded as she struggled to her knees, crawled to him, and jammed her fist onto the open wound. There was blood everywhere, and despite her best effort, she couldn't stop the bleeding. "I need bandages!" she yelled.

'Be careful, Giselle. High grav is tricky; if you lose your balance, you could be seriously hurt.'

"Not now," she snapped. She managed to get the bleeding partly controlled, but the flow ruined the bandage adhesive, rendering it useless. Her arms were shaking from the strain, and her knees ached from pressing into the hard deck at multiple G's. "I need bandages! Now!" she sobbed. There was nothing: in the mad scramble to get away, they left everything including the priceless first aid kit on the runway...

§

"They're approaching critical reaction range, sir." Defense was on the edge of panic. "I need to activate now."

"No. Wait until they reach half critical range, then hit them with everything you have."

Defense looked at him anxiously, then focussed on his screens with his hand hovering over the master power button. The two missiles continued to gain, arcing over to follow them. "We have tactical lock. Missiles are tracking us, sir."

"We're at maximum thrust, sir," the pilot said.

I'eiBida said nothing, watching the screen calmly.

§

Her knees and shins were in agony from the increased acceleration, but she ignored the pain as she fought to save the defender's life. Something bounced off the floor next to her, hit her in the face, and almost got away before she grabbed it: a roll of duct tape from some tool kit. She tried to tease the end of the tape loose, but couldn't grab it with her bloody fingers, so she gripped the end with her teeth, ignoring the dense taste of blood, and pulled enough out so she could work with it.

§

"Critical reaction range." The missiles were closing fast; only seconds remained to use their countermeasures. "I need to activate now, sir!"

"Hold your position!" I'eiBida snapped.

Defense almost protested, but discipline held his rising panic in check. He hunkered down and focussed on his instruments, his ears laid back and tail twitching as much as it could on the

280

crowded flight deck. I'eiBida ignored the tail slapping his shins, and tried to maintain an outward calm while silently praying to his Ancestors to get them through the next few minutes. The shuttle continued to climb way too sluggishly, and when the co-pilot cut in the ramjets as they gained altitude, he left the turbines running until they wheezed and failed in the thinning atmosphere. Despite which, the missiles continued to gain, now clearly visible in the defense view screen.

"Half critical range!" Defense hit his power without waiting for further orders, and began punching his systems as fast as he could. On the stern of the shuttle, a panel fell away revealing a gatling gun which tracked on the first incoming missile and opened fire. At the same time, the electronic countermeasures came up to full force, and a string of flares dropped from the rear of the ship. The first missile was hit and exploded, shaking the shuttle...

§

The duct tape helped, but the bleeding wouldn't stop no matter how many turns she wrapped around his neck. His normally warm brown complexion was waxy gray, but she couldn't wrap the tape any tighter without choking him. Blood spurted out from under the tape, soaking the adhesive and pulling it away from the scaly skin. She looked around desperately at the defenders watching her struggle to save one of their own. "I need something for a compress!" she yelled. But there was nothing: they abandoned all their gear when they boarded. In desperation, she tackled the casualty's footwear, and managed to get one of the flexible, glove-like shoes off. She hastily folded it into a wad, and tried using it as a compress, but to no effect. "Dammit!" she yelled, her tears streaking her blood-spattered face. "I need a compress!"

The blood was spurting erratically, the flow diminishing as he bled out...

§

The gatling gun immediately tracked on the second missile, which was wavering as it tried to overcome the jamming and reacquire them. It never had the chance: a rain of shells exploded it close enough that they could hear bits of shrapnel bounce off the hull.

"Both incoming destroyed, sir," defense said in a shaky whisper.

"And we're too far away for them to launch any more missiles," I'eiBida told him, evenly. Defense gave him a blank look. "Live and learn, mister. They would have if they knew we had countermeasures."

"Sir?" someone called from the cargo deck. "One of the casualties needs help!"

I'eiBida and S'deMnveb looked at each other in dismay. "Great," I'eiBida muttered as they clawed their way back into the crowded cargo compartment.

The defenders had pushed to the sides as far as they could to give Giselle and the casualty a bit of room. She knelt on the bloody deck over the unconscious defender, her prison tunic soaked, one fist pinned under the layers of duct tape as the life-saving compress as she added another winding with her free hand. She looked up them when she finished. "I have the bleeding stopped, but he needs immediate medical attention."

"We...should dock with the ship soon." I'eiBida was distracted and a bit sickened by all the blood. "We will alert their physich to be ready."

"He needs immediate surgery, and blood, too." I'eiBida nodded, and went forward to the control deck.

Silence fell over the compartment, broken only by the muted rumble of the shuttle's engines. Giselle sagged as her tension eased with the passing crisis. She shifted to ease the pain in her knees, keeping her fist pressed firmly against the wound. As far as she was concerned, the worst was over, and she was resigned to whatever came next. They would make their escape from orbit, or the transport would be destroyed. Either way, her fate was out of her hands. She had a patient to attend to—her first ever—and she was free. For the first time since she was arrested by the 'Tan Shirt' goons a year ago, she was no longer afraid.

"Thank you," S'deMnveb mumbled to her at last.

'Damn,' the voice echoed faintly. *'That was slick.'*

*****

"Chapter Eighteen"

Life aboard transport 186 had been hectic ever since they were ordered to prepare for the breakout they were warned about in their mission briefings. The ship was already filled to capacity and beyond with people evacuated from Singapore, and the last shuttle brought word that they could expect another forty-two as the two defender sections and a few odds and ends made the final break. That was a lot to fit into one shuttle; where they would put them all aboard the ship was beyond understanding.

Right then A'vberBenn floated in the center of the command circle in an impromptu staff meeting with his elders. They needed to keep their voices down and watch their tails, as all stations were crewed, but he couldn't bring himself to move the meeting to the lounge deck below, where there was no room anyway.

"I *told* them this isn't a colony ship," he complained. "*How* will we cram them all in?"

"Our logistics are still a mess, sir," the Second said. "Water is critical, and we're not much better off for oxygen."

"They should have used a liner for this mission," the Fourth grumbled.

"I should have stayed at home and called in sick." A'vberBenn shook his head in dismay. "And to *think* I could have been an accountant."

In addition to the forty-two crew, they had over one hundred evacuees from Singapore, eight embassy personnel rotating home, and another eight originally bound to Geneva. The last shuttle brought the few remaining Intel personnel; still to come were the two defender sections holding the landing field and a few hangers-on. Two hundred bodies would strain their life support to the limit, to say nothing of having to stack them like cordwood in the cargo holds.

"We will have to go four rotations in the few hammocks we have, sir," the Second told him. "Including the crew. The upper cargo bay is set up for sleeping quarters, and as soon as we can clear the lower bay, it will be the day area. Where we'll put them until then, I have no idea."

There was still a fair amount of cargo, mostly human freight meant for their embassy in the World Nest, which needed to go. Word from Singapore was the Specials were about to raid the 6th Office laboratory, and hoped to be back before dawn. Off-loading had ceased, and the rest of the cargo would have to be dumped on the run.

"Once we get under way, round up all the able-bodied tails you can find and put them to good use," A'vberBenn said to the Fourth. "Zero-G training or not, I want that cargo cleared before we leave the system."

"Well, it should be easier under acceleration at least," the Fourth muttered.

A'vberBenn gave him a sympathetic ear twitch. "You and your people have done a fine job. It's not our fault we were tail-knotted like this."

"Four rotations," their physich sighed. "We're all going to be seriously short on sleep."

"They'll get plenty of sleep in a human internment camp!" A'vberBenn snapped at her. They were already seriously short on sleep, and tempers were frayed.

"Still, these civilians aren't used to this, or the short rations, either. We'll have to watch their health carefully."

A'vberBenn sighed. "I know. What about the shuttle?" he asked his Fourth.

"The loading is complete, sir."

"Right. As soon as I give the word, jettison it, and the other one as well."

"Yes, sir."

"Did you finish sorting the food stocks?"

"Yes, sir. I packed as much as I could into the frozen food locker. We should have enough to make the trip home."

A'vberBenn sighed at the thought. Their stock of endurance rations was nowhere near enough for so many mouths, so on top of the sorry state their filters would be in, the ship would be filthy with crumbs and scraps by time they got home. Assuming they *did* get home. "Very well. Thank you." That brought up another worry. "What about our water supply?"

284

"The tanks are full, and my section is completing an overhaul of the number three filtration unit," the Third reported. "The other two are running at full speed. Depending on how often we have to dump sewage, we should make it, although we'll be mighty thirsty by time we reach d'enchia." They would have to dump their septic tanks at least twice as well; which brought to mind the bizarre image of masses of raw sewage hurtling through hyper-C to the ends of the Universe.

"Mighty smelly too," the Fourth noted. The zero-G showers would be secured for the duration, and drinking water would only be available in the galley.

"Adventure on the far frontier," the Third grumbled, parodying the classic recruiting slogan. That got a sour chuckle from most of them.

"Speaking of which, who came up with this tail-knotted maneuver they expect us to pull off?" Fourth asked. "Can the ship survive?"

That would be the Second, who handled navigation, but he forbore to comment. "Ask me tomorrow."

"I told them this isn't a colony ship," A'vberBenn said for the umpteenth time.

The duty Communications rating interrupted their gripe session. "The shuttle has launched, Eldest."

"All right, stations, everyone," A'vberBenn said. "Get the defense system on line and stand by to maneuver."

They broke up and moved cautiously to their stations; the command deck was more crowded than ever with an extra control station for the suite of passive defenses installed just for the occasion. The status reports started coming at once.

"Defense standing by, sir."

"Power board ready, sir."

"Maneuvering ready, sir."

"All crew at stations, damage control on standby, sir. Emergency decompression herd set."

"I have the shuttle in sight, sir," the Second said as he feverishly worked the navigation computer. "I have the rendezvous programmed," he added a moment later.

285

A'vberBenn took a deep breath to steady his nerves; this ship was not designed for what they were about to do, and it went against all his training, years of experience, and common sense. "All right everyone, this will be tricky, so keep your tails tucked in. Initiate attitude burns, capacitor on standby."

The ship's plasma drive would take far too long to move them clear of the human defenses.   Instead, they would use the maneuvering thrusters aided by the mass polarizer to jump forward, then brake sharply back to orbital speed.   Aside from having to cut a shallow chord through the planet's upper atmosphere—something their ship was *not* designed for—they ran the real risk of hitting some random bit of space junk, of which there was plenty in earth orbit, but it was their one chance to outrun the humans.

The horizon shifted slowly as the ship's computer adjusted their attitude.   "The courier is maneuvering, sir," the Second reported. On one screen, their companion ship was turning to match them.

"Anything from the humans?"

"Not yet, sir," Defense reported.   "They're tracking us on their traffic control system."

"Maneuver completed, sir," Helm reported.   The center pip in the view screens was aimed well below the planetary horizon.   It was an unnerving sight for all of them.

"Let's hope this works," A'vberBenn said fervently.   "Forward on thrusters.   Thirty percent discharge on capacitor.   Take the lead in front of the courier."   The Second entered the commands on his keying column, and turned the key to unlock the drive...

§

The Duty Officer aboard Space Dock had received the alert about the Ic'nichi shuttle launch, and was just picking the rogue shuttle up on his ground scan telescope when the maneuvering thrusters on both Ic'nichi ships suddenly bloomed, followed by the automatic squawk from the traffic control computer as it detected movement.   He stared back and forth at the two monitors in confusion, then hit the General Quarters alarm.   Within seconds, the station Commodore was on the horn.   "What's going on up there, mister?"

"Ah...the Ic'nichi, sir, they're all over the place! Both ships are maneuvering, and they have a shuttle coming up..." He hesitated as a new report came over his monitor. "...And Singapore reports they've been attacked, sir!"

"Alert the ships! And go to battle status!"

"Yes, sir!" He was already on it.

There were three human warships in orbit: a cruiser and two destroyers. The cruiser and one destroyer were on one hour status, but that still meant an hour before either could bring their systems on line and get under way. That didn't mean they couldn't fire missiles.

The alarm tone changed as the computer picked up something which should be impossible. The Duty Officer stared in disbelief at the courses projected on his display. "*Sir?* Both Ic'nichi ships are under way, *into* the atmosphere!"

§

Down in Singapore, dawn was just breaking, but the Admiral was at his desk busy with paperwork, as usual. His phone buzzed, and he picked it up without thinking about it. "Yes?"

"Here is a recording of a recent conversation which might interest you." The voice had a crisp, faintly British accent; he realized immediately it was an Ic'nichi. "You will want to consider this carefully."

"What?" He was startled out of his dreary predawn routine. "Who is this?"

"The Admiral and his Chief of Operations are causing no end of trouble, sir." He recognized the voice as Volmer. "They seem to be on to us, the Flag Ops in particular."

"Indeed?" Alvarez said, coolly. "That is only to be expected. The time will come soon enough do something about it."

"It's going badly, thanks to *them*."

A voice came over the line. "Who is this? Who are you?"

"Vandemere? Is that you?"

"Yes, Admiral. What is this?"

"...impress on you how critical this is?" Alvarez was saying. "We have to move now. The information the Lizards stole could destroy us unless we preempt Space Fleet."

"Is it that bad, Colonel?"

"You do *not* wish to fail in this matter, Volmer!"

By now the Admiral, his Flag Ops, Security, and Fleet Intel were all on the line. "Sir?" Security asked. "What is this...?

"Quiet! All of you!"

"...what about the Lizard evacuation, sir? They clearly intend to get the information back to their world."

"No doubt, but we will allow their pretense for now. You focus on securing the spaceport so we can move swiftly against the renegades."

"But..."

"You have your instructions! As for the Lizards, once we take over Space Fleet, I will order them to destroy the transport, and the courier as well. Let them run for now; the trap is already set."

"I am on it, Colonel! And the traitors?"

"Borneo is a fitting answer." The Admiral blanched at Alvarez's threat, then his anger rose. "This crisis will soon be under control, and we will no longer need to put up with them."

"What about Geneva, sir?"

"I will deal with Geneva. *You* make your preparations! Do *not* fail me, Volmer! My patience is at an end!"

The line went silent except for the faint sound of several people breathing. "You all heard?" the Admiral asked at last. There was a chorus of affirmatives. "My office. Five minutes!"

§

The view screens glowed as they hit the upper atmosphere, and they could hear the thin scream of air friction as it tore at their hull. The command herd waited silently, watching their instruments and praying to their Ancestors as the ship rocked and buffeted. As feeble as their maneuvering jets were, they provided enough kick at near zero mass to push the ship well past escape velocity. There was a heavy *THUD!* from somewhere below; lights were blinking, and alarms sounded. Everyone tensed, ears laid back as they cut two blazing tracks across the nighttime Asian sky.

"Structural alarm in the central column, sir!" Engineering reported. Another alarm went off. "And we lost pressure in the astrogation dome!"

288

Their passage through the wispy upper air would only take seconds, but there was no guarantee they would last that long without crippling damage. There was another dull *THUD!*, and the ship shuddered as something was torn away.

"We lost our comm laser," Communications reported. Thankfully they were already through the fringes of the upper atmosphere, and heading back up toward vacuum.

"Reversing thrust!" Helm yelled as the howl of air friction faded. The capacitor surged again as the forward maneuvering thrusters fired. They never used this particular braking method in ordinary service, and had to grab whatever handholds they could as pencils, clipboards, and odd junk unexpectedly went bouncing around the command deck.

Then, almost as fast as it started, it was over. They hovered where they came to rest for a moment, stunned by the rough ride, the silence broken by the creaking and popping of the heated hull.

"Damage reports!" A'vberBenn snapped.

They all spasmed at that, and studied their instruments nervously. "Navigation blister's gone, sir!", Engineering said. Thankfully they shut the overhead hatch as a precaution. "Pressure holding otherwise."

"All power systems show good, sir," Power Board reported. "Capacitor is down to forty percent. Not enough to hyper-jump."

"Fleet channel is out. Tactical channel is erratic..." Communications fiddled anxiously with her controls. "...but I'm picking up the shuttle."

"What about the courier?" Half their view screens were dead, and without the navigation telescope, they needed to rely on radio communications to know the fate of their other ship.

Communications adjusted her controls. "I have a faint signal, sir...they took major damage...but they are able to maneuver."

By the grace of their Ancestors, their dip into earth's atmosphere only cost them a couple antennas carried away and the plastic navigation blister melted.

"Ancestors, it worked!" the Second said in amazement.

"We're not out of this yet!" A'vberBenn snapped. "All right, where are we?"

The Second shook off his bemusement, and studied his panel. "It looks like we're roughly in position to recover the shuttle, sir."

"We may pull this off yet. Get the recharge started! Get those defense systems on line! And get damage control to work!"

With the capacitor nearly flat-lined, they were stuck in earth's defense zone. It would take days for a full recharge, and the plasma drive delivered about 1/8th standard gravity without it. They could live-feed the reactor's power into the polarizer, but that only reduced the ship's mass by about ten percent; much better acceleration, but not enough to outrun earth's defenses.

"Tracking is active, sir! No sign of a reaction yet."

"Defense systems active, sir!"

"Drive standing by, sir," Power board added. "Reactor at full power and charging the capacitor."

"How soon until the shuttle docks?"

§

"There's the ship, sir," the shuttle pilot said to I'eiBida.

"Hmph! We might get away with this after all," he muttered to himself. From the visible damage the transport sustained, that could take some luck. "How soon do we dock?"

The pilot spared him a glance. "How neat do you want this, sir?"

"Just get us there."

The pilot gave him a raised eye ridge. "Then we should be docking momentarily, sir."

"But it won't be pretty," the co-pilot added.

§

The Commodore arrived on the Orbit Dock bridge as the last battle stations were reporting in. "What happened? he demanded.

The Duty Officer gave him a frazzled look. "Those crazy Lizards jumped both ships *through* the atmosphere, sir! They're roughly thirty degrees ahead of us in orbit. It looks like they plan to grab that shuttle on the fly, and make a run for it."

On the long range view screen, the two ships were low on the horizon, with the triangular sliver of the shuttle closing on the transport. "Order them to surrender at once."

§

They were closing fast—too fast—aimed straight in rather than parallel, but there was no time to carefully maneuver the shuttle to the docking ring on the ship's central column. The pilot uttered a vivid curse, cut out the flight computer, deftly rotated the shuttle by hand and eye, and hit the main engine. It was rude, crude, and vulgar, but he was one of the best shuttle pilots in the fleet. The shuttle stopped about three lengths from the column—facing aft.

"This is embarrassing," he sighed as they drifted toward the docking platform.

"You'll have nothing to be embarrassed about if it gets us home," I'eiBida said.

The shuttle collided with the ship rather than docking. The pilot hit the mating collar perfectly, but the impact broke two of the docking clamps and bent the mating seal. The cargo specialist pushed through the tumble of bodies to the access hatch leaving a trail of vivid curses in his wake. "We have pressure loss, sir!" he called after trying the test valve.

"How bad is it?" I'eiBida demanded.

"It looks like a slow leak, sir."

"Open up. We have no choice, so we'll have to gamble."

§

"Ancestors!" the Second muttered as the ship whip-sawed from the impact on the spindly central column.

"Damage report!" A'vberBenn snapped.

"The stain gauges show over-stressing, sir. Systems seem to be functioning, the dampers are kicking in..." Engineering gripped his console to steady himself as the habitat module swayed back and forth, and studied his instruments anxiously. "...and there is an air leak in the access tube. They damaged the lock seal."

"*l'cc'vn!*" A'vberBenn studied the aft view screen in dismay. "And we can't maneuver while they're hanging on us tail first like that!" The shuttles normally rested on a support girder while the ship was under way; without that support, the main engines would rip the shuttle loose, sending it crashing into the capacitor, and possibly snapping the central column. He called down to the cargo decks. "Fourth! Get that hatch open and get them, aboard!"

§

The hatch in the shuttle's roof opened with a whoosh of outrushing air. "Move!" one of the crew yelled down to them. "We're leaking!"

"Steady!" I'eiBida yelled from the back of the herd struggling toward the damaged lock. "Don't panic!" He fought his way to the hatch and shoved the frightened defenders back. "Get the wounded out first!"

Getting Giselle and the wounded defender through the hatch in one awkward package took some doing, and if it wasn't for her slender build and willingness to be bent any which way, they couldn't have done it. They were all gasping by then, and the casualty was limp despite the portable oxygen cone over his snout. I'eiBida shared his breather cone with Giselle, which was enough to keep her conscious. "Are you all right?" I'eiBida asked once she was fully in the docking bay.

She was blood soaked, her prison tunic tattered, and she was still duct-taped to the casualty, the two of them surrounded by a fine bloody mist. She flexed her knees, and winced. "*Si*. But I think we just invented a new form of kinky sex."

"All right, get them topside." The other wounded Special was mobile enough to help as she and the casualty were sent up the elevator to the equipment deck above.

"We're losing air fast, sir." The Fourth hefted an emergency silicone sealant gun. "We need to plug the seal."

"No time. We have to unload and jettison the shuttles before the humans fire on us." The elevator returned, empty. "Let's go!" he yelled down the docking tube. The elevator normally held six, but they managed to cram ten aboard, standing practically on each other's shoulders. "Watch your tails." I'eiBida hit the button, and the elevator climbed up the shaft with its motors whining.

§

Three decks above, the ship's physich was dismayed as the major casualty was floated into her cubical in a cloud of blood with a *human* duct-taped to him. "Gunshot wound to the right lower neck!" the human fem snapped. "Major artery severed! He needs oxygen and blood, stat!" If she was shaken by recent events, as she had every right to be, she didn't show it.

The physich didn't understand half of what she said, but the situation was obvious. She stared in amazement at the human's fist *taped into the wound* as a makeshift compress, then she turned and fumbled a unit of artificial blood out of a locker. "Give me that!" The human snatched the end of the feed tube and deftly slid it into a vein. "Get the oxygen!"

§

"That's the last of them, sir!" the shuttle pilot reported as he came up the docking shaft. They'd sent four loads up to the habitat above, and now the last stragglers were squeezing through the access tube. Most of the air was gone; there was still enough to make do with breather units, but they had to act fast.

"All right, seal the hatch," the Fourth said.

As they rode up the elevator, the Fourth examined the buckled hull plating and bent ribs of the central column in dismay. Several major pipes were broken loose from their brackets, and the elevator trolleys squealed as they scraped past buckles in their rails. "*l'cc'vn,*" he muttered as he studied the damage. "We're lucky to be in one piece." He turned to the shuttle pilot. "That docking was *cc'v'renk.*"

The pilot was unfazed by his criticism, being too weary and wrung out to care any more. "This whole tail-knotted operation is *cc'v'renk.*"

The Fourth twitched his ears, bemused. "You have no idea."

"I just hope it holds together when we accelerate."

The elevator reached the habitat, and they were hit with a welcome whoosh of air as the upper lock opened. "That's it," the Fourth said to his people. "Jettison both shuttles, and get to work moving the cargo out."

§

"The load-out is complete, sir!" the Third reported from the equipment bay. "We took some structural damage to the column, so be careful with the main drive."

"Thank you." A'vberBenn turned to the Power Board. "How much on the capacitor?"

"Forty-one percent, sir!"

"Both shuttles have been jettisoned, sir."

"Right. Get us out of here as fast as you can. Drain the capacitor, burn it all."

The helm rating gave him a worried look. "Sir?"

"We have to risk it."

The helm rating replied with a nervous ear twitch, and turned to his controls.

§

"They're under way, sir!" the Duty Officer reported.

In his screens, the two Ic'nichi ships were hidden by the glare of their drives, but they seemed to jump ahead as their capacitors were flat-lined. The speed burst only lasted moments, but it was enough to push them to escape velocity.

"Stand by on missiles!" the Commodore said.

"Missiles armed, sir!" Weapons reported. "Locked on!"

"Fire one through four!"

The station shuddered as four long range guided missiles leapt from the launching rails and streaked toward the fleeing ships.

"They're jamming us, sir!" Weapons reported as a wave of electronic interference came up on their scanners. "Missiles have lost lock." Not good: if their ships were armed, that meant they planned this move for some time. The Commodore gnawed his lip as he wondered what surprises they had in store...

"They jettisoned their shuttles, sir!" Weapons said as the two tumbling craft emerged from the drive glare. Two of the missiles locked onto one shuttle, blowing it to bits, while the other two went wandering off at random.

§

Once the oxygen was flowing, the physich cut the tape binding the human; they were greeted by a burst of crimson which soaked both of them. The physich recoiled in dismay, wondering what she could do for the wounded defender who was covered in blood.

Giselle uttered a vivid curse, grabbed several artificial blood units out of the cabinet, and started plugging them in wherever she could find veins. "I *will not* lose you!" she muttered as she worked. The physich couldn't understand her, but the tone was unmistakable, and it galvanized her to a renewed effort.

§

"One shuttle destroyed, sir," A'vberBenn told I'eiBida when he arrived in the command circle. "The countermeasures worked, and we're close enough to their atmospheric horizon that they will be hard put to hit us with any further launches."

"Good work on that, but we still have to get past the orbital weapons platforms, not to mention being pursued by those ships."

Aside from Orbit Dock, the orbital ship yard, and the supply depots, earth was ringed with radar pickets, missile batteries, and minefield spreaders remotely controlled from Singapore. There were established minefields further out in synchronous orbits, but they had been mapped by Ic'nichi Intelligence, and could be avoided. Thus far none of them showed any sign of life beyond traffic control radars, but if they opened up, the two fugitive ships would be lucky to get very far.

"How long do we have, sir?" A'vberBenn asked.

I'eiBida shook his head. "Unknown. We're depending on their reaction time down in Singapore."

They were pulling about a quarter standard G, and earth was beginning to show its spherical shape, but they had a long way to go. A faint metallic groan came from somewhere aft, and caution lights blinked on the engineering board. They all held their breath, ears laid back nervously until the strain gauges steadied. "Keep going," A'vberBenn said to Helm.

§

Having failed with their missiles, the Commodore fell back on his most accessible resource: the ships parked nearby. "You and the *Visigoth* get under way as soon as you can," he said to the captain of the *Verdun*. "Overtake them as fast as possible."

The *Verdun* was the latest addition to the fleet, a new class of ship sometimes dubbed a 'heavy cruiser' which carried more firepower than most known Ic'nichi ships. And while the *Visigoth* was an older destroyer, she was thoroughly modern, and had a first rate crew.

"How soon can you get under way?"

"Forty minutes, sir!" the *Verdun's* captain said.

"Make it thirty, mister."

"They refuse to answer, sir," the Duty Officer said.

"The damned fools! What do they hope to accomplish?"

"Message from Singapore, sir," Communications said. "It's the Admiral, and he isn't happy."

"No one gets to be happy," the Commodore told him as he reached for the comm phone. "Admiral? We weren't able to stop them, so I've ordered the Verdun and Visigoth to pursue. They should be under way in half an hour."

"Ah...no, don't take any undue risks, mister. Have those ships follow *strict* procedure in getting under way. We don't want any accidents."

The Commodore was confused. "But sir..."

"By the numbers, mister! Do I make myself clear? We can't afford any operational losses now."

This was completely out of character for the Admiral, who was a hard-case in the fleet's cherished MacKenna tradition. The Commodore and Duty Officer exchanged dubious looks. Then it sank in. "Ah...yes, Admiral, by the numbers."

"Sir?" the Duty Officer asked once the link was broken.

"You heard the man: by the numbers."

The Verdun was first to break orbit, an hour and a half later, with the Visigoth twenty minutes behind her.

§

"Come on, move!" the Fourth yelled as the crew and assorted ground force struggled with bales and boxes and tubs of frozen food. "The sooner you get it out the air locks, the sooner you'll have a place to sit down."

The deck under them swayed gently; a harmonic set up by the buckled central column which the dampers couldn't contain. The Fourth gauged the sway uneasily, wondering how long it would take for metal fatigue to set in. The elevator from the shuttle lock returned, and they began hustling heavy cargo aboard. Their best hope to prevent a catastrophic failure was to lighten ship, but cramming some hundred tons of cargo down the elevator shaft and out through the two shuttle access locks would take forever.

"Put your tails in it you *hro'n'nad riv'Agna*! You don't get to quit until it's all gone!"

§

296

The *Verdun's* Captain was dismayed by the reports they were hearing over the fleet communications: an Ic'nichi force had raided the 6th Office compound inflicting major damage and heavy losses. What's more, their landing field at Singapore was abandoned after a stiff fight with Peacekeeper troops. The raiders and base staff were obviously on the two fleeting ships.

The two rogues were well ahead of them and pulling away steadily, while the *Verdun* and *Visigoth* had just left orbit. They were pursuing as fast as their engines could push them, but couldn't overtake them before they went into hyper-C at this pace.

"Power systems! Draw down the capacitor faster! I want to close the range."

"It's no good, sir," the Exec said. "They're too far ahead, and we're already risking debris strikes this close to earth."

"Plus we have to skirt minefield layer number twenty-four, sir!" Weapons added.

"*Do not take any undue risks, mister!*" the delayed demand came from Singapore.

The Captain cut the connection without bothering to answer. He could smell a rat, especially since the 6th Office was involved.

§

"We are running out of blood," Giselle said, grimly. The ship's limited stock was all but exhausted, and the physich was stymied by the pulsing flow as she fought to stitch the torn artery. The monitor next to the table was fluctuating wildly as the casualty's hearts fluttered. Giselle watched her struggle, then grabbed the casualty by the neck just below the wound, choking off the flow. "Hurry! We cannot do this for long!"

The physich was a bit unnerved; this was her first time this close to a human, especially one drenched in blood and sporting all the ear-twitches of a fanatic. She redoubled her efforts, making progress against the reduced flow.

§

"Two human ships are after us, sir," A'vberBenn told I'eiBida.

"Not good." He studied the two small pips pursuing them in the rear screen, and his ears sagged in dismay. "I didn't figure they could react so fast."

"And we're still in range of the orbital batteries, sir."

"What about our defenses?"

"Both we and the courier lost our comm lasers in the atmosphere, sir."

"*I'cc'vn!* I was counting on those." The comm lasers were modified to deliver full power at close range, making them decent anti-ship weapons. Without them, they were left with their countermeasures and the gatling guns which could only fire aft. "We can't outrun them, or out-fight them, and we can't charge the capacitors..." I'eiBida's ears sagged again. "Unless we have a stroke of luck, they'll overtake us eventually. There won't be a blessed thing we can do then but surrender."

"Why don't they shoot?" A'vberBenn muttered. They were passing less than a million lengths from an orbital platform bristling with long range nuclear-tipped missiles.

"They may not have given the word to their ground controllers yet," I'eiBida suggested. "Communications lag."

"Or her recording perhaps?" T'thReptn suggested.

"It's our only real hope."

"Well, either way, let's pray for more human inefficiency."

§

Another elevator load arrived at the shuttle dock from the cargo bays, and two vac-suited cargo handlers began feverishly stuffing boxes into the shuttle access tubes. They were both weary, and working in the heavy vac suits under acceleration was draining, but they kept doggedly at it knowing each box ejected was that much less strain on the damaged central column.

It didn't take long to fill both access tubes to capacity. One of them slammed the hatches shut and hit the chamber compression inlet valves, charging the access tubes from their priceless reserve air supply. Then he hit the outer hatch buttons; the explosive decompression vaulted the cargo away from the ship and the bulky capacitor just below.

On the equipment deck above, they heard the faint thump and hiss as the cargo was ejected. They had no choice about it if they were to offload on the run, but everyone involved wondered gloomily how much air they could afford to lose.

The elevator returned. "Right," the Fourth said. "Let's get the next load moving." The work party turned to, hustling more material into the elevator.

§

The physich added one more round of surgical tape to the stitched neck wound, and watched carefully for any sign of renewed trauma. Her cubicle looked like a slaughterhouse, but the bleeding was stopped, the patient's blood pressure was creeping upward, and his hearts rhythms were stabilizing. Barring infection, he would live. The two of them stared at each other over their patient, bewildered by their struggle. "We...do it," the physich mumbled in her limited human.

Giselle stared back at her, gasping and trembling in a state of near shock. "*Si,*" she whispered at last. "*Madre de Dios,* we did it."

§

"They're out of range of the orbital batteries, sir," Sensors reported to the Verdun's Captain.

"We can't catch them unless we jump, and the odds of coming out within range would be pure luck," the Exec added.

"That won't save them," the Captain muttered. He knew the Admiral was up to something, but he couldn't risk running afoul of the 6th Office. "Weapons! Charge up the special torpedos and lock them in." The Verdun carried four mass polarizer equipped torpedos—another Ic'nichi invention which proved useful—and the Visigoth had two. Their polarizers would give them all the acceleration needed to overtake the two fugitives, and by time they closed, they would be moving at a sizable fraction of the speed of light: the Ic'nichi would have no chance of countering them.

"Torpedos ready, sir," Weapons reported a few minutes later. "Both targets acquired, well enough for nuclear shots, at least."

"They aren't responding, sir," Communications reported.

"All right, we gave them a chance," the Captain grumbled. "Missiles! Stand by to..."

His order was interrupted when one of the cases of 'machine tools' impacted on the astrogation dome, cracking it and setting off the decompression alarm.

"Suits!" the Exec howled. The crew forgot the impending battle as they struggled frantically to close their vac suits and hook up to the ship's emergency air system. Seconds later, a bale of *uf'thoka* finished the job, sending them scrambling for handholds as the ship decompressed. Out of the corner of his eye, the Captain saw a blinding flash on one screen as the Visigoth's capacitor was shorted out by another wooden 'machine tool' crate, half-vaporizing their drive section.

There was another impact. "Tracking antenna carried away, sir!" Further impacts; the lights went dead, and the stars began drifting across the surviving view screens as the ship tumbled out of control.

§

Nearly four days later, once the ships were able to jump out-system, all aboard were able to relax. After the two human pursuers were wrecked, they hid in the Oort Cloud charging their capacitors and discharging the last of their cargo, and when more pursuing human ships were off elsewhere, jumped to hyper-C.

A'vberBenn finally made his way down from the command deck to the galley level where the surviving Specials were gathered. "Well, we did it," he told I'eiBida. "We escaped from earth, and are on our way home. Ancestors, how we ever managed to pull off this tail-knotted, earless excuse for an operation is beyond me." He offered them an exasperated look and a perturbed ear twitch. "They'll either promote the lot of us or send us all to a penal nest for life. Bless me if I'm not sure which would make me happier."

"You're alive," I'eiBida told him pointedly. "Your Ancestors must think highly of you."

"You call this living?" The Eldest was coming down off his panic and exhaustion high, which made him cranky. "Do you have any *idea* how much paperwork I face after this *p'quas'tka*? Not to mention they may well take all the damage we suffered *and* those two shuttles out of *my* pay."

"*You* should complain!" I'eiBida gave him a humorless smile. "You won't have to explain this little adventure to my bondmate!"

"Prison might be easier, sir," B'monTrea said with a wry grin.

"You may be right." I'eiBida was so bemused by recent events that he couldn't fault B'monTrea's presumption.

"Yes, well, maybe so," A'vberBenn allowed. "In any event, we will reach *b'vem'n'uii* Great Nest in twelve days. Ship number 140 is due there by then, and we can transfer enough oxygen and other supplies to make it home."

"Home," I'eiBida sighed. "Ancestors, we really pulled it off."

B'monTrea offered a sardonic ear twitch. "We should take sworn testimony from everyone involved, sir. No one will believe our after-action report otherwise."

I'eiBida gave that a derisive chuckle. "We better get it endorsed by our Ancestors while we're at it."

S'deMnveb came up the elevator just then, looking a hundred years old. "How is your defender?" I'eiBida asked.

S'deMnveb sagged on one of the hard plastic belly cushions with a weary sigh. His uniform was still filthy, and bloodstained, and he was emotionally drained. "They both will live; L'kneDrum especially, thanks to her."

It was touch-and-go, but Giselle and the ship's physich stabilized the critically wounded defender, although the physich swore to all and sundry he should have died there on the runway in Singapore. As for Giselle, once the physich pronounced the casualty out of danger, I'eiBida gently lead her away and insisted she delve generously into their limited water supply to rinse herself clean. After which he deposited her in an out of the way spot near one of the viewports on the galley deck, about the only room which could be found for her, and left her to get over her shakes.

"It's a shame the other human didn't make it, sir," B'monTrea said. "We owe him a lot, and I can see why you admire him so."

I'eiBida shook his head in bemusement. "For sheer *l'fru'ng*, you'll have to trot a long way to find his equal. We could all learn some valuable lessons from him." He paused and looked idly at Giselle, who floated near one of the windows staring at the emptiness beyond. "We raided their most important military base, destroyed their secret laboratory, liberated their captive MacKenna subject, killed their mind program specialists, and got away with minimum casualties. It's hard to believe."

"Not to mention those two wrecked human warships," B'monTrea added with a grin. "Talk about luck! We shall have to recommend frozen food as a new tactical weapon."

I'eiBida answered with a derisive snort. "It's a shame about him, though." He was silent for a bit as he brooded over Mac's death. "This is the second time I haven't been able to fulfill my promise to him," he said at last. "I hope my Ancestors will understand."

"There's still her, sir." B'monTrea gestured at Giselle. "I understand you promised to take care of her."

She was watching them silently now as she floated by the window. I'eiBida pondered her as he contemplated the future. "Yes, I did, and I'll try to do what's right for her, although Ancestors know if I can. I suspect we'll need her: we may have contained the threat posed by the mind transfer program, and knotted the 6th Office's tail, but I'm afraid we touched off the war we were trying to prevent."

"Will she be able to do any good, sir? From what you said, her MacKenna implant is greatly weakened, and no doubt will fade further by time the hostilities get rolling."

I'eiBida sighed. "We can only hope for the best."

"*No se preocupe, mi amigo*," Giselle said, evenly. "I know how to defeat them."

*****

"Denouement"

The young woman in the video trembled; tears rolled down her cheeks; the words coming from her lips carried the ring of Command Authority which evoked instant obedience, tolerated no fools, and was known to eat junior officers alive:

§

"And if they can do this to her, they can do it to anyone: your parents, your spouses, your brothers and sisters, your children.   You.   They can suborn any public figure: legislators, teachers, judges, activists, priests.   They can erase anyone's mind, and replace them with a Secret Policeman, so they can even infiltrate your homes and school playgrounds."

§

Despite their apprehensions, the war I'eiBida expected didn't *quite* break out.   The Arbiter in Geneva, alerted by a secure transmission from the courier before it jumped out-system, informed the Chancellor of what was going on in the 6th Office, and sternly threatened them with public exposure.   That blunted the wrath of the warmongers for the moment as they turned their attention to doings in Singapore.   It couldn't buy much time, but it was all Ic'nichi Intel needed.

§

"Ladies and gentlemen, I fought through the Collapse; I've seen seventy-five years of war up close and personal; I watched through the periscope of the submarine I commanded as Singapore was nuked flat: and I can tell you that this is far worse than the bomb ever was.   With this, they can create the ultimate, permanent Totalitarian state."

§

She went on like that for over an hour, laying it down in stark, grim detail.   And on top of the undeniable facts, generously backed up with photos and other intel, her words carried a skin-crawling, nightmarish quality which touched people in the darkest corners of their fears.

§

"This is your last chance! You have to stop them now, or it's all over for our civilization. Humanity will sink into a Dark Age which we'll never rise from again.   If that happens, if you can't stop the Purity Movement, then the Ic'nichi will do what they must to protect themselves."

§

Her eyes were sick with fear, and she gripped the podium with both hands to steady herself. Despite the steel in her voice, she was on the edge of losing it. Millions were, all across earth at that moment.

§

P'tveb'n'ii T-ggr'tian Medical Institute
The World Nest, d'enchia
325 Common 13th t'n-bran'm'brn:

Giselle was finishing breakfast with Doctor Eddington when I'eiBida arrived.   They were seated at the small table in the courtyard of the top security research lab where Mac was reborn, and where they spent the last year putting her mind back together. The morning was unseasonably mild, and it promised to be warm later, so she was dressed in shorts, a tank top, and sandals. Eddington had been regaling her again over tea and sweet rolls with tales of his youth in East Africa, which put her in a relaxed, wistful mood. Despite the wariness in her eyes, she looked more at ease than ever—with just a hint of the nightmares haunting her dreams. Eddington's bedside manner had progressed by leaps and bounds over the years.

"Doctor Eddington tells me you are cured, Giselle," I'eiBida said.

"I guess," she muttered.

"Her neural scans show clear, and her word association tests come up within predictable norms." Eddington paused to finish his tea.   "As near as we can tell, the last traces of the implant have been erased by this new round of anti-psychotic drug therapy."

That hurt in a way, although I'eiBida was expecting it. He took comfort in knowing that Brian would have wanted it like this. "That's good. It was a burden you should never have had to bear."

304

"So what is progress back home?" Eddington asked.

"Things are moving fast. The public reaction has become a ground swell, and it's taking on a life of its own despite the efforts of the Alliance to quell it. Believe me," he said to Giselle, "your broadcast got attention."

"All those ships you sent did not hurt, either," she said, pointedly.

§

Thirty Ic'nichi warships came out of Sol's corona and took up a tight double-layered ball-of-yarn blockade orbit almost before anyone realized what was happening. The humans had four ships and the Orbit Dock defenses, but they weren't anxious to start anything against the bulk of the Ic'nichi fleet. The Ic'nichi replied to their challenge by saying that they came to deliver a message, and asked the Commodore to hold off until he could hear what they had to say. Clued in by the Admiral in Singapore, they listened to Giselle's recording, and her invocation of the legendary MacKenna, and shut down their weapons systems.

§

"According to the latest dispatches, the uprising has turned into all-out Civil War," I'eiBida told them. "The Parliament has been dissolved, and the Alliance is being run by decree by a 'Select Committee' of Purity Movement fanatics. Two more Alliance states have outlawed the Purity Movement, and we have reports of Peacekeeper units defecting to Space Fleet. They're relying more and more on their 'Tan Shirts', and it's turning into a Reign Of Terror in many places. Finally, the Alliance Chancellor was killed by a mob two months ago; we just confirmed that."

"So how's it look?" Eddington asked.

"It's too early to say for certain, but my guess is that the Purity Movement is finished."

§

The combination of MacKenna's strategic cunning and Giselle's knowledge of current affairs on earth gave them a weapon none of them anticipated; a weapon far more devastating than the mind erasure process: the truth.

305

The Alliance tried their damnedest to suppress the broadcasts, but thirty starships blaring away around the clock in a dozen languages with their planetary-range transmitters made that a futile effort. Her words touched a raw nerve among earth's population, whose nerves were already rubbed raw by the growing excesses of the Purity Movement. All they needed was one spark; all they needed was to see someone else take the first step—and Giselle's words were that spark. The explosion she ignited was unstoppable right from the first.

§

"So...will I be able to go home soon?" she asked.

I'eiBida shook his head regretfully. "Earth is in for years of chaos, and there is no guarantee that the uprising will win," he said. "We are hearing reports of organized terror activities in many places. It looks like local elements of the Purity Movement are digging in for a long term guerrilla war. It won't be safe for you to return to earth for a long time to come, if ever."

"Not surprising," Eddington muttered. "What about here?"

"We've cleaned out the last of that *p'quas'tka*, so the threat should be taken care of."

Acting on the intel Brian provided, the 'Dark Grays' staged a lightning raid on the human diplomatic compound, and uncovered a trove of weapons and munitions. Some one hundred recent arrivals—all suspiciously tough young mals—were summarily deported, triggering a similar expulsion of personnel from the embassy on earth; which played right into the Ic'nichi's hands.

"Despite howling in the Chamber, things have settled down."

Eddington nodded. "Good. There's been enough of that nonsense lately."

"So what happens to me?" Giselle asked, warily.

"That's what I am here about, in fact," I'eiBida told her. "I plan to hand in my placard tomorrow, but before I retire again, I have one last duty to perform; one I've been looking forward to. I'm here to take you to your new home."

*****

"Epilogue"

Six hours later, an executive jet touched down on a small landing field at the North end of a largish island just below the equator.

"This is *ff'eD'brin'tt* Great Nest," Eddington told her as they watched through the viewports. "It's a fairly obscure place, with nice climate and scenery. They have a low key, laid-back attitude here. Tourism is their major industry; a pleasant lot, all told."

The airport was your typical small town facility, with a few basic structures and a tarmac for private aircraft, including several of the colorful, archaic pedifliers which were popular hereabouts. A couple Ic'nichi waited impatiently for the jet to settle so they could take off with a glider in tow.

Two humans were waiting for them with a large open-air electric vehicle like those outlandish golf carts used in tropical theme parks. They were tall, slender, and elderly, dressed in tropic casuals and floppy hats.

"Hello, Omandi," the man greeted Eddington warmly. "So this is our new family member?"

"Indeed," Eddington said. "This is Giselle. And these are Professor Pierre Roubidoux, and his wife Jeanette."

Pierre gave her a gentle bow. "Welcome, Giselle. We have been expecting you for some time now, and we all look forward to you joining our little community. There will be a welcoming party for you this evening."

"Um...*gracis*." She looked around uncertainly. "What is this place?"

"The Ic'nichi established a colony here for humans who ran afoul of the authorities on earth, and whom they have seen fit to grant asylum to. I'eiBida came up with the idea about twenty years ago. We were the first to arrive, which makes us the unofficial *Les Magistrates*. We have around two dozen residents now."

"Everyone here has done us a great service," I'eiBida said. "Often unwillingly, but great nonetheless. We honor our debt to those who help us."

"But all I did was..."

"Ah..." Pierre held up an admonishing finger. "We have a rule here: we never talk about the past, and we never ask."

"Sorry."

He smiled. "Not a problem. Most of us do not care to remember the past anyway."

"Is there any word on Anne-Marie?" Jeanette asked.

"Yes," I'eiBida told her. "She reached the embassy, and we're working on ways to get her and the hatchlings out." He gave her a wry grin. "And there is more good news: your first great grand-hatchling was just delivered."

That brought a heart-felt sigh of relief from both of them. "Then we have triple reason to celebrate tonight," Pierre said.

§

They passed a chain link fence a short distance from the airport through a gate guarded by two Ic'nichi. "The 'Dark Grays' provide security here," the professor explained. "Our relations with the locals are good, but we would be a major tourist attraction if they weren't kept away. It's just to insure our privacy."

"Actually, we have a lot of interaction with them," Jeanette added. "We go into town for shopping, if you'd like to come along, and Pierre teaches a human language course at the local Institute."

"We also have close professional ties with the Learnéds of the Institute; mainly sociologists and philosophers," Pierre said. "This has become a major center for Ic'nichi-human sociological research."

The electric cart had left the highlands, and was winding along a narrow asphalt road which worked its way down toward the sea. The afternoon was warm, and the tropic foliage around them buzzed with what looked like oversized dragonflies. The air was heavy with the tart aroma of flowering plants and the distant scent of the sea.

"I understand you were a student nurse?" Pierre asked.

She frowned at that. "*Si*, first year."

"Perhaps you would like to work with Omandi in our clinic. There is not much demand, but it will give you something to do."

That thought warmed her. "*Si*, I would like that."

"Good," Eddington said. "I know Bethany will welcome you."

They stopped at a round open-air bungalow, one of a line along the road on a low rise above the beach. "Here we are," Pierre said.

The bungalow was done in typical Ic'nichi fashion: about ten meters' diameter, with an electric fireplace built into a central pillar, and an overhanging roof. The exterior half walls were mostly open, and could be closed off with shutters. The room was divided roughly in half, with one side having a small kitchen, an enclosed restroom, and a bedroom alcove. The other half was a living room with a computer station in one corner. It was done in a sophisticated-primitive tropical motif, and was deceptively light and airy: occasional storms came in from the West; there were steel beams under the wooden falsework.

"This is mine?" Giselle asked incredulously as she stood in the main entrance.

"It is not fancy," Pierre said. "But it is comfy, and the amenities are all here."

"It is nice." She moved around the place, poking here and there to familiarize herself with her new home, then turned to face them. "This is kind of you. I did not expect this."

"It's a small price to pay," I'eiBida said. "After what you went through, we owe you."

"After..." She blanched, and stared at nothing.

"Well, we'll be moving along," Eddington said. "The community center is right down at the end of this road, Giselle. Come down and meet the others." They headed for the door. "Coming, I'eiBida?"

I'eiBida considered Giselle closely: something he had seen building up on the trip down here was starting. "You go on, I'll come along later." He and Eddington exchanged knowing looks, and the others trooped out, leaving the two alone.

They stood silently for a while, watching each other uneasily as she wrestled with the demons she kept bottled up all this time. As Eddington predicted, this wasn't the first time she'd had these episodes. She was venting the horror as best she could.

"Let it go, Giselle," he said at last.

"I...I wanted...them to k-kill me," she stammered as her barriers finally crumbled. "I wanted to die."

309

"Talk it through, Giselle. It helps."

"They...did those *horrible* experiments on me...I kept dying...again and again...b-but I kept coming back."

"Work through it, Giselle. Bring it out."

"I...prayed for death...each time they gave me those shots...I prayed to God to take me..."

"That's right. Let go of it."

"...A-and there were...those...*recuerdos terribles*...in my head..." She sobbed and clutched herself, fighting for self control. "...so much bloodshed...so much death...I...prayed they would kill me..." She was trembling now; post-combat letdown; he knew the sensation well. "...but that *voice* was there...in my head...he kept me going even when I wanted to die. H-he would not let me quit." She turned to him in anguish. "Why would he not let me die?"

"That was his way. He had to protect you: he couldn't accept your death, even if you wanted it."

"But why?"

"He was a creature of duty, sworn to protect the weak. His whole life was devoted to that. All the deaths he witnessed, all the deaths he caused, millions of them, were personal to him."

"He kept me going," she muttered to herself.

"I knew him back when he was still alive, and later when we reactivated him the first time. He was strong, but brittle. You may have helped him get through that as much as he helped you."

"I am glad he is gone. He was a monster!"

"He was a good and honorable human, as frightening as he must have been to you. He once taught me the meaning of duty."

She was silent for a while, avoiding his eyes. "I know," she said at last. "It...just...he terrified me."

"He terrified himself."

"How could one man have so much horror in him?"

I'eiBida sighed and shook his head, and wondered how an innocent young fem like this could absorb even the residue of Mac's lifetime. "I don't want to know. Ancestors forbid I ever do." He brooded on that, remembering. "He was a product of his time. Hopefully earth will never see the like again."

§

Finally, after she regained control, they went outside so she could get a bit of fresh air. A short flight of steps lead down from the back of the bungalow to the beach. A spread of coarse sand curved along a small bay enclosed by headlands at either end. It was late afternoon by then, and d'enchia's sun was dipping toward the horizon. The air along the beach was busy with insect-like flyers, and a pack of vaguely reptilian creatures on some rocks off shore set up a chorus of belching noises. There was a short pier and a couple grounded sailboats about half way along the beach. The shore was lined with bungalows perched amid the trees, and the larger community center crowned the headland in the distance.

"This is lovely," she murmured. "Like this little inlet I knew on the Mediterranean."

A light Ic'nichi patrol ship was anchored in the entrance to the bay, its radars turning slowly, searching for intruders.

"I know Brian would have wanted this for you; both of them."

She turned and looked at him. "You should be ashamed of yourselves for inventing that mind-thing," she said, softly. She was calm now; the nightmares were filed away where, hopefully, they would fade away in time. At least she would have help here.

"Rest assured, Giselle, we are. We will do whatever we can to help earth get past this."

It pained him that despite his strenuous protests, they weren't going to destroy the recording. Some things should never be, but for all the havoc it unleashed, it was just too critical to let go. They finally back-trailed and rooted out the compromised staffer who copied it. He was now carefully isolated and being used to feed disinformation to Alliance Intelligence; something else they learned from the human 'spooks'. As for the recording itself, at least it was moved to the most secure place imaginable: buried deep down in the admin archives where no one would think to look for it, and would play a merry tail chase finding it if they did.

"So, are you alright?"

"*Si.*" She stared at the fading horizon. "He is gone. *Los diablos* have been driven away. There is nothing left but old nightmares." Then she threw her arms around his neck, giving him a heart-felt hug. "Thank you. Thank you for everything."

"Ah...um...that's all right. Happy to oblige."

"Well, I better go," she muttered awkwardly. "I must not be late for my own party." She glanced down the beach toward the distant headland, now lit by the soft glow of the community pavilion, then she turned and looked at him again. "What did he teach you? About duty?"

"He taught me that duty is when you step up to do the job because it has to be done."

She thought about that for a moment. "Oh."

"Will you be alright?"

She stood looking at the fading horizon. "*Ahora ando un nuevo camino,*" she mumbled, half to herself.

Without a further word, she headed down the beach toward the headland. When she reached the water's edge, she pulled off her sandals and splashed along through the small wavelets rolling up the beach, leaving a weaving path of footprints as she followed the ebb and flow. Further on, she began kicking at the wavelets as they rolled in, and at one point she paused to examine something washed up on the sand. A larger wavelet swirled around her ankles, and she retreated up the sand with a faint squeal of laughter.

I'eiBida nodded thoughtfully to himself as he watched. "Good bye, Brian," he muttered.

To Be Continued...

*****

"Appendix"

Ic'nichi terms

chasing their own tails.
        Slang term for desertion, incompetence, cowardice.

ear debt   Slang term for a debt owed by the soul; similar to the human term 'a debt of honor'.

Hand   A military formation of four; equivalent to a human squad. Four Hands plus a commissioned Elder and Worthy make a section of 18; equivalent to a human platoon. Four sections in turn, with supporting elements, make an echelon of 120 to 130; equivalent of a human company.

lengths   Rough measure based on Ic'nichi body length; about two meters.

Stellar bomb Ic'nichi term for the hydrogen bomb. They refer to atomic bombs as 'radioactive' bombs.

Ic'nichi words

cc'v'renk   Literally 'dishonored before ones' Ancestors'; acute embarrassment; disgraceful behavior; inability to make a decision; inability to see common sense; slang term for mental retardation.

er'trxxda   Literally 'haunted by the Ancestors' voices'; obsession; insanity; delusion; raging temper; vulgar habits.

hro'n'nad   Slang term meaning clueless or ignorant.

l'cc'vn   A mildly obscene adjective.

l'fru'ng   Brazen audacity; annoying habits; body odor.

nn'etd   Literally 'distinguished elder fem', a courteous formal greeting.

p'quas'tka	A particularly vile obscenity.
rai'tru'na	Small sour berries; a popular snack.
riv'Agna	A mythical spirit, similar to the earthly 'demon'.
t'plk'asira	An ornate formal plaque given to defenders upon retirement which bears symbols representing their various achievements.
uf'thoka	Analogous to bean sprouts with a spicy garnish.
un'tdar	A crude, vulgar person; a pig-like animal; bad breath; slang term for an unpopular person.
V'liz	A popular beverage containing a mild stimulant which can be prepared either like coffee or soup.
x'mnnb'	Literally 'dead fish'; slang for annoying, stupid behavior; comparable to the human term 'bullshit'.

Human terms

Hash	Uniform insignia.
Hula	Activity, move about, exercise, engage in sex.
Godown	Chinese term for a warehouse or factory building.
Goy	Guy, fellow (verbal drift)
NINS	Now If Not Sooner.
Pukers	Political protesters, the protest movement.
Sausages	Slang term for mixed race individuals.
Step in it	Hear rumors.
Ugly, the	Facts, news, confirmed rumor.

*****

314

An excerpt from
MacKenna: A Knight Of Ghosts And Shadows
Part 6 of the Interstellar Concord Saga

Some time later—it was hard to say how long—there was an abrupt change. The formless void drew back slightly, and a figure emerged. He eyed it uneasily, as it evoked a sense of dread in him for some reason. This newcomer was man-sized, vaguely reptilian, a horizontal biped dressed in a yellow tunic and brown slippers on four-toed feet. There were some pens in a vest picket; jarringly *normal* by comparison. Who, or what, was this? A memory clicked into place: this was an Ic'nichi. Another memory: this one was male, and elderly. Another memory: the yellow tunic was worn by physichs—this was a doctor. The yellow tunic stirred a memory; he looked down again, and all of a sudden he was dressed in a suit of bottle green and oxide brown picked out with various badges and insignia.

The Ic'nichi halted and studied him in obvious surprise, then circled him cautiously, looking him over from several angles. His ears were cocked back, his motions were awkward, tense. This one was afraid, clearly as ill at ease as he was, if not moreso. Why did he feel such a sense of alarm? He searched his memory for some reason they should be afraid of each other, but got nothing but a vague sensation of ominous danger.

Finally their eyes met. "You are clearly an intelligent being," the Ic'nichi said. "But...what are you?"

"What do you mean what am I?"

"What is your species?"

"Is this some kind of joke?" Evidently it wasn't, which unnerved him a bit. What was his species, anyway? A memory clicked into place. "I'm a human. You ought to know *that*."

The Ic'nichi pondered him doubtfully. "We've never heard of your race before."

More memories came bubbling up, leaving him bemused. It seemed there was history between the humans and Ic'nichi. "Come off it. We're not exactly forgettable, you know."

"One would presume, but in fact we don't know."

This was getting them nowhere. "You mean you've completely lost eight years of interaction with us? The treaties, the war, all of it? What about all those books your people wrote about us?"

The Ic'nichi pondered him in plain confusion. "One would assume the record of such events would be extensive, but in fact there is nothing. Until I came here this moment, we expected to find...something else." He took a deep breath, almost a sigh of relief, and shook himself all over like a wet dog. Another memory clicked in: this one was vastly relieved not to find his 'something else'.

Not that he shared in his relief. "Okay, I give up. What th' *hell's* going on here?"

"There is the crux of this mystery." The Ic'nichi seemed more relaxed, but still cautious. He settled in a squatting position on what would be the floor, if there was one. "Honestly, we have no knowledge of your people or the extensive relations you claim. We must discuss this! I, for one, am at a loss."

"That's bullshit! You expect me to believe you people forgot about us altogether? We're not a set of car keys to be lost in the wash!"

The Ic'nichi raised his arms in a placating gesture. "I don't understand it either, but that seems to be what happened. I can't imagine how, but we have no knowledge of your kind at all."

"This is one *monumental* SNAFU, mister! You may not remember, but it happened, trust me!" More memories came pouring up in a chaotic blur: he got the impression the Ic'nichi figured mightily in human affairs and his life over the last few years. He could hardly keep his head above the flood.

"I don't doubt you in the least," the Ic'nichi said. "Although I have no idea about any of it, and it is my business to know such things. Could you give us some details about this interaction you mentioned?"

"Us?"

"This conversation is being monitored by our research herd. Please? Some facts?"

This was getting them nowhere, so he decided to pull in his horns a bit. "Um...sure." He racked his memory, but came up with nothing. Great: just when he needed it, his mind went on the fritz again. "Ah...I'm drawing a blank here." *What* was wrong with him? Why was his memory so erratic? All of a sudden he was afraid: this was something huge; perhaps even bigger than this alien realized. "Ah...I've got nothing."

"Evoke the memories."

"Huh? I don't follow you."

The Ic'nichi hesitated, and his ears twitched back and forth. Another memory: this one was upset or worried about something. "That brings up a matter which you will probably find distressing. Perhaps we should put this off for another time."

"The hell we will! No matter how bad it is, not knowing is worse."

The Ic'nichi mused on that. "An interesting outlook. Very well, I will go on, but I caution you, this will be unpleasant."

He didn't doubt it for a moment, and steeled himself for bad news. "Lay it on me."

"Your...conscious identity is held in a computer. The software contains a search function, which you activate by requesting data."

"Huh? Wait a minute! Run that by me again."

"We found a recording of your memory engrams. Evidently it was misfiled, and was only rediscovered recently." The Ic'nichi made a sweeping gesture taking in the nothingness around them. "This is a computer-generated virtual reality we are using to communicate with you."

That was a lot to swallow. "This is *too* weird!" He shook his head, dumbfounded. "I'm a recording? So what about the real me? Am I dead, or something?"

The alien seemed a bit nonplussed. "I suspect so. The recording was made some two hundred years ago."

*****

Titles from The Written Wyrd
2021-22

The Diplomacy Trilogy - Science fiction humor.
First contact from the aliens' perspective in a trio of lurid tell-all memoirs written by a team of alien diplomats sent to earth to open an embassy.

The MacKenna Trilogy - Science fiction military drama.
He was earth's greatest soldier; they needed his skills once more, but they didn't realize how wrong bringing him back from the dead was.

Nature's Way - Environmental disaster / apocalyptic horror.
This is the last day of our last stand against Nature out for revenge!

Trial - Science fiction political thriller.
The aliens demand justice for their murdered ambassador while right wing extremists plot revolution; which is the greater threat?

Overland - Period science fiction drama / romance.
He was trapped between a beautiful genetically enhanced revolutionary from the distant future and the inhuman monster sent to destroy her. Can he survive caught up in their titanic battle?

Playing God - Apocalyptic horror.
Brenda discovers she is the Dream Girl of a mad scientist capable of altering the past. Can she find a way to undo the disaster he wrought and prevent a nuclear holocaust?

The Big Snow - Environmental disaster / adventure.
A passenger train is wrecked at the top of Donner Pass in the worst storms in recorded history. Can the railroaders get the passengers to safety?

(continued)

Young Adult Demi-Novels:

Diplomacy's Children - YA humor / adventure.
A young alien space fleet recruit faces his greatest challenge in a self-centered, foul-tempered human youngling he is ordered to keep in check.

Star Flight - YA adventure.
She was an outcast, cursed with supernatural powers. She was offered a reprieve, a chance to start over, but could she survive the challenge?

Short Story Anthologies:

Deus Ex Machina - Humorous fantasy short story collection.
From bungling wizards to moronic barbarians to redneck elves, here are the old tales of epic adventure as we would love to see them told - just once.

Ghoulish Good Fun - Macabre short story collection.
Reality is a cruel practical joke. Laugh along with it if you dare!

*****

Available in print and Kindle from Amazon.
Visit our web site for details.

http://www.the-written-wyrd.org/shopping.shtml

*****

A Brief Note From The Author

Thank you for reading this novel. I hope it entertained you, and that you will follow the continuing exploits of Admiral MacKenna. I would love to hear from you, my readers, to let me know how I am doing as an author. Every bit of input helps me to make my next effort a better product for your enjoyment.

All my best,

Bob Boyd

You can learn more about me, and keep up to date on my efforts through our Blog:

Facebook.com/The Written Wyrd

*****